Butcher's Folly

The Wrecking Squad Book 2

Nick Snape

NICK SNAPE

Copyright © 2025 by Nick Snape

This is a work of fiction. Names, characters, places, and incidents either are the product of the author's imagination or are used fictitiously. Any resemblance to actual persons, living or dead, events, or locales is entirely coincidental.

All rights reserved. No part of this book may be reproduced or used in any manner without written permission of the copyright owner except for the use of quotations in a book review. For more information please use: nick@nicksnape.com

First Edition

First edition May 2025

Book Cover by Getcovers.com

www.nicksnape.com

(No generative artificial intelligence (AI) was used in the production of this work. The author expressly prohibits the use of this publication as training data for AI technologies or large language models (LLMs) for generative purposes. The author reserves all rights to license uses of this work for generative AI training and the development of LLMs.)

Also by Nick Snape

Weapons of Choice Series
Hostile Contact
Return Protocol
Zuri's War
Finn's War
Alien Rebirth
Invasive Species
Legion Earth
Nemesis Earth

The Wrecking Squad Series
The Wrecking Squad
Butcher's Folly
Warmonger's Wrath

The Scorching Standalones
The World in My Hands
Just Press Play

Warriors of Spirit and Bone
A Dragon of the Veil
A City of Ashes
A Queen in Blood

Praise for the Author

'A masterful voice in modern sci-fi' ★★★★★ SPR

'Nick Snape's creative storytelling, rich world-building, and engaging characters make this book an unforgettable journey.' ★★★★★ **Literary Titan**

'Stunning series. Very highly recommended.' ★★★★★ **Goodreads**

'Sci-fi with pace, heart and unafraid to tackle deeper questions of what it means to be human.' ★★★★★ **Amazon Customer**

'Wildly creative' ★★★★½ **Self-Publishing Review**

For Ceres Station

You know who you are - thank you for keeping me going through the dark times and the good

CHAPTER 1

"Arin, Savvo, are you done?" Rebekah said, running her hand through her closely shorn hair. "How long does it take to pat a bot's head and rub its tummy?" She checked the orbital telemetry, and satisfied the *Sunstar* was still where it should be, took a bite of her toast before sliding it back into its mag-container on the console. She chewed, waiting on whose turn it was for the sarcastic comeback. Mentally, she had a bet on Arin, but Savvo had woken up in a tetchy mood.

"You want to do this? Huh? Sat in your nice comfy cockpit sipping coffee." The comms were terrible around R6, the metal composites full of radiation. However, the real source of Savvo's foul temper lay in the residual impact of a massive solar flare. The constant crackle and frequent drop offs adding an edge to Savvo's complaining. A bet lost. Wouldn't be the first, nor the last.

"Hey ..." she coughed, crumbs of toast tickling at her throat. She hacked them up. "You were the one who wanted to try working this side of the field for once, see something a little different."

"You eating?" chipped in Arin. "I mean, coffee was bad enough, but chowin' down while we're being fried is not the example a captain should be setting." The sub-engineer's snort and barely contained chuckle were not masked by the crappy comms.

"Give me some credit. I didn't ask you to take any eggs out with you." Savvo near choked.

"Only because we ain't got any," hit back Arin.

The smile in his voice overrode the hiss filling her headphones. Somehow it was getting worse, but the next wave of particulates from the flare weren't due yet. It niggled at her.

"Seriously," she said. "Send me your readings for the last five minutes. And how much longer are we talking?" Rebekah eyed the console's screen. The cabin of the huge excavator her two crew members crawled over, dwarfed them on the drone-cam. Their suits covered in grime, the charged dust camouflaging the pair against the door they were unlocking. As the camera rolled back, three more of the magnificent mining machines slid into view, their drills and self-contained extraction belts jutting out like the arms of a giant. Hovering to one side, the auto loading train trundled inexorably by, winding its way about the asteroid collecting the recovered ore. Arin and Savvo were the only two human operatives on the entire rock and could have walked around its circumference in thirty minutes if the gravity and radiation allowed. And, of course, Savvo's mood.

Both sets of readings pinged in. They were edging out of the green, but still well within expected parameters. Once inside the shielded cabin, the excavator's anti-radiation system would soak up whatever the suits managed to dump.

"Looking fine from here," she said, her toast hovering in front of her lips. The smell of melted margarine drew her in, and she bit down, chewing quietly. She nudged the monitor menu, and Arin's eye-view popped up.

"You mean fine ... munch, munch, munch ... from here, don't you?" teased Arin, the crackle worsening. "I'm expecting a Danish when I get back."

"Not the one you hid in locker 3c? Please don't tell me that's your go to hiding place? I'm sure I saw Tremil hanging around there earlier." She heard Savvo snort this time. Bingo.

Arin's gloved fingers tapped away at the excavator's keyboard, and Rebekah could make out half of Savvo's helmet while he watched the data streaming across the screen. "You are kidding me, right? Those little thieves. Just you wait."

"I mean, if you will use the same hiding place all the time, what do you expect? It didn't have sprinkles on it, by any chance? Rainbow-coloured and full of sugar." Savvo's tone lifted, as if whatever gloom he was under had decided to call it a day. "Because you know how much Dricks likes her sweet stuff. I bet Tremil was on an appeasement mission."

"Appeasement?" Arin replied, his voice close to a whine. His fingers stopped, and both he and Savvo tapped the excavator screen on a single line. "Got it."

Rebekah could almost hear the grin as Savvo continued. "Yeah. You not know? The girls acquired one of the sump tanks. When I say acquired—"

"You mean stole in the middle of the night," finished Arin. "Sump tank?"

"For their new project." Savvo's glove slid beneath his helmet and waggled like tentacles. "You know, the symbiote. I think they said it was getting out ... *hunting* for dreamers."

"Har fucking har," replied Arin. "ZZ3, repair protocol, flag sent, action code Wrecking Squad."

Rebekah checked ZZ3's tracker and activated the camera feed. The bot lifted up from its station attached to the outside of the cabin, thrusters flaring brightly against the dull grey dust that covered everything. In a few seconds, the bot reached the motorised tracks Arin had flagged as an issue. The massive machine usually inched forwards on the tracks as it dug, but the internal rollers had seized. Once ZZ3's plasma torch seared into view, she flicked back to her two crew.

"How many more issues?" she asked.

Arin was whistling as the data scrolled. "Three more. Easily within the given time parameters, Captain, so you can eat toast and stop fretting."

Rebekah ran her eye over each one. Routine. This was the third of the excavators they had repaired, the whole area having been washed by the remnants of a solar flare that had caused the entire Karal mining operation to batten down for a week. The crew were on anti-radiation meds just in case, but give Karal their due, they had plenty. The company, however, was desperate to get the repair and rescue crews out, their financials still dire and any delay costly. A good company, but struggling. Unlike the Emperor's Enforcers, who were neither.

Our new handlers.

The alert blared through the ship, and Rebekah's startled reaction knocked the mag container, sending toast crumbs flying. She would have to worry about that later, and tapped at her screen.

The sensor arrays were struggling. The flare's aftermath had negated much of anything beyond the nearest rock, and now it was limited to the bounds of the asteroid's surface. Increasing interference was not a good sign and left her crew and the ship vulnerable. Pike's team had tracked the incoming particulate shower within the bounds of sensory and comms limitations. Had something changed? Many sun flares were unpredictable. Variable output, without a single peak. Was there something they missed?

"Dricks, need you up here," she said over comms. "Hurry."

Switching to the surface, her comms responded with a violent hiss. "Arin? Savvo? You copy?"

The clomp of Hendricks' magboots echoed behind, and the co-pilot's chair swung around as the engineer took her place. Wordless, she began tracking through the ship's sensory data, clicking through the information with a shake of her head.

"Anything?" Rebekah glanced over, cracking a thumb joint as she did so.

"Interference across the spectrum," Hendricks replied. "It's telling me shit." She switched over to external cams, magnifying the images from different angles. "There."

Rebekah eyed the images as they flickered on her screen. A dust cloud, but not from the surface. The asteroid, and the *Sunstar*, were entering an unmapped area of dense particulates that, by the look of the readings, emitted a haze of radioactivity.

"What the hell? How?"

"Dunno." Hendricks tapped through a menu and sent the data elsewhere. "Maybe the girls can find out."

"No. I need them on comms. I want contact with my crew. There's a second wave of particulates from the flare due, according to Pike, and Karal's data is as erratic as hell. And I want an evaluation impact of that cloud on the engines. Now."

The roar over comms dumped Savvo slap bang back into his sour mood. "What the hell's going on?"

Arin remained focused on the job, running through the software and uploading the patches Karal had tasked them with while they were out there. "Just a fritz. It was a flare, after all. Chill."

"Chill? We can't raise the *Sunstar*." Savvo slammed a gloved hand on the cabin console, receiving a rare stern look from Arin in return.

"You okay? Are you going cold turkey or something?" He stopped what he was doing, turning to face his crewmate and friend. "Cos, I kinda depend on my buddy when I'm in space, you know."

Savvo shook his head. But he had been feeling it, the call for the stims raising its ugly head as the days returned to their previous dull monotony. Yet Arin was right. They relied on each other, and he needed to calm. For a second, he considered activating his chip, but dismissed the thought. Self-control was key. Numbers counted down in his head as he tried to centre himself.

"Happy thoughts," he said out loud. "Yeah."

The comms hissed violently, a crackle of unintelligible syllables amid the noise. However chilled he needed to be, something was wrong – he could feel it. Then his HUD pinged, a flag in the heads-up display pulsing for attention.

Arin had clearly got it, too.

"Fuck, Savvo."

An image of a dust cloud sat amid the text. A warning, alongside the *Sunstar*'s need to withdraw.

"Too dangerous for them to hang around in that shit," Savvo said, as much to himself as to Arin. A glance to his HUD informed him the scrubbers would maintain O2 for another twelve hours. A non-issue. Food? Gels. Taking a shit? The usual, lovely experience in a suit. They could sit safe and—

The cabin alarm blared, the screen flashing its own warning with Arin shoving himself back into his seat as it flooded red.

"Shit," was all the sub-engineer said, focused on the screen.

Savvo ignored him, heart racing as he read the monitor. "We got some heavy rad coming this way and a threat to life warning. We can't stay in here." He checked his HUD, bringing up the most recent map of the asteroid. The drone's secondary role was to remap the surface, but there hadn't been time yet. The old version would have to do, despite the likely changes due to micrometeor impact and space weathering. The excavators would survive. They were exposed to all sorts of cosmic rays and radiation blooms, but humans ...

A second message dropped; the twins' signature 'HT' attached. Savvo clicked through via his wrist control, praising Heki and Tremil with every word read. An extract from the original asteroid works, ringed and focused. A safety shelter. The mining site had been built way before their time with Karal, and humans had been part of the original crew setting up automated pre-mining operations. Savvo cross-referenced it with his map, the area shown flat and bare. It didn't make sense. With a tap, he brought up a probe image, one from an old mapping run. Again flat, barely a change in the smooth rock of that section. The alarm blared again.

"Fuck," said Arin, both fists slamming into the cabin console.

"You see this?" Savvo said, sending the information over. "We're getting short of time."

Arin focused on the image, his head shaking slowly. "What choice we got? Stay in here, we neutralise what, forty percent of the shit coming our way? If we're lucky, we come out medium-rare in the centre. A little seasoning, and we'd be perfect for a barbeque. A little salad on the side..."

"Not the bloody time," growled Savvo. Sweating, heart racing, he checked ZZ3's position. The bot was still working on the tracks. Plasma torch saddled against his back; attachments engaged and adjusting the stuck roller. He could make out the dust in the background, with the ghostly glow his mind added, not helping. "Call ZZ3 back. I'll send the drone over to have a look."

"On it," replied Arin, and he stood, boots clamping to the deck. His movements were staccato, nervous. Unlike how Arin usually behaved in the face of something dangerous. But then his mood swings were famous.

And everyone feared radiation. An unseen killer, unlike tentacled freaks or autobots.

Savvo called the drone, the data pulse taking three attempts before gaining a response. The small, zero-g machine confirmed the coordinates, but he had little confidence it would be able to get images through. He swore, but there was no alternative. It didn't have the software level to discern a building from the rock, so an image was vital. He downgraded the picture quality to a bare minimum data packet, then sent the drone on its way.

"Three minutes," said Arin, now tapping at the screen. "Before the rad levels start rising. Five before the cabin shielding may as well be tinfoil, and we baste ourselves in olive oil while kissing our arses goodbye."

ZZ3 appeared at the cabin doorway, red eyes focused on nothing, forelimbs outstretched. The bot could carry them both, but the flight time meant it was a one-shot deal. Even ZZ3's shielding would succumb to what rode the flare's particulates. If there was no shelter, either removed by the original setup crew, or destroyed by space weathering, they were screwed.

"And if we survive, cancer. Rotting from the inside out. Remember, I'm red-haired and fair of skin. Susceptible to sunburn. In all likelihood, I'll be sizzling. You know, *All* over."

Savvo toe-clicked Arin's nearest magboot, shoving the sub-engineer towards the door. He staggered, and released the other, hands twisting the lever to unseal the entrance.

"I'm babbling, I know," Arin stated. "Just let me. It helps."

Savvo nodded. Taking a breath, he activated his wetware. A chemical warmth filled his brain, soothing his fractious mind. He would pay for it later, vowing to be alive long enough to tell Rebekah about why he had no choice.

Arin swung the locking handle, and the door refused to budge.

"Ahhhh!" shouted Arin, slamming his fist.

Savvo could see things were rapidly going downhill. Give Arin something ridiculously dangerous he could observe and understand, and he was insanely fearless. Or just insane. Radiation, however, was untouchable. You couldn't beat it off, pummel the vicious stuff with a machine gun, or depend on your buddy to cover your back.

"Chip," he said through the hiss of comms, tapping his friend's helmet. "That's an order."

Arin's body relaxed, his movements more settled. A familiar sign, one he was experiencing.

Savvo gave him a role, a focus. "Now, get ZZ3 to open the bloody door."

"Aye," replied Arin, and spoke through comms to the waiting bot. Amid the crackle, ZZ3 must have discerned the command, and two metallic limbs slammed into the edges of the cabin door. Arin yanked the handle down, and the seal parted but refused to release. Another shove from ZZ3, and the door gave, dust fluttering from the synth-rubber seal.

Savvo flinched, though he knew this was the asteroid's own detritus. Charged and annoyingly cloying, but not as dangerous as what seethed their way from the flare.

"ZZ3, rescue protocol, target defined, action code Wrecking Squad. Get us the hell out of here." Savvo sent the target, the supposed safety shelter, and ZZ3 paused before two of its arms wrapped about them both. A third limb slammed the door shut, and the bot's thrusters engaged. They rose swiftly, with an ominous shimmer of diffused light looming to their right. The asteroid was entering the vast dust cloud that had forced the *Sunstar* to leave, abandoning them to the flare's particles and whatever radiation the dust carried. His suit began a countdown, Savvo wishing the clock's start point was far higher.

ZZ3 shuddered as it levelled off, thrusters spluttering. They dipped and weaved as if flying through a maze. Excavators shut down below them. The huge shovels and drills spinning to a stop, emergency lights flaring inside cabins. But the train rolled on, trundling across the surface, its precious ore hardly in danger from the incoming radiation.

Savvo checked the data flow, nervously eyeing the rad count and avoiding flicking through the spectrum. It would only up his stress.

A faint crackle in the comms scraped his nerves. He desperately tried to home in on any possible words, hisses and pops his only reward. No packet message, no hope, dropped into his visor. The *Sunstar* would be safe. Rebekah had no choice other than to preserve those aboard. Savvo only wished he and Arin were by her side.

A second flurry of crackles echoed in his comms. A pause followed. No hisses or pops. No rescue.

"Fuck."

And a packet dropped. An image. At a strange angle and with poor definition. He squinted, fervently trying to work out what it showed, until it dawned. The drone must have crashed, and the lower half of the picture was mere rock, the upper black – space. Between them was a small ridge of dust, uniform and straight.

Something was there.

"Under the fucking ground," he muttered.

"Eh?" replied Arin. "You mean we're going caving? Is this the time? You know, we have pressing … Oh, you mean the shelter."

"I do."

Alerts flashed – the countdown neared the end of its cycle, and the rad monitor entered the feared red. Savvo growled, his HUD flickering in and out of focus. For a second, he thought he'd taken a strong dose, only for his suit to adapt and the screen to return. A creeping inevitability took over. A fear that even if they made it, death would still come on the wings of an invisible killer.

ZZ3 adjusted. Limbs pulling them in closer, and the bot twisted to fly on its side. Its torso plating now between them and the assumed direction of the flare's particulates. A double layer of shielding, and ZZ3's thrusters burned brighter.

Thirty seconds pinged into Savvo's HUD. A new countdown, the numbers a faded green. Blinking away so slowly as ZZ3 counted down the time to safety. On ten, a jolt shuddered along Savvo's spine, and the bot hit the rocky floor, limbs wrapped protectively about them. ZZ3 rose to its hooked feet, grasping at the rock as it lumbered three steps towards a dead drone and a line of dust.

Everything flashed deep red.

Rebekah adjusted her gas stream, decreasing the jetpack's thrusters so they didn't throw up too much dust. Her feet settled onto the asteroid, boots leaving a print as she stepped forwards and fired a pinion into the rock beneath. She hooked on a lifeline and then jetted three metres before driving another into the ground. Between them, she attached three more tethers, all the while praying to whoever would listen.

Comms remained compromised, but she refused to believe the lack of response was for any other reason than residual radiation. She sent the drone up, letting it sync with the navy suit's HUD, mapping the layers of dust. The HUD defined a rectangular patch whose density was different from the surroundings. Rebekah flew over and drove a third pinion, her last, into the rock on the other side. With that, she cast a synth-rope between and lowered herself down amid the triangle of lifelines strung around the anticipated hatchway. Rebekah used the jets to blow away the dust, revealing the door beneath. With a surge of hope, she yanked on the tethers, pulling herself down, and tightened them off so she was stable. Finally, she extricated the pinion sheath, rapping it against the hatch, and waited. The pause filled by the thunder of her heartbeat. Would ZZ3 sense the vibrations?

Dust slid in a line, filling the gap along the hatch's edge as it lifted. ZZ3's eyes focused on her, glinting red, giving hope. The bot lifted the thick concrete and polythene skimmed door and cast it aside. Beneath, Arin and Savvo's suits were curled about each other, the glow of their HUDs filling the three-metre square shelter.

As dust hovered above, Rebekah spotted movement. Her HUD pinged, two life signs streaming in.

"Got any toast?" asked Arin.

CHAPTER 2

"Mr Erikson," said the cashier, counting the chips piled on the counter. "You appear to have had a fine evening."

"Fine? I suppose you could call winning *fine*." He leaned in close, piercing eyes connecting with the cashier. "But there are times this place can be ... thrilling. Not just gaming on the table, but playing those around it." He winked, hating himself and the false impression wasted on a lowlife. Always a façade to show, whether to those on the periphery of the Court he had spent the last four hours stifling a yawn around, or to the bald-headed cashier who hung upon his every word like a starving dog.

"I do hope that was as successful as your gambling." The cashier swiped a card, wiping it clean and placing it on the desk beneath a golden cloth for Erikson to collect – no noble would deign to touch a sullied card.

Erikson picked it up and swiped his wrist, enjoying the moment of monetary victory before tossing the card nonchalantly onto the desk. He walked away, not looking back, adding a swagger to his hips, masking his usual efficient walk to emphasise power and success. His mark stood near the casino doorway, grey-eyed and black-haired. The Almaarian nobilities' ultimate combination, though Erikson had quickly established this minor noble's family had resorted to gene therapy to accentuate the finer traits. Viscounts were in that middling position, always vying for more, never quite satisfied with their place among the elite as they jostled for Court status. Some, like the Honourable Dexter here tipping his glass in a hopeful goodbye, had been raised as a weapon. Educated and physically manipulated to appeal to the excess of anyone mummy or daddy pointed them at. Erikson should know. He'd been raised for the exact same role.

Tonight had been an undoubted success. Sowing the seeds for a later meeting and the start of a new investigation into the comings and goings of daddy-dearest, whose murky dealings in the City State of Jota had come to the Enforcer's attention. Bribery was no surprise, but extortion was something of interest. So here he was, and a welcome return from the hated bleakness of space.

The gentle throb against his upper left pocket was an unwelcome disruption. Ignoring it, he stopped at the carved doorway of the casino, feigning a glance to the intricately woven carpet, before releasing a knowing look back over his shoulder towards Dexter. The Viscount's son gestured with his drink again, a perfect smile breaking out below chiselled cheekbones that Erikson so wanted to smash with a hammer.

The peak of nobility.

He left with the briefest of smiles and a coy tilt of his head.

Descending the steps, the concierge called for his transport, and his car rolled out of the car park, coming to rest level with his outstretched hand. Erikson didn't speak or acknowledge the woman. She was too far below him for that. He accepted the wiped clean electronic casino tab before entering the vehicle.

"Code 492/A," he said, and rested his hand against the internal palm plate. With a green flash, his command was noted, and the vehicle silently slid away. He cleared the casino tab's memory, ditching it in a storage pocket ready for next time. With the seat set for a gentle massage, and a little warmer than the current temperature, he eased back and drew out his comms slate from his inside chest pocket. Erikson glanced out of the transport window, the sway of perfectly manicured trees in the wind catching his eye with their steadfast resistance despite their artificially created beauty.

"No surprises," he whispered, his handler's call code flashing back on the screen. With a swipe, the comms sought a secure connection while he engaged the transport's jamming net.

"Erikson," said the androgynous voice. Again, a change in tone. He had wondered when the next one was due, and now he knew.

"Yes," he said, trying not to sound concerned. If the call sent him elsewhere, weeks of work would go down the drain. To rebuild that would take guile, which he had in spades, but he loathed wasting time.

"How are things with the Honourable Dexter?" His handler must have been monitoring on-grid. A teaser of an opener to display their power. It put him immediately on edge.

He sighed, deliberately. "I am close to opening a line of communication, shall we say? I am hoping this conversation is not about to throw away all the preparations I've set in place. This identity took an age to evolve into something useful."

"Not at all. That mission is a priority, and luckily for you, I have another you are more than capable of running alongside. The Breakers—"

"I have not the time to go into space," he interjected, kicking himself for the outburst.

"I said before, Enforcer, that operations can be run from Almaar once established. Though if I command, you will jump into the nearest spacecraft and ask how far. Understood?" Synthesised androgyny or not, there was an undercurrent of impatience in the tone.

"Understood."

"Good. I have a cargo I require recovering. Wetware, from Benetai."

"Benetai? I am not familiar." Erikson was tempted to apply a quick search, hating not knowing and being at a disadvantage. He made a mental note instead.

"A garbage-dump of a space station we barely tolerate in the Windward System. Useful in some ways as a mine of transient information, but full of the lowest of lowlifes. Senti, Bustan and those Almaarians who wish to avoid the hand of the Emperor."

"And wetware?" He tried to word the next part without sounding condescending. "That's mundane equipment. Army kit, and not so useful since the Senti forced the cessation."

There was a pause, gnawing at Erikson's nerves, but his not questioning validity could also be regarded as a dereliction of duty.

"And?"

"Excuse my ignorance, but we are the Emperor's Enforcers. Our role is to keep the nobility in line, and I struggle to see how such a cargo is of concern."

Again, silence. This time with an ominous feel. Erikson considered it deliberate, to keep him guessing and on edge. But what if it wasn't?

"The wetware pertains to the activity of a noble, and its acquisition by anyone other than them, or us, would be to the detriment of the Court. That should sate your curiosity and the veracity of the mission."

He thought on that, a root of recklessness wheedling its way into a crack. "Would it help to know which noble I am defending?"

"It may make you less galling. You will be protecting a *countess* from outside influence." There was a hint of triumph, as if the pronouncement of a higher class of nobility should shut Erikson up. It nearly worked. Not a lowly baron acting above their station.

"The Warmonger? Countess Segfi?"

"I couldn't possibly confirm or deny. But now can you understand the stakes? The wetware is a priority recovery item, and you have the ideal team to return it to us. A bunch of lowlifes with the skills to take it if they can't acquire the wetware by other means. And not connected to us should it go wrong. Sending an Enforcer onto neutral ground has been done before, but in seek of information, or assassination. For this we need—"

"—Breakers." Almost as if the crew of the *Sunstar* had been groomed for this moment. Too perfect, perhaps. But then, sometimes life gifts you something sweet instead of sour, and being on the right side of a countess, especially if it was Segfi, was a priority for all the Court and their minions. That particular battleaxe had a taste for blood, and still railed against the cessation of the war as the great betrayal of the Emperor and the nobility.

And she's running out of time if rumours of her illness are true.

"Okay. What do we know?"

"I'll have the details sent securely. But for now, the wetware was put up for auction anonymously on Benetai. We got wind through a few contacts, and at first thought little of it until its uniqueness was flagged." The voice had flattened again, down to business. Erikson tried to focus while the transport pulled up at his gated temporary accommodation. They opened automatically, and the vehicle restarted, house lights switching on in the distance as they approached.

"Uniqueness?"

"Unused. These were not extracted from dead Marines."

"I don't understand. The Senti design and surgically add wetware ..." he trailed off. Segfi would use any angle to win a war, whatever lives it cost or toes she broke. "You mean the wetware isn't Senti approved?"

"You're getting it. If it's revealed that the wetware, or its adaptations, are of Almaarian origin, then we could be risking all future access to their FTL transport. You know how touchy they are about their tech. Inter-system trade, diplomacy, could all grind to a halt. There's a long list of people whose hands we don't want on this kit. Senti included."

Erikson had to agree. It would be tumultuous for the Court, embarrassing for the Emperor and, despite the forced cessation and reduction in Senti 'Faster Than Light' transport usage, could jeopardise future access. Even if that was only for the short term, the ramifications were huge. But then, the Senti still craved human memories and dreams. The war they had enabled through FTL passage had, however, flooded their worlds with the replayed memories and emotions of human death and destruction. By all accounts, it had brought their colonies close to collapse. Forcing the cessation had stemmed the flood of both official and bootlegged mind-sucked gore, allowing them to stabilise their worlds.

"Are the Bustan involved?" he asked. A potential clash would not help relations.

"Not as far as we know. But we can't rule it out. Benetai is as known to them as to us."

Back to business. The Breakers were physical brutes, though in Rebekah he had detected an intelligence unfortunately affected by emotional flaws such as loyalty. He needed to know everything of import, and from his handler, not a dry summary. "You said it was up for auction. Any buyers?"

"It was withdrawn after a few days, without notification of sale. We don't know why, so this is a job in a hurry. Nothing gets to Benetai easily. The Senti have no Orb connections there, so we're talking private contracts or the mind-sucking Senti parasites who hang around the fringes looking for opportunities. We have a little time, but not much leeway."

"Agreed. Anything else I need to know?" Erikson asked.

"*Failing* acquisition, destroy all traces of the wetware. If that's unachievable, we *need* the next link in the chain."

His handler's tone left no room for doubt. This was a no fail situation, and his role felt too convenient for its own good. They could plausibly deny the Breakers if it went wrong, and if they found him at fault, he could be equally as deniable when they recovered his body full of holes from a lonely river – or not at all.

But what choice did he have? And despite the initial downplay, this was much larger than it had first appeared.

"Okay. I'll check through the details and get on this ASAP. I take it my request to the Directorate has been prioritised?"

"It has," replied his handler. "And will go through, have no doubt. You need this Connors to act as proxy, and the Incini Directorate know that. Use her. But be warned, there'll come a time when she will have to be burned."

"Not a problem. Erikson out."

The transport pulled up outside the rented house, its full-length windows shining brightly with the auto-lights. He stepped out, palming the door, and watched as it self-garaged. Within a few minutes he was sitting with a whiskey at his desk, tapping away at the slate connection to Davina.

While he waited, he took a sip, the sour drink matching his mood as he contemplated a next move. He'd need a lie for Rebekah's crew, one with a thread of truth. The last thing he wanted was for them to become a problem for his handler, and therefore him, by default.

"Earn your keep," he said, and sent off an encrypted request. The Incini the perfect person to find a rogue Senti willing to transport the *Sunstar* to the Windward System, and also contact a human crew beholden to him for their little secret. All that in Duboit's name. An Incini, a keeper of secrets, especially about a sleazeball baron masquerading as Duboit and what the noble had really been up to out in the black.

His private slate vibrated, the image of Dexter appearing on the screen. With a sigh, he swiped to receive the call.

"Dexter, what a surprise."

CHAPTER 3

"This is Karal Mining Control," said the familiar voice over comms. "Come back RCKN5QD. Who am I talking to?"

"This is Rebekah, Pike. We in the clear for entry?"

"Ooh, let me check the work log," replied Pike.

Rebekah sighed. "Don't be a dickhead, Pike. No, nix that. Don't be any *more* of a dickhead than normal. We need a rad scrub."

"Always the kind words, Beks."

Rebekah winced, choking back the sour retort that rolled along her tongue.

Oblivious, Trent Pike continued, "The reports from R6 seem rather exaggerated. Did you get someone else to do the repairs? It says here you spent twelve hours in a rad shelter. I mean, do we pay Calc for sitting on your arse?"

Savvo cut in, one hand on her forearm, trying to calm his captain as she wound up for a full tirade. "Come on, Trent. You wind and wind, then complain when you get a bellyful of acid in return. Are we cleared for docking? The scrub is scheduled, and we got crew who need a bath."

"You used to be fun, Wrecking Squad. Since when did you get all serious? M4 clearance activated, docking area 32b. Right next to the primary scrubber, as I'm a nice guy."

"Check the mirror, Pike. Think you mistook yourself for someone else. Wrecking Squad out." Rebekah grimaced; her fingers balled tight. The man was an insufferable pain in the arse, but – and it felt odd saying it – the evidence suggested he was on their side. He had been caught up in the events with Duboit, and later their Enforcer handler. Somewhere in that shitshow he had dropped in a few warnings, for which she forgave a multitude of sins. To a point.

A quick scan of VERT, Karal's virtual-control system, showed their berth, and who paid for it. Duboit. An upgrade, and a hint at the speed of their likely turn around.

Damn.

She clicked on the ship's comms. "Dricks, draw up a needs-must repair list for the ship. Arin, a wants-and-desires list. Got a feeling we might need to do some shopping. HT, you two listening?"

The comms crackled. The sound of a quick breath rasped in her ears. "Loud and clear."

"You know the drill. Let us know what you would like from M2, and we'll meet in the galley in thirty minutes. I think Savvo and Arin owe you big time for getting that message through, so don't skimp."

She stood up, stretching her back, and dropped a smile on Savvo. "Nicky on the tower?"

Savvo's embarrassed grin was enough of a hint. He nodded.

"Better see us in then," she said. "I'd advise enjoying the moment. I don't think we'll be here long."

"And that's all," Dricks stated. "Just need the extra shielding around the repair where the *Maverick* sliced and diced my baby." She stroked the galley table, causing them all to smile.

"Well, I'm not going to be arguing over any of that," Rebekah replied.

"Naah," said Arin. "Don't know if you can be as generous with this addition to the list, though." He put the drawing pad on the table, the joys of M4's grav keeping it in place. Rebekah recognised the pad, and the care with which the previous paper had been removed. The twins. She eyed Arin, who shrugged. "So, we have a special request for an industrial printer."

"You've lost me there," replied Savvo, with Rebekah agreeing alongside. "You mean, like one of those factory models they have on the dock? Firstly, what the hell for, and secondly, where is it going to go?"

"I can answer the *where*. Those on the dock are for ship printing and repairs. You know, full plate shielding, damaged crane hooks and that. I would like one for component builds. The small stuff, so a compact printer. There's enough room in the machine shop." He raised his eyebrows to Rebekah, cracking out a grin that was half real and half forced.

Tremil and Heki were shuffling on the bench, trying desperately not to catch Rebekah's eye, but the emotional wave hit her like a train. Her earworm fired up for the first time in days, and everyone at the table shivered and shook their heads.

"And what for?" she managed to squeeze out. "I need to justify this to … to …"

"Us? It's our creds we're spending," said Savvo.

Arin seemed to sink into himself, but Rebekah suspected he was visualising a list concocted with the twins through a background of the girls' raging emotions. "Also, ZZ3 attachments, minor component replacement, perhaps weapons and armour refinement on the fly. That is assuming we will be on mission sometime soon."

"And maybe a bio-environment for the symbiote?" she added, raising an exaggerated eyebrow.

Arin pressed his lips together, shaking his head slowly. "Well, yeah. It might be able to do that. *If* we had anyone who wanted to devise such a thing."

"Send me the specs. On a proper list, you know, by slate." Rebekah squeezed herself out from under the bench, pointedly looking at both girls. She had said don't skimp. "Anything else?"

"Chocolate. And a Danish with rainbow sprinkles."

"I want to stay on board," Hendricks said, rubbing her newly shorn hair. "For the twins' sake. I'm not so sure it's a good idea to leave them alone." She lifted her flask of sweet, milky coffee, taking a sip before placing it back on the galley top. She sighed.

"We all need a break, Dricks. We agreed to maximise our time off the *Sunstar*, especially if we end up being sent away somewhere and are cooped up on the ship again." Rebekah made sure the concern showed. Hendricks was as stubborn as they came when the mood took, and would find an argument she wouldn't be able to bypass. But she was also right.

"Aye. Doesn't change what happened last time we berthed on M2. This Victor is out there, and no doubt looking for payback. He will have lost face, and the woman with him is still a mystery. ZZ3 ripped their strike team apart, but left enough to know that they were all male." Her lips twisted, as if the words were sour in her mouth. "And I'm not so sure the twins are able to discern the real difference between events on the *Maverick* and here. Heki talked of death following them, you know, no matter where they went. I was thinking maybe I should stay, and they might open up a little."

Rebekah chewed over Hendricks' point. The extremes of the girls' reactions were a dilemma. Yet at the same time, they had appeared more relaxed. Part of the team. They had protected the ship, and then themselves. Saved Dricks and Davina – and in all likelihood, the rest of the crew – by taking control of the *Maverick*.

"We take it in turns. You have the first night shift, as you'll only mither if not. Savvo can have the second, and so on, until we're out of here." She stood and squeezed the engineer's arm as she made for the passageway. "But you and Arin need some time away from the ship. Understand? No argument."

Her ex-captain blushed. Blushed. It left Rebekah a little ashamed until Hendricks broke out in a small smile and nodded.

"Agreed. What are you going to do about the despicable Mr Duboit?"

Rebekah stopped and faced her. "What do you mean?"

"I know you got a message. He'll turn on us in the end. They all do. When they decide we are more of a liability than an asset, and I worry we won't see it coming. We're combat Marines with a new trick, and when they have no more use for us ..." Hendricks left it hanging, her shrug and knowing gaze finishing the sentence for her.

"I hear you. We need to be ready to run. And if the opportunity comes, take the chance while we can." She sighed. "I'm not going to deny that it's felt good these last few weeks. Like we've been a crew again, rather than a bickering family. But I'll find a way. You know the consequences as well as I if Segfi gets wind we're alive. And also, if we bug out without a plan."

"Aye, fucked if we do, screwed if we don't. I know. We all know. That needs to be on your radar too. We all *understand*." Hendricks shrugged, arms held wide. "Yet here we still are."

Rebekah squeezed her lips, the thin smile accompanied by a nod as she turned away. She left to the sound of two thumbs cracking.

Rebekah dropped her night bag onto the bed. The room matched the one she'd slept in the last time they'd been billeted on Minx 2. Level 5 in the same district, so not boasting quite the same grav, but far better than the alternatives deeper in the asteroid. She contemplated unpacking, but what was the point when she would be back on the ship in a few days? The bar was calling her, the draw of a cold beer and different faces than those she peered at all day long.

With a sneer, Rebekah pulled up the message she had been avoiding, the decoding having run its course about half-an-hour ago. With a sigh, she sat on the bed and scanned the topline.

Time to earn your keep.

It dripped of servitude with an unhealthy dose of noble attitude. The Enforcers were supposed to keep the nobility, even the Court, inline with the Emperor's desires and wishes. Rebekah had never considered how they achieved compliance, assuming in her ignorance, that they tapped the noble on the shoulder and wagged a finger, while the other hand threatened their burgeoning bank accounts. Apparently, what they wagged from time to time was a little more aggressive than that. A squad of ex-Breakers, Marine black ops, with a penchant for smashing their way through an issue. Well, at least they used to.

"Earn our keep?" she growled.

A shower, a change of clothes, and fifteen minutes later, she was at the door when its alarm pinged. A glance up at the camera left her hand hanging over the handle. Davina, Mr Duboit's and now their Enforcer's Incini. Not what she needed right now. But there was little alternative.

She opened the door. "I'm heading for a bar, so this had better be quick."

Davina, her hair as elegant as ever, tilted her head down the corridor. "Let me stand you a drink. For old time's sake."

"Old?" replied Rebekah, locking the room behind her. "It's not even been a month."

Davina wrinkled her nose. "Felt longer." She coughed, though it was a much healthier sound than the last time they had talked. "Still on the road to recovery."

Together, they walked along the metal floored corridor, the walls wide enough for two while leaving room for others to pass by. Rebekah set the pace, the taste of a beer on her tongue.

"I thought Mr Duboit would be contractually required to provide the best care for his pet Incini." Rebekah winced as the words left her mouth, trying to cover her indiscretion with a smile and a laugh, as if it were a joke. Davina clearly saw through it.

"Yeah. Best available on M1. Which has been good, but I feel like I am just an asset whose value stops at being an Incini, rather than a human injured in the course of their contract. Patch me up, set me back to work. But that's the life I live, I suppose."

They reached the concourse to the lift, which Rebekah reluctantly called, saving Davina from the stairs. "Doesn't sound like you have much influence going on. Isn't that what you do?" she said as the doors opened. "Shape the narrative."

"I did."

They were silent until the bar, the neon glow of its sign declaring they had missed happy hour. They took a booth facing the window out onto the thoroughfare, Davina ordering two beers and an alcohol-free cocktail with her wrist ID.

With a knowing smirk, Rebekah downed the first beer and sat back against the bench to peer out at the milling citizens and temporarily berthed crews who walked by. She lifted her second glass, the foam covering her lips.

"So, not a social call," she said, taking a sip. "And you chose the least viewed table in the bar."

"Did I?" Davina replied. She smiled and lifted her glass, turning to face Rebekah. "You need to know I can't protect you."

Rebekah froze, the beer halfway to the mat on the plastic table, and returned it to her lips for another sip. She couldn't prevent the anger flushing her cheeks, nor the narrowing of her eyes. It was all she could do not to glare at the woman next to her.

"That's not a threat," continued Davina, and took a drink. "But my newest employer is curious, and dogged. And I might say, ambitious. This is not about the twins. That I can promise."

"Then what?"

"He thinks I'm ruthless, and as an Incini, he's not wrong. There are those from the Directorate who work with *his* kind. I am to be his go-between within Karal, and anything related to Minx organisations. I cannot disclose his dealings to you in any way. You can't trust me." Davina faked a smile and a slight laugh as she lowered her glass onto the table. She tapped it twice, before settling the drink on the mat.

"Nothing's changed then?" Rebekah took a sip, then gulped the rest down, her eyes never leaving Davina. "And thanks."

"I am to inform you that your meeting was originally to be at 9am. I rescheduled it for an hour later, as I'm guessing you may need some recovery time." Davina eased off the bench, leaving a hand on the backrest, eyes on the *Sunstar*'s captain. "I hope that is agreeable."

"They're innocent," replied Rebekah, examining the dregs in her glass. "And not an *asset*."

"I'm glad we agree." Davina dipped her head as if to say goodbye, and left.

Rebekah sat against the bench, eyes watching as the Incini joined the throng heading to work or home outside the bar. She never looked back, keeping her eyes ahead. Rebekah didn't know if she wanted to strangle her or send thanks. A curious meeting, but then her life's change of direction was full of fresh surprises.

Except one.

She remained thirsty.

She ordered a beer, and with a glance at her wrist, another two with Arin and Savvo messaging their imminent arrival. By the time the drinks arrived, she had moved booths, taking one central to the bar and in the middle of the hubbub. She settled into the noise and camaraderie of her fellow customers, recognising a few of the captains and their crews as it filled for the evening. Level 5 could attract those who subcontracted out, especially when that paid well, and it looked as if the pickings had been good. Revelling in the competition for the tallest tale of danger, Arin drew a crowd of like-minded people, enabling her to push thoughts of Davina to the back of her mind, drowning out her warning in a sea of beer, and later, whisky.

Savvo and Arin saw Rebekah to her room, their own a few doors further along the corridor. She stumbled in, half-reaching the bed, with her knees still on the floor, and wondered if it was possible to sleep in that position – only to awaken sometime later in darkness with a sore back.

She checked the time, the glow of the room clock creating shadows about the room, and stripped for bed. Something in the ambient light caught her bleary-eyes. With care, she stretched out her back and argumentative knees, and collected the slip of paper lying on the floor next to her clothes. In her addled state, she couldn't work out how it got there. All the doors on M2 were sealed, a precaution should the airlocks fail, unlike the cheaper miners' accommodations on M3. Eventually, it clicked. The paper had been slipped into – or onto – her clothes somehow, either in the bar, or somewhere between. Blinking, she read the words.

I haven't forgotten.

A cryptic message on untraceable paper. She wasn't in the mood, and screwed it up, dropping it in the bin. With a sigh, she rummaged in her night bag and extricated a small drone. She set it on guard, primed to activate should anyone but crew enter, and messaged Arin and Savvo to do likewise. A toilet trip and a flask of water later, and she managed to hit the bed this time.

CHAPTER 4

Heki shifted the newly buffed and adapted sump box to the table. With her face lit by a smile, she placed her hand on the lid Arin had fashioned, despite his grumblings about a vanishing Danish. Inside, the symbiote responded with a wave of metallic colours that pulsed along its skin like a rippling pond. Tentacles slipped into the air holes drilled exactly to the girls' specifications, and Heki let her fingers dance along each, the metallic rainbow brightening with every touch.

"How does it feel today?" said Tremil, leaning over Heki's shoulder to watch the display. "Any different?"

"Weaker." Heki's smile wavered, but returned as she alighted a single fingertip against the largest tentacle. "Definitely weaker. We need to find an answer, and soon."

"And your dreams? Mine have still been … calmer. More peaceful." Tremil reached past, her fingers upon the box, delighted as the tentacles reached for them. She calmed her mind, knowing as they touched, the symbiote would leak some of Heki's memories that would bleed into her own. A problem for them both, especially when they already struggled to separate their tangled emotions.

"The same. But it won't last if we don't find a way to feed TB."

Tremil tilted her head, watching the symbiote's colours, identifying the difference between her touch and Heki's in the patterns. Subtle, but there. All their research about the Senti had fallen down a big, empty void. Most of what was recorded was basic supposition from their appearance, gravity preferences and mannerisms. Little had been recorded about the symbiotes, so finding their nutritional needs had been next to impossible. They had experimented with everything organic available on board, with the symbiote not only disinterested but actively avoiding whatever they provided. Often, in fact, appearing distressed by its mere presence.

"Then it's time. There's only Dricks on board. I've let her know we plan to release TB so he can explore the ship. See where he goes and whether there is any hint of what he may be interested in." Tremil checked her monitor on what would have been the captain's personal station in the corner of their room. A tap on the screen revealed Dricks was in the engine workshop. Probably clearing space in the hope of a component printer.

"Dricks," she said over internal comms. "We're releasing TB. That okay?"

"Yeah, no problem. I'll lock down the door. Let me know if it wanders this way. Got a lot of dreams that'll keep it awake all night in this noggin," Dricks replied.

"Will do." Tremil stated, then turned off the comms.

"He?" said Heki. "Since when did *we* decide TB was male?"

Tremil shrugged. "Can't keep calling him 'it'. Doesn't feel right."

Heki shook her head, but failed miserably to mask her feelings. Tremil knew she agreed, but wouldn't admit to it. Heki lifted the converted sump box gently and headed for their door. Once through, they put the box down on the galley table.

"You go to the far end of the ship," Heki said. "And I'll release TB in sixty seconds and follow *him*. It's a shame the tracking tag keeps shorting out." With one hand on the lid, Heki peered at her sister, waiting.

Tremil huffed and walked off down the corridor, opening each doorway along the way except personal cabins, and engineering, where Dricks was working. On reaching the cargo hold, she froze – a barely audible but obvious scraping setting her on edge. With memories of the dead gang members on her mind, she turned to leave, when the noise repeated. It seemed vaguely familiar, and despite knowing she was emitting anxiety that would stream through the ship and into Dricks' mind, Tremil entered. Keeping low, she ran between the storage containers used for smaller items until she reached a corner view of ZZ3. The robot's eyes were dull, giving the impression the bot was on standby, but there was a tremor to one limb by its side, and another rattled against the deck. A strange sight, as if the robot was having a nightmare. Oddly, she could almost feel ...

The pounding of feet broke the strange spell, Dricks' concern rolling along the corridor as fast as the sound itself. Tremil stood, not wanting to cause more panic in the engineer, and calmed her thoughts – setting her features, and recounting her personal litany in her mind. As Dricks entered the bay, she made to turn, except ZZ3's behaviour drew her back. The tremor had stopped, and the strange aura gone. She blinked, unable to process whether it had been real, or she had imagined it. Had she placed human emotions upon a machine in addition to an alien symbiote?

"You okay?" said Dricks. To Tremil's surprise, she had her carbine in hand, wrapped in oily fingers.

"Fine," she answered, her voice monotone. "S-sorry Dricks. It was all the excitement about letting TB roam. I think I'm a little on edge." Tremil stepped away, back towards ZZ3. "Thought I heard a noise, but there's nothing here."

Dricks lowered the rifle, relaxing, and followed her into the hold. "Stuff shifts after re-entering grav. Happens all the time. Arin never quite gets used to it." She wandered over to ZZ3, slapping the robot affectionately on the arm. By its side sat the inert black containment box, two thick cables protruding from its sides lying on the deck. "Could be these," said Dricks, lifting one. "I told Arin to batten them down, but he gets easily distracted unless I'm on his back." She shoved them tighter to the box and removed a snapped cable tie from the deck nearby. "Unless he did, and the damn plastic was faulty. You know, printing ain't perfect. You have to test whatever you make before using it. There can be issues with the bonds." Dricks pocketed the cable wrap and scanned the hold.

"Duly noted," replied Tremil. "I'd better go see where Heki and the symbiote are."

"No worries." Dricks shouldered the carbine and followed her out, sparing a glance back towards ZZ3 before heading for engineering.

Tremil strode through the ship, carrying out her assigned role for a few doors, only to walk into a wall of emotion. Immediately, she knew exactly where Heki was. The pulse of her twin's mood drawing her like a moth to a flame. Resisting the pull was impossible, especially as the emotions were so different than normal.

The galley.

Had they even moved?

Heki sat at the bench, her back to Tremil. The wave of love, tenderness even, was so different. Tempered, perhaps. When she reached her sister's side, the symbiote rested on her biceps below the sleeve of her striped skinsuit they both wore under a crew t-shirt. Heki was running her hand along the creature's tentacles one by one, and the motion created myriad patterns amid its skin. Brighter, and to her shock, Tremil sensed the symbiote's emotions. They were a match for Heki's, not perfect, but close. An off-kilter element to them she allied with his differing biology.

"Heki," she said. Her sister didn't respond, mesmerised perhaps by the symbiote, or the new type of feelings she was emitting. It was hard to tell. "Heki," Tremil repeated, and placed her hand upon her shoulder. Heki flinched, her heart rate jumping to match the sudden wave of surprise and fear the touch caused. A shudder ran through Tremil, the powerful connection almost knocking her off her feet. The symbiote's colour-display stopped, and TB turned greyish-green, releasing its grip upon Heki. As the alien disengaged, he left a livid red mark on her forearm.

The shift in Heki's mood was instant. The calmness gone, replaced by a flare of anger. It hit the ship like a tidal wave.

"Hek, you need to go to our room, now," she ordered, grabbing her sister by the arm. "Before Dricks sees your arm. Now." Dragging Heki up, she shoved her towards the corridor. "Hurry. Or they'll take TB away, understand? Move."

Heki stumbled, but caught herself. The glare towards her sister full of venom that dissipated as Dricks' voice echoed down the corridor and into the galley.

"Hurry, Hek."

And she did, running lightly along the deck, reaching her room before Dricks appeared from engineering. At least this time she had left the gun behind.

Tremil eyed the symbiote, which lay on the galley table, dragging itself towards her.

The gravity.

That's what they'd forgotten. And why Hek had carried the symbiote. It couldn't cope. What was M4? About 0.6 standard. Far too much.

Stiffly, she reached out, and the symbiote pulled himself onto her palm. She cupped her hand, laying the other on top and turned her back to Dricks as the engineer entered the galley.

"Now what?" said Dricks. Tremil turned her head, catching the concerned look and the set of subtle earphones the engineer wore. The anger must have been raw. Perhaps close to overpowering for Dricks to succumb to the music.

"We fell out," replied Tremil, a tear appearing as she filled her mind with a bad memory – the aftermath of the events on the *Maverick*. The suicides they had caused perfect for the role. "Over the symbiote."

Dricks shook her head. The look, however, a little fearful. "Can I help?"

Tremil used a sad smile, hoping it appeared as it did in her mirror. "No. We just need a moment apart. We'll be fine."

"Okay," said Dricks.

Tremil could feel her relief. It almost made her smile, despite the deception. Not a lie as such, but close. She didn't feel good about it, however. Dricks was her family now, but perhaps the symbiote was too.

Pick your battles, as Arin would say.

Dricks took her sense of relief with her as she headed back to engineering. Tremil imagined the engineer muttering to herself about teenage girls and their moods. When safe, she opened her hands, the symbiote having settled on her palm. The colour ripples were slow and gentle in rhythm. The word that came to her mind was *content*. She stroked it with one finger, each touch tingling with shared delight.

After a few minutes she stood, shifting the alien to her other hand, eyeing the red mark it left with trepidation though admittedly mingled with more than a little hope.

At least we know what it eats.

With a slow, steady sigh, Hendricks walked down the corridor. The gravity sat heavy on her shoulders, yet felt light on her feet, which were thankfully devoid of magboots. But the girls? They were a weight she could never shift. A falling out? No surprise in children who lived their lives in each other's pockets, and she had always assumed they had their spats privately. But this was the first either of them had shared. A step forwards, perhaps.

They had briefly talked of the deaths on the *Maverick*, and those here on M4. But very little, as if the trauma needed to be locked away, and only revealed a piece at a time. She could understand that, after her own horror-filled revelations four years ago.

A scrape caught her thoughts, and she glanced into the cargo hold. ZZ3 stood inert where it had before, the Butcher's containment box sucking in any light by its side. It felt wrong to have the general's body aboard, but she agreed with Rebekah. A bargaining chip that no one but Davina suspected they had, and that's hopefully how it would stay. Incini were supposed to keep to their contracts, though Hendricks had little faith – after her encounters with Almaarian officers – about how nobles viewed dealings with lowlifes.

With the hold quiet, she fingered the cable wrap in her pocket and discarded the broken plastic into the nearest recycle pod. Her thoughts on Arin, and tomorrow.

CHAPTER 5

Rebekah sat in the office waiting room for a third time, wondering how often she would have to repeat the visit. Of course, Hendricks was right. At some point the Enforcers would betray them. All they had was a stay of execution. A delay on revealing them to the Warmonger and her Inquisitors. But for how long?

Savvo's leg shook a little, his anger still present from their last session with Mr Duboit's replacement. She had considered long and hard whether they had been played from the off, and Davina had either lied, or was lied to. The meeting in the bar hinted at the latter, and her actions in saving Hendricks and ultimately the girls. Some clear air amid the fog.

Davina slid the door open, her face neutral though she greeted them both with a smile.

"Mr Duboit is ready," stated Davina, keeping up the pretence of who they were dealing with.

Rebekah caught a hint of frustration. Also, a promising sign.

"Good," she replied. "Come on, Savvo. The hound master has whistled, let's see what he wants his dogs to do."

On entering the room, she was relieved to note the new Mr Duboit was a hologram. The movements were too perfect, mirroring the first meeting she'd had with the Duboit holo, and the voice familiar.

"Captain Khan, and Savvo. Take a seat," said the Enforcer. "We have much to discuss."

Rebekah sat, scanning the room, her chip engaged and checking for any tells of sensor arrays, or potential weaponry. It remained clear, as it had on the last two visits.

"Mr Duboit," she said, tilting her head.

"Yes. Good. Straight to business. I have signed you off Karal for a month. Mr Pike was most accommodating." The Enforcer leaned closer, eyes only for her. "You know, I think he quite likes it when you're not around."

"Probably less swearing and hassle. And cheaper, until they want a dirty job to be done," she replied, adding her own false smile and wishing he'd get on with it.

"Perhaps. I need you to go to the Windward system." The words were blunt, clipped.

"You are f..." Rebekah bit back the swear word, pressing her lips together, "joking. It's a sea of ingrates, murderers, addicts and smuggling gangs."

Duboit nodded along, a smile breaking out. "So I've heard. Perfect for you. I want a cargo retrieved, or failing that, ensuring no one else has their filthy hands on it."

"Where?" she asked, knowing the answer, and wishing to hell she didn't.

"Benetai," he replied, easing back in his chair. "You should fit right in."

Benetai. A shit heap of a space station orbiting one of Windward's seven moons. She knew it by reputation, legendary – almost – among the miners and repair crews who claimed to have been there. She doubted any had ever left the Almaarian System, never mind visited scum central.

"Benetai? And how the f... how the hell are we supposed to get there?"

⚜

"Scarva? You have to be bloody joking," Savvo said, kicking at the recycling bot and missing as it dodged aside. He aimed for the wall instead and succeeded with a hefty *thunk*. "Fucking Scarva? Surely somebody shot that bastard."

"Apparently not." Rebekah checked over her shoulder. The feeling of being followed annoyed her, especially as she was convinced that was the purpose of the paper note – to ruin her downtime with little effort. If anyone had tried their luck at that moment, with the mood they were both in, it would turn ugly. And bloody.

"Which unit was it?" asked Savvo, ramming his hands into his jumpsuit pockets. "Jumney's?"

Rebekah shook her head. "Carmen's."

Scarva was a scum sucking piece of shit. Simple as. A Senti with less ethics than a nanite, who would leave you just as devoid of memories and life if it could. The Warmonger had used the exiled Senti sparingly, mainly for covert ops so secret, only she had access to the mission parameters. Word was Carmen's unit arrived at Bustan 8 on Scarva's dump of a ship, but the bastard had failed to turn up afterwards for dust-off. In truth, there wasn't a Marine around who didn't believe the Senti had sold Carmen out. Dropped the squad and took two payments, one of them Bustan. The unit's dropship disappeared off all comms. Lost? Taken? Who knows? The only certain thing was every Marine they knew assumed the alien had a hand in it. Whether Rebekah truly mourned Carmen was another matter entirely.

"And we get to trust the fucker will be there for pickup. The joys of our new life. I need a drink." Savvo pointed to a bar, but it was out of their league. She doubted they'd get past security with how they were dressed, and their sour mood would likely alert the guard way before their appearance.

Rebekah checked her wrist-link, Arin enquiring if Savvo was ready to relieve Dricks yet. She looked at her co-pilot, doubt settling in her mind.

"Tell you what. You find a spot on Level 5 at Chense's, and I'll take your shift on the *Sunstar*. Nicky's free, isn't she?" His altered body language calmed her worries. Savvo glanced over, the scowl replaced by the slightest of smiles.

"You sure?"

She squeezed his arm, directing Savvo towards the lift. "Yeah. I'll go over the deets. Do a Dricks and break it all down ready for the morning. Then we can meet on board with a takeout and analyse what resources we're gonna need. How's that?"

Savvo grinned, punching Level 5. "Hey, that bloody dust cloud? On R6. Nicky let me know what it was. R89 broke apart. A rubble asteroid that proved too unstable to mine. They must have left behind some shit that blew during one of the flare's particle runs. We only hit the edge. Lucky, if you think about it."

"Yeah, lucky." She winked as the door closed, despite not feeling it, and took the next lift alongside several office workers heading for lunch. Saddled in the corner, she watched the back of their heads, trying to work out if she was envious of their mundane lives. Yes, they were in space, but did they ever really experience it? Live it?

And did she live it too much?

Benetai was wild, simple as. And the job far from a standard recovery run. Barely used wetware, apparently removed from a dead unit on their first run and intercepted on the way back to the Senti. Stolen from an innocuous autoship transport, according to Duboit, years beforehand. Then pirated and sold on, only to raise its head when Almaarian intelligence identified its location after a failed auction.

So why was this an Enforcer-led mission, and not the intelligence service? Or a covert Marine black ops team? Duboit shut that conversation down. Mentioned an officer-noble's embarrassment at the loss, someone a little higher up now in the echelons of the Court. Like she gave a crap. Besides, he had emphasised they were his dogs, to be unleashed on whatever he decided. She concluded that meant a combination of expendable and ... expendable. It stank.

All they had was a cargo freight number, thirty sets of wetware and that the frequency was classified. So, in the unlikely event they were operational, the tracer HUDs wouldn't show them up.

Find the kit, buy it, steal it, or destroy it. She preferred the last one. Simpler. Duboit didn't.

"Fun times," she said to herself quietly. The man in front looked over, and to her surprise, she recognised him.

The smile was warm. He pointed to his temple. "How's the head?" he asked.

"Fine," she replied, "And thank you. I was a little drunk."

"A little? Stig had me swear off the stuff for a week afterwards." His accompanying laugh was genuine. "You on R&R?"

"Downtime, yeah. Not for long. Get our grav quota and back out." She felt awkward. Strangely out of her depth in a simple conversation. "You know how it is."

"Actually, I don't. Hardly ever get off this rock. Working life kind of sucks the joy out sometimes." The lift stopped at Level 4, and the man whose name she never got, started to leave. "I will mention you to Stig. I'll tell him you're doing fine. And sober."

She laughed, and watched him exit, wondering who would be there to greet him when he went home. A perfect partner, perhaps. One who made it all worthwhile. She brushed away an unexpected tear.

Not her life.

Nor could it ever be.

But maybe for the others, if she could keep them alive long enough.

Rebekah squeezed herself into the oddly shaped chair, trying to work out if she knew any human it would fit. The concourse was half-empty, with only a couple of crews waiting for the shuttle to M4 like her. She nodded to the occasional one she recognised, and displayed enough *piss off* and *leave me alone* aura to be sat by herself. As the shuttle's airlock tunnel connected to the arriving shuttle, billowing then tightening as air was pumped in, she caught someone's eye – not hard when they were staring right at her. With her chip engaged, the woman's holo-mask flickered, and Rebekah wondered if she had come to collect on her promise.

Rebekah smiled and raised her eyebrows, causing a flare of anger in response as the woman strode over. Rebekah glanced to the airlock; aware it would soon be open. This was not a place for a fight, and under Karal jurisdiction, would likely end badly for both of them.

She stood, her stance loose, ready. She had to admit, letting off a little steam was tempting after her encounter with Duboit. A flex of her forearm was rewarded with a familiar pressure against the scar on her wrist.

The woman was within a few metres when she spoke, her words almost a hiss. "I haven't forgotten my promise," she said, the mask perfect, syncing lip movement with the words. "I will have those eyes."

"You have issues," replied Rebekah. "And I have friends in high places." She moved towards the opening doors, on the half-turn, yet fully focused on the woman.

"Sometimes the reward is worth a little pain. I owe you, bitch. For more than a single beating. The *Maverick* is now top of the list, and then there's the *Hatton*. You have a lot of backs to watch, and there's only one of you."

Rebekah turned sharply, and the woman backed off, hands up. An ugly smile on the holo.

"See. I know what makes you weak. Your crew. Your friends. Your eyes will be last, understand? When I've stripped you of everything, I'll take them." She turned away, and the urge to drive the wrist knife into her kidney washed over Rebekah. Only the thought of the twins stayed her hand.

Just.

She allowed the chip to calm her thoughts, and entered the airlock, cracking a thumb knuckle along the way.

When she reached the ship, Hendricks was already waiting, her overnight bag packed and a hopeful gleam in her eye. Rebekah decided against explaining the mission, but advised her to watch her back with the return of Victor Goncho and whatever gang members were about.

For a moment she considered contacting Davina, to pass on the same message to Duboit. Instead, she called Arin to ensure he met Dricks off the shuttle, settling down afterwards to an afternoon and evening of deets, mission briefs and teenagers.

Fun.

"Hey, you two," she said over comms. "I have chocolate."

CHAPTER 6

Rebekah watched the camera feed, head tilted with her eyes lidded. Trying to work out what Arin's concern really was.

"There," said Arin, pointing at the slate.

"What am I looking at?" replied Rebekah. "I know what I'm seeing, teenage girls eating in the middle of the night. But that's no real change." She switched the slate off, giving Arin a half-bemused look with a tiny shake of her head.

"They're eating more," he replied. "More than I planned for, anyway. Did you see how much was piled on that plate." He tapped the screen for emphasis.

Rebekah let out a small laugh. "If you're telling me you're worried about two stick-thin girls *eating*, we're going to have an issue. If it's 'what the hell is going to happen to my secret stash', then I get it. Hide your stuff in your room. Or in Dricks' cabin, she won't mind."

"Humph. She'll have licked the sprinkles off before I get a second look," he replied, pushing himself up from the galley table. "Don't say I didn't warn you." He made towards the coffee pot when she took his arm, gently pulling him back.

"I'll keep an eye. Maybe being a parent isn't as easy as being a Marine." Rebekah tried to make it sound light, but instead it felt like she had voiced her own worries. Not that eating was one of them. They had also logged an extra half-an-hour each in the ship's gym.

Arin twisted his mouth, looking to the deck with a nod. "Yeah. I get it. And no, it isn't. Dricks was worried about the *Maverick*, and the rest. All that death. The trauma. Downloaded a few books."

Rebekah smiled at the red-haired sub-engineer, blinking back the emotions that welled up before she shoved them down. "Yeah. I get the feeling books and doctors won't have any answers for ours. I'll talk to them."

Eventually. It's not as if we haven't got enough worries.

She let Arin go. The sub-engineer rubbed the back of his neck, and his fixed gaze on the deck broke. With a rueful smile, he prepped a flask of black coffee before sitting back down.

"I've been through the cargo our new Mr Duboit provided. This hush-hush shit hasn't made things easy. Got a restock on the navy suits' patching gel, which, considering a certain captain's predilection for getting shot, is a good thing. No new carbine grenades, but unless we're in a full-scale war, we should be okay. Surprisingly, the request for a Navy-issue plasma torch couldn't be fulfilled." Arin grinned at Rebekah's raised eyebrow and swiped the screen before spinning it around. "I asked for the electronic mines from our Breaker days. The directional explosives. That was a no-can-do, but Davina acquired enough parts that I should be able to build our own versions."

"Useful. And the printer?"

"A few years old, but serviceable. I inputted the engineering schematics, and it's still processing, but I can't see an issue. The simpler parts it spat out in seconds. What's key is getting the right resources for it to build with.

Anything big is limited by its size and speed, as well as what we have in the way of materials. And whether we have the correct structural schematic." He sighed, taking a sip of the black coffee and wincing in a mix of pleasure and surprise. "Davina sent some great coffee. That's a boon."

"And suits," she laughed. "Don't forget those."

"Yeah. Hypoxia kind of focuses the mind on different things. Brand new, Karal-branded survival kit with scrubbers. Purloined from Pike's private store, no doubt." He stood, finishing his coffee and placing the flask inside the cleaning unit under Rebekah's watchful eye.

"You know the drill," she said. "Service the navy kit, make sure it's ready at the drop of a space helmet. And let's hope we don't need it."

"And Savvo?"

"He may need a hand. Apparently, the old armour has a few old kinks and dinks."

"Like Dricks then," he said, eyes raising to lock with hers. "I never got the chance ..."

Rebekah shook her head. "Don't. It's took most of the past month to box all that shit up. Don't open the lid again. The operation, the implant, was the right thing to do, whatever the circumstances. And nor do you go round thinking you both owe me. Dricks means as much to me as to you, but it doesn't colour what I chose. We're locked in with this Enforcer until we find a way out. Want to thank me? Think on how the fuck we get out of an agreement with no contract. One where that bastard holds all the cards."

Davina ran through the long list of messages, prioritising as she went. Those related to the true Mr Duboit's dealings she filed into a secondary sub-category, and then divided them into a hierarchy of need. Once complete, she turned her thoughts to those of her new – what was the word? – subcontractor perhaps? Relating to resource provision for the *Sunstar* and her crew, as well as a pressing list of coded messages she couldn't access. Yet.

Davina clicked on a personal message. Her sensory wetware pinged, which the flash in her brain translated into a visual stimulus, though in truth it was far from it. The top line of graphics were embedded with a structural code that alerted her array. She swiped the message, sending it to her Incini encrypted slate.

"Just say no, and I can get back to my life," she whispered, and opened the message. The old saying was 'in black and white', taken, if her pre-Senti history was correct, from when paper was in vogue and the written word was trusted. Back in the days of ink.

Unfortunately, the words on the screen – or to be more accurate – the shapes on the message that her wetware interpreted, were from the Directorate, and not good.

"Fuck," she said, choosing the *Sunstar* crew's favourite expletive. She scanned the encrypted message again. An agreement to the sub-assignment that condemned her to a life of Enforcer servitude. Yes, it was wrapped up in 'circumstances', and commendation for her service so far. But in truth, her soul had been sold. She was to carry on her work as Mr Duboit's Incini, dealing with Karal and the other mining companies with a clear subtext that these were to be less controversial to the Court. All the while, to also act as the hand of the Enforcers. A shadow on board M1, and over her future. Once you were sucked into the emperor's agency, there was no going back. At least her indenture to the Directorate would be paid back sooner, if she didn't burn out, or get burned.

It left her hopes dashed that the temporary service she had been forced into would be negated by the real Mr Duboit. Perhaps with a demand that he got what he paid for. Apparently not. She wondered if he had been coerced, or bribed. Probably a combination of the two.

With a sigh, she closed the message, eyeing the blink on her office slate. She stood, smoothed down her clothes, and engaged her Incini training as a smile bloomed. Elegance returned, she knocked on the door and entered to the sound of the holo firing up.

The fake Mr Duboit ignored her, staring at whatever was in his hands, she assumed a slate though the holo showed a book. Eventually, he put it down, clasping his hands together and placing them below his chin. The smile was hard to interpret. Some would say triumphant, but in truth, when did an Enforcer *not* have their wishes met?

The holo phased, and she was presented with the image of a different man. She stored it, but trusted the image as much as a *bastardo*.

"Sit. Now that you are fully in my service," said the holo, "you may call me Mr Erikson. Understood?"

She nodded, and took a seat, hands in her lap, an expectant smile in place. "And how may I be of service?"

"I am sure you are aware that Mr Duboit's presence on M1, and his dealings with Karal, are to continue for the betterment of himself and the Court. So, a continuation of contract negotiations, mining rights, the automining systems, and on and on ... yawn. How interesting. For that, you will maintain a line of contact. Be aware, that this is monitored." Erikson smiled. A cat playing with whatever it had caught – disinterested and bored.

"I understand."

"I'm certain you do. The business with the *Hatton*, I am sure, is something Duboit would like to keep hidden. I am not of the mind to delve, but I'm more than positive I wouldn't like what I found."

"I can't comment," she stated. He knew this. All the contract negotiations, whether with a criminal organisation or not, were Incini registered. Therefore, sealed as per the Directorate's tenets. Only an act of the Emperor, where treason was surmised, could change that, and that had never been the case yet. Such dealings shouldn't pass through the Directorate's scrutiny, but corruption is as corruption does.

"Yes. You can't. However, I am curious about events around the *Maverick*. Assuming, as I do, that this was all under contractual obligation via Mr Duboit, are you still bound by the tenets?" He leant back, steepling his fingers now so that only the tips touched his chin. If it had been a face-to-face contact, she would have read much into that. But on a holo? And with Enforcer training? She didn't ignore the tells, just mistrusted them.

"I am. The Directorate have agreed with my report." She kept her face neutral, hands still, her gaze on the holo. Underneath, she squirmed. Her warning to Rebekah had meant something. A measure of what was to come with no prescience required.

Mr Erikson's smile was tight, and he leaned forwards. "They did. However, that does not sate my curiosity. I want to understand who I am dealing with a little more – this crew of Breakers. I want you to acquire the investigative evidence for me, in full. I am sure Mr Duboit's name and involvement will open those doors required. And his money."

"Simple enough," she replied. And it would be. Not quite the normal work for an Incini, but then, she wasn't one anymore. The advantage was obvious. If she negotiated the agreement, Duboit's apparent side of the deal was guaranteed to be silent. It opened so many more lowlife minds to bribery, especially when they knew that it would lead to serious implications for Duboit should he renege. "Anything else?"

"No," he replied. "Not yet. But there will be once I've analysed the evidence. You may go."

The hologram cut out, leaving an empty desk behind. Davina stared at the space where Erikson had been. A life tipped upside down. Is this how the Breakers had felt when they took on Heki and Tremil? One moment their life set, with purpose and order. Then thrown into a spin drier, never knowing where it may get tangled next.

She pushed herself up from the decidedly uncomfortable chair and left the office, her visual memory system extracting the names of the investigation panel, and from there, branching out until she found a likely contact with access to the evidence base. Davina had no other choice than to trust the crew's alteration of the evidence, and the panel had taken little time to come to the correct conclusion about the actions of the *Maverick*. They hardly had any upstanding support to appeal, after all. But would it stand up to an Enforcer's eyes and resources?

Davina sighed. Like she had told Rebekah, she could not be trusted. The Incini tenets bound her to the Enforcer's demands. Back in her office, it wasn't long before the details of her contact were up on the slate. With a tap, she began her new life.

CHAPTER 7

From space, the rear of the ship carried an air of alien advancement. The looped curves of the rear engine compartments interwoven into an organic design that eased a human eye. It appeared capable, sleek and crafted. As if the creator of such a spaceship had a vision of the beholder gaining trust and belief in its capabilities simply from its appearance. This was in stark contrast to the bow, its bulbous nose mired in a multitude of hacked together aerials and protrusions which Rebekah would normally assume were comms systems and sensor arrays. However, Senti uniformly kept their tech a close secret, especially scum buckets like Scarva, who relied on the technological marvel of Faster Than Light travel to keep goods and payment flowing. Therefore, they could have numerous unguessable purposes. Unlike the rotating centre where Scarva berthed spaceships looking for passage. Those who sought to avoid paying official fees or prying eyes. There was a single shuttle docked right now, and by the look of it, as ill-kempt as the main Senti ship.

"Has the ship responded yet?" Rebekah asked, adjusting the trajectory for another slow sweep past the ship. It all cost fuel, and gnawed at her patience. Efficiency, a mark of her dealings with the Senti as part of the

Marines, absent from their first contact with Scarva and the alien's ship, the *Unpronounceable*. It wasn't the Senti spacecraft's true moniker, but with the name more akin to the crash of a wave against a sea wall, it would have to do.

"Transponder beacon has activated," replied Savvo, and he duly locked the *Sunstar*'s navcom to the signal.

Rebekah felt the ship slip from her guidance, and eased off the controls to let the computers work through the finer details of docking one missile hurtling through space, with another. The thrusters kicked in, and they slowly adjusted until aligned and their speeds matched. To give Scarva its due, the transition was smooth, everything working fine until the docking clamps attempted to engage. Hendricks' swearing filled the comms as the scrape of metal upon metal reverberated through the hull. A second attempt had her in near apoplexy until the Senti changed tack and used a nose clamp to steady the ship and ease it into place.

The navcom signalled its release from Senti control, and the false gravity created by the *Unpronounceable*'s central spinning core engaged. Rebekah felt her inner ear argue about the change, and cheated, stabilising her system via the wetware. Arin would do the same, leaving Hendricks disorientated initially until she eventually adapted, and Savvo if he could maintain his discipline and avoid using the chip.

"Half standard," her co-pilot said, unbuckling and standing up gingerly. "Lovely."

Rebekah smirked and ran through a navcom system check. Once complete, she joined Savvo in the galley, leaning against the units while trying not to find Hendricks' flushed tirade the least bit funny.

"Fucking Scarva. I told you; I told all of you, that fucker needs a carbine up his arse and ..."

Arin was trying desperately to look the other way, avoiding Savvo's gaze as if eye contact would leave them both in fits of laughter, and the next target.

Rebekah collected a flask and took her place at the galley table. She placed her slate directly in front, the coffee on the upper right, and proceeded to clasp her hands together on the table edge. She eyed the engineer, stoney-faced until Hendricks finally caught her gaze. The engineer stopped in mid-word, open-mouthed and then clammed up.

"Finished?" Rebekah asked.

A single nod confirmed she was, Hendricks apparently not trusting herself to speak.

"Good. Because we're depending on this shit to give us a ride there, and more importantly, back. Right now, all Scarva knows is that we have business in Windward and we chose *it* to take us. So that means we're fucking shady. Going in all guns blazing about Bustan 8 is not going to cut it. So swallow all your crap, lock it away, and take whatever comes. We're gonna have to pay our dues, all of us, and that means dealing direct." Rebekah leaned closer, making sure Hendricks knew where her words were aimed. "Understand?"

Her ex-captain nodded.

"Dreams?" said Savvo. "We paying the old way?"

"I doubt it. This mind-sucker feeds the black market wherever the Senti finds it. Those of us with wetware will be fine. I hinted at memories of the *Hatton*. That should be enough to get us passage. You okay with that, Dricks?" She wanted to take the woman's hands, but here and now, she needed to be a captain, not a friend.

Hendricks grimaced, pulling at her collar before responding. "Yeah. Don't need them. I'll put memory markers in. I've got this."

"If there's one thing I've learned, anyone who says that ..."

"Got shit," replied her squad, but there was humour there and Dricks managed a slight smile.

"Are we dressing for the occasion?" asked Savvo, a glint to his eye that she well understood. From here on in, everyone they dealt with was untrustworthy. Scarva was an unknown despite the reputation perpetuated by bitter Marines, but as far as they were all concerned, that Senti was the most dishonest of them all. Maybe it was worth demonstrating they were going to take no shit from the start.

Rebekah longed for a combat vest. Rarely worn by the Breakers – dropping into a war zone required the powered kit Savvo had been checking over – so they had added vests to the list when the mission brief suggested making a deal with their target before resorting to more forceful means. Pirates and thieves, gang members and drug runners. Good times ahead, requiring a little more protection if they could get it. Slim-fitting, they were designed to prevent projectile ingress. Or to be blunt, getting shot and stabbed. This was, of course, relative, and on an asteroid mining centre, impossible to acquire – but anything would make her feel less naked than she did right now.

The second-hand flight jacket she wore wouldn't stop a drawing pin, never mind a knife or bullet, so her shield had to be the aura she projected. A handgun at her hip, and a 'don't mess with me' attitude that powered armour, and a carbine usually helped with.

Rebekah added combat vests to Arin's printing projects.

The airlock corridor stank. Old cabbage and mould, with a faint whiff of stagnant seawater. The latter, she wondered, perhaps triggered in her brain by the ship's Senti name. Already on edge, stained walls and fouled decks were adding to her mood. The sight of the Senti in a clearly old but functional encounter suit wasn't helping either. Four limbs hooked into the deck gave the impression of reversed legs, but she knew they contained tentacles supported by the liquid-filled suit. Three limbs protruded from the torso, one at the chin and the others from what the human mind assigned as shoulders. The elongated head sat inside a plexi-glass helmet, with the flat face central and set back.

The chin tentacle held an ancient slate. Screen cracked, modded edges frayed. Another Senti appeared on the screen, gestures and voice wholly misaligned as it spoke. It wore no encounter suit, the upper half of its body spread wide in folds of blue and green skin.

"Welcome to (sound of crashing waves) crew of the … what was the name again? It slipped my mind?" The voice was clear, concise. Not human, but familiar in tone to the Senti Rebekah had encountered previously. She had never thought about it before – to a Marine it was useless information – but Rebekah wondered how it spoke. Nothing moved on the face and the possibility of it being manufactured came to mind.

"*Solar Flame*," replied Rebekah, stepping closer to the slate. "As you know." She added a smile filled with disinterested malice. At least, that was her aim. "Scarva, is it?"

"In your language, yes. *Solar Flame*." A tentacle hovered in the background, grasping or tapping off screen. "Yes, yes. That's what your transponder is saying. And you are the captain of this vessel? Khan, is it?"

Rebekah nodded, then remembered the Senti couldn't read body language. Well, that's what the Marines had been told.

"Yes," she growled. They had toyed with false names, but Scarva was about to drain their memories, and no one in the Windward planetary system would know who they were. The ship would be on a docking record, assuming Benetai had one, hence the adapted transponder code courtesy of Davina.

"And three crew. Hmmmm. There are more of you aboard." The Senti's chin tentacle waved at the screen, almost as if wagging a finger. Along the inside were hooked barbs, like needle-shaped teeth. Rebekah suppressed a shudder and batted away the image of crimson sacs with emerging hybrids. "*All* must pay."

"They are too young," said Savvo, interrupting, his voice low and hard. "Understand."

"If you're going to quote some bullshit agreement or other, you're on the wrong ship," replied Scarva. Rebekah could detect no anger or enmity in the voice, adding to her assumption it was manufactured. "No Senti tariffs here."

"They won't be paying," cut in Rebekah. "You were willing enough when it was four. Price agreed. You ain't touching my kids." She forced herself to relax, while holding herself still and stony-faced.

"Then someone pays extra. You need to work out who by the time you reach my lab. Shame, youngling's memories are sought after. The price high." The three black eyes of the Senti glistened, and the mouth slit beneath them quivered slightly. "Always the same when the *rules* get in the way of such delights."

Rebekah's stomach roiled, acid-bubbling in disgust at the Senti's reaction. A hand squeezed her arm, and a glance back told her it was Hendricks. The engineer dipped her chin towards her right hand, Rebekah finding she had gripped her gun. Letting out a slow breath, she let go, flexing her fingers.

Scarva refocused on them. "Follow Yat to my lab."

The Senti, Yat apparently, lowered its slate and turned away, magboots clanking along the metal deck. The smell didn't get any better the further they walked into the ship. At least there was air, though the pleasure of grav reduced as they moved closer to the central hub. The rotational speed was higher than she was used to, but tolerable, and after thirty metres or so and passing a multitude of rooms that on a human ship may have been cabins, stopped. Yat stood aside, its elongated head bobbing in the liquid, while one limb scraped at a door shaped as a square with a rounded top. It opened inwards.

Rebekah had been hoping for a scrubbed and sterile lab, only to be badly let down. Two thumb knuckles cracked as she took the lead, disgusted, her elbow scraping across the mouldy architrave as she entered the room. A quick scan allayed any initial fears of a double-cross, but gnawed at her nerves. The room was as cobbled together and metal-stained as the rest of the ship. None of the smooth membranes, or absorbent floors they had encountered when transferring to the war front.

Scarva was not there, but she motioned the rest inside. Arin took a seat on a battered-looking chair that reminded Rebekah of a dentist's, while Hendricks and Savvo took station in the corner, eyes on the door, and plainly on edge like her.

A scrape of tooth on metal emerged from the doorway, and a Senti entered. Folds of blue and green rubbery skin layered over a puffed-out body hovered above four thick tentacles hooked onto the decking. The side tentacles slid along the edges of the door, as if feeling their way, and pulled the bulbous Senti into the lab. The three eyes retained their glint. Wet, expectant, not dead like the other Senti. The skin, however, looked far more aged than she had seen before. Wrinkled and dry in places. An assumption, but a sense of age hung about the alien. There were two more Senti in encounter suits behind, one possibly Yat. Guards.

"Aha," said Scarva. "Ready and waiting. Good, good." Tentacles emerged from behind the elongated head, a symbiote scampering over the Senti with an eagerness that belied the alien's appearance. Perhaps the symbiotes were longer lived, or not, and they had many such relationships during their lifetime. "Hmmmm. A pleasure to meet such upstanding fellows in person. And who is paying the younglings' share?"

Hendricks nodded, as agreed, and approached the Senti. "I am."

"Well, I've had a thought. A delivery I need making on Benetai. Perhaps a deal — requiring the one extra memory set, in return for this favour?" Scarva stared at Rebekah, its frill quivering. "Yes?"

With a glance to Hendricks, she nodded to the Senti. One less donation meant there would be more to give later. And a package? That could provide an element of truth to their cover. "Agreed."

"Then ..." began the Senti, its tentacles pulling it further into the lab and towards the chair.

"This ain't my first ride in a mind-suckers saddle, Scarva," growled Hendricks. "I know what I'm doing." She shoved Arin from the chair, and sat, swivelling her legs to lay down upon the long back support. "Scan me. I have placed the memory markers. Both sets. Scrape any more and I'll ..."

"Dricks! Shut the fuck up," snarled Rebekah, though she leaned back on to the stained wall, arms crossed. "Stop your bitchin'."

Hendricks' mouth twisted; a scowl heavy across her brow. But she did as she was told, playing the part they had both agreed. The Senti glided closer, shoulder limbs wrapped either side of the chair, while the symbiote scurried down its chin tentacle. Colour flowed over the cuttlefish-like creature as it rested on Hendricks' skull. The Senti stroked the symbiote, a quiver to its upper layer of skin unsettling Rebekah.

"You are broken, old soldier," said the Senti. "And the wetware's empty."

Hendricks rumbled deep in her throat but said nothing.

"Yes. You are experienced. Those markers are well set." The Senti turned to each of the crew one by one, finally settling on Rebekah. "Are you all broken?"

Rebekah made to speak, when a tentacle rose, as if to hush her.

"No. I will find out soon enough. If this mind is anything to go by, you carry memories I would pay well for. The human war still sells so very well. All that blood, and emotions. Quite thrilling to the right buyer." The odd eye wetness returned, and the slit she took to be a mouth, opened and closed.

Rebekah pushed herself off the wall using her back, uncrossing her arms. "Those we're saving for when they're needed, Scarva. We know their worth, and you will soon enough. Think of them as a promise for when we need your services in a fucking hurry. Yes? And ..." She drew closer, forcing herself to deal with the alien's odd smell. "Everything we've marked as off-limits, stays off-limits. Understand? We're already paying well. And I trust nobody. Human, Senti," she nodded to the symbiote, "or their pets. Touch them, and we'll know, and you will never get your tentacles on our war. And they are good, Scarva. Blood-filled. *Painful*."

The Senti's skin bulged, and the alien off-gassed from its upper frill.

"How good?" it asked.

She leaned in. "Frontline," she whispered, and turned away.

"Tease," replied the Senti. "But I will keep to the contract. And I never forget a promise."

"Keep to the right areas of our brains, and neither will I," Rebekah said, Arin snorting with a barely restrained chuckle in the background.

CHAPTER 8

Heki rubbed at her forearm. The skin had healed with no scarring, but it itched as if dry. TB sat atop his tank, tentacles waving, though his colours were muted to shades of green. Heki had expected the symbiote to act strangely when they docked with the Senti ship, but nothing had changed at all. The little alien remained passive, seemingly content with their company, and much healthier.

Tremil stirred the pot of dried fungi and hot water on the galley top, the nutritious soup it created anathema to both twins. Her nose wrinkled at the fusty aroma. She poured the contents into two bowls and brought them over.

Heki took a sip, her lips twisting at the taste. "Yum."

"In hindsight, we should have chosen something more appetising," said Tremil.

Heki nodded in agreement. "It was all I could think of when Arin asked what we were feeding TB. I don't think he'd have gone with chocolate cake and cream."

Tremil laughed and sipped the soup, then held her nose. With her eyes to the galley ceiling, she poured the concoction into her mouth, swallowed, and choked a little. She quickly snapped a chocolate bar in two, sucking on her own half before munching it down.

"That work?" asked Heki, and at Tremil's affirming smile, did the same with hers. The chocolate took away the taste, with added benefits. "Better."

Tremil poked the symbiote affectionately. "This is your fault."

Heki couldn't help but smile when TB wrapped his tentacles about Tremil's fingers, and was about to do the same when a muted crash echoed along the corridor. Immediately, they were up and out of the bench seats, their emotions rolling around the ship in a wave of anxiety.

"Cargo hold?" Heki said, a question that didn't need answering.

They headed along the passage, cautious and on edge. A second clatter confirmed the direction, and together they checked the camera feed along the corridor. It appeared still, nothing out of place though the field of view didn't include the hold's internal door. They watched the screen for a few seconds, and with nothing altering, Heki dinged the door open. The internal airlock was disengaged as expected, and where it would have stretched across the doorway, sat a half-open metal container. Optical wires and component boards were strewn across the deck.

"A mess," Heki said, and jumped over, turning about to start tidying up.

"Hek," said Tremil, her voice uncertain, causing her sister to look up.

Heki followed Tremil's gaze, which appeared focused on ZZ3 towards the centre of the room. "What's up?"

"ZZ3 has moved," she said.

Heki tutted. "I'm sure Arin will have been doing something. Are you going to help?"

"No. I mean since we checked the cam." She glanced back over her shoulder, towards the viewscreen on the wall. "I'm sure."

"Too many mushrooms," replied Heki. "Grab hold, will you?" She held the far edge of the now full box and indicated Tremil to take the other.

Between them, with the low grav, they managed to tip it back level in its allotted slot.

"I am sure," said Tremil, wiping dusty hands on her crew jumpsuit. She glanced at the bot and shook her head, as if clearing her thoughts.

"Paranoia," said Heki. "Not good for empaths. Can you imagine what that'd do to Old Lady Dricks?"

Tremil snorted, and a faint buzzer sounded in the main ship. The crew were returning, and they were under orders to keep TB locked away.

"I'll get TB," said Tremil, and headed down the corridor before Heki could argue.

"Typical," she mouthed, and then checked the box lid. A sudden presence, as if being watched, loomed in her mind, with an accompanying noise at the edge of her hearing. Like breathing, but not. She spun, eyeing ZZ3. Had Tremil spooked her? Put thoughts in her head? Something they often did to each other. The bot stared back, inert. Heki blew out a sigh and turned away, closing the cargo hold door behind her as voices bounced down the passageway.

By the time she reached the galley, she had control of her thoughts. With her face set hard, her movements stiffened while she managed her emotions. Their increased contact of late had enabled them to practise with greater regularity, and devise increasingly effective strategies when not under stress. Distraction helped; often task focused. But when facing less rigid social interaction, they had to be constantly focused, and the strain took its toll.

"All okay?" asked Rebekah, whose emotions Heki could taste as if they were on her tongue. There was relief there, and anger, mixed with an edge of stress.

"All good," Heki replied, and clasped her hands together.

Rebekah smiled back and the captain's emotions switched to love. Heki basked in its warmth for a second, though it broke her resolve, and her own smile slipped, falling further as her eyes fell on Dricks. The woman looked ill, her face drained and sweat beaded across her brow.

"I'm going to go lay down," Hendricks said, and headed towards her cabin.

Heki followed, concern forcing her feet to follow. "You okay?" she asked, her voice monotone, and in her mind, safe.

Hendricks waited for her to catch up, then carried on. "The Senti ... when they take a memory from wetware, it kind of doesn't physically hurt you in any way. Your memory remains intact, you just feel violated, you know. Like someone's rifled through the most private version of you, exposing who you are."

"And if they take a real memory, you get the same but worse?" asked Heki, blinking as she thought of that being done to her.

"Kind of, yeah. I have a hole in my thoughts that wasn't there before, filled with that violation." Dricks stopped in front of her cabin, hand resting on the door. "I know what they took, because we discussed it before we went. So not only have I been exposed, violated, I can't remember why. That hits you hard."

Heki paused for a moment, trying to imagine such an absence. She understood the debasement, being used and your emotions ripped raw from you. That had been a daily occurrence in the lab as they tested how far she could be pushed before she snapped, and the emotional tidal wave poured forth. But the absence was foreign to her, alien, and she couldn't put herself in Dricks' place.

"Did you give them us? When ... when we hurt you?"

Hendricks slowly shook her head, eyes on the floor. "No. That's a part of me I treasure. A rebirth, if you will, after being dead inside for so long. That's staying with me until the day I die."

Heki couldn't help it, and lost control, the wave of stress and love from the engineer too much.

"Woah," said Dricks, squeezing her ears as if she could block out Heki's burst of need. "Calm down. I have enough to deal with."

"Heki!" shouted Arin along the corridor, the voice strained and pleading. "Please."

"S-sorry," she said, and found herself hugging the engineer, before striding towards her room as fast as possible. She burst through the door, throwing herself onto the bed. Pencils and her drawing pad bounced off in the low grav, landing on the deck, and she tried to restrain the sob rising in her throat.

Tremil perched next to her, a hand against her back. The touch felt like acid, unwanted, and she bucked it off only for soft, dry tentacles to replace it. They edged along her spine, distracting Heki from the raw love for her family overwhelming her mind. Alighting on the back of her head, the symbiote pulsed gently.

Heki felt the emotions slide away. No, not all. A little, as if the symbiote sipped at the edges, smoothing them, enabling her to regain some control.

"Tremil," she whispered between the tears. "Can you feel that?"

"Some," her sister replied, and Tremil's finger graced her head next to the symbiote, edging one of the tentacles aside. "But he's not feeding off you. There's no mark."

Heki calmed, her turmoil triggered by Hendricks settling as the symbiote lapped at her emotions. What had the engineer said? Violated? This didn't feel like that. TB wasn't draining her thoughts and memories, more calming stormy waters as he drank. Admittedly the Senti symbiote was familiar with them, and though she was in danger of giving an alien human traits as well as gender, there was a sense of companionship. A togetherness exemplified by how calm TB had been in the galley.

"There's something in this," she said, half to herself. Tremil's hand returned to the small of her back. No longer a touch of acid, but warmth. "For us both."

Rebekah moved through the ship quietly, the magboots set low with the grav as it was. She tapped on the twins' door, and with no response, eased it open. Heki and Tremil knew she would be checking in and had left it disengaged. Once inside, she scanned the dark room using only the residual light from the corridor. The girls were completely out, their breathing regular.

According to Scarva the journey might take longer than the transference modules used by the Senti Orb. Those trips the Marines slept through, and on the run from Bustan when they had deserted with the twins in tow, it had only taken a few days. Rebekah harrumphed, stark memories of Heki and Tremil's stress came flooding back. Their first sight of the needle gun for the sedative, their fear. Everyone had been under pressure. Newly deserted, with the causes of that decision both traumatised. That day they had all taken to headphones, even Hendricks, in an attempt to cope. It had been the first step in truly understanding the future they had chosen for themselves.

"Only for a short while," she whispered, smiling down at the twins. Just enough time to get them through the transference into void-space – as Scarva called it – and back out the other side. Pure emptiness, where anything with an imagination would suffer horrendously as they ripped through. Rebekah had her doubts. More like a Senti trick to ensure humanity didn't learn their secrets, and become independent of their mind-stealing. You put the travellers to sleep, and they learn nothing.

A scrabbling drew her attention, and a waving tentacle tip, her eye. She wandered over, the blue glow from the top of the box joined by six others as the symbiote recognised her presence. Rebekah touched a single tentacle with a finger, sensing the connection. Scarva's symbiote had been no different from her past experiences, whether that was due to the wetware or not was an unknown. But her involvement with TB, as the twins named the alien, always felt different. No revulsion. Two beings making contact and perhaps taking comfort from that. The alien appeared healthy and content, if she could risk such a judgement.

She turned about and closed the cabin door, palming the lock. With her boots clicking, she toured through the *Sunstar*, or *Solar Flame* as it was to be known for the next few weeks, enjoying the quiet and low light.

Peaceful. A moment before the storm to come.

Should she feel guilt at being secretly excited about the mission? Stretching their potential, Major Ren, their former officer-noble, would have called it. Doing something out of their comfort zone. One of the better nobles, but still a bastard. Ren wanted his Marines back in one piece, but only so he could throw them into the next meat grinder.

Once past the cabin doors, she eyed the cargo hold. Scarva had reiterated the transfer affected gravity in weird ways. Twisted it into spheres of high and low effects that the Senti steered around as they were just as susceptible as humans – and more so to high grav. Even so, she had tasked Arin and Hendricks with ensuring everything in the hold and engineering was secured, while she and Savvo checked the remainder of the ship.

With a sigh, her need to be *sure* playing on her mind, Rebekah entered the hold. A quick tour reassured, and she cast a final glance to the Butcher's box-cum-coffin and the inert ZZ3. Despite the robot's rescue of Arin and Savvo, and its usual role since the *Scourge* and that ship's foul secrets, she still didn't feel comfortable around the bot. Being chased and threatened with dismemberment kind of did that to a person.

"When we're out of void-space, I'm going to see about having you moved. Creepy storing you next to that corpse." She made to slap the bot's nearest limb, exactly as she would have done in the past, and changed her mind. "Not ready for that yet."

She left, the hold door closing behind her and clicked her way towards her own cabin, and whatever the future held.

CHAPTER 9

*G*unfire rattled off the dropship plating, bullets flying by the narrow cockpit window. Dunst eased back on the stick, guiding Phoenix 4 away from the green space in central Shimmi. Below, a truck burned, with the shrapnel covered dead and dying of the Bustan Army strewn on the road. Arin and Savvo had taken the wheeled transport out, but unlike the old ways, they had disarmed and dragged away those with a chance of surviving. A sign they were changing, killing to survive rather than the automatons the officer-nobles so prized.

Dricks stood by the pilot-sergeant, Dunst, with an eye on the co-pilot who was plotting a course for the Segfi, the Warmonger's flagship and their base of operations. On the ground their backup squad, P4, would be waiting for the dropship's return. Holding out against the mustering Bustan Army after their shock attack on Bustan 7.

Rebekah eyed her captain. Blood ran from her nose, her armour scraped and battle-worn, leg plates in a mess. But her eyes were clear, focused. And after encountering the two girls huddled beside Savvo and Arin, full of something akin to life. And about to snuff out one, possibly two Marines locked into the fervour of battle by the wetwear wrapped about their minds, and the drugs in their veins.

Desertion had a price.

A look her way, the tilt of a head, a hand upon a sidearm. It was time. With a glance to the girls whose eyes were wide yet strangely blank, she unbuckled, and walked steadily over, riding each nuance of the dropship's movement. A dread rose. A moment of realisation. They were about to announce the price of their emotional freedom, but the fee was high. No doubt Dunst and his co-pilot were the instigators of hundreds of deaths in the name of war, but it still sat heavy. Dricks pulled the gun, placing it against Dunst's neck. His reaction took them all by surprise, throwing the stick downwards, and to the side, as if he'd been ready for just that moment. The captain fired, the bullet hitting the pilot's shoulder, blood spraying across the co-pilot.

Rebekah crashed into the hull, the sudden movement casting her aside, while Dricks hit the floor. Mayhem ensued, the girls screaming, Dunst slamming into the console, the co-pilot wrestling with their own stick to keep them in the air.

And then it hit.

Fear.

Pain.

Anger.

A desperate need to live.

A tidal wave of emotion swept over the Breakers and smashed into the pilots. Pleading for everything to stop.

Dricks was up, holding onto Dunst's seat, scrabbling for her weapon. The pilot got there first, agony-filled eyes on the captain as he blew his own brains out. Rebekah's motorised armour shoved her up, powered her grab for the co-pilot. He had hold of the stick, ramming it downwards, aiming towards the edge of Shimmi and a collection of low buildings. A suicide run. She wrapped an arm about his neck, and yanked. Even amid the chaos, the snap *was audible, but she hadn't the time to hate herself. Stretching across the body, she pulled back on the stick, sensing hands pulling the co-pilot away.*

The dropship's nose rose, but she needed to be in the seat, accessing the thrusters, steering it clear of the roofs and high fences. The slap of a body on the floor and the seat was clear, Rebekah squeezed in and dragged the thruster controls back. The engines roared, burning the pitch roofs, undercarriage scraping tiles and satellite dishes from their apexes. She eased the stick back further, feeling the dropship respond, and they began to rise.

A second wave of emotions rolled across them. Hope tinged with fear threatened to overwhelm her mind. The ship juddered, and alarms sounded – heavy weapons fire. A second strike set the console flashing red, half the thrusters kicking out, forcing Rebekah to up the power to the main engine. And nothing responded. Flat and dead.

In a moment of clarity, she remained quiet. The girls were emitting enough raw emotion as it was without her adding to it. A glance to Dricks, a narrowing of the eyes, and the captain moved to the back.

"Buckle up," she ordered. "We're going down."

Woodland emerged ahead, the edge filled with saplings and thick bushes. A stroke of luck, perhaps, and with the remaining power in the thrusters, she steered the dropship, fighting gravity, hoping to live long enough to experience a new future. To save two frightened girls from their fate.

And then they hit, bouncing off the earth to smash into bush and tree, scarring the woodland as the dropship's momentum buried them deep among the branches. Rebekah's armour battered against the console, the seat, hull and window, until the ship came to a rest a hundred metres past the edge.

"Fuck me," she said, realising she had come through relatively unscathed. Breaker armour. The best. Moans from behind garnered her attention, and Rebekah pulled free of the co-pilot's chair. The rear was filled with swear words, but that meant life, and as she peered into the murk, she marvelled at the two young girls wrapped inside a cocoon of Marines and a warbot.

Rebekah groaned, her head full of memories that were half-cherished, and half-feared as she woke up. The death of two dropship pilots sat badly, the Breakers desperate escape causing casualties on both sides of a fruitless war.

Groggy, she unbuckled herself from the bed, and swung her legs over, her body sensing the lack of gravity. With a gentle shake of the head, she dragged herself through the cabin via handholds, heading for the joys of a zero grav toilet trip and a shower. Apparently, they had re-entered real space, and if Scarva was true to its word, were on approach to the Windward System. She just hoped the bastard would be there on their return.

At the first touch of the water, she washed away the dream – the memory – and their treachery. Why now, after all this time, had it returned? Perhaps it was her worries about where they were headed. Another place where betrayal and lies held sway.

"Happy travels, *Solar Flame*," Scarva's voice echoed over comms, flat, un-emotional. The refrain sounded almost sarcastic. "And deliver my package, as agreed."

Rebekah growled in her throat, keeping her feelings from the comms. "Just make sure you're here, and responding to our call."

"The agreement was one week. I have some business on Durnat in the outer system, so will be in the vicinity until then. After that, our contract is void."

She heard the comms click, as if those were the alien's final words. "Don't forget what we have …" But the Senti was silent, their conversation at an end. It galled her to be at the mercy of that mind-sucker, but there was no alternative. Besides, they had to survive what was to come first.

"We got a visual?" she asked, turning to Savvo.

He wriggled in his chair, an unreadable look on his face until he raised an eyebrow, and sent the image over.

"That's it? How the hell does it stay together?" she said, moving closer to the screen as if it would improve what she saw.

The space station orbited a small icy moon around Windward, an orange-hued gas giant whose atmosphere roiled and eddied under constant movement. The planet was stunning, the station less so. If there had been a piece of space debris in the system not attached to the station's core, she would have been surprised. It reminded her of a sucker ball she used to play with, if the suckers were replaced with derelict ships and spliced mining transports, all spinning merrily in the void and staying, somehow, attached to the central hub.

"I take it we're not masquerading as Health and Safety," Arin said over comms. "We wouldn't last five minutes, clipboards stuffed up our arses and spaced for good measure. And our ride would be added to the junkyard."

"At least we can wear something less formal," added Savvo. "Like a carbine, or maybe the Hammer."

"Hey, you made me leave that beautiful piece of weaponry behind. Still miss that."

Rebekah pushed herself up from the pilot's chair, eyes to the ceiling. "Going to need those combat vests," she said. "And a thick skin." She clomped through to the galley, heading for a coffee while mulling over the possibilities. "Savvo, let me know when they pick up the transponder. Dricks, meet me in the galley."

She made two coffees. One white and full of sugar, then sat with her slate and flask in their usual places. The engineer arrived, smiled at the proffered flask, and took the seat opposite Rebekah.

"Shall I start the conversation?" Dricks asked, taking a sip before letting the flask lock to the table.

Rebekah twisted her lips, and nodded. "If you know my mind."

"Well, it doesn't take much to work out. Some old ex-captain with a dicky back needs to stay behind and corral the horses."

Hendricks' smile was genuine, despite the content of her statement. Yet somehow, she knew her ex-captain was not happy.

"By horses, you mean the twins, I take it." Rebekah found her hands were on Hendricks' somehow, far from the act of a Marine squad leader. But they weren't that anymore. Maybe a variant, having evolved into something new. "I don't like working in threes, I'm not going to lie, but I think it's necessary. Look at it differently. We need human backup. Sending ZZ3 in is going to be a last act, one that'll mean we failed somewhere along the line. Whereas a canny Breaker with years of experience, that's a different prospect. If you're here, ready to intervene, strategically I think it's the right call."

Hendricks tilted her head to the side, musing over the suggestion. "And that's not placating an old woman, then? Watching her crew from afar, not being able to help. On the *Scourge*, in the bloody void, I got it. But here?"

"We'd be dead and forgotten out there without you, don't forget. The twins need watching, and I trust your judgement over who we deploy – a warbot or a Breaker – and when." She didn't feel good about it and had thought long and hard over whether Arin should be the one to stay, his mood swings a potential hazard. Besides, if they needed to leave in a hurry, Hendricks could have the ship prepped and ready.

The engineer finished her coffee, standing to place the flask in the cleaning unit, and leant both hands on the galley top. "I can't be a liability forever."

And there it was. "You run the engines. Keep Arin in line, and have our backs. This isn't about being incapable, it's about the best person for each job. You asked me to lead, so I lead. But a squad, a crew, is like a machine. Each part working in unison."

"You're quoting me at me," she said, turning to face Rebekah. "I like that, shows you listened."

"And learned. Now stop your bitchin' and maudlin' and get to work." She stood, arms spread wide. "Agreed?"

"On one condition. Arin. I ..." Hendricks paused, a small blush appearing on her cheeks. "ZZ3. The *Scourge*. All that shit. It's on his mind. I know you know. But an extra eye would keep an old lady happy."

"You know, there are times I could hug you."

"Don't push it, pilot-sergeant."

CHAPTER 10

Rebekah checked the transponder. The connection with Benetai was more consistent than she would have suspected, the link guiding the *Solar Flame* carefully into the docking station. But then, there was nothing more likely to impact a spinning piece of space garbage than a crash with a spaceship. The dock was attached to an ancient frigate, its hull completely hollowed out, with their ship sliding between to engage with a waiting docking clamp. A rumble announced their imminent arrival, and the clamps gently gripped the top of the hull, while the rotational gravity effect pushed the crew onto the deck.

"We're at 1.1 RPM," said Savvo, tapping through the data packet from the transponder link. "And right here we're only a little under standard grav. Reckon this heap of shit is about 1.5 clicks across. Hope you know what we're looking for, 'cos that's a lot of haystack out there."

"Me too," Rebekah replied, and checked the pricing streaming onto her console. Expensive didn't cut it, but they didn't have a shuttle, and no one wanted to be suited up for transfer. Out in the black, a parking cluster sat in orbit. As with her encounter above Bustan 7, there were fewer transponders signalling their presence than actual ships. And she trusted none of them.

Savvo noticed her gaze. "Seventeen," he said. "A lot of them are further apart than strictly necessary. Guess they're not all pals out here."

"Copy that." She sent over enough extortionate creds for two days berth. "Lock the navcom down. I don't want any connection with the Benetai while we're in dock. And make sure Heki and Tremil are monitoring any intrusions. I want us sealed off."

"If they're too good, they'll get suspicious," he replied.

"Yeah? Tough shit. We're paying for docking, at, I guess, mistrusted stranger rates. I think we have a right to tell them where to shove any hacking crap. Be ready in twenty." Rebekah headed for the workshop, to find the twins in the galley, waiting.

"Chocolate?" They both nodded, a smile shared between them.

Heki spoke, her voice less monotone than usual out of their room. "And we heard. You know, about the hacking. We can see how good it is, maybe give it a false entry point and send them in circles."

"They could be better than you think. The *Maverick*'s lame efforts won't be anything on these f…" Rebekah stopped herself.

"Ingrates? Pirates?" suggested Tremil, her grin almost mischievous.

Rebekah paused, recognising the subtle shifts, but unable to categorise what was happening.

Growing up?

"Yeah, those."

"Copy that. We'll be careful. Trust us," Heki said.

And Rebekah did. She realised she hadn't stopped trusting them from the moment they had helped with the *Hatton*. Well, as far as any teenager could be. There would be secrets, or things they didn't want to bother her with that they really should. Normal stuff.

Normal?

"I do. But you are crew, and like any crew member, let me down and I reevaluate. Understand?" For a moment she found herself stunned. Her earworm in full effect, but nothing crashed against it, nor was there the abyss they created when walling in emotions behind their own personal mantras. What was happening?

The airlock cycled, and Rebekah stared at the patched and repaired tunnel. Arin muttered ahead of her, and started to climb up the handholds, unable to keep himself from touching the material, as curious as ever. By the time Rebekah had reached the far end, he'd decided it was an older form of adapted polythene, explaining to her they'd last seen it in the protective shelter back on R6. Not exactly robust, hence the patches. But it would keep out most of the rad flying about the station.

Rebekah had no idea if there would be a greeting party. Information was scant – no, scrub that – non-existent, about how Benetai operated. There were rumours, of which she believed precisely none.

She cycled the airlock to find a pair of locals waiting on the other side. Gangsters was a loose term, but it was the best she could come up with. Give them their due, they must have bathed within the last week, and their clothes had seen a wash unit within a month or so. Their tattoos, however, were most definitely homemade. Pinpricked and scarred, like a brand gone bad. Rebekah eyed the hand cannon each wore strapped across their waists. A sensible choice, powerful enough at close quarters to shred a body, but unlikely to penetrate any decent thick hull. She hoped.

"Aha. Yes. Fresh meat," said the first of the racketeers, his shaven head scabbed from the latest tattoo attempt. "Duty."

"Duty?" she played dumb. Extortion round one.

"Hannos payment," said the woman, her head shaved at the sides, with a slit of a smile to accompany the Mohican hairstyle. "You give; your pretty ship stays safe."

Rebekah chewed at her tongue, eyeing both the racketeers in turn. "And what if you fuck up? You know, some other gang-shit gets in? Where's my guarantee I'm getting my creds worth?"

The male patted his gun. "Not gonna happen," he said. Before he could move, Rebekah had kicked in her chip and had a powerful grip on the man's weapon arm. She resisted the temptation to free her wrist blade, a secret worth keeping. Besides, Savvo and Arin had already drawn.

Rebekah shook her head, mouth in a lopsided smile. She wanted to tut, but decided it was a step too far. "I hope these *threats* are shittier than you. How much?"

"A hundred. Per day," said the woman, a little less sure.

"I'll go for fifty," she replied. "And you had better be worth it. And Hannos? That your boss?" The man nodded, and she released his arm. She sensed the twitch, his urge to pull the weapon, and deliberately met his eyes. The mood shifted.

"Yah," he said. "You got some shit to learn if you don't know that. Hannos leads the cartel right now."

"Good to know. Signal my ship, they'll be waiting to sort payment. And don't piss Dricks off, she has a nervous disposition and a love of heavy weaponry." Rebekah strode past, knowing Arin and Savvo would follow, weapons still drawn with eyes on their new friends.

A few strides along the curved connection tube, and Arin was chortling to himself. She tried to ignore him, but had Savvo joining in.

"What?" she said, but refused to turn around.

"Ooh, you were hot. I mean, a notch up from dealing with Scarva. I thought we were going to be, like, undercover," replied Savvo.

"We are. I didn't kill them." Rebekah let that stew. They hadn't announced their presence, merely shuffled their position from bottom of the pack 'dead meat', to 'arseholes with attitude'. It was a start.

"Could have asked them the way," said Savvo. "Before pissing them off." She didn't bother with a glare.

The tubular corridor was relatively new, the workmanship *robust*. As in functional, the welds thick and obvious, layers of lava-like metal declaring where each seam lay. It was appreciated after the outer appearance of the station as a whole. There were no portal windows. Anyone who spent time aboard a station of any kind, and the battle transports with their own central spinning sections, even Scarva's ship, knew that wasn't a good idea. Combining being able to watch yourself turning through space, while walking in any direction, but especially the opposite way, was a one-way trip to vomitsville. The eye, the brain and the inner ear all fighting for precedence, the loser being you and the contents of your stomach.

What was clear, however, was the health and safety on the station came down to self-responsibility. They passed through a bulkhead door. A deadlock, no electronics or auto-closing systems. Manual, with old signs declaring it was your responsibility to ensure it remained sealed. Strangely, it both took her by surprise, and in a way, didn't. Aboard any type of vessel in space, especially one as vulnerable as a space station, maintaining hull integrity and containing breaches was essential. Placing that responsibility onto everyone aboard from the off, set a standard – a mindset for survival. Almost self-policing and making you aware just how dangerous stupidity could be. That also lay with the weapons their welcoming party displayed. Lethal at close range, but far from deadly beyond five metres or so. Their benefit lay in not killing yourself by piercing the cobbled-together outer reaches of the station.

Savvo sealed the bulkhead behind them and joined Rebekah as the first smells of Benetai crept along the tube. There was a pungent taint of spice, sweat and, if her nose was to be trusted, ash in the air. They reached a junction point, where the cylindrical corridor had a set of metal ladders bonded on one side, with another bulkhead set in the ceiling. That way lay the inner core of the station and anyone heading there would have to climb until they reached another cross-section or inner ring with lower gravity. This door had an electronic pad, an add on, with a gang tag scrawled on its surface.

"Hannos?" asked Arin, gesturing towards the symbol.

Rebekah squinted. The symbol appeared to be a severed hand holding a knife. "Guessing that's not the way."

She gestured further along, towards the source of the scent. As the passageway curved upwards, there was another bulkhead wheel-lock poking out from the side, this one continuing along the outer rim of the station. Her mental map, formed by assumptions from their visual scans, hinted that this led towards the bulk of the space scrapyard welded onto the core. Arin spun it open, and there was a second bulkhead a few metres further in. They closed one, opened the other, and the full gamut of pungent aromas and human noise assailed their senses. From the quiet of space, they entered the tumult of a market.

Vibrant colours were on full display in the clothes, fabric stall dividers and signs that declared their wares. Amid this, the chatter between customer and vendor, or huddled conversations by those sitting at tables mended a hundred times with cards or game pieces strewn about, added to the hubbub. With the chink of glass and cup fanning enticing aromas of coffee and tea, life appeared in all its chaos.

"Wow," said Arin, his eyes alive amid the sensory overload, flitting from vendor to table, unable to focus on one thing without being drawn to another.

Rebekah tried to make sense of the layout, but the constant movement of the human tide was off-putting. They were at the edge of a much larger cylindrical section of the station. She estimated that it was about thirty metres wide, and to the 'curved ceiling' around fifteen high. She expected there to be at least four small ships connected to the outer hull – whether they held their integrity was another matter. With that in mind, there would be another ring similar in size to this one further along, and then a final ring that served as a docking station. This, Dricks and Arin insisted, was likely a repair works. Ring was a loose term with the welded add-ons, but it would have to serve, giving a sense of robustness to the station in her mind.

"We stay together. No bright ideas and falling for any of the delights of this place," she said, turning to face Savvo, her eyes, however, on Arin. "Understand? This is a mission; we need to watch each other's backs. Pay attention. You may not see the enemy coming, whether it's to pickpocket or to stab you in the back."

"Aye, El Capitaine," replied Arin, employing a grin accompanied by a swift nod of his head. "Loud and clear. Mr Distracted to stay focused."

"We have a name?" asked Savvo.

Rebekah assumed the question was for Arin's benefit. "Scarva called the dealer *Pshwa*, as far as I could tell."

"And it peddles to the Senti, the addicts. So, either they'll be in encounter suits or ..." started Savvo, raising his eyes to the ceiling. "Further inwards. Maybe we should look first, then ask around. Get the lay of the land before we draw any attention."

"Agreed. And how the hell do they pay for stuff here?" Arin glanced around, eyeing the vendors. There were no cred scanners in sight.

CHAPTER 11

Why am I doing this?

Adjusting his rings, Erikson intertwined long fingers and stretched his arms into the air. A neck twinge caused him to roll his shoulders, and then his head, kneading out the knot amid a hint of annoyance. With a last grimace, he straightened the nape of his polo shirt and rubbed his eyes. Late nights with the Honourable Dexter were playing havoc with his patience. As was the new mission for his team.

"Are you sure?" he muttered, partially under his breath but the slate beeped back at him, wanting to know if it was a genuine question. With a second roll of his shoulders, he tapped the query. "Are you positive there are no alterations to the *Sunstar* files?"

The slate pinged back a negative.

In a way, it seemed wrong. Any crew worth its salt would have said or done something inappropriate when being attacked by a group of salvagers. Not just the once, either, but initially sabotaged by a cam-bot, their scrubbers then disabled, and finally an attempt to kill the crew via cutting a huge hole in the *Sunstar*. It was only natural for the Breakers' response to be violent, and having *nothing* of note on the recordings, drew his attention far more than if there had. Especially from ex-Marines with a reputation like theirs. He could barely watch the Bustan invasion vids, the violence almost banal in its repetitive efficiency. But then, exposing the *Maverick* to space was definitely efficient, and in a way ironic. Rebekah Khan claimed it had been an accident during boarding, desperate to save her remaining crew dying aboard the *Sunstar*. But surely, they would have torn them apart? Perhaps they had, and that was the missing piece. Taken out their revenge, and somehow smoothed the evidence. As good a reason as any as to why it felt *too* perfect.

"There has to be something." He returned to watch as Davina rescued the ageing engineer, amazed, he had to say, at her reckless bravery. In that act, he saw a spark he could manipulate. A will to survive that set her apart from the Incini he often dealt with. Their combination of mental rigour and sensory augmentation made them uncomfortable to deal with, as did the Directorate and their tenets. So often they placed barriers in his way, a frustration most Enforcers took as simply being part of their role. But to him, they were like a hand grenade thrown into an investigation, blowing apart a carefully built case for bringing a noble down low by the bonds of their rules. It seemed counter-intuitive to have an agency tasked with keeping nobles in line, while providing them with the means to hide behind.

More pieces to the political games of the Court, perhaps. Keeping everyone busy looking over their shoulders, checking their ambitions by default.

Davina. Yes.

He checked through her deposition again, knowing there wouldn't be a chink of light in there. It was the omissions he sought, much like the *Sunstar* recordings. What wasn't there perhaps more important than what was.

Something to hide? Or contractual obligation.

Everything tallied. Her rescue of Hendricks, the use of the medbay, keeping them both alive until the early return of the *Sunstar* crew. The condition of her lungs after oxygen depletion. Even the med report matched the events.

So, what is that nagging at the back of my mind?

That it was all still too perfect?

"No," he said out loud, staring at the slate. "Be honest. It's not the Breakers that bug you." Erikson sighed and rolled his neck. He leant back in his chair trying to push intrusive thoughts about what Baron Stimpson had really been doing to the back of his mind.

Had it really been a lure? Entrapment?

Focus.

The crew had access to both ships, and amid their set of particular skills, he had little doubt surveillance tech would be high. Yes, his inquiries with a few officer-nobles outside of Countess Segfi's inner circle showed Angel Markez, the Breaker with those abilities, had died. But they all doubled up. No doubt their sub-engineer would have such skills.

What about the dock details? By reputation, VERT was as secure a system as any. Required to keep a whole community safe out in space, as well as linking far-flung asteroid mining operations.

The cargo manifest he knew was false. The weaponry and powered armour Baron Stimpson supplied had been part of his initial fact-finding investigation into the noble's dealings. A long list.

"Code EE4529BN." He thumb-printed the slate, and the Breaker's recent resource request pulled through. It was comprehensive, and surprisingly full of ammunition requirements that Davina could only partially fulfil. According to *his* handler, they had sent them to a war grave at best. A derelict out in the black with little to trouble a Marine group. Duboit had thought differently, expecting a gamut of autobots that would require some serious firepower to deal with. Any attack squad would want more than they need and overstock. It was the army way. But the requests suggested more than that.

"Is that it?" he asked himself.

The anomaly. Everything scrubbed clean to hide that the mission *had* been carried out? The details of which were buried in the Incini tenets.

"Stimpson," he said, the words slipping out unbidden. The intrusive thoughts wormed their way back in, infuriating him. A baron whose punishment amounted to a slap on the wrist and being called a naughty boy, while he picked up the pieces. If Stimpson had been baited, what had Khan and her crew shot at? Ghosts?

This was dangerous territory. His handler had sworn him off that line of thinking. Demanding that should *his* new attack squad raise the issue of Duboit/Stimpson's target, they were to be swatted down with threats of exposure and talk of desecrating war graves. Two sides deliberately avoiding what was actually out there, and Erikson shut down when he mentioned it. Passing it off as an enticement for an errant baron who needed bringing back into the fold.

It smelt of a cover up. That Baron Stimpson, in the guise of Duboit, had stumbled across something too big to expose, or at the very least, had contacts willing to shut others down in case they discovered his actions. It gnawed at him. How important could it be for it to screw up *his* career, while a noble baron wrote off his losses and carried on wheedling his way in the Emperor's Court?

And now dealing with a countess, possibly the Warmonger herself.

A new mission to wipe clean a countess' mistake, recover wetware that had fallen far too conveniently into his new remit. Almost as if the perfect team had been assembled. Off the books, and who could be burned in the background somewhere far, far, away if need be. If Erikson's handler had covered up for Duboit, the chances were this was another pile of dirt they wanted sweeping under a carpet. And if things went wrong, Erikson with it.

His mind itched with worry, and an anger at being *used*.

There was of course, another possibility. That the Baron's ambitions had not only stepped on the toes of someone high up, but had uncovered something they desperately wanted to remain hidden. Stimpson was a noble. Yes, he was on the fringes of the Court, but nevertheless in the eyes of the Almaar media on a regular basis. Bringing him down publicly would be embarrassing. It was why the Enforcers were there – to shove errant nobles back in line. The Emperor wasn't above a public show, or even a show trial. But a baron had not suffered such a fate in fifty years, and treason could come in many forms. Perhaps such exposure was too dangerous to risk in such a public show. So, a quiet slap down, a reminder of their status, and don't make too much of it.

Oh, and burn my career during the cover up if necessary.

Does that mean I'm expendable? Or just more expendable than before?

He had been the Enforcer sent in to set the noble straight. And now, if this was a cover up, he retained knowledge that could be regarded as dangerous, and conveniently moved into a role where his handler could keep an eye on two potential sources of embarrassment – the Breakers and their controller. Safely kept together should they need to meet a sticky end.

Have I just convinced myself I'm screwed both ways? Or, at the very least, that I can't risk letting it go? If the baron was guilty and had been pulled from the shit, don't I deserve some payback? And if what is being covered up is treason …

He checked the time, then his slate. It would be 11am on M1. He ran through Davina's itinerary, pleased to find she should be in the office. What he was about to do held a hint of danger if he veered too close to treason – but Stimpson's dealings as Duboit apparently hadn't, in the Incini's opinion, so he could piggyback off that.

Hopefully.

Erikson checked himself in the mirror, then sat back at his desk, aligning himself with the holo camera and its rear projector. An image shimmered in front, replicating Duboit's office. He spoke into the camera and called Davina in. The lag was minimal. Laser comms would normally take an hour, one way. The baron, of course, had Senti tech. A system of communication point to point that the Court used to keep its finger on the pulse of the system. Restricted to nobles, obviously. And in this case, an Enforcer acting in their place.

A minute later, Davina was sat before him as if she were in any normal meeting. Hands in her lap, face set ready for what was to come. A slight smile and trained interest in her eyes. It amused him to wait. Using the precious technology in this way may be decadent, but he couldn't help it, pretending to read something off to his right.

Eventually, he turned his attention to the Incini, wearing a smile as fake as hers.

"I have been reviewing the *Maverick* files." He watched for a twitch. None came. Annoying. "Interesting. Clean." He leaned forwards. "Too clean. But I suspect you know that and couldn't possibly comment."

"By the tenets," Davina replied. "No."

"Well, perhaps that's not entirely true. You see, it's obvious there are elements missing from your report, and of the *Sunstar*'s crew, that don't quite tally." There, at the corner of her eye, was the tiniest of twitches. Had he imagined it? Something to review later. "And you're going to tell me that you can't comment on it, blah, blah, blah."

Davina didn't respond.

"Not helpful at all. Here's my take on it, so you appreciate where we both stand. You know things I want to know. Perhaps, more than that, I *need* to know if I'm to handle this crew to the best of my ability. My review of the recordings hint that you have an attachment ..." Erikson noted another twitch, but this time the Incini, in his opinion, had recognised her own fallibility, and cut in her wetware.

"Whether that is true *or* not, is irrelevant," Davina replied. "I am assigned to devise any contractual arrangements you require by the Directorate. You ask me to find a gang willing to do a hit on, say, Hendricks, then I will – within the rules, of course."

The mask remained in place, but the chosen ex-Marine was an interesting choice. A score, perhaps.

"So, here's the thing. I don't care. They do their job; they get to breathe another day of freedom. That's the deal. What I am interested in, is the contract with Duboit. What they went out to find." He held up his hand, blocking whatever tenets or Directorate crap she was about to throw out. "I'm not asking you to divulge anything. What I am asking for is a report on the *Maverick*. All the evidence from the investigation points to them attempting to stop the *Sunstar* reaching the *target*. But then, when they get there, allowing Khan's crew to make the attempt at recovery, while they try to murder you and Hendricks and wait for their return. That speaks to me that they had made an attempt upon this *ghost* ship. And failed. *That* is of interest to me." He smiled, imagining himself as the tiger on the hunt for a deer that knows it is about to be eaten. Enjoying the sensation of power. He watched her wilt, and thrilled in it. "What could the Breakers do, that the crew of the *Maverick* couldn't?"

"Be specific in what you wish to know," she replied. "Otherwise, I cannot judge what I can or cannot divulge."

"Did the crew of the *Maverick* make an attempt to board this ex-Navy ship?" He kept it short.

He watched as she mulled over her thoughts, eyes unfocused, lips trembling very slightly.

"No," she replied. "Let me save a little time, and my patience. They attempted to get through an asteroid family surrounding the ship. It was broken up, orbiting at speed and in thousands of pieces. They sent unmanned and remote-controlled spacesuits to try to find a way through the debris. And failed." Davina's shoulders were tighter, her eyes distant, as if attempting not to engage with Erikson. To prevent displaying any tells.

That was interesting. His knowledge of asteroid fields, space in general, was scant. But such a phenomenon in the outer system seemed odd. Suspicious. Especially if it was only a lure. But then, being impenetrable would ensure any probe or autoship employed by Duboit would report back on the potential of it being true. A reason to employ the Breakers.

"Natural?" he asked.

The lips twisted. "No."

"Okay. As part of an Incini contractual negotiation I declare this discussion a provisional exploration of possibilities. Agreed?" Erikson waited for the nod with a victorious smile, enjoying the moment when it came. Sealed. "I want all the data available on the *Maverick*'s journey and find me an autoship to do the same run. It will require camera and sensory probes. It is to scan the entire asteroid field, and return. My eyes only."

"Agreed," Davina said, the glint in her eye setting Erikson on edge. "I assume this is to come from Mr Duboit's account?"

"Yes," he replied.

This couldn't go through the Enforcers, that was obvious even if he could tie it into his current role. Someone, including his handler, had been part of a cover up. And Davina would not know he was on dodgy ground, assuming, as he was, that Erikson was actually trying to find out whether Duboit had flown too close to treason. But he was potentially exposing himself to Incini rules, going against Enforcer diktat, and should his machinations appear treasonous, she would talk. He needed to keep the connection to Duboit.

He could pull back. Sign it off as a failed contract she couldn't divulge.

But the nagging was there. It was a long fall from the Enforcer ladder he had climbed rung by rung, but if he was now marked as expendable, or the fall guy for Duboit, he wanted to know why. And maybe knowing more could keep him alive. If he was wrong, and the potential tech had simply been bait, then what was the harm? Insubordination wasn't something that would cost his life, just his career.

Am I doing this?

"And what am I to class it as? For the files?"

"Exploration."

CHAPTER 12

Rebekah glimpsed down the series of steps bolted to what technically could be classed as a scaffold, though that would imply a sense of safety. Arin was at the rear, glancing back every now and again to check who was watching them. They had a tail, that was certain, probably several. Whether they had been targeted as new, and therefore easy marks, or a threat and being watched for the benefit of the gang factions, she couldn't say – yet. But few humans were climbing the rickety steps towards the bulkhead. The one they had been guided towards by a market vendor desperate to be rid of Arin's constant questioning. While climbing up revealed they were seeking the Senti enclave to those interested, it had the benefit of anyone following also being exposed.

"There's a couple of local ruffians eyeing each other at the base," called Arin, his voice full of humour. "They seem to hate each other. It's like a big stare off."

"Ruffians?" said Savvo.

"One of Dricks' favourite words. Uses it to describe the girls when they piss her off. And you, first thing in the morning."

Savvo glared in response.

Rebekah looked back the ten metres or so, wishing for a HUD and a zoom option. One was of Bustan origin, stocky and young. Maybe sixteen. The other in his thirties, definitely Almaarian by the willow-thin body shape. She couldn't make out the tattoos that adorned their necks, but their demeanour left her in no doubt they were dealing with two rival factions and both unwilling to follow.

"I'm sure they'll be waiting for us when we return," she said, and started back up the stairs. They had been operating at standard grav, and the effort was telling despite the steady drop. A return to a planet-based life seemed less appealing with every step as the weight slowly lifted from her body.

The bulkhead was open, a young woman waiting patiently for Rebekah to arrive before continuing her own journey along the ladders pinned to the connection tube. A woven basket was strapped across her back, more attached to hips and lower thighs. They didn't appear heavy, and were filled with a very thin, gauze-like material of multiple hues.

"Thank you," she said, and took hold of the hatch. It was surprisingly light, possibly due to it being a regular throughway. The girl smiled, a warmth spreading across her face that reddened slightly.

"No problem," she replied, her voice more a sing-song of pitch and tone. The accent was similar to that of the market vendors, Rebekah assuming it was a station specific. At least among the ordinary folk. She let Savvo past, then carried on after Arin arrived. Another fifty metres and she emerged to find Savvo holding on to the upper hatch, again lightweight, but this had a bulkier 'over hatch' splayed to one side with a hefty engagement lock on the other. There was a low barrier around this section, and as she stood up from the ladder, familiarity of the new space rolled over her. It had the green-blue colours and smooth materials of the massive Senti Orb, the FTL hub the army used for transport between the Bustan and Almaar systems. The floor mimicked that of the mind-suckers' inner space, where they were taken for memory extraction. The same bouncy feel, but she very much doubted it had the same absorption properties. No disappearing encounter suits here.

Pulling herself together, she could hear voices amid the swirling materials. The same tones as Scarva and the other Senti she had met, but amid them, a chorus of splashes and splat-filled noises she understood was their true language. The ring mimicked the one below in width and height, but the curve of the floor was more pronounced. Not a problem to a crew used to Level 8 and above on M2. Nor the lowered grav.

They made their way slowly, adjusting their stride pattern and speed of movement to the curvature. Here, Senti hovered amid stalls and fabric-curtained shop fronts, their wares contained within caged containers or woven baskets. Rebekah could not work out how they were delineated. The membranes they passed through on the Orb replaced by a fine material similar to what the girl had been carrying. These wafted in the stream of air that constantly breezed through the concourse, leaving how each vendor marked their territory a mystery to the uninitiated.

There were a few humans amid the Senti, most carrying baskets or pushing trolleys. Few were buying, the rest mostly workers she assumed, and not one with a faction tattoo. What they could provide, however, was information.

"Savvo." She lifted her chin towards a teenage boy carrying a yoke of baskets across his neck. His clothes were well kept, and eyes bright. Again, not matching Benetai's reputation. Perhaps there was hope in all the darkest places.

"Hey," said Savvo. "Got a moment?" He stood in front of the boy, who barely looked at him as he stepped aside. He tried again, the boy glancing up with a furrowed brow, then moving on.

Arin intercepted; his grin as wide as the arms he held out. "Hey, man. Need a little direction. That's all."

The boy stopped. Whether it was Arin's demeanour, or their persistence, was hard to tell.

Rebekah stepped to his side. "Sorry. Where a little lost. Looking for Pshwa. Know who I mean?"

The boy nodded, pointing back the way he had come, though his face darkened. "That way." That tone again, lilting. Local. "The building." He glanced down at Rebekah's holstered gun, then towards her shoulders and neck, searching, she assumed, for gang marks.

"We don't know him." Rebekah didn't know why she said it. It was as if the boy had judged her and found her wanting. "Just a delivery."

The boy nodded, the darkness spreading to his eyes. He turned away, saying no more. Arin made to move in his way, but Rebekah shook her head, and still with a grin, he waved him on by.

"Hey, thanks," she said, but the boy had disappeared into the milieu of whirling gauze.

"Not exactly hardened pirate talk," said Savvo behind her.

"You prefer fuck you and thanks?" Arin replied. "What is it with this place? I can't get my head round shit here."

"Hopefully we don't have to." Rebekah eyed the structure the boy had pointed out. The two-storey metal walls and roof were painted lurid versions of the blue and green, verging on neon, in a swirl of patterns that she couldn't quite follow. She engaged her chip as they walked closer, the disconcerting patterns slipping away every time she looked to another. Her augmented vision threw up no other anomalies. None of the worrying heat signatures or potential sensor arrays to indicate a wary drug-dealer was protecting their patch. Just a weirdly painted Senti building on a cartel-run space station.

After emerging from the constant touch and swish of cloth, the front of the building felt oddly natural. Its place on the ring wall providing a sense of gaudy calm. There were three sets of barred windows along the front, all with internal shutters, their height more akin to where a human would place them. Another set sat on the second floor, again shuttered. The door hinted at solidity and appeared newer than the windows. Its square shape with a curved top hinted at Senti origin.

"Subtle," said Arin. "You know, if you had said look for a drug den, I would never have thought of this place. Just walked on by."

"Blinded by its beauty." said Rebekah. "Knock."

"Me? Do I *look* like an addict?"

"No. You look like the type of human desperate enough to sell his memories for money. They're all lonely in that empty skull." Savvo watched the rear while he spoke, lifting his chin towards the Senti vendors. "And we have been followed."

"It's the older man," said Arin, pointedly not looking around. "Marked him after we spoke to the local. Keeping his distance. Watching, but that's all. Couldn't catch his gang mark."

"Knock. Savvo, watch the gangster." Rebekah turned to face the door, feeling vulnerable. As a Breaker, you dealt with each situation through extreme violence, or the threat of it. Your presence and armour enough to mark you as powerful, and to be feared. Here, she was just another human. Soft-bodied, and committed to staying alive, to be there for those who needed her.

Arin knocked, and was answered with silence. "I think they're out. Maybe gone for a picnic, taking in a movie."

Rebekah drew her gun, using the butt to hammer on the door. Each strike died upon the metal. Dull thuds. It was definitely solid.

A noise like buttered toast slapping against the floor slid from the door. Rebekah glanced down to one of the unusual sets of patterns. Focusing, her chip helping, she began to make out a uniform shape. A square within a circle, and she ran her fingers over its raised edges.

"The patterning, its camouflage. A sensory well." She glanced up, trying to discern more amid the strange whirls only to stagger with a sudden sense of vertigo.

"Clever," came a voice. "Now fuck off, human."

"Pshwa?" she said, mangling the name. She tried again. "We're looking for Pshwa."

"No one here by that name, or any other garbled variant your human lips can come up with. Now, what was it I wanted you to do again? Yes. Fuck off." There was a second sound of buttered toast, and a click to follow.

"Okay. I'll go take this package of Scarva's and give it to a random Senti. Oh look, there's one now. Bye." Rebekah pushed herself away from the door, running her hands over the metal, feeling for a hidden handle. But then, she'd never seen a Senti use a handle. Not even on the low tech *Unpronounceable.*

"Scarva?" came the voice, but Rebekah ignored it, turning away. "You said Scarva. You don't look like his usual crew. Fewer tentacles. Show me."

Rebekah drew out the silvered rectangle of metal, about the length of her palm and as thin as her finger. Though it appeared heavy, it was light even in normal grav. Assuming the Senti wanted it positioning near the square, she lowered it. A flash of light hit the metal, and a familiar swirl rolled over the surface.

"Scarva," said the voice, and the door clunked. A hiss followed, and a pungent scent flowed out – a strange mix of spice and earthy forest that had Rebekah's eyes watering. "Come in."

Rebekah checked behind. Arin was at her shoulder alongside Savvo, both watching the ring. "Savvo, Arin, wait here. Make sure we have an exit."

She sucked in a breath, and pulled the door wider, expecting the gloom of a drug den and getting a wash of blues and greens instead. A flat-bodied

Senti waited the other side, the gravity a little higher than they preferred, the frills overlapped rather than bulbous. No encounter suit.

The Senti looked her up and down, the elongated head tilting in a strange, mechanical way. There was no symbiote, which took her by surprise.

"Come in, come in." A shoulder tentacle took her gently by the wrist, and the Senti ignored her flinch, guiding her inside. Once over the threshold, the door began to close, and the feeling of vulnerability returned. New life, new rules.

The proportions inside again spoke of human occupation, Rebekah assuming the building had been repurposed. The tentacle slid off, and Pshwa dragged itself ahead, dripping liquid. Not walking on its lower tentacles, more half dragging itself a few metres, before turning off into a side room. Here the floor was wet, and as she rounded the entrance, three barrels of a brownish liquid appeared in each corner, at their sides a smooth box of the same metal as Scarva's package, with two sets of what appeared to be reshaped wetware attached.

Without any formality, the Senti entered one barrel, almost pouring itself in as it slid over the lip. Immediately the scent increased, Rebekah coughing as it scraped her throat.

"Ahhh. Getting too old to be dragging myself about this place." The frills filled out, a burp of gas rose from within the liquid, releasing another bout of the powerful aroma. "If you would?" The chin tentacle reached out, its tip splayed into three squirming tips, like a snake's tongue. Rebekah held out Scarva's metal slug, watching as the tentacle wrapped itself about the metal and pulled it towards the smooth box. Once placed on top, she was finally reminded of the power of Senti tech, as the metal lid bobbed and stretched, and absorbed Scarva's package. When she looked back, the Senti had wrapped the wetware about its skull, and the dead eyes glinted wetly, similar to Scarva's reactions during the drawing of the memories. Excitement, maybe? Anticipation?

Noises emerged from the alien. Burbles and waves, syrup dripping, distant thunder rumbling. Amid it all, Pshwa off-gassed with greater frequency, and Rebekah felt dirty. Almost ashamed to be there.

"Yessss," said the Senti eventually. It had probably been a minute, that stretched interminably longer. "Good. Powerful. This will draw back some of my lost customers."

Rebekah desperately wanted to leave, eyes downcast, trying not to look at the Senti nor the way out.

"This yours? Yes, it is. Scarva always seems to find the very best, somehow." The Senti's shoulder tentacles quivered, then rose out of the brown liquid to remove the wetware and place it aside. "He would do well to keep you close."

"I'm sure he would." The words were strained, harsher than she intended. Pshwa hardly seemed to notice. "I have a favour to ask." She eyed the wetware, wondering what the human kit they were looking for could be repurposed to do. Could this Senti be a dealer too?

More of the moaning sounds slid through the door, Rebekah realising there would be rooms like this one throughout the two floors, probably filled with Senti who were about to get a new fix.

"For bringing me this, I feel a little generous for a change. What can I do?"

"I'm looking to buy wetware," she said, pointing to the basket of electronics sat at the barrel's side. "Human. The recording kit Marines use."

Rebekah, as with most humans, couldn't read Senti body language, certainly not the more subtle reactions. Pshwa's was obvious, his upper tentacles all rising into the air simultaneously, the slit of its mouth wide.

"Old tech? You think there's some here? On Benetai? Interesting."

The words didn't seem to match the reaction, but then that was a big assumption. She had shocked him, that was clear.

The tentacles relaxed back into the water. "For Scarva?"

"Yes, yes. For Scarva. And for me, a cut of the creds." Had she agreed too fast? The opportunity was too good to pass up.

"And now me." Pshwa wrapped its chin tentacle about the wetware at its side, lifting the woven electronics into the air. "Yes? If Scarva is branching out into wetware, making his own recordings or some other heinous plan, then I want a slice. That Senti's a devious bastard. Just the type to find a new angle. Are you able to agree to that?"

"Depends on what you're asking for."

"Twenty ..."

Rebekah shook her head, and again on fifteen. "Ten percent." She crossed her arms, hoping the signal was read.

"Okay. Come back in three hours. I'll dig a little, see what rises to the surface."

CHAPTER 13

Rebekah watched Arin, who was deep in conversation with the teller. The ancient ship in which they stood was cold, her worries about its structural integrity not helped by the dragon's breath streaming from her nose. There were three counters, each with the same gang mark scrawled above the thick plexi-glass window the tellers huddled behind. Hannos.

It was one giant scam, and now she understood why Benetai had a reputation for thievery. It wasn't that you'd be mugged, or your personal items stolen, though that may still be a possibility. But how they controlled the flow of creds in and out of the station. They had simply set up an exclusivity deal. One nodal point for each of the three gangs where you exchanged creds embedded in your ship's slate for physical monetary cards. On the one hand, it enabled commerce in their enclosed world. Travellers to the station from Bustan, Almaar, even the Windward System and beyond, able to pay for goods and services on board, and in another it enabled a cartel tax on the exchange in both directions. When you acquired your Benetai card values, and when you returned them. For those living on board, they didn't have to pay the tax unless they left and needed creds.

Arin walked away from the teller, slightly red-faced and clearly ruffled. He was tapping his chest and jacket pockets. "Did he steal my belt when he took my pants down and spanked my cred account? Shiiit."

"Should be used to it by now after the prices on M2," replied Savvo. He nodded towards the ship entrance, the busy market in the ring beyond still teeming with humanity. "We have one of our two friends back. Should we say hello?"

Rebekah glanced over, with the older Almaarian leant inside the ex-airlock that connected the bank ship to the ring. He wasn't hiding, his arms crossed beneath a blatant stare. They had planned to explore the ring, walk its circumference before returning to the ship. Get a better feel for how it operated, and the layout.

"Come on," said Rebekah, and walked directly towards the gang member. He pushed himself away from the corridor wall, wiry arms hanging by his sides. She kept her hands well clear of her handgun, but flexed her forearm, feeling the familiar stiffness and pressure against the scar beneath her skin. She dismissed activating the chip for now, her advantage lay in the dual backup following her.

Locking eyes, she knew immediately he wasn't going to run. Probably pleased she had initiated the contact. Rebekah stopped two strides from him, flanked by Arin and Savvo.

"You going to tell me why you're following us? Or do we have to guess?" Rebekah demanded.

The man huffed, recrossing his arms. "Hannos would like a word."

"I ..." Arin started to say.

Rebekah glared, shutting him up before he could provide one. That mouth.

"What guarantees are there that it'll just be a word. Had my boots buffed, wouldn't want to get them scuffed if I had to kick your arse." Rebekah was tempted to mimic his posture, choosing instead to keep her arms loose at her sides. Something told her he wasn't alone, and she needed to balance the bravado with understanding their position.

"Hannos has no guarantees, but a rep to keep. You're here as a guest on our station—"

"A paying guest," cut in Arin.

The man broke into a smile, revealing a set of cracked teeth on one side of his jaw. "Yes. But still a guest. Hannos is curious about you, your ship and why you are here. It would be a courtesy."

Rebekah cracked her thumbs, mulling over her options. There didn't seem to be an alternative. They needed to move about freely and be as inconspicuous as they could. Pissing off the lead faction of the cartel would probably be a mistake. Besides, if Pshwa couldn't find any leads, where would they be going next? Possibly to the gangs, though she'd had a mind to start with the smallest and work her way up, not start at the top.

"Lead on," she said, gesturing back to the market.

The Almaarian glanced to Arin and Savvo, and with a tilt of his head, turned back towards the ring. Alone or not, he had exposed his back and clearly didn't perceive them as a threat. Not yet, anyway.

It wasn't difficult to work out where they were heading. In ten minutes, they stood beneath the bulkhead door with the Hannos gang mark and the only electronic pad they had seen. Their guide tapped and spoke into the comm at its side, and the door spun open. Having the access through what was effectively the ring's roof provided a weird kind of security, and the narrow connection tube beyond doubled up on that. Of course, powered armour would negate most of that advantage.

The waiting gang member pushed her ponytail out of the way as she peered down. She narrowed her brown eyes, a scowl to her face that appeared almost theatrical. Rebekah didn't need to play that game having already established their position.

"For Hannos, Lena. Yes," said their guide.

"Okay, Penta. They armed?" She gestured towards Rebekah's handgun. Penta, their guide, nodded, baring his battered teeth. "Hannos knows."

The woman stepped aside, balancing on the frame of the doorway, and Penta passed her, clambering onto the ladders. Rebekah followed, refusing to respond to the continued scowl and hoping Arin and Savvo would do likewise. After a few minutes, she judged they were parallel with the Senti enclave by the grav, and emerged inside the belly of a ship. By the hull plate, and her memory, this was likely an ex-corvette. Not a bad place to protect should any gang war erupt. Not that there had been the slightest sign of one.

The inner ship was virtually intact. The rooms divided much as she imagined they would have been when it functioned. They were on the lowest deck, behind her would be engineering, and ahead, where Penta headed, crew quarters and possibly weapons control and the missile tubes. To her surprise, that's where they ended up, though shorn of the weaponry. It had been cleared, with a galley and mess on one side, on the other a large table built from a piece of ship's hull. Four sat at the table talking, glasses clinking on the top and vigorous hand gestures between the words. Not an argument, but close.

"Wait," Penta growled. "Until you are addressed, okay."

Rebekah wasn't well known for her patience, Arin less so, but she swallowed it down and kept half-an-eye on the red-haired ex-Marine whose eyes flitted about the room. Savvo's gaze was more measured, but no less intense. Finally, the conversation ended, and two of the four squealed chair legs against the decking as they stood up. A clink of glasses, and the smallest of disinterested looks their way, and they both left.

"Yah. Merchants," said the middle-aged woman. Almaarian. Her skin tinged orange, her hair blonde but grey at the roots. Her eyes, however, were full of life and wrapped in creases that deepened as she smiled. "Sit," she said, and pointed to the chairs opposite. The younger man at her side twisted his lips into a form of a smile, a scar along his cheek preventing complete success. Rebekah had no doubt they were related, and by the age, mother and son seemed likely.

"Thank you," she replied, and took the central chair, hands on the table where they could be seen. The woman, Hannos she assumed, eyed both her crew with a raised eyebrow. "Savvo, Arin, sit the hell down."

Arin snorted a laugh and sat. So did Savvo, a little more measured.

"Good. Drink?" she proffered the bottle, the scent of a clear and strong spirit wafting over.

"Too early." Rebekah smiled, trying to keep her tone apologetic.

"Never too early." Hannos poured herself a glass and took a sip. "Now, this feels like a fucking corporate meeting. I just had one of those. Don't want another. Why don't you tell me why you have business with that mind-sucker Pshwa, and then we can go on with our days." Hannos gestured with her glass, one finger in the air, and knocked back the remaining liquid.

"The stock answer is none of your business, to which you say everything on board is my business, and then I say not this." Rebekah gave a tight smile.

Hannos let out a barked laugh and poured herself another drink. "You got some balls, girl. Like that. Okay. Let me make an educated guess. You took that shit some new mind-sucks to play with. Am I right?"

Rebekah didn't answer, keeping her face placid.

"Not going to start our relationship off on a good footing by being silent. Let me fill you in a little. I don't want that shit on my station, but the Tensei and Baja clans seem to think he's cool. That translates into they skim his loot. Even if *I* skimmed the fucker's loot, I'd want him kicked off without a fraggin' encounter suit."

"Popular then," Rebekah replied. "I delivered a package. That's it. End of."

"That scar on your wrist tells me doing that hurts. Hurts bad."

Rebekah flinched, rubbing instinctively at the scar where her wrist blade emerged, mind full of the Senti's sickening response as it delved into her memories via the wetware.

"That, at least, is a good sign. Which unit?" Hannos leant in, grabbing the bottle and offering it over. Rebekah nodded, and one glass each was poured. One. Recognising her status.

"Can't say," Rebekah replied. "Too many ears."

Hannos growled in her throat. Not at her, but the response. "Copy that. Some advice," she pointed around the room. "I have Bustan and Almaars alike, understand? Don't give a flying shit which side of a noble's war they were on. Only that they're loyal, and like getting paid. The Tensei and Baja sit on the opposite sides of the divide. Hate each other, and in turn hate me. Small, but not small enough for me to crush them. But it keeps the balance. Keeps my people safe enough."

"People? You mean your faction."

"No, my people. I head the cartel, run the station. There are generational families that ride the Benetai. Maybe go back seventy years. *My* people. I keep the balance. Keep them as safe as I can. Don't want anyone upsetting that." Hannos threw the shot down, grimacing at the liquor before replacing the glass on the table. There was a tremor to her hand. "So, as you've paid for a berth, do you have more business to attend to or are you here for the grav and the booze?"

Rebekah looked directly at the woman, not wanting to lie, but knowing she needed to keep things close to her chest until she had a grasp of how the station ran, and the best way to find the information she needed. She wanted to trust this woman, but wasn't ready.

"Booze and grav. If we pick up anything else along the way, that's a bonus."

Hannos shook her head, closing her eyes as she did so and mouthing an expletive. "Girl, you don't want to make an enemy of me. I'll accept your words, but I'll have an eye out. Next time you're in here, I'm hoping you'll be a little more open. Time to go."

Rebekah slugged the drink, alcohol burning the back of her throat. She refused to cough, swallowing every drop and standing up from the table. She made to leave, Savvo and Arin at her side, when an urge took hold.

"What was your unit?" she asked, turning back.

Hannos snorted, and unzipped the top of her jacket, exposing the upper half of a pair of wings, a sunrise in the background. "Skyriders."

"Shiiit," said Arin, his voice low but Hannos heard him.

"Better believe it. So don't mess. Hear me?" The cartel leader wore a fierce grin full of pride.

Rebekah wanted to talk, desperately needed to sit this woman down and grill her about the *Scourge* and the Skyriders they had uncovered. The *Moonstrip*. All of it. Shit, and if Hannos hadn't been there, she deserved to know.

But she couldn't. At least not yet. There was a mission to complete, one getting more complex minute by minute.

"I hear you," she said. "Never an insaner bunch of soldiers this side of the void. Proud to have served alongside you."

CHAPTER 14

Heki focused as the data stream poured over the screen, her fingers intertwining absently with TB's while the symbiote sat happily on her other forearm. He was covered in slowly pulsing ripples of metallic hues. Heki perceived it like a cat purring, the alien being content. She wasn't sure if TB slept, but there were down times when no colours flowed along the skin.

"Trem," she said, pausing the screen and highlighting a line of code. "I have a secondary attack piggybacked on the first."

Tremil wandered over, collecting her slate from the table and adjusted one of the anime figures. "Where … yep. Got it. Send it over and I'll lock it into the naughty code prison along with its buddies."

"That's three so far. All different," Heki said, sliding a finger across the screen and sending the errant code to Tremil. "I traced the first two back to different nodes on the station. I'm thinking the third will be yet another."

"Why?" asked Tremil, her fingers working swiftly over her screen.

"Arin's call in said there were three gangs. Makes sense that they're all trying their luck, especially as they use slightly different methods." Heki's tongue poked from the corner of her mouth while she swiped away at her slate, adjusting the on-screen data on her console. "Tracking … got a tracer program running … sheesh they like their firewalls. Pity they're paper thin."

Tremil sat back on her bed with a sigh and tossed her slate aside. "Done and done. Got them running in a circular loop. By the time they've worked out they're not in the really real world, I'll have a kill switch in place."

The console flickered, and flashed red, lines stretching across the screen before thinning out and disappearing. Heki stared at it a second, dumbfounded. She had just discovered the nodal address. Had they been detected? Launched a response attack.

"Trem." But her sister was already up, her eyes narrowing as she leant over her shoulder. The console flickered again and leapt back into life. The same code hung there. She reached for her slate, horrified to see the same thin lines now running across the screen. Again, this blanked out, and after a breath, the original data reappeared.

"This them?" Trem said.

Heki tapped at the screen, isolating the address and flagging it for later. "No. It's something else." TB's ripples changed in intensity and hue. His tentacles waggled and withdrew from her left hand to crawl slowly up her arm. She caught the change and assumed it was her mood shift that drew the alien.

"Something different? What do you want me to do?"

"Check the navcom, isolate it from the internal systems in case this goes wrong." Heki glanced over to her sister. "Isolate the ship while I try to figure out what's happening."

Tremil collected her slate and sped out the door. Heki sensed her turmoil, and her twin's attempts at dampening the emotional noise with her usual refrain. It was working, for now.

The pattern of the attack was very different to the norm. The code structures interpreted by the ship's computer so foreign to her ordered mind. Rebekah and Arin had let them study Almaarian and Bustan computer systems. Both being from one original source before the two planetary systems fell into mutual isolation and later war, they were similar but had diverged and branched off. Such evolution had seen multiple coding languages emerge around similarly evolving computing architectures. Heki knew how all of it worked, linked and conversed. Most, though not all, intimately, but mainly through simulation or their own hacking into Karal and VERT databases. None of that was on the screen. Or if it was, so hybridised it made no sense.

TB reached her head, and settled against the back of her neck. The rising sense of panic quelled. A calm, a warm blanket, settled on her mind. Not a fog, her sharpness remained.

"Code I've never experienced before," she muttered.

Tremil returned, her face set hard, trying and failing to contain the worry. "I've isolated the navcom with our firewall. But short of unplugging it from the system, I don't know what else to do."

"Fetch Dricks," said Heki, hating having to ask. Would they always be calling for help? Never be truly independent. A burden, rather than an aide to the crew.

Tremil left, and Heki sensed her sister's own doubts. But what else could they do? If they tried to work through this on their own, and failed, it might be too late. She considered contacting Rebekah and dismissed the thought. Hendricks would make that call.

She eyed the console, the clash of the strange code washing over the screen. It had no immediately obvious structure. Almost like someone had thrown up all the algorithms they knew into the air, forcing them to tangle together. No rules, or perhaps all the rules happening at once.

All.

Hendricks tapped at the door, then walked in. Another of the crew to enter their domain.

"What you got?" she said, and her hands rested on Heki's chair, peering over her shoulder.

Horror struck Heki then. Not from the attack, but the realisation TB was still wrapped about her neck. How would Hendricks view that? Playfulness? After the conversation with her about Scarva's memory-drain, the bitterness and pain Hendricks had suffered at the touch of the alien's personal symbiote, it could only end badly.

Tremil came to the rescue. "Come on TB," she said, her hand alighting on Heki's neck, the caress gentle.

Heki sensed the symbiote's reluctance, but the alien wriggled free of her neck, and wrapped itself about her sister's arm. She heard the lid of the sump box open.

"We're under a hacking attack. But it's not like anything I've seen before. Whatever it is, breaks all the rules."

"I'll be honest, Heki, I have no clue. I only use the damn things, no idea how they work. An engine, it has a feel to it, a sense of what's right. All that gobbledygook on the screen means nothing to me." Hendricks' emotions poured over Heki, A deep-seated ill ease. She feared it was because of TB, but the engineer appeared focused on the code.

"How bad is it?" Hendricks continued. "Can you stave it off?"

"I don't think so. It's tearing our defences apart, or rather, finding gaps we didn't know existed. Trem's isolated the navcom, but we'll have to do that physically if this continues. Do you know how?"

"I—" Hendricks stopped, open-mouthed.

A clang reverberated through the ship. Memories of the scavenger attack struck Heki, and she struggled to hold back the sudden fear and revulsion they triggered. Hendricks staggered from her emotional wave. Tremil grabbed the engineer and handed her a set of headphones. A grateful and green-looking Hendricks put them on, but was beaten to the door by

Heki's sister. Tremil peered out, and a second and third clang rolled down the corridor.

"ZZ3?" whispered Tremil, looking back to Hendricks and Heki. "It's ZZ3."

Hendricks pushed her aside, striding out to face the bot. "ZZ3 protocol stand down, action code Wrecking Squad."

Heki stood, entering the corridor alongside Tremil, peering over Hendricks' shoulder at ZZ3 as the bot paused. Its eyes flashed in a whirling pattern. Had it been compromised? There was nothing more isolated than the warbot from the ship's systems. Rebekah had insisted they couldn't risk any cyber attack taking over the huge bot. It could kill them all in a blink of an eye, tear the ship apart piece by piece. Voice command only, and even those were stripped back by Arin's pacifist program.

Except, of course, Tremil and Heki had meddled – a little more than the crew knew.

Unconditional love was so hard to come by.

"ZZ3 unit is under pacification. Threat assessment nil." The bot's voice was as monotone as theirs, but it didn't *feel* that way to Heki. An undertone, from a bot?

"Yeah, buddy. I know. I say again. ZZ3 protocol stand down, action code Wrecking Squad. Return to the cargo hold." Hendricks stepped in the way, hands spread wide, and Heki's heart thudded in her chest.

The warbot's lower limb jiggled, sliding forwards. "ZZ3 unit is under pacification. Threat assessment nil." A second limb pushed ahead. "External threat detected."

Heki blinked. Again, an undertone. Not of threat. Concern? She glanced over to Tremil, and she could see the confusion in her sister's eyes. And her decision to act. Tremil eased by Hendricks, who made to pull her back.

"No, Dricks," said Heki, and she affirmed that with a wave of focused intent. The engineer paused, her fingers merely on Tremil's shoulder, as if caught between thoughts. Tremil's fingers flew, the complex pattern garnering the bot's attention. Heki sensed its limbs stiffen, a slight tremor amid the lights. Tremil was attempting their safety override. She loved Arin, and he had completed a fine job of restructuring ZZ3's software considering his limited skills. But they had done the opposite, refined the software including the pacifist program, added additional computing power and storage. Turned the bot into a playmate, albeit one with a fierce level of protection.

No need to fear this toy being taken away.

Until now.

The captain's console in their room sounded an alarm. A fizzing beep that exuded panic. Ahead of her, Tremil repeated the safety override, wide-eyed as the bot didn't respond.

What was happening here?

"External threat detected," said ZZ3 again. "I repeat, ZZ3 unit is under pacification. Threat assessment nil. Please get out of the way."

The bot strode closer, a gentle arm pressing against Tremil, moving her aside. Her sister's panic rolled over Heki, forcing her to absorb it or leave herself incapacitated. Hendricks made to stand in front of Heki, the engineer's emotions immersed in the need to protect and survive.

Her own fingers repeated the same pattern, remaining in the bot's eye-line as she backed away. ZZ3 was clearly aware of her, and made no attempt to ignore the gestures, but nor did it respond. Instead, a second, almost tender movement, saw Hendricks pushed towards the corridor wall. The engineer fought back, anger flushing her face, kicking and striking the bot. ZZ3 ignored it all and strode on towards Heki. Her hands fell to her sides, aware the gestures were having no impact, Tremil's panic intertwining with her own rising fear. Both limbs released, leaving Tremil and Hendricks nonplussed, until the ex-Marine growled in anger and charged at the robot from behind.

Heki found herself past their cabin door, and the bot stopped, ignoring the engineer's attempts to drag it back. Red eyes flashed, the same whirling pattern, and the huge bot separated, lowering its upper half to the deck and dragging itself inside.

"What?" she said.

Hendricks, as nonplussed as her, stared at the lower half as it settled on the deck.

"Threat to life detected," came the monotone voice from within the cabin. "ZZ3 protect."

Tremil made to move towards their cabin, only for Hendricks to stand in her way, face-to-face.

"No. Me," said the ex-Marine, and turned away, easing past what remained of ZZ3, and entering their cabin.

Heki knew neither of them could keep away. Curiosity was their shared trait, and TB was inside. Heki reached the door before her sister, peering around to find Hendricks passive, standing behind the bot. The snick of wires and the familiar sound of metal-to-metal maglinks pinged. ZZ3 was attaching to the console. She couldn't remember the bot having that modification, and then an image dropped in her mind from Tremil. The box tipped onto the deck in the cargo hold.

"Oh," was all she could manage.

"ZZ3, action protocol assess, action code Wrecking Squad," said Hendricks, the engineer stepping aside to peer at the screen. Heki was frustrated, unable to watch what was happening, and eased herself into the room – ignoring a fierce glance from Hendricks.

"Cyber attack. Senti source code," replied the bot.

How the hell would it know?

"Senti?" said Hendricks. "Explain."

Heki felt the ex-captain's adjustment. A re-evaluation, on the fly. Making a tactical decision when and where it was needed. She was still on high alert, but realigning the threat's source.

"Scarva, that bastard," swore Hendricks.

The bot didn't respond at first, Heki making out the flickering screen and new code that pulled apart the structure, overwriting, rebuilding it into a form she began to recognise.

"Station," said ZZ3. "The cyber threat comes from the station. Not Scarva, or the—" the bot repeated the crashing against a cliff face that signified the *Unpronounceable*'s Senti name. "Threat level reducing."

"How?" said Tremil. She had snuck in, and was removing TB from the box, one eye on the bot,

Heki joined in. "How are you doing this? ZZ3, explain, action code HT." She ignored Hendricks' glare over her shoulder. Another secret bared, though they'd known the girls had reprogrammed the bot, they just failed to mention this part of it. And of course, the physical mods.

"ZZ3 is actioning protection protocols."

"You are not connected to the ship," said Heki, squeezing in beside Hendricks. "So how did you know?"

The bot was silent, and the screen blanked out, rebooting swiftly to reveal the code had been pacified. The attack at an end. ZZ3's eyes reflected in the screen.

"ZZ3 is now connected. Ability to protect those I serve has increased. Please leave the room so I may reassemble."

"Not until you answer my last question," said Tremil, TB resting against her forearm. "How do you know about Senti code, when we don't?"

CHAPTER 15

"Senti?" said Rebekah. "You're sure?"

"*How* are you sure?" added Arin at her side, eyeing the twins on the slate's screen.

Heki and Tremil looked at each other, and then behind where Hendricks appeared over their shoulder.

"Long – excuse me – fucking story," Hendricks growled, her eyes constantly glancing over the edge of the slate.

"Quick version," said Rebekah. "Now. We're on short time here, due at Pshwa's in ten minutes."

"Cyber attack. But not like the others. Tremil isolated the navcom, but it kept coming. ZZ3 ..." Hendricks' eyes flicked up, glowering again. "Rebekah, ZZ3 self-activated. Refused to return to the hold, and proceeded to shut down the attack."

"Bullshit," cut in Arin, receiving a dual glare from Rebekah and Hendricks. "With respect. That's fucking impossible."

"As I was saying before PYP interrupted, ZZ3 fought off the attack. The rest I'll tell you later, when I get my head round it. But I'm told it wasn't Scarva. I'm not convinced." Hendricks eased her back. "And these two ingrates need to explain a little more about what the hell else they've been meddling with. Screw the chocolate, Rebekah. Bring more of that mushroom shit. TB is about the only one with any sense left aboard." The girls blushed, looking anywhere but the screen and their furious captain.

Rebekah shook her head slightly, hoping they could feel her glare through the inert electronics. "You sure you're safe?"

"Yeah. ZZ3 has returned to the hold. I may, however, be up on a few charges after interrogating these two."

Rebekah wanted to say to go easy. But perhaps now was not the time. Hendricks loved them as much as she did, and she had to trust her ex-captain would only go as far as necessary. They had come such a long way. But trauma was a bitch, and could sneak back up on you, blinding you to reality in an instant. They all had more than their share of that.

"Gentle," she mouthed, though she looked away from the slate. Hendricks would have to make that judgement. She had a Senti to visit.

"You catch that?" she asked Savvo who had been watching the immediate area of the market they were sat in.

Savvo dipped his chin, glancing back briefly. "Enough. Screwed-up shit."

"Dricks was saying the girls had been interfering with ZZ3 more than we knew. Put that crap aside, we still have a Senti cyber attack. I ain't heard nothing about them doing stuff like that. And how would they know?" Arin clattered his metal bowl on the table, the soup dregs splashing in the bottom. "I mean ZZ3? Shit."

"So we're in the crap, and the robot is still the first thing on your mind? Are you sure Dricks can handle a three-way love triangle?" Savvo didn't look back as he spoke, but Rebekah expected there to be no accompanying smile. Her second was goading Arin into focusing on the current issue. The Senti.

Rebekah finished her soup, savouring the scent more than the taste. But she needed the nourishment to help focus. Was Pshwa involved? It seemed too much of a coincidence. They had come across dozens of Senti in the enclave, any of whom may have seen them and their ship as an easy mark. How many times could they have succeeded before and been undetected? Few others had the ability of the twins to not only fend off attacks, but to identify them in the first place. Pshwa was Scarva's contact, and apparently as filled with greed, so that added a layer of mistrust. And the three-hour wait? Was that a delay to check them over? See if what she had divulged was true, or the chance to hack their ship?

Self-preservation would dictate returning to the ship, getting the full facts, then acting. But this was the only lead they had short of banging on Hannos' door.

Time to find out.

"Come on. Get your shit together, we have a lead to follow. Savvo on point, Arin watch our fucking six and stop fretting over ZZ3. Dricks will tuck your bot up in the hold." Rebekah slapped them both on the shoulder, standing to the scrape of her chair.

"It's not love," said Arin, taking his station at the rear. "More ... shit, it's love. But in that kinda 'I need a pet' way. You know, or your best friend when the rest of the world are just mean bastards who show you no respect. I mean none. Look at you two, for instance. Would ZZ3 bad-mouth me like that? Of course not. Living with people like you drives a man to find love wherever he can."

"Good to know," said Rebekah, eyes roaming over the market-goers as they headed for the scaffold. "That I show you no respect, I mean. I was wondering if I was being too nice."

Arin choked. "Nice? I don't think they put that in a captain's manual. What's the word? Redacted. And any of its synonyms you wish to apply."

"Back on the big words," interjected Savvo. "Got gang tattoos in the crowd ahead and to the left. Think it's that kid again, the Bustan."

"Copy that," said Arin. "Eyes on. I bet he has similar issues. Gets bullied by his fellow gang bangers, forced into the shitty jobs, talked down to. But like me, keeps going back for more, hoping his competence will be noticed."

"You done?" Rebekah followed Savvo's lead as they reached the scaffold, cutting through the four others climbing the steps to the clearer air above. "Got it out of your system?"

"I'm done. He's hanging back, but I'm thinking he's edgy. Reckon he might keep tailing us."

Rebekah stopped, turning with Savvo to gaze down the scaffold. She pointed at the teenager, two fingers, twitching her thumb like a gunshot.

"Got you," she said quietly.

The boy winced and Rebekah shook her head, turning away, Savvo retaking point.

"Why a teenager?" asked Savvo, ten steps from the top and eyeing the hatch. "Why not someone experienced? Or even devoid of the tattoos. Kind of obvious."

"I was thinking the same thing," replied Rebekah. Opening the hatchway was the next vulnerable moment, and after that the climb up with anyone wanting a guaranteed shot waiting at the top. They were being watched, but under threat? An attack on the ship had their hackles up. Was this just another gang keeping an eye, making sure their assets weren't in danger. What had Hannos said? The other gangs skimmed Pshwa, got a cut of his addiction-inducing gains.

Maybe ensuring their creds were safe.

"Savvo, open the hatch." She laid her hand on the gun at her hip, watching as her second wheeled the lock open. It dropped, Savvo stepping aside. There was no one there.

Paranoid? Probably.

But alive.

"Up," she said. "And have your weapon handy."

He nodded and went ahead. With a word to Arin, she followed, climbing hand over hand until she was at the top. With a signal, Arin followed, a last growl of 'wait' to the queue of complaining locals he'd formed.

Rebekah emerged from the hatch, with Savvo at the barrier, hand tapping at his hip as he surveyed the upper ring and its billowing sheets.

"Clear," he stated. "As far as I can see."

Rebekah waited on Arin, gesturing down the connection tunnel for the waiting humans to follow once he dragged himself clear of the hatch. She received some interesting hand gestures in reply.

"Pleasant lot," she said.

"Yeah. They were alright. They were curious why we weren't sporting tattoos. I think if we had, the gestures may have been a little different." Arin took his place next to Savvo. "Thinking about getting one of ZZ3, right here." He pointed to his heart.

"Let it lie," replied Savvo.

"Oh, you start something and then you expect me to be magnanimous. That's another big word, means 'fuck you' in posh speak." Arin choked back a laugh.

"Savvo," said Rebekah. He nodded, moving out with a brief glare towards Arin who grinned in return.

"I'm going to tell Dricks," she said on the way past. "Word for word."

Arin choked again, this time without the laugh. With a tut, he peered back down the tube, catching sight of the boy at the bottom calling for the others to hurry up.

"Persistent," Arin said. "Tail's back."

Rebekah threw him a thumbs up and carried on walking between the Senti stalls. The Breakers would have levelled the lot, given themselves a clear view of the target, and gone in hard – informant or not. Acquire the target, question them and do next whatever their orders demanded – often a kill. An execution.

Instead, they were walking through a flurry of material that hid any assailant and left them vulnerable. More so without their powered armour.

They emerged at Pshwa's strangely coloured dream-den, its patterns as indiscernible as they had been before. It creeped her out. Before it had felt strange, but now threatening. What lay camouflaged behind those brain frying hues?

"On guard," she said, and approached the door. She knocked, activating her chip and watching the edges of the comms square emerge. Attuning to it, she swept the rest of the door. There were no more devices, but she could make out a couple of unidentifiable protuberances above and below each of the windows. Rebekah bet herself a drink or two on their function.

"Fuck off," said the comms square.

"Pshwa? We talked earlier today."

"Ah. Okay."

"You got what I need?" It seemed a reasonable thing to ask a drug dealer, though not a drug of any use to a human.

"Come in. But only you." That raised her paranoia, but then that'd been the deal last time.

She agreed, and the door unsealed. The same scent of spice and earthy trees tickled her nose. With a signal to Arin and Savvo, she entered the corridor, though no Pshwa waited for her. His voice echoed from the barrel room, and she followed it, checking the room opposite before entering. More barrels, all empty, the basket of wetware at their sides and no liquid splashes on the floor. A glance ahead confirmed the upward leading stairs were empty too, but there were recent stains on the steps.

"Come," said Pshwa.

Despite her unease, Rebekah kept her gun holstered and entered the room slowly. The Senti sat in his barrel, the headset placed nearby. There was, however, another presence. Human, Almaarian by his body shape, his hands empty and held wide to show they were weapon free. However, the tattoo across his neck and head spoke of the real danger. At a guess, it wouldn't match the boy's outside. Tensei and Baja, two gangs on the opposite sides of an old war she'd rather forget.

"Captain Khan," the gang member said, taking the lead. "We need to talk."

Rebekah resisted the urge to draw her weapon. She was alone in a Senti drug den, and at a disadvantage.

"We do?" she said. "I can't remember asking for a meeting."

"No. But we're having one, anyway. I represent the Tensei. I'm unarmed, but should tell you that I have my foot soldiers upstairs should you take badly to our conversation." The voice held more than a hint of Almaar, and far from the local accent. He held himself with wary confidence. Again, not the rough gang leader she had expected.

"Are *you* Tensei?" she asked, not knowing if it was the leader's name, the gang's or both like the Hannos.

The man tilted his head. "One and the same."

"So why do we need to talk?" Rebekah took a quick glance behind, and placed herself half into the doorway, her back to the entrance. She didn't make any attempt to hide her wariness.

"Isn't it obvious? Pshwa tells me you are looking for wetware. I have wetware." He opened his arms, his eyes and smile snake-like – trust me they said.

Shit on that.

Rebekah turned to Pshwa. "This your ten percent? Bringing someone else in without consulting me?"

"My understanding of human nature is that you would stab me in the back for a bigger percentage. I simply got there first. Humans can't read Senti body language. See that twitch around my third eye? That's a Senti shrug." Pshwa off-gassed, its frill lifting within the brown liquid, bubbles slowly escaping the barrel. Rebekah suspected that spoke more than the conniving alien bastard's eyes.

"Is done," said Tensei. "And just asking around would alert me. No harm. I have, what did your army grunts used to call it? Chips, yes? I have some that happen to be hanging around gathering dust. They are for sale."

"Of what origin? And how many?" asked Rebekah, trying to keep her voice steady.

"I assume an Almaarian's dead body. I am no expert. Cargo that an acquaintance of a dead pirate used as collateral on another deal. Not worth worrying about. I have thirty-three sets if you include others I have acquired elsewhere. A thousand a piece should cover it." Tensei smiled, one step short of sticking out a forked tongue. Rebekah assumed ninety percent of his words were lies. But the ten percent was either a hook or the truth, and she had little choice other than to take the bait.

"We need to see them," she said, "before any deal can be made. Especially as that figure can go fuck itself."

Tensei laughed, and more bubbles rose from the brown liquid. He eyed Rebekah, assessing her. Looking her up and down with a touch of admiration on his face. Feeling sickened, she drew on her chip.

"Ballsy. You can see the wetware tonight." He handed a piece of paper over to Rebekah, a number written on it. "That's the containment unit on the next ring up. Be there at eight. And on your own."

Rebekah grunted a half-growl, half-laugh. "Yeah. Alone. Let me put this straight. One, I won't be alone. Savvo and Arin will be along for the ride as they're my experts on the chips. Two, the means to pay won't be accessible through me. And three, the rest of my crew are a fucking vengeful lot."

Tensei made to speak. Rebekah ignored him. "You've tried hacking my ship? How did that go?"

He didn't reply, but Rebekah's chip helped catch the twitch in his left eye.

"That's the level we're playing at. Understand? Now, deal with that, or I look elsewhere." Rebekah waited, her eyes resting on the gang leader, scanning for tells. Verbal battles were much harder than battling face-to-face with a Bustan soldier. Kill or be killed. She made to leave.

"I hear you. But nor will I be screwed over by threats."

Boundaries set. She could deal with that.

"Then we understand each other. Eight pm station time. I'll be there. Open the door, Pshwa, before I reconsider your fucking percentage and take my anger out tentacle by tentacle." She kept her face flat, unemotional, and headed for the door. It unsealed without an issue, and she stepped out to find Savvo and Arin both kneeling down, hands on their weapons but not drawn. It wasn't subtle, her mood seemed to be spreading.

"Sit rep?"

"Multiple gang members on both sides. I'm thinking we've caused a stir. We have Bustan between us and the ship, and Almaarians to our right," Savvo replied.

"Nine between us and the way down," added Arin.

Savvo rubbed behind his ear. "Can't be definite, but we're talking less to the right. The Almaarians."

"Supposedly more in Pshwa's den. Just met the leader." Rebekah glanced over her shoulder and up to the first-floor windows. They remained barred, the shutters closed but there was movement, as if someone was pushing at the shutters. Or unbolting them.

"Arin, if we get out of this, how soon can you prep a simple body armour? Cos right now, I'm hankering for full Breaker kit and a carbine."

CHAPTER 16

"Schematics?" demanded Hendricks.

Tremil pulled the details, the deets as the crew called them, up onto the slate.

"Go on. Explain them to me in Dricks-ese, so I can understand what you've done." Hendricks eased herself onto the low cargo box, one eye on the passive robot as it sat next to the Butcher's coffin. Two earbuds played a soothing refrain in her ears, but it was struggling to block the angst pouring from both twins.

"How simple?" replied Heki, her own slate in hand but by her side.

"Imagine you were talking to an impatient Marine captain with a penchant for flying off the handle. Shouldn't be too hard." Hendricks ran a hand through her short hair and turned her attention to Heki. "Should it?"

Heki and Tremil let out simultaneous sighs.

"No," said Heki. "We designed an advanced CPU and operating system. Took all the bits we knew were banned by the Court ..."

"Woah. Stop there a second. Are we talking AI? Are you telling me you gave ZZ3 an independent personality, and that's the shit we witnessed in your cabin?" She felt the angst rise, tinged with a little fear at her suggestion. Tough.

"No," said Tremil. "Not AI. We know that'd be treasonous and put you all in danger. We're not that reckless."

Hendricks gave her a hard stare, and Tremil blushed, casting her eyes to the cargo deck.

"You redesigned banned processes—"

"—therefore, not banned. As these are new. Ours," cut in Heki.

"The Inquisitors won't give a flying sh… crap for that. You've said they're based on a banned design. That's enough. Think. Talk to us. Sheesh. Tell me the rest." She tucked her legs under her chin, wincing at the pain that didn't come, and wrapped her arms about her knees. "Go on."

"We added additional and more efficient memory capacity. And adapted the response program to the visual code. Then we've trained ZZ3 to mimic …" Heki glanced at Tremil, who blushed again. "To mimic all of you. You know, your voices, personality."

"Why would you do that?" But it seeped in. The reasons knocking on her skull and entering her mind without permission. Two very scared and lonely girls. Lab raised.

To practise.

Tremil nodded, still looking at the deck. "We used ZZ3 as a human model. To try out various ways to interact, and in so doing, extrapolate how we felt and responded. Assessed the data, modified our words, used different blockers for our emotional output. We couldn't hurt ZZ3." Tremil looked up from the deck. "But we could kill you."

"Hurt those we love," added Heki. Tears formed in her eyes. "Our family."

No earworm was going to work – neither an orchestra fed directly into her ear, or a thunderous storm in the other. Hendricks fought the wave of emotion by shutting her mind down, closing it off, and opened her arms wide to embrace the twins. Somewhere in there, amid the maelstrom, she fought the breaking of her heart. Soldering the cracks with an engineer's efficiency, and a soldier's need for redemption.

"Still no chocolate," she whispered.

Both girls choked a laugh and squeezed tighter.

After a while, she let them go, easing back to wipe her tears away. "Okay, extrapolators. Explain what you think happened to ZZ3, because I'm no closer to an answer."

Tremil blew out a long, self-calming sigh. "I don't think anything we built into ZZ3's architecture, either hardware or software, could have led to it knowing Senti code, nor act outside of prescribed remits."

Hendricks nodded, remembering Arin's likening of their analysis to that of a textbook. She was beginning to agree, between the tears.

"We're thinking that whatever happened on the *Scourge* – that you won't let us see by the way – and especially in the lab, is the overriding anomaly in the data, in the *deets*." Heki walked towards the bot, Hendricks fighting the urge to pull her away, to protect her from the unknown. But it had saved them from the strange hack, and countless times before. Most recently rescuing Arin from the particulates of the sun flare when she had been forced to abandon her ... her love.

Can you owe a bot? An inanimate thing?

Perhaps.

Heki stood next to the warbot, her head tilted back to gaze at the inert eyes, barely reaching up to half the bot's height. Two powerful forces of such contrasting sizes.

"So, when the Butcher took over ZZ3, invaded its system, you think it left something residual behind," said Hendricks. The thought had occurred to all of them, but Arin had swept the system, assuring them it was clear. The system, not the add-ons.

Tremil responded, as if reading her mind. "Our additional hardware, possibly even elements of the software, could have been ..."

"Corrupted." Heki finished Tremil's thought for her as she gazed up at the bot. "We can run an analysis. Check."

"I don't like that word. Corrupted sounds like ZZ3 could be a danger to us," said Hendricks, pushing herself off the box to join Heki.

"Empirical evidence suggests otherwise," said Tremil, joining them, wrapping her arm inside Hendricks to the engineer's surprise. "But we need to know what parameters this new version of ZZ3 is operating under. For all our safety."

"And for Arin."

Hendricks had mused over binding the warbot in chains, or setting multiple barricades. Even resorting to a search for an EMP grenade as they had the bot's ever-switching frequency patterns. But after that proved fruitless, she realised their only choice was to wrap the bot in the jaws of the cargo loader. Hold it long enough for them to escape should it prove threatening. Hendricks was half-tempted to place the Butcher's box the other side, maybe accidentally catch the foul thing in the cargo loader's arms on the way past. Possibly crush it a little.

Glancing up at the ceiling mounts for the massive jaws, she had her doubts they would hold the bot should it turn on them.

Why do this now?

Why not wait? Do this in the void, or just space the warbot, anyway?

Because the twins would be fretting. Because the crew were absent and couldn't be harmed.

Because I need to know.

Heki and Tremil were at the rear of the bot, their slates connected to its core system underneath a back plate. They were talking between themselves, the excitement palpable despite their attempts to lock their emotions down.

"There." Tremil tapped her slate, spinning it about for Heki to see. "That's not our code. In fact, it's more like the Senti algorithm that attacked us."

"Something I should know?" asked Hendricks, her hand over the emergency button she'd rigged up. Wired in with no way to intercept any signal except by ripping it out.

Heki responded. "All our additions have been ... mutated. Corrupted isn't the right word. Redesigned and repurposed."

"Can you purge it?"

As soon as the last word left Hendricks' lips, ZZ3's eyes lit. The swirl was instant, way faster than normal, until the rhythmic pulse took hold they had last seen in the girls' cabin. Limbs twitched, and Hendricks' hand dropped closer to the button.

"Step away," she said, her voice hard, and expecting nothing but agreement.

ZZ3's upper limbs swept upwards, held high, twisted about as a human would to show they were unarmed.

"Protect protocol. ZZ3 under pacification, threat assessment nil. ZZ3 will not harm any of the crew."

Hendricks twitched, eyeing the girls who had stepped back, open-mouthed. Their fear was centred on the bot. No, not fear, though it was an undercurrent. What battered at her mind was *awe.*

By rights, she should be sending the girls out and introducing the warbot to the cargo loader.

Shit.

"Talk to me girls. Sit rep. Now."

"ZZ3 ... it has an aura. Not like the emotions we see in you. But something is there." Heki took a step forwards.

"No!"

But Hendricks was too late, the twin had taken hold of the bot's elbow. A touch. And the warbot readjusted, turning about as it could to look behind, limbs folding back on themselves.

"Threat assessment nil. I will not harm my crew."

Tremil joined her sister, touching the bot to Hendricks consternation. Oh, for a squad of Marines who did as they were told.

"Who are you?" asked Heki. "Explain protocol, action code HT."

"I am ZZ3, but more." The voice was monotone, but not the same. Nuance lay there.

Hendricks' skin crawled. "She said explain," she growled. "Protocol do as you're fucking told, action code Wrecking Squad."

The bot turned its attention to Hendricks, the eye pattern intensifying. A stone sat heavily in Hendricks' stomach. It wasn't fear. Though the bot was all metal and wires, it had gained something. Habits?

Mannerisms.

"I have been adapted. I have melded with the partial code from a brain patterning." ZZ3 tilted one rear limb, an almost human gesture. Mimicking, to Hendricks' mind, a person who bent one knee when they stood still. A habit she had enjoyed drilling out of the occasional Marine on the parade ground.

Both girls gasped, seeing something that Hendricks couldn't, their awe superseded by raw curiosity that infected her own mind. She fought for sense amid the storm.

"That would be the Butcher," said Hendricks, squeezing her eyes tight with her other hand. "General Asham. He, who murdered an entire cruiser's crew, and most likely that of the *Moonslip*. Step away girls, now."

"There is a third part. Please, Tremil, Heki. Check my code. Look between the patterns."

Please? What bot says please?

She watched them swipe and tap at their slates. Happy that they were backing away as she asked, despite remaining at the limits of their slates' wired connection to the warbot. This was a mess, regret at allowing it increasing by the second.

"Pacification code," said Tremil, Heki nodding at her side, looking over her sister's shoulder. "It's embedded throughout the architecture. Amid ours and the Senti algorithms."

"Yes," said ZZ3, a hint of nuance again in the voice. Relief?

"Explain." Hendricks didn't know who she was asking.

"I can't," said Heki. "It's like the Senti cyber attack. Lots of broken and blended lines of code that make no sense on their own. The pacification is active. ZZ3 is right that the threat assessment is currently zero, but whether that can be changed is difficult to ascertain."

"When our glorious leader engaged the pacification protocol, it overrode Asham's brain pattern, and my parameters. He fought it. I shut him down. Forced him to comply. During that process, this me, the new ZZ3, was created." ZZ3's leg limb straightened, its arm limbs wrapping about its upper body. "Part of me is Asham, part ZZ3 and the bond embedded in the pacification protocol. I can do no harm to my crew. My threat assessment is zero."

Hendricks stared at the bot, the steady rhythm of its pulsing eyes intensifying. It knew she was assessing, mulling over what the bot had become. A human would sweat, their bodies reveal tells a Marine could pick up. These were absent, and so it remained the eyes and the odd mannerisms of the warbot's limbs the ex-Marine had to judge by.

Though Hendricks had a not-so secret weapon.

"Heki? Tremil? This aura thing, can it lie?"

The girls looked to each other, exchanging quiet words, then at Hendricks.

It was Tremil who spoke. "It is as new to us, as to you. But we detect only truth and self-loathing."

"Self-loathing?" said Hendricks. "That I can relate to. Explain, ZZ3."

"The Asham part of me has been examining memories. It hates itself. What it has done."

Hendricks' hand dropped, not to the button, but to the cargo box lid by its side. Holding herself up. Life, they said, was a circle. Things come back, turning on themselves to complete the cycle. She remembered the taste of the gun barrel, a young girl's red-rimmed eyes watching, needing to be saved. Urging Hendricks to overcome her self-loathing at the senseless death and destruction she had wrought.

"Damn."

The warbot looked away, back to the twins.

"Thank you," it said, and then the body relaxed against the deck. Entering an inert state, or at least, appearing as if in one.

"Hendricks?" asked Heki. "What now?"

She blinked in response, clearing her mind of the lab. With a sigh, she pushed the emergency button away.

"We extrapolate the data. Analyse, and present what we know to the Captain when she returns. And you need to rest, sort those tangled emotions out, as my head is reeling. And yes, I know you're trying to hold it all in." Hendricks smiled at the girls. "And I need a shower."

CHAPTER 17

Rebekah walked with her hand resting on the butt of her gun, eyeing the Senti in their stalls and the occasional human who moved along the concourse. The gang members stood out. Their bodies muscular, broad shouldered and thick-legged. The result of Bustan's 1.1 standard grav over time. They stood aside as all three walked towards the down tube, forming a curtain behind them. A threat, and she wasn't in the mood.

Savvo was on point, Arin at her back. Threat was something she understood, but this felt new. They were armourless, and it was for the last time. A vulnerability that overrode her thoughts, and she suspected, would lead to decisions she could be forced into. It did not sit well on her shoulders.

As expected, two waited ahead of them, arms crossed, a scowl to their faces. One would either be the Baja leader, or their proxy. Expendable.

It was that type of day.

"This is turning into a busy day," she said, keeping her hand on her hip and close to the gun. "Whom am I going to tell to fuck off this time?" She quirked her eyebrows towards the pair, judging the slightly taller of the two would be the leader. She was wrong, not for the first time that day.

"We are Baja," said the shorter one. Probably in his late twenties, brown eyes filled with red veins.

"And you are their leader, and we need to talk," she replied, failing to keep her voice level as she intended. The whole process was gnawing at her. Up to now, they had effectively kept up an impression of a 'don't fuck with me' attitude through words, posture and the struts through the market. But it was wearing, and Rebekah needed a mental break before having to return that evening. Patience was thin.

"No. I am Neend, I speak but do not lead." His Almaarian was good, but the inflections were wrong. Nor was he station born and bred. The arms were still crossed, the eyes narrow despite the proxy's attempt to keep them wide. At least she had intimidated him. The only problem was that those lacking in confidence, or feeling threatened, often responded with aggression.

She forced herself to calm, engaging the chip's help. "No disrespect, but if your boss can't be arsed to present themselves, then I see no reason to speak." She gestured with her chin towards his guard. "And if you haven't got what I need, then there's no point in a conversation, threats or not."

She kept her eye on the taller guard and began to move past Neend. As expected, the guard shifted into her path, blocking her way. Rebekah stood eye to eye with the muscular man, aware of where each of his weapons were.

"There is no need for violence," said Neend, and he slid a hand between the guard and her. The guard backed off, eyes full of pride and now hurt at having to stand down. Rebekah tried not to laugh, but a smile betrayed her, and he growled in his throat.

Neend slid into the space, having the good sense to keep his distance from Rebekah. "Baja knows you have creds to spend. You have seen Pshwa, and the Tensei scum hang around you like a fart in a space station. You are here to buy; we like to sell."

"My understanding is that you skim from Pshwa, as do the Tensei." Rebekah glanced behind, noting both Savvo and Arin were back-to-back with her, eyes on the rest of the gang. She gestured towards the Senti's addict-inducing den. "As far as I know, you should be asking him what we're after. But I guess the alien bastard cut you out from the deal. Not my problem."

Rebekah sidestepped and walked on. She knew it was a mistake as soon as the guard grabbed her arm. Instincts kicked in, enhanced by the already active chip, and she punched him in the throat. The Bajan gangster hit the station floor like a sack of spare parts. Decision time.

"No fucker touches me, understand?" she barked, focusing her anger on the guard, not the proxy. The swish of guns from holsters filled her mind, and the potential loss of Arin and Savvo to her stupidity.

"Woah," shouted Neend. "Guns down, guns down."

Rebekah turned her head, keeping the anger on her face as she swept the Senti enclave. Every Bajan had a weapon out and pointed her way. In response, Savvo and Arin had closed, shoulder to shoulder, their own weapons in hand.

"Learn some manners," she said, and turned away, heading towards the descent ladder. No gunshots rang out, only the voice of the proxy echoing above the billowing gauze. On reaching the ladder, she risked a turn, finding her crew with their handguns lowered and backing her way.

"Hey, Neend. Keep your dogs on a leash. Talk to Pshwa. If you got what I need, stop trying to hack my ship and fucking call instead." Rebekah started down the ladder, Arin waited a heartbeat, then followed.

"This Rebekah I like," the sub-engineer said on the way down. "Makes me look refined and subtle."

"Not a chance, Arin." It was Savvo from above, his eyes on the hatchway. "This is simply a new way to blend in with the locals. You know, have a fist fight, slap them down so we don't draw attention to ourselves. Can't see a problem."

Rebekah took a glance down, the way clear below the bottom hatch, and slid down the final few metres of the ladder. On her haunches, she scanned the immediate area, moving aside as Arin joined her.

She sighed, her shoulders relaxing as she stood. "Okay. An overreaction."

"Who am I to judge?" said Arin, his lopsided grin grating with her, compounding her annoyance with herself. "I'm just the one protecting your back. You see robots are predictable, you can trust a robot. People? Naah."

Savvo climbed down the last few rungs, a look up, and then he was by Rebekah's side. "From what Dricks said, ZZ3 is as haywire as you."

Rebekah caught the intensity in Savvo's glance, her second checking on whether she was alright, calm. He didn't need to say anything more. She shook her head, more to herself than anyone else.

"On point," she said, eyeing Savvo. He nodded, locking eyes for a second, and set off down the steps.

She followed, Arin muttering away to himself amid the clangs on the steps.

After a few steps, he spoke again. "Was I too much?"

Rebekah couldn't help but smile. "No. Just right."

"Good ... You sure?"

"Sure."

Rebekah towelled herself dry after a long shower, then stood before her cabin's mirror, trying to work out how tired she felt. It had been an intense day so far, and not yet at an end. Hannos had proven interesting. A gang leader who cared for those on the station, or at least, that's how she came across. There would be violence and coercion in there, no doubt. An ex-Skyrider, the elite, but that didn't mean she could be trusted. Actions spoke louder than words laced with hard liquor.

Tensei regarded himself as a player, a man with his finger on the pulse who oozed confidence and leaked smarm. She trusted her assessment of him more than Hannos. He understood what he was, and so did she. A snake who knew he couldn't hide it, so didn't try. And his relationship with Pshwa was definitely stronger than the Baja's. What had played out in the Senti enclave was a power-play, a gang sensing it was being cut out. Marginalised. They were seeking the weaker faction and chose her crew, and she had overreacted. But the bastard shouldn't have grabbed her. No one got that privilege, not anymore. Not since losing her Pa and grandma had she let an unwanted touch go unchallenged. Trauma ran deep, and killing in a haze of wetware and drugs had helped, until they didn't, and two girls parted the fog.

"Fuck." She leant her forehead against the mirror, rocking gently. "Calm. You can do this. Nobody breaks a Breaker."

With a last glance in the mirror, she dressed and left, hunting for coffee and some good news. Savvo was already in the galley, nursing a tea and running through his slate with Hendricks. Rebekah poured herself a flask, and squeezed in next to the engineer as she talked through events with the twins again.

"So, give me the bottom line," said Savvo. "Safe or not?"

The engineer rubbed the back of her head, hand sliding over her scalp to come to a rest wrapped around her sweetened coffee. "Honestly? The Marine in me says blow it out the airlock."

"And what does Hendricks say?" asked Rebekah, squeezing the engineer's arm. "The new you."

"Don't feel new," she said with a slight smile. "Hek and Trem, they're saying ZZ3 is sound. That it ain't lying. Listen to that … a bot ain't lying. Fuuuuck. When did the world get so weird?"

"About four years ago," replied Savvo, tilting his flask towards Hendricks. "And every time the way seems clear, something unexpected pops up to fuck us over. At least it's not boring being in the Wrecking Squad."

Rebekah rolled her eyes, recalling Savvo's view of their mundane, claustrophobic life before Duboit had ripped it wide open.

"So, our trustworthy crew members, who wouldn't possibly make any alterations to a warbot without telling us, say its safe. I feel better already." Rebekah took a sip, savouring the slightly bitter taste. "You were there, Dricks. Your assessment. Threat points."

The ex-captain pushed herself back into the bench seat, sighing. "To be honest, it felt kind of … I dunno … hopeful. As if ZZ3 laid out the facts and hoped we'd see the sense of it all. It stopped the cyber attack, and only responded to us when it was threatened. What was the word?"

"Purge," said Heki and Tremil together, the two girls walking side by side in the corridor. Appearing as if summoned. "A self-protection response."

Hendricks nodded, taking a sip and grimacing. "Yeah. But Rebekah, I couldn't detect a threat. More a 'what will be will be'."

Swigging the rest of the coffee, feeling the slight burn of her throat, Rebekah stood and headed along the corridor, the girls parting, waiting for their admonishment. She didn't give them eye contact, but walked on past, their sighs relieved as were the roiling emotions that pushed her along the passageway.

"You don't get off that easily. Hendricks has filled me in, now it's your turn. I want to hear it from the robot's mouth. Follow." Rebekah walked to the cargo hold, pausing briefly, gathering her thoughts before entering. Arin was there, his own slate plugged into the bot, face screwed up in thought and worry. She approached, hearing the twins' footsteps behind.

"Anything new to report?" she asked Arin, who shrugged his shoulders.

"Everything matches what the terrible twosome told us. A screwed-up code I can't even begin to make sense of, and additional hardware I could possibly familiarise myself with if its staying in *my* robot." He lifted his head from the slate to look at the twins.

Their disquiet rolled over Rebekah, and she upped the earworm, staring at Arin who clammed up.

"Can we still use it?" she asked. "Can we trust ZZ3?"

"Trust? This shit has been in there since the *Scourge*, and ZZ3 saved my life. Savvo's too. Then there's the cyber attack. You earn trust, if that's what we're associating with a bot now. So far, one hundred percent." Arin looked back at his screen, then ZZ3.

"You don't suggest a *purge* then?"

Rebekah got the response she was looking for, the red eyes lighting in full neon, and the warbot rising from the floor. It was listening to every word. No longer depending on protocol triggers. Independent. Her head filled with flashbacks of a plasma torch centimetres from piercing her helmet – and her from death.

"ZZ3 under pacification, threat assessment nil," it said.

Rebekah turned to the twins.

"That's what we sense," they said together.

"But you feel threatened, ZZ3," stated Arin, stealing Rebekah's opening line. She let him roll with it.

There was a pause. "Yes."

"Protocol explain, action code Wrecking Squad," said Arin, moving round to face the bot.

"I am ... I exist. I wish to continue to exist." The lights beat a rhythm.

"Act—"

"Can't you see?" said Heki. "You don't need those anymore. The action codes, the protocols, they are defining parameters. ZZ3 has those embedded now."

"Embedded?" said Arin, but he didn't look at Heki, keeping his eyes on the warbot. "Is that right?"

Rebekah could have sworn ZZ3 nodded, a slight tilt of its body. Hendricks had mentioned mannerisms, but this.

"Yes. They are … defining my thought processes, and structuring my decisions."

"So why do you respond to a threat to yourself, what has changed?" asked Rebekah. Inside that bot was part of the Butcher, a general who had chosen to release his obscene experiments on his own crew. An act of revenge, maybe, or loathing for others.

"I am crew."

"By whose definition?" cut in Arin, his voice high-pitched, strained.

"Yours, our glorious leader."

Tremil stepped beside Rebekah, with her eyes on the bot. "So ZZ3 has extended the protection protocol, and embedded self-preservation." She turned to look up at Rebekah, a faint smile on her lips. The emotions locked away by something that felt like triumph to Rebekah. Teenagers. "And therefore, is no threat."

"Is that right? Action protocol negate pacification, action code Breakers." The bot didn't move, nor respond initially to Rebekah's words until it adjusted limbs slightly, and sunk to the deck.

"Negative response. Pacification remains in place. Breaker codes have been … pacified."

"Oh joy," said Arin. "Now your Captain's gonna be pissed."

Chapter 18

"Do I look fat in this?" said Arin, taking the rear, the rigged microphone and conduction speaker obvious only if you took a very close look. "I mean, it bulks me out. Maybe more muscular."

Savvo snorted.

"I take that personally." Arin, turned about, eyes sweeping their six as they trudged along the connecting passageway towards the upper ring.

"I would," interjected Rebekah. "But I still feel better with it on." She hitched the body armour up, cinching the buckle a little tighter, so it sat where she needed it. The plates were thin and print-bonded ceramic. Not so hot in a war zone, but from what she'd seen, most of the weapons on display were short range pellet throwers. Heavy hitters close up, not so hot from distance. The armour chafed a little under her flight coat, but it added a sense of confidence she needed after the encounter with the Baja, and her expectations about Tensei.

Savvo stopped ahead. The bulkhead door was wide open, leading into the next ring where, as far as Rebekah understood it, most of the ordinary people resident on the station lived. The opposite to how M2 and M3 operated, where higher grav was the goal. Here, she suspected, life had been built around survival. The closer to the inside you slept, the more likely you were to survive a breach. On a station that had been built ad hoc, it seemed the sensible option.

The bulkhead was guarded, Tensei tattoos on full display. Savvo spoke to them, explaining they were on business. As they conversed, a family slipped between the guards, heading their way. There was no interaction or toll to pay, they simply walked by and didn't appear concerned. Rebekah nodded to the parents as they sidled by, making no eye contact.

"We're in," said Savvo, waving them both over. "They wanted our weapons."

"And I want a hot bath, tea and toast," she replied. "Not bloody happening."

She edged behind Savvo as he went through the heavy doorway, sparing a glance for one of the female guards who seemed young and interested in what they were wearing. That information would be passed down the line, the reason they'd opted for printing thinner plated armour, hoping it would go unnoticed.

Savvo walked on to the right, periodically checking the deck for the scuffed markings that had been haphazardly redrawn. They were heading, as far as they knew, for somewhere along this outer ring, rather than internally. She hoped that was true, because going towards the hub would mean an increased vulnerability as they moved through the laddered sections.

"No eyes on," said Arin over the comms. "But as they know where we are, and where we're headed …"

"They're looking for a deal," said Savvo. "Not a war."

"Who do we trust?" Rebekah waited.

"No one but us," they replied, completing the Breaker adage.

They passed through the concourse with container after container built up along the ring walls. Ladders were everywhere, both up and across, acting as bridges and connecting levels. Most containers had a single window cut into the metal, a sheet of plexi-glass or polythene inserted to allow light into the dwellings. Rebekah estimated they ran about fifteen metres up on both sides, and were covered in various pipes and insulated tubes she assumed to be power cables. A spider's web without the uniformity, but calm. Not a slum. A home.

These briefly gave out, with double-width buildings interspersed, often with signs declaring their role as café, med centre or manufactory. It was far from normal, but in these surroundings, each new sight came less and less as a surprise. The noise was gentle, the sound of people going about the business of living their lives. The smell was more intrusive. However well the pipework and air filters functioned, an all-pervading scent of humanity remained. Sweat, musk, an underlying aroma of close living. It sat halfway between comforting and off-putting. On the ship, such conditions led to her upping the filters another notch. Everyone has their foibles.

After a quarter of the ring, the dwellings faded. Still a multitude of ancient containers, but these were a hubbub of activity Rebekah assumed was focused on making things – be it the everyday items people needed or brewing drink, fermenting drugs or sewing Senti cloth. Somewhere in all of this they needed food and water. Those were the commodities that were the hardest to acquire in the quantities needed to maintain a large population.

"Up ahead," said Savvo, ending her thoughts and refocusing Rebekah's mind. "There's an external bulkhead. Thinking that's maybe our target."

Rebekah checked the address ID Tensei had provided and the current markings on the ring floor. Apparently, they were nearing their goal, and Savvo paused another ten metres further on. She caught him up, the large entrance open and ancient. An old airlock had been ripped out and shoved to the side. Dust and debris indicated it had been there a long while. Two Almaarians stood inside the entryway, displaying a sidearm each and a machete holstered at their other hip. Gang tattoos were on full display. There was no need to check the address marker, but she did so anyway.

"Looks like an old freighter," said Savvo, pointing past the entrance to the wide interior. "I mean, really old."

"Then let's hope it's still sound. Watch our backs, Arin, and don't get twitchy," she said.

"Me? I didn't flatten a Bustan a few hours ago."

"*Now* it's too much," Rebekah said. "Stow it."

"Yes, Captain. On your six."

Savvo walked at her side as they approached the entranceway, one guard stepping across and pointing to their weapons. Rebekah had expected as much, and handed over the handgun at her hip, with Savvo and Arin following suit. It was shit, but they were prepared as long as they weren't searched.

"Unzip," said the guard, gesturing up and down as if undoing her jacket himself. She complied, letting the coat hang wide, and spinning around. He made to pat her down, but the other guard intervened, grabbing his wrist, shaking their head.

"You see Pietr's throat? Fuck that."

Rebekah stared back at the man, daring him. The hands returned to their sides, and he twitched his head to the side. "In."

Savvo and Arin were not treated the same way, and the tap on their body armour didn't go unnoticed.

"Rough neighbourhood," said Arin. "Can't be too careful."

Apart from the armour, he was clear, and all three entered the old freighter. Rebekah checking the one-shot ceramic handguns were still under her back armour. Not much use other than as a surprise take down of your opponent with the aim of acquiring their weapon. At least they had some element of self-defence.

The freighter had been attached so the hull ran alongside the ring. They walked into the upper deck, and what she guessed had been the ship's galley that now functioned as a bar. Music blared, and several gang members sat around tables playing cards, while another helped themselves to a plate of food. Rebekah marked each one, where they sat, what they wore, and any visible weapons. Each threat point noted, expecting Arin and Savvo to be doing the same. Tensei sat at a far table, cards laid out before him in a regular pattern, tapping one against the table while eyeing those face up.

The snake-like smile returned when he spotted Rebekah, returning to his game briefly to throw the card on a pile with a self-congratulatory flourish. Rebekah was mightily impressed by the perfect timing, wondering just how long he'd been tapping that card while waiting for her to arrive.

"Captain, a pleasure," he said.

"Tensei," she replied, deciding against adding a description.

"And friends. Good, and on time. I like that." He stood, scraping his chair against the old metal deck. Four of the card players took the hint and stood, some hitching up their belts with the hand cannons holstered across them jiggling.

Subtle but effective. Not a warning, more a reminder.

It left three of Tensei's members in the bar, and two more at the entrance. With the threat points noted, she followed Tensei through a seized bulkhead door that led to a short corridor. They bypassed a lift, its lights dead, and went through another hatchway to a set of stairs whose age didn't match the ship's. They descended; the clink of each step dulled by the detritus strewn about the stairs. The ring had been surprisingly tidy, as if the people cared where they lived day in and day out, and this was a marked contrast. Gone was the smell of spice and ash, replaced by the tang of rusting metal and uncared for age.

Rebekah estimated they had dropped a standard deck, and they emerged into an old cargo hold. Not as big as she expected, but often the older freighters would have a number of holds for separate goods transport. This one, however, was used for more than just cargo. When they entered through a chained-back bulkhead, there were four booths immediately to their right. Two were occupied, a woman laid back on a rigged-up chair in each, a basket of wires and electronics wrapped about their heads. Rebekah suppressed a flinch, scanning the women for any signs of coercion. The only thing of note were the tab guns on a table at their sides, and the gang tattoos.

Tensei caught her glance. "Live stream," he said. "Dreams, though the Senti have grown more demanding of late."

"Live?" she asked, unable to help herself.

Tensei stopped by the last booth, hand upon the smoked plexi-glass wall. "No one has figured out the tech for recording." He turned to Rebekah, and likely reading her scepticism. "Pshwa thinks Scarva may have found a way to get the old wetware to play ball, why else would he want the kit? Unless he's going to livestream from that crappy ship."

Tensei clearly knew more about the wetware than any other human she'd met, and despite the mission, she wanted to know more – especially with a symbiote on board her ship. But she didn't want to appear ignorant.

"What about the symbiotes?" she said, leaving that as open as she could. She sensed Arin stir behind her, but ignored him.

Tensei didn't seem fazed, letting out a huff. "Way beyond our operation. Little monsters can draw from inside the skull and keep the source feed pure. But no Senti is going to share, are they? And Pshwa's little tentacled pal died a long time ago."

Tensei pushed himself away from the booth as one of the women stirred, releasing a moan, and rolling to one side. Rebekah could see her rapid-eye movements, and a twitch in her shoulder. There were tab bruises on the upper arm from repeated use of the gun.

Twisting her lips, she followed Tensei, thoughts on why they were here rolling about her head. At first look, the mission brief appeared to be a basic recovery run. Some noble having lost a cargo that had garnered the Enforcer's interest. Was owning wetware illegal? If it was, hardly an Enforcer issue. So, something about this particular set had piqued their interest, either as leverage against the original owner, or ... more than that. If it was used, did they contain recordings of something the Enforcers wanted? That made sense.

Beyond the booths was a table piled with various gadgets that had been sorted and labelled. They all looked new, and the labelling, at first glance, appeared systematic.

"For auction," said Tensei on the way past.

"Of course." Duboit had mentioned the station feed, and the constant advertising of goods for sale on one section. The wetware they sought had been put up and then taken down quickly – within the day, but they had got wind of its existence.

More cargo boxes had been broken open, and lay discarded along the far side of the table. Without her HUD, she couldn't scan the codes, but suspected everything in the room came from a multitude of stolen or illegal sources. Space piracy was a fallacy. Boarding a ship was dangerous business even when in orbit, hence the Skyriders, never mind when in flight. Toms had sent his salvagers to cut their way in, kill her crew, before even attempting to board. If so-called space pirates attacked a ship, the crew knew they were going to die unless they fended them off. It kind of heightened the desperation, and freighter crews often included ex-Marines in their ranks for that very purpose. The higher end the goods, the more likely they would have a set of reconditioned powered armour to heighten the deterrent.

No, most theft happened at the warehouses, and after that the docks. Easier pickings, and manifests were notoriously poorly filled.

Tensei stopped by a lidded metal box. Blank, no marking, and lifted the top to reveal a pile of wetware wrapped in individual clear packaging. It was a graveyard, full of dead soldiers. A first glance told her the kit was basic army and navy issue, much like those Savvo had adapted to track live crew on the *Scourge*. Duboit hadn't been clear on what to expect, only that it was definitely Marine wetware and would have the additional chem add-ons. And, of course, the cargo coding on the box.

"Good kit," he said, taking one of the bags and starting to open it. "Tested. Pshwa adapted a few for my live booths."

"Savvo," Rebekah said, gesturing him over. He approached, taking a glance around, scanning the hold, before accepting the half-open bag. He glanced at it, putting it aside, and began to dig into the box. Rebekah saw his face shift, a tremor at the corner of his eye. Savvo emerged with two more sets, still wrapped, but sections of the wiring had deteriorated on one, the other had two sensors hanging free.

"Tested," Savvo said. "With a fucking shovel?"

"Those are repairable," Tensei said quickly, taking the bags from Savvo. "Look at some others."

Her second trawled through the cargo box, separating ten of the sets out from the others. With a side-eye to Rebekah, he flipped open his belt pack, exposing the breaker kit and toolbox. A few connections later, and the wetware thrummed, settling after a few seconds. Savvo examined the data streaming over his toolbox's tiny screen.

"Sound," he said. "Want me to test any more?"

A gunshot, dulled by the stairwell but clear enough, thudded above. Followed by two more.

CHAPTER 19

"Hold," said Rebekah, the whisper only for the hidden comms.

Tensei drew a handgun from inside his jacket and cast a withering look towards her.

"Not us," she said, hands open but holding her ground. "I'm here to buy, not steal and ruin any chance of returning to this corner of paradise."

Tensei grunted, the snake-like smile replaced by a scowl of mistrust. The barrel was aimed her way, and Rebekah ignored the temptation to step closer and rip it from his hand. The difference between a Breaker in full powered armour, and one wearing a thin vest.

"Point that fucking thing at whoever's shooting," she growled. A glance to Arin and Savvo confirmed they still waited on her order. "Or you'll be fighting on two fronts."

"Samir, Davyd, Babik go. Hanna, stay with these three. If they so much as twitch, shoot them."

"Us ...?" started Arin, a glare from his captain causing him to trail off. Tensei followed his three guards up the stairwell, more shouts and gunfire sounding from above. As the gang leader disappeared up the stairs, Rebekah backed away towards Savvo who stood by the open wetware box.

"Any of these what we need?" she asked, half-an-eye on Hanna, the woman's heavily muscled shoulders too tense for her liking.

"No boss," he replied. "These are army. Basic shit, and some older Mk. 1's at that. Not worth the effort. I don't think this is what Scarva is looking for."

True enough.

"Hanna, is it?" More gunfire made her hurry, it was getting closer. "Any more wetware stored down here? You know, the good stuff Tensei was only going to show us if we blew him off? Save some time."

With her chip kicked in, and senses heightened, she watched the woman's face. There was a tremor in her cheek, and the slightest of eye movements to her left, Rebekah's right. That was something. The temptation to go for the stunner was there, but Hanna held a hand cannon, a flechette version packed with glass needles. The right shot would tear anything vulnerable to shreds.

Tensei flew through the door, clattering in a tangled heap before the dream booths. A stocky Bustan stomped in after him and swung an enormous bat at his legs. Rebekah winced as it struck, though the blow could have been a lot harder. A softening up. Hanna had spun towards the fracas, weapon raised when a second Baja appeared, their hand cannon aimed squarely at Tensei's head.

"Drop your weapon girl." The drawl was all Bustan, the owner's smile full of teeth and malice below a bald pate. "He doesn't want to die, and nor do you. I've come for what's mine. Nothing more."

Hanna's face rippled between confusion and loyalty.

"He'll be dead before you squeeze that trigger. Lower it," said Savvo. "No need to die when you've already lost."

Rebekah noted the shake to her gun arm, the finger flexing, the bad decision she was about to make.

No.

She slammed in at hip level, driving her down, hitting Hanna twice about the ears as she landed on top. "Stay down."

There was applause from across the way, a slow hand clap. It grated on her, the sarcasm she imagined within it.

"Good," said the Baja. The soft click of his weapon being dropped into a holster caught her attention. "I don't like senseless death. You'd be the captain of the *Solar Flame*, yes? Khan, is it? Welcome to Benetai, home of thieves and cutthroats. I much prefer the first, but indulge in the second when forced, eh, Tensei?" He shoved the other gang leader down with his boot, pressing between the shoulders as more gang members appeared behind him.

"I am. Here to buy some goods," she replied, both Arin and Savvo stepping in at her side, hands loose.

"Well, it's you I've got to thank. Would never have guessed it was Tensei bastards who had my goods without you being here." He strode past Tensei, the Almaarian's scowl aimed directly for Rebekah. She ignored it for now, nothing to be done.

"I told your proxy shit," she replied.

"No," he said, having reached the cargo box. "You told me to check with Pshwa, and eventually the windbag coughed up the truth of things, yes? That you wanted wetware, and my rival had some. Funny that, because my shipment got fucking intercepted a few months back." The Baja leader checked the open bags, and casting them aside, lifted the wetware Savvo had tested.

"I told you it was Hannos," spat Tensei.

"Aye, you did. And lied, no doubt." He threw the wetware down. "And my buyer is mighty pissed and steaming this way. So, Tensei," he spun around, drawing his gun. "Where the hell is *my* shipment? Cos this crap ain't worth nothing, and I'm on a short timescale. My wetware is clean, new. Not like this ancient shit."

Rebekah glanced over to Tensei, his lower jaw was tight, grinding away. The tension in the room impinged on her senses, her instinct to fight her way out gaining ground. She clambered off Hanna, only to realise her mistake.

The distressed woman kicked her knee, and Rebekah went down as it collapsed from under her. No damage done, but she was vulnerable as she hit the deck, and Hanna was up, holding her weapon unsteadily. A single shot filled the hold, and Hanna flew back, hitting the table and collapsing into Arin.

"Not very helpful," said the Baja. "A waste." He walked over, paying no heed to Rebekah, and knelt next to Hanna. Blood seeped from her shoulder and upper arm, multiple pellets having penetrated the flesh. "You'll live, girl," he pressed his fingers into the wound, grinding at the bone, "if I get my wetware."

Hanna screamed, and he dug deeper.

"Please talk, or I have to do this to Tensei, and then things get messy."

"There, along the wall" she replied through sobs of pain. A Benetai accent, through and through. She tried to point, only for Baja to drag her to her feet and shove her forwards. "Show me."

Hanna stumbled, catching herself against a wall of boxes, before hobbling over to a pile against the opposite wall. She shoved some aside one handed, clearly light, and behind it sat an Almaarian Navy stamp.

Bingo.

Hanna stepped away, collapsing to the floor.

Baja approached the box, a smug smile on his face. "See how easy that was. No need for all this pain. Zeta, Neend, get over here."

Rebekah rose from the floor as the proxy and a sidekick entered the hold, followed by another with a bruised and swollen throat. Pietr, by what Tensei's guards had said earlier. His glare full of hate and spite, and for once she didn't throw any back. Baja had shown no threat to her, and exacerbating that wasn't on the agenda. What was, however, was in the box the three of them dragged out from amid the others. There was a digilock on the side, ripped open, wires hanging off. A less than subtle entry, and Baja lifted the lid.

"Yes. My shit, Tensei. Stolen by you." He had one set in his hand, Savvo tensing at her side, the softest of nods affirming her suspicion. Baja walked over to Tensei, the wetware gleaming in the hold's light.

It was new, unused. Perfect kit.

One theory shot down.

"Now, if I was a vengeful man, I would steal something back." He paused as if considering it. "But I'm going to let this lie, understand? The bad blood ends here, or else next time I finish it. Wipe your ass from this station. Get me?"

Tensei's jaw ground, but a nod followed, the lowly gang leader's stare up from the deck hate-filled.

"Good." Baja smiled; teeth glinting as he nodded to Rebekah. "Pleasure meeting you, Captain. Now my advice is to leave Benetai. Tensei here may feel he has a grudge with you, though it would be ill-placed. And Pietr would like a piece too, though he only has himself to blame."

She took the cue, signalling to both Arin and Savvo to follow as she bypassed the two gang leaders, starting up the stairs as the clatter of a metal navy storage box rattled behind.

The stairs held a couple of surprises. Tensei guards stunned, and propped up in the corner, and as they entered the bar more of the gang members sported low-level injuries. The attack had been rapid, but not brutal. Restrained. The two external guards suffered the worst of the wounds, bleeding profusely from leg shots. Nicked arteries, maybe worse.

Arin swiftly collected their weapons, throwing each over from the safe box where they'd been stowed.

Savvo gave her a look, and she shook her head. They were Breakers no more, but there was too much risk in helping the wounded. Rebekah had taken two strides, when she turned back, Savvo having not moved.

"Fuck it. Be quick."

He didn't reply, dropping to his knee while drawing out a simple med-pack from inside his coat. He showed both guards the medpads and bandage wraps, making his intent clear.

Savvo checked each leg. "I'll staunch them, but they need attending to immediately."

Their answers were in local accented Almaarian. A picture of a station controlled by outsiders building in Rebekah's mind. The strongest led, criminals bringing their muscle to bear and dragging those with little future on the station into their web of theft and extortion. Yes, a lot of the people seemed far happier than she expected. Her preconceived idea of a floating garbage dump, heightened by how the place appeared from space, inaccurate. Perhaps Hannos spoke true, and she maintained the balance while having to show strength in equal measure to keep it.

In two minutes, with the banging of feet and a metal box ringing from the internal bulkhead on the rise, Savvo signalled he was done. He stood, and with a grimace to both guards, followed.

Rebekah felt a knot of pride in her heart, despite the threats from Baja. *Buying back a little piece of lost humanity each day.*

"Move. Arin take our rear, I'll take point," she didn't wait for an answer, doubting Baja would be patient a second time. However, in his eyes she was a trader, someone looking for a score, and therefore a potential customer.

Getting a rep for killing your main source of income wasn't going to be on his preferred agenda. Nor hers.

Calming her movements, she moved through the ring, eyeing the high units that served multiple purposes for threats. She assumed this was Tensei's patch, or at least on the edge of it, and therefore under his protection and watchful eye. As they emerged into the main living district, she slowed. Again, Tensei influence would remain, but this was not a place for a gun battle, nor to create alarm by barrelling on through. A gang boss who wanted to remain in control by fear, could spark an opposite reaction if bullets began to fly around families and children.

Savvo closed behind her, and a glance back confirmed Arin was watchful.

"Sit rep. Call in," she said.

"All clear," said Savvo.

"We had a tail until we entered the beautiful Benetai suburbs. A Baja, but they've stopped. Don't think it's to admire the pipework," said Arin.

"Keep an eye," she ordered. "Savvo, any way we can track that kit?"

"Not without the frequencies, and only when powered up," he replied, his voice a little distant, as if mulling over the possibilities.

"What about testing? Baja said he had a buyer. The kit was pulled from the auction pretty quick. I thought because they had been made. Now it seems it had been fucking stolen." Her thoughts were meandering and unfocused. Rebekah hated that, needing Savvo to bounce back on her theories right now. Being on the edge of violence, but not engaging in it, had made her thoughts raw.

"They'll test, but again, no frequencies, no way to track them. He mentioned a buyer steaming here. And he was on a short time frame. I don't like that." Savvo was at her shoulder. He rubbed behind his ear, a habit of old when stressed, usually followed by him engaging his chip once too often.

Rebekah nodded, keeping her eyes sweeping ahead as they approached the outer ring bulkhead that would eventually lead to their ship.

"Steaming. I don't like that word and what it implies. And was it me, or did his urgency come from more than just satisfying a customer?" Rebekah turned about as Savvo spun the wheel-lock open, watching the strange mix of people who were heading home to bed, or out to find a little nighttime fun. Spend some of those Benetai cards.

Something clicked.

"Ah shit." Rebekah slapped the side of her head. "Maybe they had something of more worth to bidders who wouldn't or couldn't risk engaging in an auction. They pulled it, because it was bloody sold. Someone with a lot of creds."

"I hate not being able to playback shit," cut in Arin. "Having to remember stuff. But yeah, he was more than bothered. On edge. Remember he attacked another gang and didn't see it through. Back on Almaar, he would be eaten alive for that. You kill and take in the slums, or die. To some, leaving Tensei and the guards alive appears strong. You know, restraint in the face of provocation. And maybe to his faction and those under his wing, it is. Thoughts of blowing all shit to hell sat inside an eggshell with only cold vacuum waiting the other side, may stay the hand."

Savvo pulled the door wide, checking the way ahead was clear and glanced back at Arin, head tilted with a grin.

"What?"

"You been thinking again? You know how that hurts."

"Har fucking har. Tell me I'm wrong." Arin kept his eyes on their rear as Savvo went through, taking guard a few metres down as the rest followed.

"Not wrong, just thought you might need a rest afterwards," Savvo replied. "With a soothing wet cloth on the forehead."

Rebekah let the banter fly; they were focused on their roles. It was a symptom. They had been in a dangerous situation, and not in control.

Amid the flow, however, Arin's first words cut deep. A gang boss on the edge trying to show restraint, keep the balance while being forced to act.

That was important. How big was his buyer?

And what had Baja said?

Clean, new.

No surprise Erikson had lied, but why?

CHAPTER 20

Erikson settled into his seat. A nervous tap of his ring upon the edge of his simple but expensive wooden desk, vibrating about his office – his SCIF – a secure compartmentalised information facility. In here, he was supposedly safe from being monitored. But could he truly trust that? The last few days had seen a growing seed of paranoia in his chest, taking every communication or Enforcer directive as a potential slight or setup for his impending fall. It felt ridiculous that he was viewing his employers with such mistrust after years of toeing the line. Yes, the potential limitations of failure had always been there, the long tumble down. But the constant, gnawing hatred that boiled inside him for the self-serving nobles he briefly brought low, had been epitomised by Baron Stimpson. Erikson forced to take the heat for his indiscretion, while the baron had his servants wash off the shit so he could carry on as if nothing had ever happened.

"Now I have some space," he said to himself, snorting gently at his own joke. "Space." He angled his slate's stand, manipulating the external mods that set – at the cost of two months' salary – a second and personalised SCIF around his desk. A box within a box.

He pressed play.

Davina Connors appeared, her red hair and smooth skin doing zero for him. A façade, inside of which sat a scheming Incini mind. Always thinking, always checking the fine print and finding you wanting. Akin to the nobles she served – and he hunted – constantly questioning whether you were good enough. He hated that line of a smile, her mask, more than his own version.

"I have sent the information you requested," she said. "It should be with you now. I will be awaiting your call."

The pictures began to stream in, with sensory data running in a window alongside. The autoship was fast, able to travel without concern for any squishy humans inside. Most that Karal operated were relatively simple machines, a block of metal that could auto-navigate their way around the asteroid belt using the beacons and transponders that took partial control whenever close orbit or docking was required. Davina had procured one that worked the planetary runs. Fast ships designed to transport refined metals back to Almaar, or the colonised planets. A good choice.

The slate transcribed the data into understandable facts. As the images of the asteroid family-cum-field appeared it highlighted and modelled the orbital pathways and provided an analysis of its current state. Deterioration was predicted, but likely not for another decade or two, and as it stood, the complexity of the maelstrom protected whatever lay inside.

"Is this a natural phenomenon?" he asked, receiving a fourteen percent likelihood in return. He made a note to check who had the capability to produce such an effect, all the while watching the rock swirling with avid interest. It was frustrating. He could have taken what he had to any number of experts and got answers, while being exposed to the eyes of his employers. He swiped the slate, forwarding the imagery until the probes started mapping the field. The complexity to him was breathtaking.

"Calculate the likelihood of a human penetrating the asteroid field," he said. Ten percent flashed up. Simplistic, but that's what he'd asked for. "Ten?"

No wonder Toms had chosen to take down the *Sunstar* rather than retry. But that smacked of the Breakers being successful. The attempted sabotage couldn't be pinned to them, the cam-bot having self-destructed, the cargo manifest bereft of evidence. But the actual assault on the ship was, and he had no doubt they intended to scuttle the *Sunstar* or find a way to hide their murderous intent. In space, who the hell would know?

The Breakers *must* have got inside. The restock requests indicated they had taken a serious battering on the way. They fought and survived. His handler had expected them to return, but looking at the screen, Erikson was certain that judgement was by default – an assumption they would fail to gain entry. A mistake.

"What did the Baron find? More than just a war grave, that's for certain."

The baron had hinted at illegal advanced tech – how advanced? AI? It couldn't be. Hellfire, it would explain the Enforcer's involvement, and the need to cover up the baron's role. But that would crack the Court wide open, even if Stimpson was ignorant of it. And why engage the Breakers afterwards? To keep them on a leash in case they knew? Or a convenience for the new mission – deniability.

"Any analysis of what's inside the field?" he said, allowing the slate to interpret his intent. The camera view swept around the entire field, building a 3D model of the external rocks before imaging what it could of the inside. It flagged up a number of issues and some interference, the images blurred by radiation, and switched over to extrapolate through the electromagnetic spectrum. The results, marked as within seventy percent accuracy bracket, struggled to interpret their composition. There were hundreds of possibilities, of which the vast majority were common materials. There was no sign of any ex-Navy ship.

With a soft, frustrated tap of his ring, he considered his options and then called Davina.

"Yes, Mr Erikson. How can I be of service?"

"Extending the contract remit. I want you to have the sensor sweep analysed on M1. Quietly. Again, my eyes only," he stated, annoyed he had to use her as an option. Keeping her eyes off the data minimised the opportunity for the Incini to see any treason within his actions – if there was any. But she had been there, and frustratingly knew what he wanted to know.

"I have contacts. How soon? Payments go up when requiring silence *and* speed," replied Davina.

The baron's pockets were near bottomless. On the other hand, he needed to make sure that noble bastard never got to see what he was doing.

"No limit, but under Incini contractual silence."

"That opens many doors," she replied.

"I bet it does. Get to it."

I'm still doing this? How deep am I willing to dig? Deep enough to pull myself out of the well? Or so deep, I'll never get out?

Davina clicked off her slate, silencing her own SCIF and wondering where the hell Erikson was heading. A sensory analysis meant he wanted knowledge of what was inside that asteroid field. He was a dog with a bone, but why? Rebekah and her crew were under his control until he burned them, or they ran. They were not a threat. But the information inside that crashed ship must be. Rebekah and the rest had said little, keeping their counsel about the events aboard. Yes, there had been a battle and yes, they had recovered the target containment box. Beyond that, they hadn't trusted Davina, and rightly so. The contract had been achieved, Rebekah wanted the twins safe, and the less an Incini knew the less she could be forced to divulge outside of the contract's bounds. But the hints were there, overheard whispers between sedative-induced sleep, yes, but there. What was in that box was definitely tech related, and had them reeling. And they feared a repeat of whatever they had fought on board.

And Erikson wanted the analysis for his eyes only. Bound by contract. There was nothing she could do.

Davina checked over her slate, swiping past a number of likely candidates ranked by their level of knowledge, willingness to subcontract and above all else, a love of the finer things in life. Of the two remaining options, one stood out above the rest – a Karal scientist named Geghid. Not too brilliant – otherwise why the hell were they working for Karal and not the larger corporations – greedy, and had overseen the analysis for the precious metal load aboard the *Hatton*. Someone already subject to an Incini contract who had proven capable and silent.

With a swift swipe and tap, she sent a request for contact with her personal signature. Enough of a hint that there were creds in the offing and guaranteed, iron-bound, privacy. It bounced back in seconds, with a contact request.

Accepting it, Davina drew up the screen and Geghid appeared. Mid-forties, lines around her eyes and mouth, with luxurious hair she was clearly proud of. The white lab coat was an affectation, probably put on before making the call. This wasn't a scientist who got their fingers dirty.

With a sigh, Davina laid out the expectations as decreed by her new boss. "A full spectral analysis of the field. Whatever can be discerned from the data at hand."

"And this is sealed information?" came the woman's hoarse reply.

"Bound by Incini contract, and for Mr Duboit's eyes only. I will have to change the code reference, Mr Duboit has had some eye surgery and retained a new retina scan." A lie, of course, but she was an Incini and lies were not an issue, only the binds of a contract and the tenets mattered. Duboit, to all intents and purposes, was now two people. One who maintained their interests in asteroid mining, but no longer risked their noble standing by sabotaging shipments to undermine Karal before a takeover bid, and Erikson – the version controlled by the Enforcers to whom she was equally bound. The tenets were the same, whatever the façade.

"Send it over." Geghid relayed a secure data depository. Davina wiped the coordinates from the information, running a variety of checks, before sending it over and waiting on a reply – the scientist calculating a timescale on-screen as she ran through the data.

"Hmmm. No more than a few hours but I've a long backlog. You need ID?"

"Sorry?" replied Davina.

"On the ship." Geghid spun her slate around, sweeping a finger to highlight a section of the visual field. Davina recognised it. The entry point the crew had used as the smaller asteroid spun about. "This is Almaarian Navy plating. There's a possibility I can identify the ship if it's unique enough."

Damn. But I am bound.

"It's in the remit. Yes."

"Then I'll get the initial data over by the morning. This may take a little longer." The cost appeared on Davina's slate, and she confirmed the price. High, but not overly so. No doubt, someone looking for a long-term financial relationship. Sensible choice considering where this was all going. Geghid smiled and cut off the connection.

Davina swore, slamming her hand down on the table. If the plating could be identified, then Erikson would continue to dig. But why? What could be worth such interest? Not just illegal tech, there was enough around after the war. Rebekah had discussed the potential of a Battle AI on the *Sunstar*, was that it? If he suspected that there was an AI on board, then his investigations would infer he was looking for sedition.

To bring down Duboit.

The Court was devout in its determination to kill any AI development, one of the intricate and murky reasons they had gone to war with Bustan. They, and the Emperor, saw AI as a threat to their status, to control, and therefore within the bounds of treason. If Erikson discovered the Breakers had taken the containment box and suspected it contained an AI, her contractual silence would be shattered. The twins exposed, and the Breakers not only expendable, but likely to take her down too.

The Directorate had not been privy to that conversation, and she had dismissed it as fancy. Besides, everything else went to crap afterwards. Nothing in her contract with Duboit had indicated its existence. Only an advanced and illegal tech. But a creeping sense of the inevitable hung heavy on her mind. A trap closing in.

CHAPTER 21

"What the hell?" shouted Rebekah as she stomped down the corridor, ignoring the proffered flask of coffee from Hendricks. "What bloody time is it?"

"About 06:00 ship time. That's a little out of sync with Benetai. Call it 06:30 for my benefit." Dricks took a sip of her own coffee, still holding Rebekah's out.

She swiped it from Hendricks' hand and headed through to the cockpit.

"Want me to join you?" asked the engineer. "Moral support?"

Rebekah growled in response, gesturing towards the co-pilot's chair, and Hendricks sat with a sigh into the comfortable seat. She took a sip, then attached the flask to the edge of the console before putting on the comms set.

Rebekah already had hers on and clicked over the channel. "This is Captain Khan. Do you know what time it is?"

"I don't give a fuck what time it is, Khan. There are a lot of things I do give a fuck about, mostly my people." Rebekah winced, the rage in Hannos' voice seared into her head.

A strange click came through on the channel, and another voice leaked in. A local accent amid the pleading.

"Please ... no ... please help me. I don't want to die like this ... Please Tensei. He hurt me; I couldn't help it." The voice broke out into constant crying, the fear pouring over the comms and sending a chill down Rebekah's spine.

"Hanna," she whispered.

"That's right," replied Hannos. "I knew her father before he died. A hard man, but solid. A sterling worker who provided for his family. She fell in with Tensei after the rad cancer ate him away."

"I need to help her," said Rebekah, her emotions raw in her throat.

"Too late. That was a recording of a live feed. The fucker spaced her in an old suit, and made sure the whole station knew," said Hannos, an undercurrent of sadness in her voice beneath the already inherent anger. "She mentioned your crew. What the fuck happened in there? What did you do?"

"Are the comms secure?" asked Rebekah, knowing the answer, but point made.

"No. You have an hour. No weapons, and I'm not in the fucking mood to argue." The comms cut off. Rebekah rubbed her eyes and slowly stretched as thoughts of Hanna and Hannos impinged on her mind. Guilt. Frustration. None of it about the mission, yet. But that would come as a sense of things running away from her began to rise.

"From what you told me, slap the guilt down, Rebekah. I can see it in your eyes. If we hadn't come, maybe Baja would have wiped all of the Tensei faction out instead. Especially if he's as desperate as what you think. Resorted to extreme violence without the benefit of your distraction." Hendricks squeezed the outer rim of her coffee flask and took a sip. "Going to be a point where you might have to choose sides."

"Our side," she replied.

"Beyond that. The station was in balance, now it's out of kilter. Redressing that is Hannos' role, but I'm going to make a guess she'll pull you in. Use you as an excuse, or even a tool, to get the job done, so she can point fingers elsewhere."

"You think?" Rebekah pushed herself back in her seat, two thumb cracks bouncing off the inner hull. Her ex-captain was placing a seed in her mind, a hint that she needed to be wary. You listen to that type of advice. "Then you're coming with."

"Me and my big mouth."

"Better believe it old lady." Rebekah slapped Hendricks on the shoulder as she got up. "And we leave Arin to get shit prepped. I'll call a crew meet."

Arin nodded. "I checked the whole lot after we docked on M3, but I'll run through and spec up. Anything I need to prepare for?" His voice was low, focused. Rebekah had stopped short of replaying Hanna's death; they'd all seen and experienced enough to know the attached emotions. And working in space gave you a heightened awareness of what type of agony, both mental and physical, Hanna would have gone through. The atmosphere was bitter in the galley, vengeful. Just the mood Hannos would feed off, and Rebekah wasn't sure whether she disagreed.

"Both sets of kit. I may move the *Solar Flame* out into orbit if we end up involved."

"*If?*" Savvo said, leaning in his usual place against the galley wall, arms crossed. "We need that wetware. Standing in the way is a gang leader, I don't see an *if* there. He would have killed us if it served a purpose. As for Tensei, surely there's no 'if'. That bastard needs some Breaker justice."

Rebekah couldn't argue. But there was a time and place, and Savvo's reaction underlined her choice for the meeting.

"We'll see. Prep for leaving, Savvo," she said, waiting for the ripples of confusion to run through the crew.

Arin spoke up first. "We're leaving? We can't stir a hornet's nest and then buzz off without the honey." His hands slid back along the galley table, and he wiped his palms on his crew jumpsuit.

"Mixing your metaphors," said Hendricks. "I think. Listen with your head."

Savvo pushed himself off the wall, uncrossing his arms. There was tension there, but he nodded. "That steaming comment got you thinking?"

Rebekah nodded. "That and the prospect of being involved in a gang war. If any of those ships out there are Tensei's or Baja's, then we're sitting ducks. If they're for hire, then maybe we are just as fucked. Plot us an orbital and thinking on it, a fast-burn trajectory to rendezvous with Scarva."

"And the girls?" asked Arin. "Why haven't they come for the crew meet?"

"I think I have some bridges to build," Rebekah said, standing and downing the last dregs of her coffee.

"You didn't knock them down," said Hendricks. Rebekah eyed her ex-captain, closing her eyes to blink out the stress building behind them.

"No. But they're young and bruise easily, as we all did at that age."

And still do.

She walked along the corridor, pondering over how to make this approach. Not so long ago, her relationship with Heki and Tremil had been such even contemplating entering their room would have triggered a wave of turmoil across the ship. So why did it now feel so much worse? Doors had been opened, exposing what lay behind those walls – both physical and emotional.

With her earworm beating a steady rhythm, she raised her hand to knock. As usual, the door slid open, though it was Heki who greeted her, not Tremil. The expected mask was in place, her face set taut, but she could sense the worry because the void between them was huge. Deeper, wider.

Damn. Give me hybrid tentacled monsters any day.

"I—," was all Heki could manage. She froze, as if holding everything back took all her energy.

Rebekah's glance behind revealed Tremil pointedly looking away, into the mirror. What worried her most were the pictures around the room. Some had been torn down, others scrawled over. She had expected turbulence, but was shocked to see it extend outwards to something beautiful they had created.

She had no idea what to do, except treat them as crew. Well, almost. Reprimanding them for not coming to the crew meet would exacerbate an already tenuous situation. If their defences broke down, already raw and risky after opening up over the last few months, she could lose them. And what would that look like?

"Have you resigned as crew?" She bit back at herself, the words harsher than she meant.

"S-sorry?" said Tremil, finally looking her way.

"I'll take that as a no," she upped her earworm, and engaged the chip, needing the calmness it brought to lower her heartbeat. "I need a comms and sensor net up and running ASAP. This ship and crew are in possible danger."

"Parameters?" said Heki, her face animated and back in control.

"Dual. I need all comms traffic monitoring between the ships parked in orbit and the station. Particularly any mention of Tensei, Baja or us. That's an immediate report to Savvo until I return." Rebekah waited, watching their eyes. There was a spark returning there, not the dead-eye shark anymore.

Tremil turned from the mirror and joined Heki at the door. "Remit?"

"All levels. If you have to break in, do so. But hide your tracks, they won't take kindly to it," stated Rebekah, her gaze moving from twin to twin. "And the same for any station comms in or out."

"And the sensor sweep?" asked Heki.

"Any indication the parked ships are warming engines, or prepping weapons, though I know that's difficult. But I also need a longer-range warning up and running. We may have an incoming ship I need to know about. If they come in dark and silent, sensors will pick them up before comms." Rebekah paused, watching the girls' usual sharp minds running through possibilities. "I'm relying on you. *We're* relying on you."

Her timing was impeccable, and she had to resist the urge to pat herself on the back. Both girls visibly straightened, yet at the same time relaxed. The void crumbled slightly – a chink of emotional light streaking out to touch her mind. The self-congratulation had distracted her, and she staggered a little, thanking the wetware inside her head for an extra level of defence. Heki's hand grasped her upper arm, and she steadied herself.

"Thank you." She brushed herself down, settling herself before eyeing them both. "If you need anything, ask Savvo and Arin. Dricks is with me. Now get to work, crew."

The door slid shut, Heki and Tremil taking a step back, glancing around the room as if in a daze. Wordless, Heki picked up the drawing pad she had thrown towards the recycling pod, and the pencils at its side. The pad flipped open to her last attempt at drawing. The marks angry and deep, almost etched into the paper rather than the light strokes she favoured. ZZ3 stared back, its red eyes patterned, about it a darkness she had perceived in her future – not in the bot.

Tremil picked up the torn and shredded paper flowers from around the captain's console, placing them one by one on the table where their figures still stood. Unconsciously, they had both avoided the printed characters in their fight.

"Sorry," said Heki to Tremil's back. "I'm—"

"—not coping well. Nor me." Tremil walked over to the pod, placing those flowers too torn to be saved inside. She wiped away a tear, then pulled Heki into a hug.

"It's time," Heki said, her heart feeling stretched, painful.

"A little space." Tremil nodded. "But first we have a job to do. Then we decide how to divide things up, and ask Rebekah for a cabin each."

They both eyed TB, who sat forlorn at the bottom of the sump box, two tentacles reaching up through the holes and defying the heavy gravity. They both touched a tentacle each, letting the symbiote smooth their minds long enough to see through the fog.

"To work," said Heki, withdrawing her finger. "Crew."

Tremil nodded. "How do we see what she's doing, yet fall for it?"

"Because ... because despite knowing what Rebekah's doing, it's the right thing, and we know it. We just can't understand that until it happens. And its real. Not a made-up role to appease the children. We are trusted, despite our—"

"—failings," finished Tremil. "Mistakes would be a better word. What would Dricks say?"

"Can't make an omelette without breaking a few eggs. Though it would be the wrong metaphor at the wrong time." Heki squeezed her sister, then backed away. "Let's go make some pirate omelettes."

Heki tore out the picture of ZZ3, the temptation to throw it into the pod high, but instead she stuck it to the hull. A reminder of a dark day, determined to make things right before recycling it and starting again. All the while, at the back of her head, wondering how she was going to share TB with her sister if they were apart.

CHAPTER 22

Rebekah restrained herself, counting in her head to calm her thoughts, trying to save the wetware for when she truly needed it. The Hannos guards waiting at the airlock were the same two who had greeted them the first time, and their smugness had returned, backed, she assumed, by Hannos' anger. The Mohican-haired woman smiled as she patted her down.

"You come prepared, yah," said the man with the scabbed tattoo, knocking on one of Hendricks' plates in her armoured vest. "Not much trust there."

"True," Hendricks growled back. "You haven't shown me any reason *to* trust you yet."

The man patted his gun like he had the first time they met. He spoke again in the patter of a local. "Hannos has belief in me, that's all that matters."

"Perhaps she simply regards you as expendable," replied Hendricks with a malevolent grin. Rebekah remembered it well, her favoured weapon during exercise drills. Could take down a squad of Marines with just one joyful promise of retribution. The Hannos gang member, to his credit, didn't step away, though he looked far less cocksure.

"Clear," the woman said. She had been thorough. But there were no stunners hidden away this time. Pissing off Hannos was not on Rebekah's agenda. "Lead on, you know the way."

Arriving at the ladder, the woman clambered up, and they went through the same ritual with the bulkhead. Eventually, they emerged into the lower deck of the corvette. This time the old ship was empty except for the large table and Hannos herself. Rebekah assumed it was too early for the others, or the conversation was going to be more personal than she had predicted.

"Karr, Scab, they are clear?" asked Hannos. She kicked her chair back, standing with both hands resting on the metal table.

"Yes, boss," said Scab, rubbing at the source of his current nickname. "Though they have armoured vests. Want them removing?"

Hannos ran her tongue along her teeth, the lip bulging as she considered Scab's words. "Naah. But fetch me some coffee," she said. "Still white and sugar as high as the rim, Dricks?"

Rebekah twitched, her prepared opening with Hannos broken into a hundred pieces. She glanced over at her ex-captain, whose apologetic smile she took as a good sign.

"Aye, Mikai. Still the same." Hendricks dragged back one of the chairs on their side of the desk, dropping down into it with a sigh. "Hannos?"

"My mother's name." Hannos shrugged and glanced over to Rebekah, a query in her eyes.

"I'm good. At least I was until just now."

"Take a chair, apparently your captain already has." Hannos leaned in, her hands clasped together. There was a slight tremor in her fingertips, Rebekah remembering the gang leader's similar issue when she had been knocking back the clear liquor like there was no tomorrow.

The coffee came swiftly, punctuating the silent atmosphere. Scab and Karr left, while Dricks stirred her mug before tapping the spoon once and laying it beside the mug. Once. At least for now, Hendricks saw no threat.

"Going to explain to me what the fuck you're doing on a mercantile run? Last I heard, you were caught up in the shitshow on Bustan 7 before the Senti pulled the plug. MIA, if my memory serves." Hannos kept her eyes on Hendricks, who sipped her coffee.

"This is shit," she said, gesturing the mug towards Hannos. "Surely any half-decent gang-banger can get decent coffee."

Hannos laughed, and the mood eased a little. "We're spinning in the middle of fucking nowhere, Dricks. I'm lucky to have the artificial shit. You didn't answer my question. MIA. What the hell?"

"It's complicated. If you owe me anything, let it stay in the need to know." Hendricks put the mug down, stretching her neck.

"And I'm the only one who needs-to-fucking-know. Got it. That comes at a price. I'm a nosey bastard, Dricks. You were a staunch Marine, a Breaker, one of Major Ren's favourites. So, either the Bustan sent you back, and I'm sure I'd have heard whispers, or your MIA began with a capital D. I find that hard to believe, but fuck it, give me a good reason to not start asking around."

Hannos' face remained all smiles, but the implication behind her final words had made Rebekah uncomfortable.

"That a threat?" she said.

"Easy," said Hendricks. "It's not, is it Mikai? You owe me, and before that, we had each other's backs. I'm going to take those words as that bloody curiosity Ren tried to beat out of you."

The tongue ran over the teeth again, and the gang leader sat back in her chair, hands still clasped. "Tell me enough that I don't eject you off this station right now."

Rebekah snorted.

"Deserted is a strong word. Better to say our circumstances changed on Bustan 7," Hendricks tapped her head, "drastically. Mid-mission. Wetware went down, and I was screwed. You know what Major Ren and the Warmonger would have done."

"Recycled meat," stated Hannos, nodding.

"My squad? Well, what the fuck do you know, those who survived decided they couldn't let that happen to me. So here I am." Hendricks spread her hands wide.

Hannos' posture altered, muscles relaxing a little. Rebekah assumed a patriot's heart beat beneath her skin, or at the very least, a soldier loyal to those she served with. "I can buy that. But this shit you've come for, ain't exactly on the level. Wetware? For the Senti? It doesn't marry with the straight-down-the-line captain I remember."

Rebekah saw a crack of light, and dived in. "If we have it, no one else does. I know how it looks, but we're not serving the Senti and nor are we dropping it into any meat auction."

Hannos sucked in a long breath, her tired, alcohol-poisoned eyes resting on Rebekah. "I don't buy that. No way. Somewhere you're being bankrolled. To come out here costs big time. Fuel, food, bribes, whatever. Half those hanging out in the black can't leave as they're shit out of creds."

She knew she'd been read and filed there and then. Hannos must have experienced every lie and deceit during her time leading the cartel, and there was no wriggle room. And Rebekah couldn't afford to underestimate her – or give too much away. Hendricks was showing trust, but people changed. Except in one area when you were a Marine.

"We know what happened to the Skyriders," Rebekah said, ignoring the flinch from Hendricks. "But you're here. Alive."

"Mikai was in the stand down squad," cut in her ex-captain. "Am I right? Two squads on active duty, one rotated out for R&R. I rec'd Mikai for the 'Riders, Rebekah. She was in the original Breakers, before the black ops.

Squad leader, and a damn fine one. Though over-bloody curious about orders from time to time."

Mikai Hannos remained silent; her mouth slightly parted. Rebekah noted the wear on her teeth from the alcohol, the slightly inflamed tongue and receding gums. That and the shake.

"You fucking with me?" Hannos said, shifting forwards, slamming her fists on the table. "What kind of bullshit is this? They died on the *Moonslip*. Blown away by a rogue Bustan ship just before the cessation. Do you know how hard it is to hear your friends are dead, and you can't even take any revenge? That you're supposed to pack up your kit and wish the pieces of your squad mates safe fucking journey into the black?"

"Every day," replied Rebekah and Hendricks in unison. Rebekah tried to add a tinge of regret into what she said next. "But that isn't how it happened. We know what did. And that's my price for the wetware."

"What?" replied Hannos.

Hendricks sighed, but caught on. "You help us recover the wetware Baja took, and we'll tell you what happened to them. Show you."

"Tensei I'll fuck up for free," added Rebekah.

Hannos pushed back her chair. The scrape along the deck echoing through the empty missile room that served as her headquarters. Rebekah understood the ex-Skyrider had been through a tumult of peaks and troughs in the last few minutes, and as the gang leader moved, there was an unsteadiness to her, an imbalance. The only thing Rebekah could see was an alcoholic who had stripped themselves of their own life, drowned their body and memories in so much liquid poison that both had begun to breakdown. For a proud Marine, a Skyrider for hell's sake, it was heartbreaking to see. But then, when the drugs wore off and the wetware slowly faded, what else could keep the memories away? The shit they'd done in the name of Almaar, its Emperor and the bastard Court.

Hannos leant one hand on the inner hull, her head resting against it as she sighed heavily. "I side with you, and the station ends up in turmoil and I may have to use a heavy hand to bring it back in line. I know, I know. It may be necessary anyway. I can't let Tensei take one of our own like that. But I *need* to keep the people of this station safe." She turned back, red eyes scanning Rebekah. "Let me think. You've screwed up my head so much I need some space. Go back to your ship. Take no action until I say. Move against Baja without me, and I'll fuck you up, Dricks at your side or not."

Rebekah went to speak, her ex-captain's hand falling on the crook of her elbow. A shake of the head stalled her words, and she nodded. The threat she was about to unload was pissing in the wind when the target was in too much turmoil to process anything.

They turned away, heading for the exit, gathering Scab and Mohican on the way. Hendricks kept her counsel, eyes locked ahead and mouth tight. Rebekah knew that face, and for the first time in four years, walked in her ex-captain's shadow. There was a weight to her shoulders, not a burden. A responsibility, one she would fulfil by hell or high water. The same one she held for the twins, and Rebekah. For all of them.

It worried her. If Hendricks disagreed with her decisions now, what would it mean for the crew so soon after they had begun to heal a little? How much did this Hannos mean to her? Stupid question, the gang leader was a former Breaker, too.

They were left at the airlock, both gang members leaving them without a word. Rebekah waited as Hendricks stared at the waiting panel, shoulders tense, a twitch to her hip where the implant ticked over inside, analysing her movements and adjusting.

"Honour," said Hendricks, the words hoarse, quiet.

Rebekah reset her feet, glancing to the floor. This moment was key, the insecurity whirling about her mind a step towards making poor decisions.

And after making them, being unable to react and redress. A killer in the battlefield. But that was behind them.

"I understand. But honour costs a lot of lives, Dricks."

"Not the lie that is the Court's version. The army, navy ... Marines. Stand by the squaddie next to you, your comrade-in-arms, have their back."

Rebekah hated herself. Tears welled that she forced down. "We're not in the Marines anymore. We're a ..."

"Family. Yeah, I know. Just don't tell that to bloody Arin or we'll have to adopt the bloody robot." Hendricks turned to face her, rubbing the back of her neck. "I get it. But if we can ..."

"The last thing I want to do is leave this station in turmoil. I've seen enough to know that the gangs are a necessary cancer. They keep control where a government and police force couldn't, and most people get to live out their lives maybe even better than they would elsewhere. Balance. Hannos has it right. But she's dying."

"Killing herself." Hendricks turned about, facing back along the ring. "I'm going to ask you for something, and as captain I will honour your decision. Your order."

Rebekah nodded. "Go ahead, ask."

"Let me tell her. Explain what happened to the Skyriders, at least our theory. Give Mikai some rest." Hendricks didn't meet her eyes, choosing to stare along the empty ring with its creaks and clangs as the stresses of its gentle spin resounded through the metal. It was a genuine silence between two friends, immersed in the reverberations of life in space. A moment of mutual trust. If she denied her engineer, she held no doubt Hendricks would seethe but accept. Not fester, like it would with Arin or Savvo.

She should say no. Giving away their ace in the hole for honour. But a different kind of honour, the type that left you dirty when it was denied.

Family.

"Take a slate. If you're doing this, she needs to see everything. Understand the hellhole we fought through. But not ZZ3. That's a can of screwed-up shit we can't have others seeing."

"Yes, and thank you," said Hendricks, blinking back a single tear but not meeting her eyes. "I am proud to call you my captain, and my friend."

Chapter 23

Arin ran the diagnostic, his slate whirring away analysing data it checked at two different levels. With an amber flag raised, he knelt, the tool roll on the floor open and exposing a multitude of screwdriver attachments, blades, oils and grease. Add into that a pile of ammunition and the less than silent chatter of the 3D printer, and he felt like a seriously busy sub-engineer. The occasional glance to the doorway and the stationary warbot beyond was not on the agenda, no. So every time he caught himself looking over, he gave himself a mental slap.

"Glorious bloody leader my arse," he muttered. "Betrayed I was." He inserted the driver into the servo motor at the knee joint, adjusting the head while watching the slate screen. The flicker into green gave a little spark of joy amid his current malaise, and he manipulated the end cap back into place.

"Work myself to the bone. Shine you, wipe the grease from your joints, top your oil up, pat you on the bloody head and this is the response I get. Silence, not a word about what's going on inside that tin head." He moved on to another set of powered armour, jacking in under the hip plate and eyeing the data screen. "Hip joint," he muttered, and started work again with a different tool, regreasing as he went.

"Fuck it." He checked the time, estimating Rebekah and Dricks would be a little longer after returning to collect a slate. Wiping his hands, he wandered through the workshop doorway, and approached the cargo hold, one eye on the girls' door and further along, the tap of Savvo's foot on the cockpit deck. A swish, and the doorway opened, the secondary airlock swept back already. ZZ3 stood by the containment box, almost as if in shadow despite the bright spotlights he switched on.

Arin heaved himself up on a cargo box opposite the warbot, mulling over the black box of death behind it.

"The twins said you don't need action codes anymore. That you have merged these with the *new* you. So how do I switch you on? Eh? No words to say, no buttons to press. And I have no idea what that finger trick flicker thing the girls do is. Come on, ZZ3, give me something." Arin's lips tightened, and he yanked his fingers through the tuft of red hair sprouting from his forehead. "I thought we were friends."

Red lights flickered across the bot's face; the painted smile lost amid the battles in the *Scourge*. Even Arin had decided it was a step too far to repaint it after Rebekah's near miss. The bot's limbs micro adjusted, enough to show alertness.

"Friends," said the bot. "A person with whom one has a bond of mutual affection."

The response reminded Arin of Heki and Tremil, how they would dive into textbook speech when social interaction was mentioned.

"Yeah, that."

"A person," repeated the bot, and its main body rose from the deck. "I am not a person."

Arin squeezed his eyes, adding a little shake to the head. "I know. But you *felt* like one."

"Analysing response," said the bot, eyes entering a repeated pattern Arin had not seen before. Eventually, the eyes settled, and the colour changed. That had also never happened before. Arin tried to remember if it was in the schematics. "Friends show concern for each other. Playback *Sunstar* recording."

"Do your job right, and ZZ3 will come through it. Otherwise, ..." The voice was Savvo's, and he recalled how the bastard had mimed a big explosion.

"To you it's just a robot." That was his voice, and he remembered how they had crossed space to the *Hatton*. ZZ3's rescue, the nanites. All of it.

The voices changed, away from the *Sunstar* to comms chatter on an asteroid, Arin remembering how the derelict *Scourge* loomed above. A similar scene played out, Arin's insistence ZZ3 was needed. A priority.

He couldn't help but stare at the bot. "Yeah. Like that."

"I am crew," said the bot. "Crew watch out for each other. Protect. By extrapolation, and connection, crew and friend are connected."

"Not always," replied Arin, thoughts impinging of more than a few frosty moments in his past. "But The Wrecking Squad, the crew of the *Sunstar, we* are friends."

And bicker like family.

"Then I accept the label, friend," ZZ3's voice remained monotone, but could he hear a tinge of emotion? Or was it simply his mind playing tricks? Or living so long with Heki and Tremil that emotional lines blurred with the constant trauma of their feelings?

"Good. ZZ3." He tried to think of a careful way to ask the next line, but he was Arin, and gave up. "You got the Butcher rattling around inside of you? Really?"

"A partial brain pattern, pacified. But yes."

"So, you have his memories, you can see some of what he did? Cos it was gross. I mean, tentacles and teeth. A murderous, sick bastard. That's gotta be hell. We've established we're friends, but I find it hard to associate *you* with *him*." Arin was unsure of where he was going, but it was eating him up, and needed to be said. From the first encounter with a freeze-dried, tentacled hand, he'd joked his way through the *Scourge* while screaming inside. Dricks understood, but he could only burden her with so much.

"Pacified. In confusion because it has been separated from its biochemical urges and – how *he* defines it – malfunctioning personality. I cannot purge such algorithms, without purging myself. I am crew. I protect crew." The green eyes whirled a second, settling back into a calmer rhythm, and the bot twisted position, face on to Arin, as if talking one to one.

Arin, at that moment, sensed more than just a bot. "Agreed. How much do you know of General Asham? What memories do you have?"

The bot paused, inert. Even the eye movement was still. "Define."

"If I asked you to, say, tell me about the experiments on the *Scourge*, could you access them?" Arin pushed himself off the box lid, the atmosphere in the room weighing on him a little, as if it had changed in that second. Not fear. Angst.

The bot's feet moved, sidling, turning the lumbering torso around until it faced the containment box. "Access? Yes. But I am crew. I protect crew."

Pieces slotted in, not quite fitting yet, but enough to send a shiver down his spine. "Those memories are in there, in that hellish box?"

ZZ3 turned his way, while sidling further away from the containment unit. "Yes."

"Shit in a bucket, you're joking me?" Arin ran his fingers through his hair again and approached the unit, walking around its narrower end, eyes never leaving the dead lights along its side.

"No joke, glorious leader."

"Is it dangerous?" Arin knew the answer before it left his lips. ZZ3 had as much as said so. Accessing it would endanger crew. It. A warbot.

"Absolutely."

"Define." Arin looked over to the warbot. "And in the future, any danger you encounter needs to be reported to the crew. Understand?"

"Understood. It retains the remaining brain pattern of General Asham. Unpacified. There have been attempts to access the ship's system which I have negated. It has attempted to bury itself in the infrastructure below the decking, which I have negated." ZZ3 tracked Arin's walk, as if wary of what might happen.

"It seeks control."

"Affirmative."

"Then we should space it."

"Negative. Reporting danger. The unit is self-contained, made of Senti plating. It would survive space, possibly a nuclear blast and the resultant radiation burst. What is inside wants to live, control, shape."

Nothing short of sending it into a sun. Arin kept that to himself.

A sudden, worrying thought came to mind. "Can it hear us?"

"My analysis of the memory fragments I contain indicate the negative. It sits in a self-contained void, pretending to be dead, until a future opportunity unfolds." ZZ3 sat back on the deck. "Threat analysis remains high."

"You can say that again." Arin whistled, turning away from the containment box, an urgent need to talk to Savvo pressing on his mind.

"Threat analysis remains high, glorious leader. Friend."

Arin wrapped his hand about the hot flask, swilling the black liquid inside before taking a sip and then a bite of the Danish. He nudged the crumbs towards his mouth, savouring the taste, mind on ZZ3 and the perpetual guard duty it had set itself.

Savvo appeared distressed. Arin couldn't think why, perhaps it was the megalomaniac patterned brain in an electronic coffin sat in their hold.

Yeah, that was it.

"Bloody hell," repeated Savvo. It was the least of his swear words in the last few minutes. "We brought the demons back with us."

"Looks that way. Some bargaining chip. Hey, we'll swap you our lives for someone who likes to make grotesque sculptures of tentacled humans. Being alive, optional."

"What do we do?" Savvo tapped his herbal tea onto the galley table, then stood, pacing. It reminded Arin of Dricks. A close living crew picking up each other's habits, quirks that crossed over into speech and their behaviours.

He took another bite of the Danish, the sugar rush from the last not pacifying his mind, but bathing in a brief moment of pleasure. "Let ZZ3 deal with it for now. Then I work with the girls on pacifying the threat somehow. You know, like a kick arse Faraday cage."

"Or a SCIF," replied Savvo. "Or chuck the fucker into the sun."

"Thought had occurred," he admitted. "Rebekah's got a shitload right now, and ZZ3 has it covered. I suggest we come up with options while she deals with Baja and Hannos."

"And that shit, Tensei. She won't like being out of the loop," Savvo stated. "It goes against everything we've rebuilt since meeting Duboit."

Arin popped in the rest of the treat, nodding. "I'm saying we should play it down a little. That we're dealing with it." He shrugged, finished his coffee, and stood up to put his flask in the cleaning unit.

"What happened to our boring life on the belt?" asked Savvo, peering up at Arin.

"Someone wished it away, and poof, off it went. Is this what you wanted? Cos it ain't dull, that's for sure." He grinned back, about to turn away and changing his mind. "Got to admit, it makes you feel alive. Can I ask you a question, and don't get antsy with me, okay?"

Savvo nodded, tilting his head to the side.

"When was the last time you hooked up? You know, the stims, when you didn't need them. Just because you needed the hit?" Arin left his gaze on Savvo, curiosity and concern swilling about his mind in an odd mix. On R6 he had seen signs, when the solar flare had threatened.

"I haven't. Not going to deny it's been hard."

"Here's my bet. Since Duboit came a knocking this time, how often have you been tempted?" Arin stepped in closer, hands on the bench.

Savvo eased back, cupping the herbal tea, meeting Arin's eyes. "None. Yeah, I get it."

"I'm the one that's supposed to be the risk taker. Says so on my uniform label and everything. Yet you need it as much as me." Arin grinned, pleased when Savvo returned it.

"Fuck off, Arin." But the light was there, life shining in Savvo's eyes.

"Savvo, Arin," echoed along the corridor from the ship's comms. "We have incoming."

Savvo stood, reaching the comms in two strides. "Say that again, Tremil. We're docked to a space station, there's always incoming."

"Bustan Navy Corvette," she replied. "Not sure that's the usual traffic."

"Shiiit," said Arin, mouthing more swear words as he stared down the corridor, mind on the suits he'd been servicing. "Demons and bastards all in one day."

"How far?" asked Savvo.

A click, and Tremil replied, "Six hour burn pattern. If they go hard, three."

"Copy that. Keep me informed. And good work." Savvo clicked off and leant his forehead against the corridor wall. "I think we just found our buyer. The fucking Bustan Navy."

"Gotta call Rebekah," said Arin. "We're running out of time."

CHAPTER 24

"Clear," Rebekah said, spinning into the ring, carbine up and eyes focused on the deck's curve for any movement. She checked her HUD, Arin and Savvo's pings coming in loud and clear behind her. The screwed-up structure of the station was likely to cause interference in places, but they'd have to deal with that as it occurred.

"Savvo," she said, the comms clear enough.

"Point?"

"Yep," she replied, and knelt on one knee, letting him move ahead. Once he dropped into a guard position, the comms crackled, and she followed. Arin fell in behind, on their rear, his Navy-issue visor halfway down to his chin and scanning like she was. They had debated back and forth, deciding against their old kit to reduce the fear factor for the innocents they were about to wade through. Full Marine powered armour screamed of a danger beyond a stray bullet. Of uncaring aggression. However, the need for a sealed suit hinted at a potential breach, and the end of all things. Families fearful for their children wouldn't cower, but fight tooth and nail. Hence, their visors were obviously open. She had promised Hannos zero causalities within the general population, but every plan went to shit in the face of reality – and the enemy.

"Approaching Hannos' ladder," Savvo said. "Scab is on guard."

"Take him down," Rebekah said.

Savvo grunted, and a shot reverberated along the corridor. A squeal followed, and Rebekah moved swiftly past Savvo, her eyes on Scab who rolled up from the floor, reaching for his hand cannon. She kicked the weapon from his hand and slammed the butt of her rifle into his face. He went down with a thud, knocked out, blood running from a shattered nose.

"Arin, take guard," she uttered, Savvo already clambering the ladder.

Once Arin was in position, she aimed her weapon up towards the door, waiting. Savvo placed the wires against the lock pad, tapping away on the screen. The wheel-lock began to spin, and it dropped, knocking him from the ladder and he slammed into the floor.

Ignoring the oomph, Rebekah shouted. "Grenade." And fired. Karr, wide-eyed, her wild hair brushing against the tube's walls, tried to pull the hatchway back. The grenade struck just inside the wall, the loud bang and flare cut out for Rebekah's benefit by her HUD visor. Karr was not so lucky, screaming as she dropped headfirst from the entryway.

"No." Rebekah dived. This wasn't in the plan, the motors of her shoulder and elbows taking the strain as she deflected the fall. Having prevented the Mohican-covered head from striking the deck first, Rebekah accepted the crack of the woman's unprotected shoulder. Dislocation at best, a shattered shoulder at worst. Hannos must have been truly inspirational to persuade her gang to agree to the punishment they were dishing out.

All in the plan. Bloody Bustan. Steaming, there you go. What steams? A fucking Navy ship.

"Up. Do your job, Savvo." The ex-Marine moaned, but rose to his feet. A quick check of her HUD showed all life signs were green. Bruising was an everyday occurrence, part of the job. He clambered up the ladder, reattaching the wires, then leaning over to the side.

"Arin, you're up."

"Yeehah." Arin spun about and headed up the ladder at speed. With a tap at the pad, the second wheel-lock began to spin.

"Good job," said Rebekah, glancing back down the ring corridor, pleased to see it remained as clear as her HUD showed. "Follow him in, Savvo."

Gunfire echoed above, and she gritted her teeth. Nothing she could do about it. The bark of a carbine followed, and then a second as Savvo rose from the hatch. Feeling uneasy about leaving their rear unguarded, she reached for the ladder, letting her suit servos do the work as she swiftly climbed to the top. More gunfire, sporadic but dangerous, ripped through the air above.

Before heading through, she reached inside a side bag and removed the handheld grenade. "Incoming," she bellowed. An agreed cue word, and threw. She heard it strike the deck, but no more than that.

"Arin?" she queried. "Sit rep."

"Smokin'," he replied. "I have three down, two more wondering what the hell has hit them and whether it's too late to leave their chicken-shit outfit. Room is prepped."

Rebekah emerged from the hatchway, and ran, following her HUD's guidance, leaping onto the metal table and kicking Hannos squarely under her jaw. She had no doubt, alcohol riddled or not, the ex-Space Marine would have dodged that move on any other day. But this was necessary. With the gang leader down, she grabbed her by the neck, and slammed it against the table, barrel to her head.

"Put your fucking guns down, now!" she bellowed, the suit amplifying her voice to reach every nook and cranny of the hollowed-out ship. "I don't want to put a hole in her, but I will."

"Do it," cut in Hannos. Rebekah wasn't quite sure which she meant – put her out of the misery she and Dricks had laid on her about the Skyriders, or to throw down their weapons. Perhaps both.

Shouts and grumbles emerged from the dissipating smoke, punctuated by the clatter of weapons as they hit the deck.

"Check everyone," growled Rebekah. "Any fucker with a weapon, shoot."

Another ring of metal upon metal satisfied her, and she lifted Hannos' head off the table.

"I want that bastard Baja's location. Got me? Or I start with these gangsters of yours," she swept the room with her carbine, "and finish with whoever else gets in my way."

"Please, not my people," said Hannos, her undercurrent of anger masked by pleading.

"Then you'd better find a way to get them out of my way."

"Talk to me Heki," said Rebekah, dropping down the last few rungs of the Hannos ladder.

"One ship is warming up, another looks like it has initiated a start up sequence," she replied.

"Any ID?"

"No transponders, but they look, as Dricks put it, like they've been through a dung-throwing contest with their windows open. I'm trying to see if I can gain any idea of weaponry." Heki breathed slowly into the comms, the tap and swoosh of her fingers in the background. "May take some time."

"Or impossible if chem based. Are the Hannos ships still stationed as agreed?" Rebekah sent Savvo ahead to the next bulkhead and kept Arin watching the Hannos hatchway as they proceeded along the ring.

"They remain the furthest away, no signs of warming up yet."

"Let me know when they do. That's our timer cue from Hannos. She can only smokescreen us for so long." Rebekah nodded to Savvo, and he began to spin the lock, Arin still at her back.

"Copy that."

"I am in, Captain," cut in Tremil. "Ready. The station systems are surprisingly well encrypted. I can't access ninety percent of it in the time given, including the heaters, scrubbers and oxygen tanks."

"I like that. If you can't get in, neither can the Bustan, if they have the mind. On my mark. 3, 2 ..." She signalled Savvo, and he yanked the door open. Arin went through, carbine up, followed by Savvo who gave a last glance behind. Rebekah could only imagine the fear running through the station right now. Powered Armour, rifles, pure threat. Only the Bustan were on the way, and she had limited time to do anything else. For all the noble corruption in Almaar and its Court, and the disdain for the lowlifes underfoot, the Bustan Navy were ruthlessly efficient. They were here for what she needed, and they would tear the station apart to get it. She had considered running, but it was too soon, and did she really want the Bustans gaining access to her comrades' wetware? Especially kit that had a special significance to the Enforcers. Decision made. "1...Mark."

The fire alarm kicked in, rising like a crescendo through the ring. It rode a tide of fear. Fire on a space station – an enclosed, sealed unit of oxygenated air. The ultimate fear-inducer. Scared yes, but out of the way of any potential conflict and allowing them to move about the station at pace.

Shouts and screams rolled along the market concourse. Desperate traders were packing their wares away only for partners to pull them from their stalls. Children and parents fought each other, the noise overwhelming patient choices and gentle coaxing with shared desperation. Rebekah could taste the sweat and fear on the air.

A Breaker would have rejoiced, applauded themselves for such a simple plan that cost zero ammo and gained them time. Rebekah blinked back the tears and engaged her chip.

"Savvo." She coughed, the words dry and hoarse in her throat. "On point. At speed. Keep up, Arin."

"Yes, Captain." No quip. He could taste and feel the same atmosphere as her.

Savvo led off, carbine up and synced to his HUD like hers. Their visors were blanked out, faces covered down to chin level with a gap beneath and wreathed in armour. The clomp as Savvo swept ahead masked by the alarm pounding in the station ring. He cut through the crowd like a Court guillotine, parting people like flesh as they realised what bore down on them. Where the fire alarm caused shouts of panic, their armour and weapons induced fearful silence. Parents shielded their children, backing away, hands up as if the skin and bone could fend off bullets. Rebekah hated herself.

"Gang members ahead," said Savvo. "Three, Tensei markings. Weapons out."

"Arin, sit rep."

"Clear, but its bloody chaos."

"Copy that, watch our six. Savvo, how's your ammo?" She knew he'd be checking his HUD.

"One third of the clip," he replied. "It was heavy-going in Hannos. She had them fired up."

"I'll take point." She moved ahead at his affirmation, raising the carbine and checking the three Tensei Savvo had flagged. There were panicked stall holders and the last few civvies running wide of her, most diving into the gaps between tables to avoid confrontation. The gang members, two men and an older female, bore the familiar tattoos. Bruising showed Baja had seen to them, possibly in the bar. They were tooled up, long knives angled in sheaths across their back, two with iron bars alongside, while in their hands were the usual hand cannons. All three were patently ignoring the alarm and, as far as she could tell, heading towards Baja's base of operations.

"Fuck. We might have timed this wrong. I'm thinking Tensei is out for a little revenge."

"Copy that," said Arin. "Two more behind have just made me. They looked ... surprised. Can't see why a two-metre-tall Marine in powered armour would do that. Permission to fire."

"Non-lethal. Permission granted." Rebekah didn't wait, nor call for surrender. She also fired, three short bursts into the small of their backs. Images of blood flowering on their clothes wiped away by the screams and cries the gunfire caused. All three were propelled forwards, flailing into the remnants of the crowd running from two threats now. Rebekah sprinted and clubbed a Tensei to the floor, pressing the muzzle of her weapon against his neck.

"You fuckers stay out of my way, or next time I'll use real bullets." The comms muffled her voice, sounding electronic and threatening. "Under-fucking-stood?"

Gunfire shuddered above the alarm, and a glance to her HUD showed Arin mirrored her actions. Two people were down, rolling onto their backs and holding chests, gasping for breath.

Rebekah left him to it; Arin would call if needed. Savvo collected the three hand cannons, and then a long knife from the third of the Tensei, making a show of scraping the edge along his armoured forearm. "Oh look, fucking useless."

"Take the rest of your shit and go back to Tensei. Tell him we're coming for him next. He needs to hole up in that crappy freighter and pray I change my mind." Rebekah denied herself the joy of slamming the man's bruised head against the deck. Her anger was for Tensei himself, though anyone who worked for the bastard after Hanna's death was fair game. Letting the tattooed head fall to the deck, she stepped over the prone gangster, a disdainful act to hammer home the message.

"Leave them Arin," she said, watching his feed as he crushed a hand cannon. "They've got the message. We're done playing."

Chapter 25

Heki ran the sensor scan again, overlaying converted comms traffic alongside in text form. All seventeen ships were buzzing with activity, a combination of worry and panic. The first layer had started with the crew's attack on Hannos, rising in tension as the fire alarm kicked in. Five of the ships had started to manoeuvre away from the station, as if the fire was a curse that could spread. Probably avoiding any potential debris if it went up, though it was unlikely wreckage would gather too much momentum considering what was *officially* on board Benetai. Risk was risk where smugglers and scavengers were involved. At least, that's what her books said.

"I have two transport shuttles emerging from the Tensei faction," she said, swiping the information over to Heki and Hendricks' slates. "Heading towards the station. Hannos are warming their engines now, but then they all are. The corvette will be on a standard sensor sweep by now."

"They're getting jumpy," replied Hendricks over comms. "Can't say I blame them. And we're sat here like ducks in a shooting gallery."

"That's cruel," stated Tremil.

"They're not real ducks ... Never mind. I'll explain later."

"Do," said Tremil, and her fingers caressed the symbiote sat on Heki's forearm. "I have an encrypted message from the corvette, hailing one of the Baja ships. Bustan code, obviously."

"Any response?" asked Hendricks, tension leaking into her voice.

"Give me a moment ... they're relaying it to somewhere in the station. Code for code, no additional decryption, sorry. But it looks like they don't want to make direct contact yet." Tremil glanced over to Heki, who understood the look and felt Tremil's tension. Despite her misgivings, she handed over TB, settling the symbiote on her shoulder. Losing contact forced her to start a refrain in her mind, suddenly feeling the pressure she was under. Being part of the crew was important to her, but if anything, that made it harder.

"I'll try to run a decrypt, though no promises," said Heki. "But it may be useful in training my program for the future."

"Copy that," replied Hendricks. "I'm moving the engines up to secondary readiness. Prep Savvo's planned nav course in case we need to engage."

"Got it in holding," replied Heki. "And Scarva?"

Hendricks swore, Heki knew, under her breath. The ex-Marine couldn't hide the hint of disdain, however, coursing from engineering. "No. If we're lucky, that bastard won't have picked up on the corvette. If the mind-sucker has, then it may avoid the rendezvous. No one wants to piss off the Bustan Navy, even in this deadbeat system. The fact it's out here, expending fuel and time, means they have a purpose worth the high cost."

"It's only wetware. I don't understand. The Bustan have their own version," said Heki. "I hadn't thought about the cost." She glanced over to Tremil, the emotion rolling off her, calm and focused. TB's influence, and it filled her with jealousy she couldn't hide. Tremil nodded, the dip of her chin an acknowledgement of Heki's need. How quickly they had changed, become more open, had been governed first by necessity, and then by happenstance. Now, TB was a huge factor they couldn't deny. A thought wormed its way in, of Rebekah and her concern for Savvo's addiction to stims. Is that where they were heading? The jealousy a symptom?

"I don't get it either, for that matter," replied Hendricks. "There's more at play here. But we are in the Enforcer's net, and they keep their secrets close to their noble-hunting chests."

Tremil tapped her screen, swiping across a marker. A reply burst, and not coded.

"Dricks, the reply has been relayed through the Baja ship. No encryption, asking for immediate assistance and that the agreed cargo is in danger."

"From the fire?"

"No. From unknown assailants. They've picked up on Rebekah," replied Tremil.

Heki scrunched her lips, a sense of worry rolling off her in waves. "Entering hard burn, corvette ETA adjusting ... We have forty minutes. Hannos ships are manoeuvring."

"Understood. I'll contact the captain."

Heki twitched, knowing she had just been superseded. But that was how crews, and squads, worked. She couldn't take it as a slight, despite Rebekah asking her to keep the information flowing. It wasn't personal.

"Rebekah, this is Dricks, come back." The comms clicked, a gentle hiss overriding the creaks of their ship. Dricks had kept the comms open and shared across the ship.

"Go ahead, Dricks."

"We have a change in ETA. Thirty-nine minutes and counting, hard burn adjustment after comms from the station. We can't decrypt Bustan code, but a panicked reply tipped us off. Hannos ships are on the move." Dricks waited for a reply.

Heki recognised the tension in herself. After the *Maverick*, any ship threat had become more real for her. And this one was from Bustan.

"Copy that. Prep for leaving."

"We ain't leaving until you're back here. Are you staying on target?"

Rebekah's silence heightened Heki's heartbeat. It was hard for her to recall the fear and trauma aboard the *Sunstar* during the scavenger's attack, and her and Trem's subsequent response. TB had been such a distraction, and the excitement of contact with the Senti, be it from a distance, and then space pirates of all things, had pushed the dreadful memories away. But Hendricks' obvious concern, and Rebekah's out-and-out attack on the station, drew such thoughts back. That, and representatives of the Bustans were approaching. People who saw her as an escaped lab experiment.

Tentacles, dry and warm, fell on her neck, TB's touch calming her thoughts, leeching the worst of her emotions.

Is this what addiction was? Running away from what you fear, rather than facing it?

Abandoning yourself?

TB squeezed tighter along her neck

"We remain on target. Keep the engines warm. Any threat from that corvette and you move out."

What had started as a simple find and collect had turned into a full-on raid with a pissed off posse on the way. Though their suits were devoid of insignia, there was little mistaking the armours' origins, and no Bustan Navy officer would hesitate to intercept on neutral ground. After that, who knew? If they took them to be Almaarian Marines, and decided to search their ship, the powered armour and weaponry on board would seal their fate. And of course, they were carrying a pair of Bustan experiments in one cabin.

Shit.

We should have cut and run.

The girls hadn't seen a Bustan uniform since they were broken out of the lab. Such an encounter would be messy, and needed to be far away from the station to reduce collateral damage. It was rapidly going to shit, and right now Duboit would be practising his plausible deniability speech.

"Dricks, scrub that order. Come back," she said. Savvo turned back, a querying tilt to his helmet.

The comms clicked. "Copy that, Captain. Are you returning to the ship?"

"No. Dust-off, park out in the black ... Prep ZZ3 as agreed. Sending location target. Just hope that twisted hunk of metal is on our side." Rebekah sighed, knowing full well the twins' stress levels would increase as things got heavy. "I want the girls to jam all remaining signals from the corvette and the station. Complete black out."

"That doable?" she heard Hendricks ask.

Heki dropped in on the comms. "We can definitely black out the station and maintain a data packet line to you." Heki paused, as if thinking over options. "I have no idea about the corvette, and they may be able to trace the origin if I try."

"Good point. Black out the station. Try to crack the Bustan code, and I want to know about any unencrypted stuff. Khan out." She blew out a slow breath, mind whirring over the possibilities, before glancing over to both Arin and Savvo. They nodded back at her. A squad in the shit, but standing knee-deep together.

"We are on a short clock. Set your timers. Thirty-five minutes on my mark ... Mark. Move, Savvo." There was no comeback, her second immediately on point and moving at pace through the straggling crowd, carbine ready, sweeping for threats.

A check of her HUD highlighted Arin behind, focused.

Four hundred metres in, and the market stalls had faded away. The return to the containers and crude adaptations of metalled walls against the curvature of the ring signalled another area of habitation. Here the Hannos mark was carefully painted and repainted everywhere. Doors and windows were banging shut, families arguing and screaming within row upon row of containers up to twenty metres high. Here the pipework was less crude and well organised, with the chaos created by the alarm in marked contrast to the hanging gardens aligning many of the walkways. A piece of green paradise the Wrecking Squad had stomped their armoured boots into.

"I have eyes on high," she said, leaving the other two to cover the deck. The fire alarm had done its job, kept the ordinary people of Benetai safe and out of their way. They'd shrug off the fear in the end. The thought helped a little as she swept over the odd tear-filled faced peeking out, waiting for the fire and the end to come.

"I have movement," said Savvo. "Behind those food stalls." He flagged the positions on Rebekah's HUD, then sidestepped to the right side of the ring. She went left knowing Arin would be on automatic cover, and crept along the edge of the lowest walkway, strewn with abandoned toys and knocked over plant pots.

"Cover me," she said. The corner of the first stall appeared ahead, tipped over, the mix of fresh and dried goods toppled to one side. She eased in closer; her servos' whir the only sound until she reached the table. Rebekah rose to full height, pushing the carbine muzzle over the stall edge, finger on trigger. A woman stared back, young, black-haired with wide green eyes. Snuggled in was a baby, no more than three months old, scrunching up his eyes and delivering a large yawn as if the world was a care away.

Restraining instincts honed by years of battle prevented a tragedy. Even the dummy bullets would have killed the child and seriously harmed the woman. The mother pulled the baby in tight, turning the child away from Rebekah's mirrored visor, plated armour and the overpowering threat of the carbine. Rebekah had forgotten the terror Marines instilled, or more likely, had wielded as a weapon of fear without thought. Shielded by the drugs and drudgery of daily combat.

A gunshot rang out. The woman immediately threw herself to the ground, covering the swaddled baby. Rebekah's armour shrugged off the bullet, but didn't protect her from the rage welling inside. Taking hold of the table edge, she leapt over, feet crashing into the deck with the woman and child now protected behind her armour. Fifteen metres ahead, two Baja ducked into a walkway that ran along the bottom row of the containers-cum-homes. Whether this was a deliberate attempt to use people as cover, she didn't know, but it had marked their card.

"Two Baja," she flagged them up. "Arin with me, Savvo get the woman and child to safety."

She strode out steering towards the middle of the concourse, knowing she was making herself a target. That was the point. With a watch on where they had entered the walkway, she checked on Arin's position, and walked on, keeping as low as the armour would allow. A head, gleaming, with a purple and swollen throat, rose from behind a plant pot, his weapon a notch up from the hand cannons most used. With a leer, he moved to fire, and Arin's bullet struck him in the centre of the forehead. Eyes widened, then dulled, Pietr collapsing to the floor in a heap.

"You have three seconds to come the fuck out, before I come for you," Rebekah said, raising the volume on her comms as the blare of the alarm in the background continued. "Three ..." The gang member rose, the skin around her tattoo a livid red, sweating. With both hands raised, she glanced over to her prone compatriot, and swallowed. Gang life had just become a little less inviting.

"Tell Baja the Tensei are not the ones he needs to worry about. Tell him I heard rumour he has stolen wetware my boss wants back. Understand? *He* wanted me to wipe out the bastard who took it, but I'm in a benevolent mood that runs out in say ... fifteen minutes." The woman nodded, the red flush spreading down her neck. "Why are you still here?"

The woman made to leave, but peered back at purple throat Pietr.

"Oh no. He stays."

She ran, not looking back, weapon forgotten on the floor as she headed towards the Baja section of the ring. Arin stepped in beside Rebekah, sparing a glance over to the unconscious man on the walkway.

"What we doing with him?" he asked.

"Bullseye," she replied, remembering how the Countess dealt with those who displeased her. Dropship target practice.

"Really? Thought those days were gone."

She sighed. "They are. He shot at me with a child and mother nearby." Rebekah slammed her armoured boot into his wrist, the audible snap echoing along the walkway as the alarm finally silenced. "Doesn't mean I want him on my six."

"Remind me not to piss you off ... well, any more than I usually do."

CHAPTER 26

"You have any insight?" Erikson asked, running down the list of notes on his slate. It was late, and Davina Connors knew that, but he had set the data analysis as a priority, and she was Incini. Everything actioned down to the fine print. Forsaking the holo, she was on his main screen, the SCIF firing up as soon as it recognised her call code.

"Is that what you wished? I have only a bare knowledge of the data, assuming you would not want my engagement with it." Erikson watched the flick of her hair, wanting to strangle the woman, though half of him knew he was projecting his growing worries about the investigation and his status onto her.

Everyone needs a scapegoat.

"I would, yes. Bearing in mind I want a factual analysis to set against the fanciful speculation going around in my mind with all the Incini smoke and mirrors." Erikson smiled, adding as much predatory zeal as he could.

Davina paused, her eyes running over a second screen, likely accessing the data set. "I'll need time."

"Fifteen minutes," he said, and clicked off.

A test. But there had been no tells he could pick up. He made a mental note to check through Duboit's array of sensors in the office at some point, including a back check to set up a baseline. His trust in the expected order of things was waning.

He swiped open the encrypted file, and the data filled out, adding detail to the scant information designed to mislead any cursory checks. A 3D model of the external field filled in, the composition of each rock locked and available at a swipe. Erikson tapped the summary provided by the scientist Davina had employed, and dismissed it just as quickly. There was nothing of note, leaving the red flag that flashed for his attention pinned to one of the larger asteroids. He swiped it open, using two fingers to zoom in on the analysis.

"Fragments of armour plating ..." he read aloud, remembering Duboit's main contact, Richarlison, had claimed to have been operating in this area with the Almaarian Navy. Knew what was there. But according to his handler, that was a ruse, though they had mentioned a war grave. He dug further down into the files.

"Plate indicates the composite metals of an Almaarian Navy Ship, used on those built circa fifteen years ago between 3456 and 3459SD."

His screen pinged, flashing a waiting message. Davina responding as requested via the Senti-designed comms. Erikson's finger hovered over the next file, but changed his mind, and opened up the screen instead.

"There is more here I need to dig into," she said. "But the facts indicate there was an Almaarian Ship involved with the asteroid field at some point. The data indicates a crash, no scorch marks or residue from a battle, though Geghid does not discount it."

Davina opened up the list of ships, sharing the screen, and crossed through them one by one.

"These are all still in operation, accounted for in shipyards or held at reserve docks." She had whittled the list down in seconds to ten, and began to work through those that remained. "These were destroyed in known battles during the Bustan war," eight were removed from the list. Though Erikson would have got there, he grudgingly admitted to being impressed at her speed.

"We have the *Ravener* and the *Assenti* as potential candidates," she said. "And that's not good."

Erikson blinked. The names admittedly meant little. He didn't want to ask – it being a display of his ignorance – but then who would know but a woman under a contract of silence? He still hated it, though. The vulnerability galling him.

"Explain," he said.

"The *Ravener* was renamed after Countess Segfi gifted it to General Asham. It was his base of operations when engaged in the war effort."

The hairs on Erikson's neck prickled, a cold sweat breaking out. "You mean it could be the *Scourge*?" The words slipped out in a whisper.

The Incini nodded in response. "A remnant. We have no evidence that the *Scourge* is within the field."

"But it could be. Is Geghid trustworthy?" he said, watching the Incini carefully.

Davina didn't hesitate. "She has proven her silence before, and she is under contract with Incini tenets."

"That doesn't quite answer my question. I'll be in contact. Note that all proceedings remain under contractual expectations."

"Noted."

Erikson signed off, staring at the file blinking on his slate. He opened it, a detailed rundown of every possible Almaarian Navy ship that could have been the source of the fragment appearing. He directed the slate to repeat Davina's analysis, finding it to be correct. No surprise.

The *Scourge*.

It has to be.

The scandal had been huge news, but from what he could recall, short of fact. Rumours had been rife that General Asham was being sent to Bustan 7 to oversee the next invasion. An open secret, designed, he thought at the time, to force the Bustan to consider the real possibility of a system-wide collapse, and an easy passage through to their home world. The war had ground on to a halt on the eighth planet, their Battle AI countering every attempt to take the planet, until Asham had responded to the Countess' request, and intervened. His coordination and incisiveness, combined with ruthless efficiency, had eventually broken the resistance. They had ravaged that world. Excessive violence and retribution followed, triggered by Asham as he let the troops loose – the spoils of war he called it – and returned to Almaar to carry on his oversight of whatever scientific program the Emperor decreed was in vogue.

And then the Senti turned off the lights. Refusing to provide future FTL travel for either side of the war. Their society under huge pressure from the wave of horror-filled memories they had sought as payment. Caught up in a chaos of their own making, the aliens had simply cut off the supply while cleaning up not only the legal trade, but those of their own cast-off criminals who had exploited the opportunity.

In the scramble to get home, the *Scourge* had gone missing. Most thought the Bustan had hunted the ship down despite the cessation and blown Asham away as revenge – the Countess, their other main target, having already fled. Others, that Asham had seen the writing on the wall, and took his ship into the black. That the Bustan wanted the general and his ship badly was not in doubt, and they openly called for him to be found and brought to justice for the excesses he enabled. A mishmash of rumours, lies and supposition, in the middle of which was a missing Battle AI the general had removed from Bustan 8.

The *Scourge*.

The centre of an asteroid field would be a fine place to hide. Or be hidden.

What have I stepped in?

Whose grave have I just opened? Or dug?

Was it treason? Or something deeper. If Asham lived, then whoever helped him would want that knowledge kept quiet. Better to let rumour assume he was out of the picture, and let the general carry on his work. Or perhaps something even bigger. Could the fabled Battle AI be involved? A second, far more deadly secret. One to keep from the Court whose hatred for the technology was legendary. If that was the case, no wonder they – whoever *they* were – wanted the baron stopped. His actions covered up quietly. And me screwed to keep it that way. And the Breakers? Where did they fit?

To clean up the messes. And then be cleaned up themselves.

The wetware being the first.

I was right. Whichever way you look, a cover up.

Erikson ran his fingers over the nape of his neck, wiping away the cold sweat. A tingle ran along his spine, though he wasn't quite sure whether it was fear or excitement. A mix of both, perhaps. Here he was with the first sniff of knowledge that had enormous power. Something nobles craved, wielding information like a sword as they cut their way through the Court in hope of the Emperor's favour. This was huge. The potential players in such a plot had to be of high noble status.

I can't walk away. The secret development of the Bustan AI would be treasonous to the Court, and its public exposure catastrophic. That slimeball Baron Stimpson has, at the very least, stumbled into someone else's secrets, and at worst into a conspiracy against the Court, even the Emperor himself. And my handler has to be involved, somehow.

He tapped at the screen, sending a response request through to Davina. The text was short and sweet.

Water lapped at her luxurious hair, swathing her head in a special warmth as lavender and camomile wafted into her nostrils. She couldn't help it, letting out a long, indulgent moan as the water soothed her mind and body. How long had she been in the bath? Half an hour? Maybe longer. How many people could indulge themselves this way in the middle of the black? Perhaps Trent Pike up on high, or some of those hidden nobles such as whoever was behind the mysterious *Mr* Duboit. Yes, the water would be recycled, but such a precious commodity. And one she had earned.

With a sigh, she sat up, and using the natural sponge, scraped her skin until it glowed. Satisfied, she rose, taking the cotton robe off the heater and wrapping it about her shoulders. She smiled at its touch, and stood before the mirror, tutting at what she had done to her hair. Geghid bent, pulling the plug from the bath, watching briefly as it burbled away into the recycling system. When she got back up, another face peered out from the mirror, and over her shoulder.

"Pretty eyes," said the woman. "I'll have those." The hammer cracked her skull, and Geghid collapsed into the bath, blood swirling as the water flowed down the drain.

"Check her slate, Victor. We need access to her lab data cache."

A flicker of her holo-mask caused the woman to swear. "This Incini's payment better be enough for an upgrade, Victor. This fucking mask is dying on me. Get that access and maybe I'll have enough creds."

She glanced down at the dead scientist, soulless eyes staring back. A handle appeared in her hand, and with a flick of the wrist, a scalpel blade emerged. "Pretty eyes you don't need anymore."

CHAPTER 27

The entrance was empty, with the twin metal doors Hannos had described lying open. The area immediately in front of the Baja's den also remained clear, most of the humanity aboard the station having thankfully stayed inside whatever refuge they had found. To Rebekah's eyes and nose Baja had chosen an area devoted to basic industry, with the telltale smells of 3D printing, small heat forges and piles of cut-offs ready to be reconstituted.

"Savvo, sit rep?" She checked his feed, her second across the way and with a view inside.

"Dark. Lights are off or been cut. I can see the odd spark, that's all," he replied.

"Arin, we're short on time. Send the drone in quickly," Rebekah ordered, one eye on the counter. Twenty-two minutes left.

"On it," he said, and the gentle whir of the simple drone broke the silence. It swept through the entrance, switching over to night vision as it entered the darkness. Death was everywhere.

"What the ...," said Arin. "You think Tensei didn't listen?"

"That wetware better be here, or spacing will be the least of that bastard's worries. Cover us, Savvo. Arin, with me."

Arin set the drone to auto, and with carbine synced, fell in by her side. Rebekah swept the entrance, allowing her HUD to adjust to the light levels. Inside was a small corridor, another hatch serving as a door that lead to a makeshift bar area. On the deck were two Baja she didn't know, their heads at strange angles and propped up against the wall. With Arin watching the bar, she bent to examine the first. His neck was oddly shaped, as if the vertebrae had been twisted back on itself. The bruising was still emerging, and the body warm according to her HUD.

A glance to the second body confirmed the same fate, and she checked the woman's hand cannon. Still holstered, no sign it had been fired in anger.

"Both dead by broken necks, brute force. Looks like this was real fast, or they knew whoever did this. Recent, too." She got the HUD to run a time of death estimation by the body temperature and visual appearance. While it ran, she took station, eyeing the bar area. Here there were definitely signs of a struggle. Overturned chairs, smashed tables. The bar top had blood-splattered shards of glass embedded in the plastic.

She signalled Arin to the left and went in low to the right. Three bodies lay broken over a table, playing cards amid the chaos. More neck breaks, though the third had torn clothing and a swelling like the lash of a whip across his chest.

"Sit rep, Arin," she said, bending over to check for life signs.

"Two down. No weapons fire as far as I can see. Both drew hand cannons but didn't get a shot off." He sent a single image, the scene similar to her own.

Rebekah stood, stooping low as her HUD provided an estimated time of death within thirty minutes for those killed at the entrance. Before the fire alarm went up, and after the change in circumstances with the Bustan corvette. She parked that thought.

"Arin, back exit," she said. Arin moved, carbine up, sweeping behind the bar, before reaching the large door. Dual dents bent it inwards, the door propped open with the remains of the barman, his body peppered with glass. Amid the blood trails were scraped prints.

"I'm thinking we missed this party," Arin said. "These prints look like they go in, then out."

"Stay alert," Rebekah said. "All dead in the front, Savvo. We're heading in the back."

"Copy that. People are beginning to wake up to the lack of a fire," he responded. "So I'm causing a stir."

"Nicky will get jealous." Arin sniggered into his comms.

"Not the time. Stow it." Rebekah signalled Arin in and took a quick look at the bloody prints for herself before following. They were odd, though she couldn't put her finger on why. Whoever had taken the Baja faction out, they were fast, strong, and by the amount of prints, numerous. There was a short corridor, the first door ajar with Arin's feed showing a storage area for the bar and a small kitchen. The door opposite, a toilet and locker room. Both were devoid of life, and they moved on to a large hatch. This had been shut. Blood stained the wheel. With a nod, Arin spun it open, Rebekah on cover and waiting as the door unsealed. After a quick sweep of the immediate space behind, she stomped through. It was a loading bay from some ancient ship, possibly an older space station, struts pinning it to the ring's outer hull and welded into place.

Containers were regimented along two walls. Again old, and filled with numerous storage boxes and pieces of equipment. There was even half an old tractor on its side keeping a container tight against the hull. At the far end was a large airlock, again bolted on and functional, thankfully.

Two more gang members lay to one side, contorted into strange positions, eyes glassy with empty hand cannons in hand. Here there had been a fight, but the end was the same.

"Cover," she said, and warily wove between two sets of boxes to reach the bodies. A pair of legs poked out, and her HUD hinted they were slightly warmer than the dead gang members on top. With her carbine in one hand, she dragged the first body aside, motors whirring in her elbow and shoulder, to expose Baja. The smile had gone, half his teeth – broken and bloody – stuck to his swollen cheek. His eyes were alive, however, and angry – though they quickly changed to fear as he took in Rebekah's mirrored visor and armour.

"You Baja?" she said, her voice still disguised, and hopefully maintaining a level of confusion for whoever might examine events on the space station. The gang leader nodded, wincing, and tried to speak. Pieces of tooth dribbled from his mouth amid the spittle and blood. Rebekah gently grasped his chin, and putting the carbine down, cleared his mouth with a finger, wiping the remains on Baja's silk shirt.

"You Baja?" she repeated.

"Yesssh," came the garbled reply. He blinked, eyes seemingly unfocused before clicking back in, pupils wide. With shallow breaths, and a sallow, greyish tinge to his skin, he was heading into shock.

"Where is the wetware you took from Tensei? Tell me, and I can help you."

Baja blinked again, another dribble of thin blood leaking from the corner of his mouth. "Bushtann?" he said, the word thick and barely discernible.

"Bustan. Yes. Where is the cargo?"

"Pssshhwa," he replied, head lolling to the side.

It was Rebekah's turn to blink. Of all the names she expected, that wasn't one.

"Confirm. Pshwa, the Senti?"

"Yessss," said Baja, his eyes rolling up into his sockets. His breathing stopped, the rise of his chest slowing. Rebekah stood, her mind running through the possibilities and coming up short. Pshwa? But that mind-sucker was up in the low grav ...

Baja coughed, rolling onto one side, a globule of blood and mucus hitting the deck. "Upperrrr rrring," drawled Baja. "Docking point two." The gang leader raised his chin, eyes still flickering at the top of his sockets. "Fuckkkerrrrsss leasssed station holddd from me."

"Arin, go replace Savvo. Now." But Rebekah knew it was too late. A final sigh left Baja's lips, and he slumped to the deck. Another death in the hunt for a box of wetware. What was so important about this kit? The deeper they went, the darker it got. "Belay that," she said, turning away from Baja's still form. "He's dead. And we have a Senti to eviscerate."

"Senti? What?" She waited for it to click home. "You mean those encounter suits? I thought ..."

"That we underestimated Senti tech? That they have FTL and can wire our brains without leaving a scratch, but the suits they wear in grav wouldn't be tech'd up? Same here." Rebekah reached the bulkhead door.

"But why?"

"I have no fucking idea," she replied, and checked her timer. Ten minutes. They were rapidly running out of time.

She clicked onto her comms, checking for a link out to the ship. It blinked; the line partial and data feed only. She eye-clicked a message, requesting acknowledgement, feeling the pressure build in her mind. They needed to destroy the wetware if they couldn't acquire it. That was explicit, but Duboit hadn't mentioned the Bustan Navy in his list of potential threats, nor a Senti mind-sucker who had thrown a curve ball into her plans. What would a renegade Senti want with wetware? To adapt it perhaps, like Tensei had for live feeds. What had the gang leader mentioned? Recording. They hadn't cracked recording.

By the time they reached Savvo, a reply dropped. Confirmation only. No query about her intent.

"Damned if I do, damned if I don't," she whispered.

"Where we going, Captain?" asked Arin.

"Going to spread a bit of your robot love. Up a ring, Docking Station 2, move out."

"They're on a bloody hard burn." Dricks tapped the slate Tremil showed her. "Gonna be some seriously battered bodies in there, with or without a drug retardant."

"How bad?" asked Heki, her screen filled with the approaching corvette and its rapid deceleration. The thruster and main engine heat blanked out much of the corvette's shape, but they had already downloaded enough data to confirm its class and armament. Point cannons that could penetrate their hull and rip out the other side. And on the run, their missile tubes had enough firepower to bring them down and a dozen others for fun. Their main advantage lay in the corvette's rapid deceleration and the projected engine cool down. Both would normally affect turnaround time. The strain would be phenomenal if they chose to pursue. Reckless but possible, and as such provided a sliver of hope.

Hendricks let out a long whistle. "The one and only time I braked like that, I lost half my squad before I even reached combat. All but one recovered, but it took time."

"So they're desperate. But why?"

"Seriously? I don't know, Heki. But a third of the parked ships have fired up and moved away. The Baja first, and the Tensei ships are preparing.

Only the Hannos are holding position. Got to give that woman some due." Hendricks stomped off, eager to fulfil Rebekah's orders. On reaching the cargo hold, she eyed the warbot. The red eyes were already alert, and on its back the plasma torch, with another pack set below it.

Make or break. I hope you really are crew.

Hendricks drew up the 3D model of Benetai station, and where she estimated the Docking Bay target Rebekah requested should be. "Tremil, we got a fix on the docking hold yet?"

"Sending." A flag popped up, exactly where she estimated it to be, and Tremil's information reformed in real time. There was a small shuttlecraft docked there. Dirty and dishevelled, the type that did interplanetary runs and were favoured by smugglers. Somehow, it looked familiar, but she couldn't place it.

One of those sent by the parked ships? Possibly.

"Here," said Hendricks, and turned the slate to ZZ3. "This is the target area." The slate hummed, and a new connection pinged up. The engineer shook her head, her world changing by the second as the warbot downloaded the details. Pacified? Really?

"I want my crew back, ZZ3. In one piece."

"Affirmative. As do I. Ready."

Hendricks turned, sucking back in the sigh and exiting the hold. The secondary airlock door slotted in behind her, and she faced back into the hold. ZZ3 rose from the deck.

"Jam all feeds and sensors," she said, Heki confirming in her comms. "Bring them back ZZ3." Hendricks punched open the cargo hold doors, and the bot sped through.

"Bring them back safe," she repeated, and leant against the airlock door. "Am I getting too old for this shit?"

"No way," came Heki and Tremil's joint reply. Hendricks winced as she realised her comms were still on. Love tinged with sympathy rolled down the corridor, forcing her to up the earworm resounding in her head.

"Thanks girls. Can you track ZZ3?"

"Not through all that jamming. We have a data link, like with Rebekah, but positional awareness will be extrapolated by line of send and receive. If we move and resend, we could triangulate," replied Tremil.

"Hold that in mind." She patted the airlock door, and turned away, thoughts of the spare navy suit Davina had worn on her mind. "Because that went so well the last time I space walked. Fuck. Let's hope it doesn't come to that."

CHAPTER 28

The bulkhead wheel spun open, and Savvo stepped through. The ring corridor was clear, the scent pervading it musty and earthy. The walls tinged with blue-green mould growth.

"Pleasant," he said. "Clear."

Rebekah followed in, eyeing the corridor, judging how far there was to go and who was likely to be in their way.

"Swap to live ammo," she ordered. "Pshwa took no prisoners, so my sympathy meter is running a little low."

Rebekah waited until the others had swapped out, then changed her own, taking care to stow the clips in the correct pocket before loading up. She wanted to send a drone ahead, but the countdown was running away from her, and it would be an obvious presence in the stark corridor.

"Savvo," she said.

"On point," he stated, and walked ahead, keeping near to the ring's inner wall.

The corridor had an empty, unused feel, one she associated with Scarva and his ship. There she had put it down to the alienness, a lack of a human touch. The familiar detritus, aroma and presence that humans tended to gather or exude, missing.

"Airlock access in sight," Savvo said, and she glanced at his feed. Here the mould was less obvious, and the corridor piled high with metal boxes. Cover strategically placed to ensure there was no direct line of sight to the doors.

"Savvo, this doesn't feel right," she said.

"Can say that again," chipped in Arin. "I mean, can't they decorate a little?"

"I'll run a check," Savvo replied.

Rebekah also instructed her visor to search through the spectrum, but nothing flashed up. No heat sources, or electronics giving off warning signals. Didn't mean they weren't there, she had no idea what level Senti tech could reach, let alone how much Pshwa had access to. Time pressed on her mind, railing against the thought of Bustan Navy Marines pouring onto the station and on the hunt for the same kit they were. What would they do?

"Nothing," confirmed Savvo.

Rebekah grimaced, worry sitting heavy. "Approach with caution. Got your back."

"I know, moving in," said Savvo, and he edged along the wall.

Movement caught Rebekah's attention, a tremor from one of the boxes, and it started to topple. A drone rose up, bulky, powerful and one she'd last seen on the battlefield on Bustan 8. Twin slug throwers hung beneath the spinning rotors, though different from what she remembered.

Savvo threw himself to the side as the drone swivelled to track, the barrels spinning up and spewing glittering needles in a stream. They shattered as they hit deck and wall, Rebekah praying they would do the same against Savvo's plate as glass raked across his leg. She fired, the bullets cracking into the drone's outer-casing. It juddered back as a burst of carbine fire from Arin battered against it. The machine's barrels split, one still targeting Savvo, the other with a bead on her. Rather than diving, Rebekah ran, upping the power into her leg motors, and throwing herself beneath the drone. Weakness lay in their inability to shoot downwards, a rapid-fire weapon designed to decimate quickly and then retreat. Arin fired again, bullets striking the rotors, and it dipped down and back, trying to get Rebekah within its field of fire. She drilled the casing with bullets, rolling away as it spluttered into fire, dropping onto the deck as flames burst from its hull.

Savvo was there, limping partially, groping inside one of his belt bags. Powder then wreathed the fire from the mini-extinguisher he retrieved, dousing the flame as the station alarm re-engaged.

"Heh. Not seen one of these bastards for a few years," said Arin, watching the airlock as Savvo doused the flame. "The Bustan love their robo-killers."

"Adapted," replied Rebekah. She bent low as the powder took effect, eyeing the slug thrower and its flechette adaption. "I'm assuming the Senti don't want to die from a station leak either."

Savvo staggered, almost falling into the drone's debris before he steadied himself against the deck.

"You been drinking? I mean it's a little early to celebrate." Despite his tone, Arin had dropped in beside Savvo, easing him to the deck. "You okay?"

Rebekah checked her HUD. Marine suits were not as comprehensive as these Duboit had purloined from the Navy, using a simple grading system the Marines had reworded to operational, injured but functioning, and screwed. Instead, the Navy-issue suit was firing out all sorts of worrying messages as it struggled to analyse what the hell Savvo had been hit with.

Accelerated heartbeat, excessive heat, lungs taking shallow breaths. There was a fast-acting toxin in his bloodstream.

"Fucking poisoned," he snarled.

Rebekah knelt, twisting Savvo's legs to the side and in and out, searching for the flechette glass. There it was, one needle broken off but sticking out between the armoured plate of shin and boot.

"You've been hit with a venom dart."

Savvo coughed. "Just the one?"

"As far as I can see. And the suit resealed."

"Without a toxin rundown, the effects are going to be unknown. I could be fucked, fucked, or fucked. And we're out of time." Savvo gripped Rebekah's forearm, pulling himself unsteadily to his feet. "Engage the slave program," he said.

"Savvo ..." she replied.

"I could be fine, but I feel like shit. You can't rely on me." He steadied himself against the wall. "Nor can I take a stim. It could do more harm than good. Do it."

Rebekah stood back, worry seething in her mind. Slaving would take command of the powered armour. At its simplest level, Savvo would be free to act until the suit deemed him incapacitated, and then he'd simply follow and be an obvious target or mimic her movements.

"I'll take him," said Arin. "I mean, once I have that power, I could keep it going for weeks afterwards. Master and puppet. Think of the fun."

"You sure?"

"Not trained for it, but I know the basics and how it works with ZZ3. Need you free to act. Just think what might happen if *I* have to lead the assault."

"You have a point," she replied, and nodded. With a click through her HUD menu, she sent the control code over. "You ready for this, Savvo?"

"Like fuck I am—"

His suit went rigid, then relaxed, the stream of expletives however didn't stop until Arin raised his hand, forcing Savvo's to mirror his as it hovered over his mouth.

"Potty language is not going to get my new pet their freedom. Say you're sorry."

"Fuck off, Arin." But no more swearing followed, only the grind of his jaw.

"I'll be a nice puppet master." He released Savvo.

Rebekah checked her HUD, noting Arin had set Savvo's suit to independence until it detected a level of bodily failure that rendered him incapable. It was the right choice, though unfortunately giving them both enough ammunition to feed a feud on the way home.

Home. It seemed a long way away.

"Well enough to get us through the airlock?" she asked, looking to her second. Slightly glassy-eyed, he nodded, and approached the lock pad. Two wires stretched from beneath his hip plate, their connectors engaging with the lock. Rebekah pointedly looked away, not wanting to hurry Savvo but aware of the likely preparations going on inside the hold – either for escape with the wetware, or for their arrival.

It took longer than normal, Savvo leaning against the mouldy corridor wall when the pad finally turned green. "It's airless, cargo doors must be open." With a shrug, he put his kit away, and engaged his full visor, the suit prepped and fully sealed for vacuum.

A glance to Arin, and a side-eye towards Savvo got a nodded response. He was aware. They copied his actions.

"Cover from the rear, Savvo. Arin go right on entry. Any Senti resistance, we fire back. No risks." The dual doors rolled open, and they entered, waiting for the few seconds it took for the system to cycle.

The door slid open, and gunfire peppered the doorway in controlled bursts. Rebekah dived to her left, rolling along the metal decking to land next to a wheeled auto-loader. More bullets penetrated its synth-rubber wheel, striking in a defined pattern. There was a lot of skill there, too much.

A check back over her HUD gave a recorded view of the hold. Built from the front half of an old freighter, it was simply a hollowed-out shell with the cargo doors open at the far end. In the centre was a clamped shuttle. Interplanetary range and a basic design copied thousands of times for simple travel between worlds and, despite the wings, ships. Reliable. Safe. And the last time she'd flown one was to escape Bustan 7 with a pair of lab experiments that flipped her life sideways. But there was something familiar ...

She checked on Arin and Savvo, the former healthy and ducked behind a large clamp used for carrying lighter loads to and from the airlock. It drifted oh so slightly with the rotation of the station, the cables oddly curved and unsettling unless you worked in space. Savvo knelt behind, carbine shouldered. Not fully slaved yet.

"Arin, have you eyes on the Senti?"

"No. Nobody."

"Cover me, I'm going again towards the left wall." On his affirmative, she peeled low to the left, heading for several large reels of cable and synth-rope stacked against the hold's hull. More gunfire pinged in, predictive bursts, forcing her to dodge awkwardly as a couple scraped along her leg armour. She threw herself behind a large reel, a good five metres short of where she'd been aiming for.

"Rebekah. They're human. Only got the rise of a helmet and a sight of their forehead."

"Watch for the Senti, Arin. Don't get too focused on the shooter."

"Copy that," he replied.

A burst of carbine fire caught her attention, muzzle flare in her HUD flagged as coming from Savvo. A check on his feed showed he had targeted a large, open-ended container. He should have called it in, a glance at his vitals telling her why he hadn't.

"Savvo, sit rep."

"There's at least one Senti encounter suit in that container. Caught a glimpse of one of those fucking tent—" The comms cut off, his feed providing a visual of the hold deck. Rebekah spun about, kneeling low, to find Arin on the turn as a Senti thrashed a tentacle towards his helmet. Savvo was laid out.

"Oh shit."

She dropped to a knee, and poured bullets into the encounter suit, praying she had enough cover from the huge wire reel to keep her safe. The rounds smashed into the Senti, driving it back, with only the tip of its tentacle swiping Arin's shoulder. He staggered, one leg striding out to stop himself from falling, his hand grasping the Senti while the other rammed his muzzle against where a human hip would be. Rounds ripped into the alien suit.

Another HUD warning drew her attention, and Rebekah swung the carbine around. She expected to be looking down the barrel of a rifle, instead the shooter had made a break, running for the shuttle with a Senti at their side, weaving between cover. Strangely, the engine hadn't seemed to fire up, yet exhaust fumes spewed below the cargo deck. The residue registering in her data flow but not the expected heat. Something for later.

"You know what you're doing," she whispered to herself. "Well trained. That mind-fucker with you had better not be Pshwa."

Another Senti emerged from the container, its four encounter suit lower limbs dragging the alien towards the spacecraft. Zooming in as she took aim, the alien's helmet came into focus, chin tentacle waving frantically towards the shuttle as it tried to speed up. Rebekah took a breath, visions of Baja's bar and the dead shown little mercy running through her mind. She had no proof this alien dream-sucking bastard was involved other than its presence here, but she was betting at low odds these bastards had stolen the wetware and sold it to whoever was on board the shuttle.

She fired. And repeated the burst. Bullets streamed across the cargo hold to slam into a set of barrels propped near the tail wing of the shuttle. The bottom one collapsed under the barrage, and the rest toppled, crashing into the alien she so prayed was Pshwa, breaking the grip of three of the Senti's tentacles. The fourth limb pulled the alien upright, and it turned, the flat face leering out from behind the encounter suit visor. Cold dead eyes that marked her for revenge. It wasn't Pshwa.

"No!" She fired again, ripping into a rolling barrel, sending it spinning into the Senti and knocking the last limb clear of the deck. Shoulder tentacles scrabbled for purchase as the Senti collapsed, desperately trying to right itself. The alien finally got a grip, rising from the deck to find a carbine muzzle rammed against its visor.

"Go ahead, give me a juicy nightmare I can sell," growled Arin, and he tapped the gun against the visor. "Make my day."

"Arin hold," she said, eyeing his feed.

Too late, the alien panicked, lashing multiple limbs at the red-haired ex-Marine. Arin fired, point blank. It got messy, and he kicked the suit into the gap being quickly vacated by the shuttle.

Heavy breathing filled her comms. "For Savvo."

"Arin. You with me? Calm it down. Show me what's in that container."

Arin glanced over, but was distracted as the shuttle dropped, released from the ceiling clamps and absorbing the rotational effects as its thrusters briefly engaged. Rebekah had seconds before their futures flew away aboard the spacecraft. She aimed, finger on the trigger, her sight zeroing in. A breath, and she lowered the carbine. A misplaced shot, a dead pilot or a ruptured engine, and she could endanger the entire station.

Their last chance had gone. And the Bustan Navy were nearly here.

Time for damage limitation.

She swore, turning about to find Arin's glare centred on the Navy storage box. From the rear, in a suit designed to absorb impact, he appeared still. But the camera feed shook.

"ZZ3," she sent, staring at the *Scourge*'s mark etched onto the empty box next to the code Erikson had shared. "Change of plan."

CHAPTER 29

The plan had been a good one until the Bustan Navy had upped their pace. At that moment, everything had gone to shit. The wetware was on some scummy shuttle heading to the gods know where, and they were trapped on board a decrepit space station they just so happened to have stormed. Hopefully, the twins had hacked any working video surveillance, otherwise their new plan would be as screwed as the last. ZZ3 had returned their suits, slowly drifting unpowered back to the ship. Rebekah hated herself for not sending Savvo back, but the energy required to keep him alive could have alerted the corvette.

"Come on. Do a bloody hard burn, put half your crew out of action, and then dawdle at the shitting airlock," Arin grumbled. One hand rested on Savvo's shoulder as he lay on the deck, the other swiping his slate as he upped the sedative, trying to keep him quiet.

"They're straightening their collars and dusting down their pants. You know the drill," growled Hannos, hands gripped together in front of her, stilling the shake as she waited by the airlock. The bruise across her jaw purple. "Preening."

"Your faction okay?" asked Rebekah.

"Sound. Think they understood what the Almaarian Marines were all about in those few minutes," replied Hannos, sparing a glance Rebekah's way. "But funnily enough, they're all sedated right now. Enjoying a little downtime, just in case."

"Thanks," said Rebekah, half-turning to the Skyrider. "For helping. For this," she gestured towards the airlock and the approaching Bustan Navy.

"The first part solved a gang war problem and maybe helped me ease my pain a little. Not that I have a fucking clue what to do about what the Scourge did to my squad. The second," she eyed Rebekah, a hint of anger in her gaze, "is for *my* people. For Benetai. The Bustan's find out I was complicit, fuck knows what these bastards will do in the name of 'efficiency'. They could tear this place apart, leave a few Marines to keep an eye, or the gods forbid, *tax* the bloody place."

The airlock cycled, and everyone standing stepped back. The first through the door was a Bustan Marine in full powered armour. His weapon was up, their equivalent of the carbine, and aiming for Rebekah. She blinked, adding a sardonic smile and opened her hands wide to show they were empty. No weapon, no armour. As naked as she had ever been before a Bustan soldier.

"Down. On your knees," the comms were harsh, electronic sounding, despite the Marines' visor only covering just below the nose. Rebekah complied, dropping to her knees along with Hannos and the muttering Arin.

A click of polished boot on deck resounded, silver tips appearing in Rebekah's field of view first, then grey, pin straight pants with the edge of a silvered jacket.

"Who is Hannos?" said the officer, his voice willowy but expectant. His Almaarian impeccable.

"I am," said the cartel leader, her shoulders shaking a little as she spoke.

"You may rise," the male officer said. "Who are these with you?"

"Mercs," replied Hannos. She then filled the ensuing silence. "Had a gang problem to solve, and couldn't trust any other fuckers ... Sorry, any of my *employees* to do the job."

"And did this gang issue involve the one named *Baja*?"

Hannos coughed, rubbing her sore chin. "Aye. You know him?"

Again silence followed, and Rebekah had to hold herself back from cutting in. She used images of Major Ren in one of his rages to pacify her mind, and when that didn't work, kicked in her chip. She hoped Arin was doing the same.

"Up," said the Bustan Officer, and Rebekah complied, helping Arin to his feet and stealing a glance. He caught her look, casting his eyes down afterwards. Savvo's condition was gnawing at his nerves, she knew, but his cause would only be helped by compliance. She had considered dropping out of the cargo hold, hoping to reach the *Sunstar* with ZZ3's help. But abandoning the station to its fate was something she could no longer do.

Rebekah kept her face neutral, thanking the wetware in her head.

"Baja sent a message asking for help. You know anything about this?" His blue eyes sparkled with curiosity, with expected compliance written in his demeanour. The switch of emphasis and target for questioning was designed to keep Hannos off-kilter. Attack the weakest link, before returning your attention.

"I do," she replied. "The fucker, Tensei, had stolen some wetware destined for Baja. I was there, trying to find what the hell was happening for Hannos, when Baja turned up to reacquire his shit. Got tetchy, a few bruises, but nothing more. Tensei took it personal, spaced one of his own who squealed."

"And my wetware?" demanded the officer. "Where – as you put it – the *fuck* is my cargo?" He stepped in closer, nose to nose with Rebekah. His breath smelled sweet; teeth perfectly white. She wanted to break each perfect tooth one by one. Where her own nobility pissed distilled self-interest, where the Court and Honour came before all else, the Bustan were merely ruthless, efficient. Their motto: *By Any Means Necessary*. Whether this was as a result of the war, or their history, she didn't know, nor care. Ordinary people just picked up the dung of those in power.

"Hannos sent us to intercept Tensei." Rebekah glanced over to the gang leader who nodded in agreement. "She got wind he was out for blood. Baja was dead when I got there, his people too. The cargo gone."

"Gone?" The officer turned his attention to Hannos, who again nodded, before eyeing Savvo on the floor and a nervous Arin.

"Gone where?" he said to Arin, then glanced down at the pale and sweating unconscious form of Savvo.

The sub-engineer's red-rimmed eyes glowered at the Bustan officer. "A Senti dream-peddler named Pshwa. We caught up to the bastard too late. The kit got burnt up in the firefight."

The officer flinched at that, anger twisting his features and a snarl slipped from behind his perfect teeth. "Burnt up?"

Rebekah wanted to step between them and take the brunt of the Bustan's anger. Arin was on the edge. With Savvo suffering, and ZZ3 out in the black if the bloody bot was following orders, this could go sideways fast.

Arin flicked his eyes to the deck. "Burnt up. Want to see? It's just my friend here got caught by one of that Senti bastard's venom darts, and I kind of want to hurry up."

"Yes. Yes, I do. With my own eyes, and all that."

"I can take you," said Hannos. "Show you whatever you need to see."

"No. You won't," said the Bustan officer. "This red-haired Almaarian bastard will show me, won't you?" He glanced down at Savvo again. "At my pace."

Arin stood at the bottom of the stairway, arms crossed, eyes locked on Tensei as he spoke to Lieutenant Ormsk. This was where their tale could unravel. The gang leader pissed off at his and Rebekah's threats of retribution, both during the run to Baja, and afterwards when they explained just how far the Bustan Navy might go to recover the wetware. The reluctance had been obvious. As far as Arin knew, it had required a promise of Baja's patch to placate the gang boss. But should he want the chance to undermine Hannos, make a play for the cartel leadership, this was his opportunity.

The tension grew as they spoke, pleasing Arin. Tensei had clearly realised what a screwed-up bunch of weirdos the Bustan Navy were. So uptight, you couldn't shove a gun barrel up their arse without extra grease. He was contemplating trying when the conversation ended, bitterness obvious in Tensei's posture as the officer turned away.

"This station is filled with scum," he said on the way past. "Looks like you should float to the top here."

Arin ignored him and fell in behind, his stomach griping at how long this was taking. If they were caught, so be it. At least the Bustan would fix up Savvo before executing him, and Dricks and the girls would have time to run. Tensei looked his way, lifting his chin and then nodding. Job done, and the twist in Arin's stomach settled for now.

They reached the outside of Baja's place in relatively quick time. The concourse clear of humanity with word of the Navy's presence preceding them. First gang war, then a fire alert, and now this. Hiding was their chosen option, and appreciated by Arin.

They entered together, two Marines ahead, sweeping the area. The officer stopped at the first pair of dead bodies, stepping sideways, looking but not wanting to touch.

"Encounter suit," said Arin, bending down to shift the stiffening neck side to side and exposing the ruptured vertebrae. "Pshwa, or whoever. They whipped their heads around."

"And this Pshwa had dealings with Baja?"

"According to Hannos, yeah. And Baja mentioned Pshwa when he turned up to take back the wetware. Want a theory from a grunt?" Arin looked up to the officer, waiting for an answer.

"No," he replied, the sneer at his suggestion unsurprising. "Show me where the wetware was stored."

Arin stood, about to turn when he caught sight of a bald-headed and bruised gang member staring at him, the wrist roughly strapped tightly to his chest. Arin could smell trouble. Pietr started walking, eyes focused on Arin, then charged, red-faced and filled with fury.

"Should have bullseyed that piece of shit when we had the chance," he whispered, and stepped between the officer and fate. Pietr made to speak, and Arin speared a hand into the man's throat, smashing the trachea, a second blow ramming upwards into the nose, before twisting the neck as he toppled. The crack left the Baja gangster dead on the floor.

A presence loomed behind him, but he ignored it, rolling the corpse over to expose the hand cannon at Pietr's waist before stepping away.

"A grunt I may be," he said. "But a damn good one."

The officer stepped in beside him, a Marine on the other with their weapon trained on Arin. "And this is?"

"One of the Baja we fell out with when we first started looking for the chips. Then shot at us when civilians were in the way. Should have done that the first time." Arin didn't look at the officer, instead turning back to survey the doors to the den. "Kind of in a hurry, you know. Not got the time to deal with grudges."

The officer paused, eyeing the dead body. "Indeed."

The sweep of the Baja cargo hold was cursory, the officer barely looking and far more focused on Arin, making him uncomfortable. On reaching the hold airlock, his curiosity returned to the matter in hand, his Marines confirming the Bustan origin of the shattered drone.

"Gustack," the officer said when he had finished. "Analyse the needles. Let's see if we can make this worthwhile for our Almaarian grunt."

The Marine stooped down again, flipping open his inner forearm guard and dropped a few of the needles inside, while the second guard engaged the cargo hold doors and flooded the bay with air. Once the airlock cycled, they entered, Arin eagerly walking over to the Navy cargo box peppered with bullet holes and scorch marks.

He glanced at the coding, swearing, and not for the first time, at the section Duboit hadn't told them about. The mark of the *Scourge*. They'd been hunting equipment originating from General Asham's flagship that lay burnt out behind an asteroid field on the fringes of the Almaarian system. It had to be why the Bustan wanted the wetware.

Inside, a pile of broken and seared chips sat amid the ash of wires and flaps. Old wetware courtesy of Tensei.

Arin lifted out a tangled set of wires. "These the chips you wanted? A lot of death-dealing for a set of useless wetware."

The Bustan officer stood a metre or so away from the box, staring at it as he circled around, Arin assuming he was recording what he saw. He closed in and repeated his actions, peering into the punctured and ash-stained box before releasing a heavy sigh.

"Analysis," he repeated, though this time he meant the Almaarian box's contents. Gustack approached, and carefully extracted contents of the box, visor sweeping over each before bagging up specific sections.

"Definitely Almaarian," said the Marine, his accent rougher than the officer's. Arin realised this was for his benefit, making him wonder. "And wetware."

"That's enough. Bring the box to the *Ansta*." The officer turned away, striding along the deck before stopping next to the holed encounter suit. The contents had melted into a blue-green puddle, only the black eyes remained intact inside the helmet. He spat on the suit, and walked away.

See. We do have something in common.

CHAPTER 30

"Where the hell did that shuttle go?" asked Hendricks.

Heki wavered, a nervous prickle rising across her neck, while fear settled in the pit of her stomach. Hendricks was wearing a set of headphones, a rarity unless things were bad, and since the arrival of the Bustan Navy, both Tremil and her had spiralled. The first sight of the Bustan markings had triggered old traumas, and on turning off the station's jamming with the ship's approach, they had sneakily watched the transfer of Marines and the officer despite the engineer's express order not to.

She squeezed the bridge of her nose, leaning over as her head spun and nausea rose.

"Here," said Tremil, and despite the consternation it may cause, Heki gratefully accepted TB across her neck. The symbiote nuzzled in, tentacles gently pressing against the back of her skull. The raw edge of her emotional turmoil eased, the pressure slowly reducing which enabled her to refocus. A side glance let her know Hendricks was too involved in the shuttle's disappearance to notice. Hopefully.

"It's among the parked ships," Tremil said, tapping away at the cockpit monitor and drawing up a view of the remaining spacecraft left hanging in the black. Heki caught the wince and tremor at the corner of her eye. They needed to hold it together or … the choice was stark, too painful to contemplate.

"We have to find it. The wetware and whoever shot at the captain are aboard." Hendricks closed her eyes, scrunching up her eyelids. "Girls, I can't focus. I feel every bit of your worry but its … oppressive."

Heki drew in as much of her emotions as she could with TB's support, but knew Tremil's concentration and her internal refrain would drift as soon as she faced up to who, and what, hung next to the space station. A Bustan Navy corvette, brutal, efficient machinery designed to be as powerful visually as internally. The front of the ship stared at you, boring into your mind. How apt.

"We could send in a set of probes," suggested Tremil. "Those we used around the asteroid field. They have visual and sensory scanning."

"They'll pick them up. The …" Heki couldn't say it. Hendricks squeezed her shoulder, showing she understood.

"Can you direct it there under low power and not transmitting? Just the one?" Hendricks rolled her shoulders as she spoke, kneading her neck muscles while worry lined her forehead.

The co-pilot's chair swivelled as Tremil turned to face Heki. "I think I could, Hek. From the captain's console I could use burst data packets. Low-level information."

"Get on it. Does it matter which probe?" asked Heki.

The engineer nodded. "It does. We'll use one of Arin's that clamp to ZZ3."

Despite the pulsing in her brain, Heki smiled, understanding the intent. "That's clever," she replied. "That old brain of yours is still pretty sharp."

"You," said Hendricks, turning to head down the corridor. "Are getting sassy, girl."

"Sassy?" asked Heki, Tremil shrugging as she looked across at her.

"I don't know, either." She eyed the symbiote, eyes rising to meet Heki's as the clomp of Hendricks' magboots receded. "You suffering?"

Heki nodded, refusing to acknowledge her fear at first until Tremil stood and headed for the corridor. "What are we going to do, Trem? If it becomes too much?"

"We can't let it," she replied turning back, her face set like stone, yet she was on the verge of crumbling. "But the ship, the flags. The way they speak. It … it …"

"Brings it back. Rakes up the fucking lab." Heki flinched at her own swear word, but she needed it. "Go. Focus on what we *can* do, not what we might. If it comes to it, we take the retardant or make Dricks sedate us."

"If we realise in time," replied Tremil, and started down the corridor.

Heki sensed TB mither; the symbiote transmitting its disquiet at Tremil leaving. The more they used him to calm their emotions, the greater TB's sensitivity to their feelings. The alien knew Tremil suffered, as did she, but couldn't help both and silently keened.

She returned her attention to the console and ran a check on the sensory image the *Sunstar* was projecting. It remained stable, providing a tweaked spectrum of responses to any scans. Presented the ship as the *Solar Flame*, via the transponder, and little else. During the process, she had noted a sensory void that the containment box created. Something that irked her. It didn't sit right, considering Scarva's *Unpronounceable* was constructed from similar Senti material, yet had appeared on their scans on approach. A concern for another time, when the fucking Bustan Navy weren't hovering with intent, She enjoyed that swear word too.

"Be safe, Rebekah," she whispered.

Hendricks removed the probe from the storage box, the fine grey sand Arin poured around them parting as she lifted the fifteen-centimetre sphere out. Its dull grey surface reflected very little, its function to absorb any spectrum data it could. The six spikes on its surface were a combination of transmitters. She activated and deactivated the mag clamp, checking it against the hold's wall.

"What is your intent?"

Hendricks shivered, her shoulders tightening as the warbot's monotone words filled the hold. She looked over her shoulder at ZZ3, the bot sat amid the navy suits Rebekah had commanded the unit to collect. A choice Hendricks admired but feared could go very wrong. She hadn't even risked sending back Savvo. Putting loyalty to Hannos and her people above their predicament.

"We need to track a shuttle. One that's among the parked ships," she replied.

"Which shuttle?" asked ZZ3, and the bot's limbs extended, pushing its bulk from the deck. "I have been monitoring, but we were jamming most comms until just before the Navy ship arrived."

"I don't have time for this," said Hendricks, and she carried the surprisingly awkward probe over to the launcher. They weren't navy, nor a survey ship, so they were not geared up for frequent auto launching of sensory equipment. Instead, they used an in-hull launcher, the probes dropped from a retracting plate, or ZZ3 took them out.

"I am crew," said the bot. "I could monitor crew conversations via the comms units. But that would be ... intrusive."

The engineer engaged the probe, a brief flash of a single LED showing it was active, and then seated it among the holding material that moulded to its shape. She cranked it into the launcher, sealing the hold from any exposure to space.

"Comms are for all crew." Hendricks pressed the comms unit button near the launcher, still not looking at the bot. "I'm ready, Tremil."

"On my mark," she replied, making Hendricks smile. Even the voice was close to Rebekah's. "Three, two, one, launch."

Hendricks pulled the lever, and the scrape of metal and hiss of the hydraulics indicated release.

"I have it," Tremil said. "We are operational."

"I can help. I am crew," said the bot. "I defended the ship from the Senti code. I returned the suits after a change of plan."

Hendricks stopped halfway to the exit, rubbing a hand across her neck and then over her head before turning about. "I don't know how to answer, ZZ3. We know what you used to be able to do, and that's how we will use you until we learn more."

"I could have retrieved the wetware faster, quicker," it replied.

Hendricks was silent a moment, trying to process what the newly reconstituted warbot meant. "You would scare people and cause a violent reaction. Warbot units had a tendency to not discern human targets well. Civilian casualties were common, and their decision-making flawed. We, as Breakers, didn't care – until we did."

Hendricks expected a reaction. An argument back, almost as if the warbot was human. A strange sensation that whatever was inside was almost alive. And if it was, how much of the Butcher remained?

"I need to process," said the bot. Limbs rumbled and bent until it sat once again on the deck with lights dimmed.

The ex-Marine turned away, shaking her head until she reached the exit.

"When did you start to care?" echoed across the hold.

How do I answer that?

"When Heki and Tremil removed the veils over our eyes and minds," Hendricks replied.

"You do it, Hek. Flying is your only high score," Tremil said.

Heki snorted half-heartedly and sent the first data packet to the probe. The response was immediate, and she guided the small machine, manipulating the momentum gained as it left the ship with minimal use of its thrusters. They had set an orbit after leaving the station that enabled them to fly in to pick up the squad at, what Dricks termed, the drop of a hat. That hats wouldn't fall in non-grav was unappreciated by the engineer when Tremil pointed it out. It had the added benefit, especially after adjusting for the Navy ship's rapid arrival, of bypassing the parked ships of whatever rogues remained aboard Benetai.

A second data burst requesting a further readjustment saw the probe fly gently between the waiting ships and engage an initial analysis.

"Checking for particulates from engine outflow," said Tremil, and Heki pictured her sister's fingers flying over the captain's console, tongue sticking out the corner of her mouth, eyes scanning the data. "Attempting to remove the manoeuvring thruster discharge from those heaps of trash they call ships. In space, no one can see you pollute with your unclean crap. Okay, I think I have the shuttle. Sending projected flight-path."

Heki checked over the data, a flash on her console drawing her attention to a background issue. She pulled that up. The Navy ship was running an active sensor sweep of the parked ships, and she immediately silenced the probe. Deadened to prevent shadowed data from its own electronics and outer shell affecting any analysis, hitting the proverbial off-button would be its best chance of remaining undetected. It would barely register on a passive sensory analysis, but an active sweep was a different matter.

"The B... The Navy are checking on the floating scrapheap," said Heki, a finger drumming on the console. TB adjusted his position. Her anxiety was rising, and the symbiote was beginning to get agitated. Had it reached a point it could no longer help? Was it 'full'?

"They're not reacting to anything," said Tremil. "Comms are silent on both sides."

"Not a surprise, unless the Navy start flying towards them, gun ports open," said Hendricks, arriving to stand behind Heki. "The first one to twitch gets blasted. Heh. Seen that film. The Bustan aren't here for them. Not worth the effort. If they're smuggling, then catch them at the space ports. Cheaper, and far less hassle. I'm betting they've recorded visual and sensory detail of every ship, including ours. Don't forget they use AI. From what I hear, they can extrapolate my underwear size from a hundred clicks."

Heki giggled, the act slicing through her anxiety as Tremil joined in.

The sweep ended, though the passive sensors would still be up. Heki ran a swift check of the probe's position as it engaged and sent a new burst command. The probe realigned, following Tremil's suggested flight-path. She risked a quick sensory analysis.

"The particulates have come to an end," said Tremil having picked up the burst data it sent back. "I think they must have shut down the shuttle's thrusters. Any residual chems will be far too dissipated to pick up."

Heki nodded to herself, scrunching her lips as she thought. "Want to risk a real-time visual and sensor sweep?" she asked, turning to Hendricks.

"Can you run a fast sweep and send the deets in a burst, rather than risk that being picked up?" replied Hendricks, her hands squeezing the seat top in front of her. The engineer was jittery, the magboots restraining her from bouncing about.

"Yeah," answered Heki. She tapped away and quickly sent the command. TB stirred, and she realised the symbiote was in Hendricks' direct line of sight. She had said nothing, but it would come.

Damn. Deal with that later.

The return data packet flagged up, Tremil murmuring over the comms as she worked her way through the information. Heki sensed her disquiet, the shift in emotions more than hinting at exasperation. Here it came.

"It's gone," said Tremil. "I can't find any sign in the data. No visuals, no EM spectral response, no chem signs, nothing."

"From that shitty shuttle," stated Hendricks. "Throw the visual up on the galley screen, overlay the EM data. I'll take a look."

Tremil did as the engineer requested, and a minute later, Hendricks called them through. She stood before the screen, squinting, not running through the data but looking at its representation.

"Now, I know engines," she started, "and I know how to storm a defensive ring. Before the Breakers we were grunts. No powered armour, only what you had in your hands and on your back. You learned to hide as well as fight. Tell me, has it engaged main engines and flown off?"

"No," said Heki and Tremil together.

"I agree. So it's here, somewhere. If you wanted to hide from a scan, what would you do?"

Heki considered the probe. "You'd need absorbent outer material, so it appears as if anything on the sensor sweep is passing through."

"And to suppress any internal emissions," added Tremil. "Though both could only be temporary. You'd need to offload before ..."

"The shit hit the fan. Yeah. So absorbent ..." mused Hendricks. "The dropships didn't use that kind of trick, but some of the atmospheric fighters did. Never as successful as you think it'll be. Atmospheric displacement, and all that. Especially in clouds."

Heki blinked. The containment box.

"A void," she said, Hendricks flinching as her excitement rose. "Rather than look for what's there, look for what's not. We'd never find it in space, at least not yet, but amongst all the floating scrap out here ..." She clomped back to the cockpit, but by the time she'd sat down, Tremil was on the comms.

"Got it," she said. "Completely inert. An absence."

Heki glanced over the data, checking Tremil had shared it with Hendricks.

"Well done. Now what?" said the ex-captain.

A voice cut in, monotone and robotic. "If it's absorbing everything, and internal systems are masked, I'd suggest the shuttle is unable to constantly monitor its immediate surroundings. That probe was one of mine, so I would advise clamping on. It works with ... Asham's containment unit."

Heki spun her chair, eyeing Hendricks whose sudden burst of worry had cut through all the roiling emotions aboard the ship. The engineer nodded, but there was distaste in the twist of her mouth, the stretch of her jaw.

"Do it," Hendricks said. "And if that shuttle runs, set it to send an intermittent signal. It ain't any faster than us going by the engine structure."

"It's already set that way for the burst packet data, I'll minimise that to reduce possible detection," said Heki, running through the commands. Once sent, she slid off her comms, meaning to talk to Hendricks about ZZ3. Somehow, the old engineer had already left, her movements quiet despite the potential ring of footsteps on the deck. She walked to the galley, finding the engineer on the bench, staring at a flask of white coffee.

Turmoil poured from the woman, her friend, her family. She didn't know what to do or say. Having spent so much of her life sorting out her own hot mess of thoughts and impulses, how to read others' needs was mired in her insecurities. Hence reprogramming ZZ3 to experiment with, and look how that turned out.

She chose a get out, and sat by Hendricks, saying nothing. To her amazement, the torrent of emotional noise dropped to a mere burble.

CHAPTER 31

"Hendricks, you there?" asked Rebekah. She let out a breath, one hand on Savvo's shoulder as she knelt by the airlock. "Come back, Hendricks. I need you."

The comms crackled. "Here, Captain."

"Bring the ship into link with Hannos airlock 3, the Bustan shuttle has our old berth," she said, adding a couple of taps on the comms microphone at her jaw. "I have Savvo in a bad way, so need the medbot up and running."

"Copy that, Captain. On my way."

Rebekah cut off the comms, and stood, sparing a glance over to the Bustan Marine who guarded the Hannos airlock.

"How long will they be?" she asked, and the Marine ignored her. She tried to shove down the anxious anger roiling in her gut. Choosing to rile whoever was in that armour would not solve her problem. "Hey, I have a man down here."

That got a response, the male Marine's jaw twitching as he turned to face her. He peered down at Savvo, the helmet briefly tilting as if listening to something. Still no words came, though she suspected he was eye-clicking his HUD by the way his neck moved. A robotic voice emanated from his helmet. Translation.

"Lieutenant Ormsk is returning. Two minutes. He has analysis of the venom dart."

Rebekah puffed out her cheeks. "Thank you." The words felt like ash in her mouth. Yeah, they had invaded Bustan 8 and outlying moon colonies. But the Bustans had been no angels, and despite the initiation of the 'war' buried deep in the murk of political bullshit, they had attacked first. Or at least, that's what the Court's newsfeed would have you believe. The resource rich moons of New Almaar efficiently stripped of life by an AI led war fleet.

She hefted Savvo to his feet as voices echoed along the ring, Hannos having greeted the officer further down the corridor, anxious for the safety of her people.

"Have you found what you needed?" she asked, not pleading, but strident in her question.

The Bustan officer wrinkled his nose as if Hannos was a bad smell he wished to avoid. Like all officers she had worked with, the man's thoughts were on everything but the woman at his side. Probably regarding her as an annoyance at best. But Hannos had a people she clearly loved and needed to protect. A sense of duty that had led to Rebekah risking Savvo's life in the name of the thousands on board Benetai.

Arin looked just as anxious as he trailed behind. His concern rising as he saw Savvo draped across her shoulders. He resisted the urge to run over, though she could see by the stiffness in his movements, he struggled to hold himself back.

"Captain Khan," said the officer, stopping before her. "Your red-haired Almaarian mercenary scum has proven most helpful."

Rebekah cast her eyes behind them, catching sight of the storage box they had been sent to find. The *Scourge*'s mark displayed before the coding.

"Good," she said, refusing to rise to the slight. "Your fine Marine here said you have something for me. An analysis of the venom dart."

"I do, yes." Officer Ormsk clicked his fingers over his shoulder, a Marine dropped the wetware box briefly to hand over a small plas-glass container. "Nasty little swines these. Devastated your armies when we first employed them. The toxin data is coded into the lid."

Rebekah reached for the proffered box, but Ormsk drew it back. "Hasty," he said, the smile predatory. "Tell me ... which unit did you serve with?"

Rebekah went to speak, but the Bustan raised his other, gloved hand to silence her. "No doubt whatever slips from those lips will be a lie, and I have not the time nor the inclination to go any deeper. But I have your ship's transponder, your scan data and now your obedience. I ask you one time, and I will know a lie, whose mark lies on that storage box?"

Rebekah paused, her eyes rising from the precious container and its potential to save Savvo, to the officer. She felt Hannos stir. If she spoke up, it was at risk of the station. She had zero doubts what would happen next if that Bustan bastard worked out she was a Skyrider. The Almaarian Space Marines were only fourth on their most hated list, behind the Breakers and Countess Segfi, with General Asham and his own personal tally of vendettas, at the top.

Fuck.

She spoke, cutting Hannos dead. "The *Scourge*," she said, keeping her voice flat.

"Good. Some honesty. Now, answer the next question with even more care. What do you know of the *Scourge*?" The officer shook the precious box, his smile accentuated by a glimmer in his eye.

Rebekah wanted to punch him, gouge out the eyes and stuff them down his throat. She felt her wrist twinge, the scar there stretch. "I know you want General Asham bad. The Butcher, you call him. Rumour has it you don't think he's dead."

"True. And?"

"I'm a grunt," she continued. "What the fuck do you want me to say? I'm here to quell a fucking gang war. Job done." She looked to Hannos, pointing. "And don't forget payment."

"I could ..." he started, then appeared to change his mind. "In the old days I could have tortured it out of you if I thought you lied. Out here though, no one gives a damn what happens to *people*," he almost spat the last word. "Maybe I should crack open this bad egg, peel the hull open and expose it to the black."

"The war is over," said Rebekah. "And word would get out."

"That it would." He smirked. "But then, the next time I asked about the *Scourge*, I'd get the truth. I have made it my life's work to *find* that truth." He tossed the box over, the malice in his gaze designed to set her on edge.

It worked.

"Scurry back to your ship, grunt. Hurry, he's not looking well."

Rebekah stemmed the acerbic words pressing for release. Everything was in balance. Her fate, and Benetai's. Words would only dig a hole, or crack a hull. She yanked Savvo into a more comfortable position and gestured for Arin to take the other side. Her second's breath smelt turgid, thick with disturbing aromas she couldn't place. He lolled to one side, eyes closed, lips trembling as they began the walk towards the hopefully waiting ship.

When they were out of earshot, Arin apologised.

"What for?" she said, hefting Savvo up a little.

"I dunno. Somehow, he must have worked it out. What we were," he replied.

"Not so hard as mercs," she said. "Not the most unlikely past, is it?"

Arin didn't reply, but she knew he was stewing over the exchange. At the moment, Savvo was the priority, and hope lay in the box in her hand. On reaching the third airlock, she let Arin take the weight, and checked for the ship. It had just slid into position, and the patched polythene tubing was making slow progress to meet it. Relieved, she checked the timer.

"Hurry, Dricks. Fucking hurry," she said over comms. The airlock began its cycle, and she slammed a hand into the ring's hull, desperate for it to speed up. When it turned green, she helped the door on its way and between them they dragged Savvo inside.

"Go ahead," said Arin. "Get the medbot set up. It'll save time."

Rebekah slid down the ladder, using the additional gravity to her advantage. She cycled the ship's airlock, knowing it would delay Arin, but speed up readying the medbot. Once through, she ignored Hendricks and headed for medbay where she found Tremil waiting.

"Let me," she said, and reached for the container, her face set like stone. "I kept Davina and Dricks alive. I know this medbot inside out."

Rebekah dithered, taken aback. Savvo needed her, he was crew, a Breaker and her responsibility.

But responsible leaders trusted those with greater knowledge, teenager or not.

She nodded, unable to speak, and handed over the box. "It's ..."

"I know," said Tremil, the words stern and hard. She opened the lid, detached it and pressed the code link to the medbot interface. Data steamed across the screen. "I need Savvo," she said.

Rebekah swivelled and got to the airlock as Arin handed over a dishevelled-looking Savvo to Hendricks. The ageing engineer shoved past her, moving at a speed that belied her old injuries to enter medbay. Rebekah made to follow, when Arin took her arm, pulling her back.

"We need to be out of here," he said. "And clear of the station. If that bastard follows through on his threat, it won't only be Savvo in danger."

"Fuuuuck," she spat, yanking her arm clear. Rebekah stomped along the corridor, stomach still churning, to enter the cockpit. Heki was there, sat in the co-pilot's chair. Their eyes met amid waves of anxiety. She fired up an earworm, with her own worries over Savvo bolstering her defences, and dropped into the seat. Strapping in, she clicked on comms.

"We're leaving. Batten down. Heki, is the airlock clear?" Heki squirmed, but Rebekah didn't have the time for her worries. "Are we clear?"

Heki checked the screen. "Yes, Captain."

"Engaging thrusters. Dricks, get to engineering in case we have to scoot."

"Copy that," came the reply.

Rebekah eased the ship away from the station, keeping her movements calm despite the urgency of the moment. Doing something she knew so well brought focus.

"We need to enter the scrapheap," said Heki, gathering herself and swiping across a suggested route. "That's where the shuttle is hidden."

"You mean it hasn't left?"

"No. But it's hidden from sensors and drifting away at quite a speed," Heki replied, and flagged its course. "I suspect its waiting until some opportunity arises, or the Bustan leave. It has to be time limited, though. They must be building up one hell of a radiation issue."

Rebekah checked the course, her mind on Benetai and its people. What would Ormsk do? And for that matter, Hannos? Would she sell them out in hope of saving the station? It was a distinct possibility, and hard for Rebekah to blame her. Until the missiles flew, or the ship was boarded.

Fuck that.

"Have we any comms with the station?" she asked.

"Not received any yet," replied Heki. "But there's chatter."

Rebekah checked their course, the *Solar Flame,* as the transponder called them, now merging into the parked spacecraft. There would be talk. Accusations flying about the specific gang ships. But many still hung out there, waiting in hope. Or devoid of fuel, as Hannos had said, and with nowhere else to go.

"The shuttle drift is altering. Not sure how they're doing it." Heki tapped at her screen, appearing frustrated.

It hit Rebekah then. "How do you know?"

"We have a probe attached," replied Heki. "Transmitting in data bursts."

Rebekah couldn't help but smile, Heki's glance over leading to a blush on the girl's cheeks. "But why now?" Rebekah muttered. "What's changed?"

"I don't know," she checked the screen, fingers tapping as she eyed the incoming data. "But the Navy shuttle has disconnected. Possibly they're getting ready to run."

Rebekah chewed over that, and the station's predicament. Nothing sat easy. She just needed the Bustan to piss off back from where they came, and all her decisions would be easier.

Fat chance.

She kept an eye on the Navy shuttle, noting the corvette engage its manoeuvring thrusters. The movement could be to provide the shuttle a smooth entry point, but she had her doubts.

"Heki, I want to know everything that Bustan ship is doing." She didn't wait for confirmation, patching into the last data burst for the camouflaged shuttle carrying the source of all their problems. She kept that window open in the top corner, her main screen on the station and the ominous corvette.

The comms crackled, a familiar voice cutting through the noise. "Khan, you there?"

Shit, Hannos didn't sound good, and it was an open line. The Bustan would hear every word. "Here."

"That fucker ... that fucker wouldn't believe me. He's convinced I knew about the wetware, brought you in to get it for myself."

"But you didn't," she replied truthfully, cracking two knuckles. What was Hannos doing? "What the fuck did you tell him?"

"The truth."

The Bustan Navy shuttle docked with the corvette having turned to face the station. Its pseudo face leering at Benetai.

"Forward missile tubes are open," stated Heki.

"No, no. no," Rebekah cried. "Open a line, get me the corvette. Now, Heki. Hail them."

Heki trembled, hands shaking as she swiped and tapped at her screen. "No response."

Rebekah opened a general line. "Lieutenant Ormsk, can you hear me? Don't do this. You have a whole set of witnesses to what you're doing. It's murder."

"Witnesses? So we do," came the self-reverential voice. "Better run. Busy."

"You fuck," she shouted. And something caught her eye, a glance to the smaller, open-window enraging her further.

"Pshwa's shuttle's engaged engines," said Heki.

"Ormsk, you fuck. Catch me, catch the *Scourge*'s wetware!" she screamed into comms. "Dricks, kick the engines in. I want Pshwa's shuttle run down. Everyone grab hold, we are engaging thrust immediately. No count in."

She slammed on engine thrust. Alarms blared. The ship shook.

As the *Solar Flare's* engines burst into life, Rebekah engaged the navcom, locking onto the shuttle's flight-path, knowing everyone on board was about to suffer.

"Sorry," she hissed through tight lips.

CHAPTER 32

The acceleration forced her back against the seat, eyes scanning the navcom's trajectory through the parked spacecraft – a prayer on her mind, a swear word on lips.

"What's the bastard doing, Heki?"

"The ba—?" Heki was about to ask, cutting herself short. "Closing missile ports," she replied, the words slurred. "Engaging manoeuvring thrusters, main engines f-firing up."

Rebekah checked the *Sunstar*'s velocity and acceleration rate, the console throwing up all kinds of warnings and threats to human life. She could predict the effect on Heki and Tremil physically, but not the biochemical reaction it might trigger in their brains. And therefore, the emotional thunderstorm to come.

And the symbiote in hard burn? Damn.

Everything was fucked up.

Ormsk had taken her bait, but there were never any guarantees such a man wouldn't go back later and finish what he started. Now they were in a chase, with the advantage of a head start, and the corvette had recently been through an extremely rough hard burn.

"Dricks, Arin," she said, finding her mind fogged by the rapid acceleration, and forgetting halfway through why she was calling over comms.

Pull yourself to-fucking-gether.

"Captain?" said Arin. Amid the vibrations and comms noise, she couldn't tell how stressed he was. "Want a sit rep? Dricks got me strapped down clomping about in those metal disco boots. She's—"

"*She* is currently watching the upper half of ZZ3 stomp down the corridor. Want me to follow?"

Tough as they come.

"I am helping crew," said ZZ3. "Tremil has fainted, according to her console."

"Shit," said Rebekah, and glanced over to find Heki pressed into her seat, eyes closed. She had her answer. But ZZ3? "Are you able to collect Heki safely and administer the retardant?"

"I can and will," replied the bot. "Will I be required to apply a catheter?"

The question took Rebekah by surprise, her mind unable to do any form of proper calculation in terms of time and acceleration. She knew they had a head start, but how much was enough? Too much, and they'd have to hard slow to prevent shooting past the shuttle.

The shuttle.

"Captain?" asked the bot.

"One second," she replied, forcing herself to swipe through the console until she had the data. "No. Just the retardant, half dose."

"Affirmative, Captain. Tremil is secured."

Rebekah remained ill-at-ease with the warbot, could define it, almost see it within her own body. But the corvette had followed, Benetai still spun, and while they lived and breathed, they still had a chance. Whatever came next, ZZ3's transformation was at the bottom of her concerns, until it wasn't.

The warbot's body, the clang of its movement lost amid the engine's effects, loomed behind. Upper limbs unclipped Heki and wrapped about her, trying to adjust for the forces acting on the girl's young body. Silently it turned away, cradling Heki, and countering the effects of the acceleration as it walked down the passageway.

If Rebekah could have shaken her head, she would have.

"Dricks, you strapped in?" she asked

"I will when ZZ3 has passed by," replied the engineer, a tapping sound echoing in the comms as she spoke. "How long we doing this?"

"Around two hours unless the shuttle ups its burn, but I'm not so sure it can if these numbers are right."

Dricks sighed, but was cut short by ZZ3's monotone voice. "Twins are secured; retardant administered. Returning to the hold."

"Strap in, Dricks."

"This ain't my first rodeo, Rebekah. Copy that."

Exhausted, dipping in and out of consciousness, Rebekah's senses twitched at the low-level alarm from the console. She blinked away her blurred vision, and eyed the data packet from the probe. The shuttle had slowed its acceleration, and the navcom had calculated a course and burn estimate as instructed. A check showed the corvette would gain on them, but very slowly.

With a glimmer of a smile, she engaged the changes, and the gentle reduction in their acceleration began. Immediately her shoulders eased, relaxed and then screamed their aches at her. A sliver of sympathy threaded into her mind for Hendricks, but it didn't stop her engaging the chip. Flooding her brain with relief and allowing her to at least shift out of the pilot's seat. Gently, she ran through the high-g stretch and exercise routine the Marines had ingrained in them and headed for her cabin. As soon as your muscles relaxed, it was a race to the bathroom.

A check on Savvo brought more relief. The medbot ignoring the effects of the hard burn and merrily administering the anti-toxin it had synthesised. His vitals hadn't stabilised yet, but his skin was less grey and sickly. The prognosis looked more hopeful than she had feared, and with a squeeze of his arm, she left him sedated and unaware of the shit they were in.

After that, she knocked at the girls' door, not expecting an answer but it was prudent. On entering, she found them strapped to their berths, eyes displaying REM. Satisfied, she left them to sleep. If ZZ3 had acted as instructed, a mild reviver would awaken them in a few minutes, but that could wait. A ship full of their stress was not what she needed right now.

As she made to leave, her eye caught a single tentacle protruding from the adapted sump box. Alive, thankfully. Curious, she went to check on the symbiote. Senti hated high grav, requiring an encounter suit even at standard. The symbiote had proven hardier, but TB had clearly suffered under the burn. A glance told her it was ill. A panic set in, images of what might happen to her crew after Heki and Tremil found out, drilling into her mind's eye. Its skin was dull grey and flaky with the alien flattened against the base, its raised tentacle weak and hardly moving. Rebekah let her finger touch the tip. A tingle itched across her skin, the tentacle easing out further to wrap itself fully around. She left it there, and though the colour never changed, the body seemed to puff out a little.

"Got to go, TB," she said quietly, almost as if the twins were asleep and not sedated. As she withdrew her finger, she felt the gentlest of tears that left a lived red mark on her skin.

Shit.

Realisation struck. She looked to the girls, thoughts of their bodies being eaten by the alien revolting her, and that she'd let it happen. A trembling hand alighted on Tremil, and gently she eased the skinsuit at her shoulder aside. She looked for marks, especially around the neck and head where, now she thought of it, TB often sat. Nothing. Trying to drag back any memories, she recalled they often stroked the alien while it sat in their palms, or on their forearms. Rolling up Tremil's sleeve, there were marks, obvious against the girl's white skin but far less red than on her finger, and only a few. Checking the other arm, and then Heki, there appeared little damage. On a normal teenager, there'd be the bruising of a normal life. Even that was absent.

She sighed, confused about what to do, and in the end turning towards the door. Both girls had been changing, and she couldn't deny it was for the better. How much was the symbiote's influence was up for debate, be it simply a focus for their love and attention, or something it was actively doing. It could wait. But not forever.

"Arin, Dricks. Meet me in the galley," she said on exiting the cabin. "No, scrub that, fetch a drink and we'll meet in the cargo hold."

"Crew?" Rebekah said, pointing towards ZZ3.

"I am," repeated the bot, "crew."

"Do you understand our misgivings?" she asked. "Can you tell how we feel about this ... change?"

"Reticence, mistrust, concern," said the warbot. "I can say the words, and that part of me, the pacified Asham element, images their meaning. I will not admit to 'feeling' them. But I *experience* them."

Arin stepped up to the huge warbot, leaning back slightly to meet its pulsing gaze. "What about trust?"

A pause followed, and the bot shifted position, lowering its gaze. "This is a known concept, but one Asham cannot image. It is … absent from his lexicon."

"Sounds about right," interjected Dricks, bitterness in the twist to her mouth, hands rising to rest on her hips. "Especially after you tried to burn a hole through Rebekah's skull."

"That was not me, this me. The one our glorious leader created by engaging the pacifist program while I was—"

"Possessed," filled in Arin. "Look," he continued, turning his back to the machine, "ZZ3 could rip our arms and legs off and play softball with our heads. There is not a bloody thing we could do about it. But it hasn't. I know that you both think I'm having a love-in with a warbot, sorry ZZ3 – check in your lexicon for 'jealousy' – but that's as clear as day."

"Why are we here, Rebekah? Discussing this now while we have a corvette halfway up our arse." Dricks crossed her arms, and began to shuffle her feet, the magboots rhythmically clanking.

"*Because* of that, and the shuttle we're chasing. I need to know what ZZ3 is willing to do, and how much we trust ZZ3 to carry out our orders. Otherwise, we're relying on just us three if things get heavy." She leant against a crate.

"I will act as crew," said the warbot. "But please understand, the pacifist program prevents initiating direct conflict. I am able to protect, and if required, damage life at the minimum level to ensure my, and my fellow crew members, survival."

Arin turned back to the bot. "That sounds like my algorithm. You know those parameters will require judgement on your part, now. For how minimum is minimum? And here's some advice: Asham is not the part of you to make that judgement, otherwise we'll have a shipload of tentacles and teeth to deal with."

"Agreed. I will need to build a baseline over time."

"Predictably unpredictable," said Hendricks. "Just like the man who programmed you."

"Agreed," said ZZ3, and the eyes swirled.

Rebekah stood, looking to Hendricks and Arin in turn. Her mind turned over the possibilities, and they were painfully few without ZZ3's help. Could a bot lie? Asham certainly would. But she needed all the shit they and Benetai had been through to mean something, to not be for nothing. To understand why the wetware was so important both to the Enforcers, as she believed Duboit as far as she could spit, and the fucking Bustan Navy. They had committed a corvette to its retrieval, with an officer on board prepared to threaten, even murder, an entire space station.

"Okay, here's the deal. I want plans, right? Get all those organic brains in gear and work out how we get out of this shithole we've found ourselves in."

"With ZZ3?" asked Arin, thumb pointing towards the warbot.

"Yeah," she replied.

I just hope that the risk is worth it.

"Right now, we don't know if Ormsk thinks we have the wetware or not. He appears to not be aware of the shuttle, or if he is, that we are chasing it down. He won't attack unless he's sure, so that gives us leeway." She waited, eyeing all three, and finding herself including ZZ3 now.

"If they have Marauders aboard, it could be a moot point." Arin raised his eyebrows as he spoke. "They're no Skyriders, but tough bastards when it comes to space combat."

Marauders hadn't been in her thoughts. Space Marines whose main role was to board ships in orbit. The hull skin felt a little less secure all of a sudden, not helped by memories of Toms and the crew of the *Maverick*.

She nodded, looking to Arin and then Hendricks. "Take that into con-sideration. How we defend ourselves, how we take the shuttle, and reserve some thought for what we do if that Bustan corvette gets wind of the other ship and goes for it instead of us. Move."

Arin and Dricks nodded, muttering between themselves as they departed the cargo hold, leaving Rebekah and the warbot facing each other. The silence was palpable, until the bot shuffled itself slightly to the side, averting its gaze.

"Mistrust is a word Asham can image. From that, I can extrapolate the meaning of trust. Imprecise."

"But a start. So here's a question, ZZ3. One that sets my crew apart from all others. Would you sacrifice yourself, so that one of us may live?"

She didn't wait for an answer.

CHAPTER 33

Davina sat with legs together, slate in front of her, waiting for the false holo of Duboit to appear. The expected qualms over Geghid's murder not surfacing. Her Incini training perhaps? Or the dulled effect of her sensory wetware? Both possibilities, but in reality, it was nothing short of what the real Duboit would have requested. It was simply *expected*, and it was slowly dawning that the emotional turmoil created by the twins, and the crew of the *Sunstar*, was exactly that. Turmoil. They disturbed the ripples of her mind, her future. The rock protruding from the otherwise glassy river causing the water to part, swirl and foam around it. Her Incini training nagged at her to smooth the flow, but in truth, those were the moments when she felt truly alive. Something worth surviving for, even with blood on her hands.

Still.

Calm.

Breathe.

The desk shimmered, and Duboit/Erikson appeared on a chair. The Senti tech projecting him in real time. A mark of how far advanced they were, though human contact had threatened to bring them low.

Because that's what we do to each other, and those around us. Even those we love. We can't help it. A big cauldron of spite and hate, while we dress up in a banal skin for others to see.

"Davina," said Erikson. "I assume all is in hand?"

She double checked the room was secure, then provided a thin smile for her new boss. "Yes, Mr Erikson. As agreed, and contracted. The issue has been eradicated, the data wiped."

"Good. I have been contemplating the information provided, and regard the issue of the asteroid field as a further area for investigation." He leant forward, steepling his fingers. "I want to know what's happening *inside* that field as a matter of priority."

"That will, of course, be difficult to achieve and retain any vestige of secrecy, if that's part of your intent." She wanted to shuffle in her chair, Erikson's intense stare making her feel uncomfortable. There was a deepness there, despite it being an image, that had not been prevalent before. Predatory, yes. A hunger, but with a different edge to it. Fervour, perhaps? So hard to tell over a holo. It could, of course, be false. Could.

"Under the auspices of the Incini tenets, I would like you to advise me on a course of action."

That took her by surprise, and she restrained any physical response in case he caught it. Being at any disadvantage in negotiations had been beaten out of her, verbally and emotionally, by the Directorate. Refusing to let it cloud her mind, she stared straight ahead, her face a mask, while her thoughts whirled. Advise?

She played along, hoping to draw out his reasons. "So contractually from this point?"

"Yes," he replied, resting his chin on the steepled finger briefly, before leaning back into his chair. "Agreed?"

There was little choice. And if she kept a modicum of control over the stream of information, and gleaned enough of what he was discovering, perhaps she could keep that special rock above the flow.

Rebekah said those girls changed their lives. And now mine.

"The Enforcer's role is not usually allied to actions in the black, so to speak." Was that disdain she could hear in Erikson's voice? Yes, and she had heard it before. "And though it pains me, you are best placed and the most experienced operative to *advise*."

Operative. Damn, I hate that word.

"Okay. Here's my first point. If you want secrecy, then I would suggest you send expendable humans only. There are companies that could get through that field, but it will be expensive and obvious, and far from silent. Their crews are also not disposable. So, I suggest you go full auto, with oversight by a salvager crew thinking they're onto a score."

"You're talking as if you know one," Erikson said.

"Oh, I do. And, if I may be so bold, one that would have a vested interest in finding out what happened to Toms." Davina enjoyed the brief look of surprise on Erikson's face. Yes, she could be ruthless. Prided herself on it in the past.

"Full circle. And perhaps, tidy a loose end. And what about the equipment? Will they have experience in such matters?"

"That I can't answer. But if they don't know someone who can oversight auto-machine access, I will dig until I can find someone looking for a little extra money. There are enough drunks and addicts out on the belt to fill several ships. I'm sure one will be clear-headed enough for as long as we need."

"Agreed, then. And the machinery?"

"Let me put the team together first, and then I can, under Incini contract, get them to advise on what we would need. I know," she said, cutting Erikson's protestation short, "I'll keep the real purpose and location hidden even with the contract. There are enough scavenger scrapyards we can scour if need be."

"And after?" Erikson asked. "Once through we will need a survey of what's there."

"Survey? Of what type?" Davina asked, but she had her suspicions. The Scourge's ship had two possibilities on board. Tech such as the Battle AI, or something more sinister hinted at by Rebekah.

"Visual, chem analysis and bio."

Davina thought a second. It would also have to be able to penetrate a ship. Humans were ideal for that. Especially disposable ones.

"All achievable."

Davina ran her finger around the glass rim, scraping off the combination of synth sugar and salt that had soaked up enough of the cocktail to leave a zing on her tongue. She licked her fingertip, then placed the ornate glass onto the faux wooden table. It clunked, the unseen maglock combination of glass base and the table taking hold. With a slight smile, she sat back into the plush sofa and took the opportunity to glance around the bar. Everything was that single step to the left of what you would call 'classy'. As if someone had taken an image of a higher end cocktail bar on Level 4, even Level 3, and redrawn it for a comic book.

"Each to their own," she said, sipping her cocktail and trying not to take in the awful chandelier above her head.

"Hey, you looking for company?" The voice grated along her spine. Her wetware kicked in, senses on full alert, and she devised a picture of the man in her mind well before he made to sit down in the chair opposite. When he appeared, she'd only got the hair wrong. Must have had had a regen. Late fifties, a paunch he hid beneath well-tailored clothes, and jowls that spoke of hard work and even harder play. She guessed at three divorces, and not noble, hence he was still having to work to pay them off without an Incini contract to wave at his former spouses.

"No," she said, and drilled the point home with a cold stare. The faux cocktail bar was one of Victor's most lucrative money-earners. Those from the high grav levels below taking a risqué punt on getting laid, drunk and likely skint. "You still here?"

"No need to be rude," he replied, and pulled the knees of his trousers back slightly before rising from the over-stuffed chair. "I was only being gentlemanly."

"And I'm only being ladylike. You don't want to make me unladylike. I promise, you wouldn't enjoy it." She added a level of malevolent glee to her smile, and he sidled off, muttering words she didn't care about. He passed Victor and the woman Davina had initially associated as his second-in-command until the report on Geghid's removal. She made a note to find out more.

"Davina," said Victor, his voice smooth but false. Hiding an accent that tickled at the edges of each syllable. He sat without ceremony, taking up the chair opposite while the woman sat by Davina's side. It was the first time they'd met, but she didn't speak. With Davina's wetware already up and running, she caught the faintest flicker of a holo-mask.

"And you are?" she inquired, looking directly at the woman.

The woman tipped her chin, acknowledging Davina. "Sabier," she replied. Davina stored the image of her face only for reference. The brown hair, freckled skin and green-flecked eyes would change the moment she walked away. What she took in was the body shape, the curve of the muscles, her mannerisms. Not so easy to mask.

"A pleasure," she replied. "I hope."

"You have business to discuss?" asked Victor. A waiter placed his drink down, an amber liquid with a chunk of ice floating at its centre. He didn't acknowledge the man at all.

"I do. I assume there are no ears."

"None. Despite my reputation, this place is devoid of any recording devices. My clientele like to be discreet, and on such a small rock ..." He shrugged, eyes flicking over to Sabier before returning to smile at Davina.

She didn't believe a word of it, and slid her hand into her purse to withdraw a dampener.

"Then you won't mind if I add a little extra Duboit-certified protection." It wasn't a question, and she switched on the device, resting it next to the remains of her cocktail. The glower from Sabier pierced the holo-mask, and Davina took a little joy from – as Rebekah would put it – *pissing* her off.

Victor pursed his lips but nodded, not that she had left him any choice. "So?" he asked.

"I want to subcontract the *Maverick* for Mr Duboit. And I think you're going to like where he wants it to go." Sabier leaned closer at her words, unable, in Davina's opinion, to hold back her interest.

"Go on," said Victor, equally curious but better at hiding it.

"Mr Duboit wants something surveyed. It'll require a mixed team of humans and bots to achieve, including the salvaging skills of your new crew." She kept the distaste for the previous crew out of her tone.

"You truly are an Incini," he said. "Does it not bother you? What supposedly happened?"

"Did happen, and no. A contract is a contract, emotions don't come into it. Besides, if Mr Duboit thought for a moment that you were involved in the assault upon his contracted ship and crew, as well as his fully paid for Incini on board, he'd have you – how would you put it? – *fucked* up by now. Literally. Up to the *Hatton*, our dealings have been mutually beneficial. You have what Mr Duboit needs, he has the creds you so love." She smiled, tilting her head, and switching her gaze over to Sabier. Davina wished she knew the woman better, her posture tight and hinting at something more than just another job. As if what she proposed was more personal.

Victor held both hands up, placating. "No, Toms was acting alone. Nothing to do with us, I assure you. So, our ship and crew, and I presume survey bots?"

"I'll arrange for those and likely an autoship to carry what you need. Entry into the asteroid field, I hear, is nearly impossible. It's going to take some serious equipment, and you'll need an expert to oversee all that kit. Someone you can keep in the dark." Again Davina noted the glance over to Sabier. What was the dynamic here?

"I think I know the right person. How soon?" asked Victor.

"As in tomorrow. Mr Duboit is not a patient man when it comes to money."

"A week," said Sabier, finally taking the lead. "If you can get the entry equipment sorted in that time. This 'expert' I can make contact with tomorrow. He won't say no, he owes me." The voice had a hard edge to it. Harsh, and Davina couldn't work out if it, too, was digitally altered.

"Agreed, under Incini tenets, this is now the basis for further negotiation," she said, moving her focus to Sabier.

"Agreed," said Victor, but Davina ignored him. The suit wasn't fooling anyone anymore. Her eyes were for the woman.

"Yes, agreed," Sabier finally said.

"Have the details encrypted to my private slate. Set me a starting price, you know how Mr Duboit works. And I will need that name once you have it." Davina stood, ignoring the dregs of her cocktail, and collected her dampener.

"Incini," said Sabier, continuing as she caught Davina's attention. "What about salvage rights? For anything we find?"

Davina stared at the woman; her gaze cold. "You are to be contracted under Incini tenets. Waiver from those, Mr Duboit and I can act as we see fit. One hint that anything from that site has been stolen from Mr Duboit, or shared, or even spoken of, and the *Maverick* will be your tomb. Understand? I'll ask again. Are we in agreement?"

Whether Sabier's pause was shock, or consideration, Davina couldn't tell. But the message had hit home.

"We are."

Davina turned away, striding through the bar, desperate for some air. Her sensory wetware caught talk of 'her eyes' as she left, a threat perhaps, but she had an Enforcer at her back and Duboit's creds in her pocket.

A cold, airless tomb.

CHAPTER 34

Rebekah stroked Heki's brow, watching the slowdown of the rapid-eye movements and the twitch of a cheek. Satisfied she was waking up, she walked over to Tremil, repeating the touch and the girl opened her eyes, locking onto Rebekah's.

"You good?" asked Rebekah, ensuring her earworm was up and running. Tremil's burst of warmth and love rolled over her puny effort, and the girl pulled her in tight.

"Jealous over here," said Heki.

Rebekah glanced over her shoulder to find the girl lifting her head from the bed.

"Hey, you missed your chance," replied Tremil before releasing Rebekah.

"I need you both on station. Five minutes," she said. "Crew don't get to lay about when there's work to be done." Rebekah forced herself not to look for the alien, trying to store that worry for another time. The list was increasing moment by moment.

"The Bustan ..." started Tremil.

"Still chasing, and the shuttle is still running. We're getting closer, but without Savvo I'm a little short in the cockpit." She noted the worry in both girls' eyes and pressing at her earworm. "The medbot has him sedated while the anti-tox does its magic."

And if we don't sort this mess out, he's probably in the best place.

"Five minutes, no more. Heki, I'll need you in the cockpit, Trem on the sensors and comms." She left them to wake themselves up and gathered a bite to eat. She quickly drank a flask of water before settling into her chair. This was going to be tough, the hole they were in deep and airless.

"Captain," said Arin over comms. "Come back."

"Here," she said. "All okay?"

"No. Well, yes and no. Dricks has talked me through that session with the Bustan tight wad. The officer. I think … I think this is maybe my fault. Why they're chasing us."

"Short of telling them the Butcher is sat in my hold having a tea party with our pet warbot, I'm not sure you can shoulder any blame," replied Rebekah, trying to quieten the crack of a thumb knuckle. She was still annoyed about the Senti he'd killed. A senseless death that needn't have occurred with more care, and a potential source of information. Though, it being alive might have destroyed their story for Ormsk.

"Wished I'd thought of that. I just said ZZ3 was having a beer with him. No … I called the wetware 'chips'."

Rebekah could sense his concern. He was right, he'd flagged them as Marines with that term and shot a hole through their merc façade, but it was no biggie. Except, perhaps, it put Hannos on the back foot with her own background. Could explain the threat to destroy the station. But Ormsk probably had 'bastard' stamped on his birth certificate.

"No worries. Consider yourself cashiered from the Marines. The Wrecking Squad, however, are far more forgiving."

"Thanks, Captain."

Heki clomped into the cockpit, rubbing her eyes and finishing a break-fast bar as she sat down and strapped in. A yawn and a sleepy blink of the eyes churned Rebekah's stomach.

"Just help get us out of this, yeah. Stay focused on us, and let Savvo fight his own battle. Run a check on the point debris cannons in case we need them."

"Copy that." The comms clicked off.

"Where is it?" said Heki, leaning in, hands on the console screen as she swiped left and right.

"Where's what?" But she immediately saw what Heki referred to. The shuttle had gone, the sensors no longer picking out its engine trail nor pinging back its signature.

"It's gone full camo again," said Heki. "As Dricks put it. Harder at this distance to pick it out by what it masks, as there's not a lot else there to compare against." Heki's sleepy expression had gone, replaced by an intensity that she exuded into the cockpit. Rebekah noted the absence of TB, and the wave of emotion rolling off the girl. She didn't have the headspace for an earworm, and adjusted the comms unit to help cut out the emotional noise.

"Have they picked us up?" she said, more for herself than Heki.

"Trem," said the twin, not looking to Rebekah. "Can you check through the sensor logs, see if we've been pinged by the shuttle out front since we were under."

"Copy that," replied Tremil.

Rebekah nodded, breaking out in a proud smile before catching herself. "Heki, can you calculate a projected flight-path based on their trajectory and the last velocity estimate?"

"On it," she replied. "I have a burst packet from thirty minutes ago. I can work off that, too."

"Captain." Trem's voice was uncertain, trembling. "We are being hailed."

Her heart sank. It wasn't the shuttle offering to surrender, that was for sure. Ormsk.

"The Navy?"

"Yes."

She tried to mask the sigh, but Heki's glance indicated she had failed miserably to shield her feelings. "Put them on." She rolled her neck and cracked her thumbs. "This is the *Solar Flame*, Captain Khan speaking."

There was a delay, about ten seconds, before the comms kicked back into response. "This is the BSN *Ansta* for Lieutenant Ormsk."

"Captain Khan, how not pleasurable to speak to you." The voice was certain, self-confident. But then, he had a Navy corvette beneath his arse, so why shouldn't he be.

"Likewise," she responded.

"Now, I'm going to cut out all the blah blah blah. You said, he said, all that rubbish. You have my wetware, I presume. I want it. I don't get it, then boom!"

"Lieutenant Ormsk, I d—"

"Wait a second, will you? Release the missile. Yes, the homing one. Sorry about that. The life of a Navy officer is never dull. Where was I? Oh yes. You give me the wetware, you don't die. That sounds like the perfect deal to me. Lieutenant Ormsk of the Bustan Navy signing off." The comms went dead.

Rebekah's heart hammered.

"We have been painted," said Heki, her words tight. "Is that the right word?"

Rebekah checked the information coming in. A single missile, locked on and burning its way across the divide. Savvo would have known its capabilities and reaction time, what few options they had. Right now, she could see none.

"Heki?"

"I'm okay," she said. "I am."

Rebekah wasn't convinced, but the girls were always better with a focus.

"Captain," said Tremil. "We were not pinged by the shuttle. I don't believe they know we were chasing. The attached probe is still emitting."

"Thank you. Heki, I need that flight-path urgently," she said. "Tremil, can you monitor the missile on our tail? I want timings, and if chance, see if you have anything on its capabilities. Anything at all."

How long would Ormsk give them? Would he prolong the torture? It was clear he had no clue about the shuttle. How could she use that?

"Model loaded," said Heki, her eyes tracking something on her screen. "Seems to be solid, consistent. But it's the middle of nowhere." She swiped the information across to the pilot's monitor.

Rebekah poured over it. "What's that?" she asked, and drew out the image along the shuttle's flight-path. A dwarf planet amid an icy belt in the outer system. Her console flagged it immediately.

No.

"Durnat," she whispered. They'd been played. "Fucking Scarva."

"The Senti?"

It all clicked into place. The mind-read. The alien must have scanned more than just the bloody *Hatton*. Rifled through their minds until it found something of interest to a Senti. Something worth the alien's time and effort. If the Wrecking Squad were after the wetware, and willing to pay Scarva for the FTL, expend the fuel to acquire the tech, then Scarva must have decided it was worth stabbing them in the back over. Either assuming it contained special memories worth a fortune on the dream-peddler's market, or the tech itself had value. More, it appeared, than the promise of their war memories.

Or perhaps the bastard had assumed he could make a play for both? She wouldn't put it past the alien scumbag.

Heki tapped her screen, bringing up an image of the shuttle before it had disappeared the first time. "Scarva? The Senti? The shuttle acts like Asham's containment unit, the Senti metal."

"The cloaking shit? That settles it. We know where they're going, and why. Tell Trem to keep listening for the probe. They'll have gone camo because they've stopped accelerating. We can take a risk and focus on Ormsk."

"Copy that," said Heki.

"Arin, Dricks. Meet me in the hold."

After outlining her theory, at which Dricks attacked a cargo box for a few minutes, Rebekah attached her slate to a maglock on the hold wall. It projected the missiles Tremil had found in an old database. Likely a little out of date, but enough to give Arin kittens.

"Locked on," he said. "Like the last dance at the school disco. No escaping if the tech is as good as ours. You have to bring it down, which, I might say, would require an Almaarian Navy ship with a hold full of defensive missiles and not a shitty repair and recovery ship spitting buckshot."

"Sounding confident," said Rebekah. Arin just shook his head.

"No outrunning them, either. Missiles don't have to give a shit about anything organic going squish. Right now, they're not even trying to catch us up." Dricks hit the cargo box again, achieving a dent which seemed to satisfy her. "Why ain't they shooting us down? Why cloak and dagger shit with a missile?"

Arin blew out his cheeks. "Because they don't want us dead yet, that right Captain? They want the cargo, the bloody wetware, and blowing us to hell won't get them that. Any stray PDC slugs could hit the wrong engine system and kablooie." He mimed the ship exploding.

She squeezed her hands together, trying to prevent herself from cracking any more knuckles. "Options? The point cannons?"

"PDC is a bit of a misnomer. They're debris canons for clearing out rocks or stray scrap metal on the belt. Too slow to react," said Arin. "By the time they pick up the missile, it'll be past them and knocking at my cabin door."

"We could lock them into the long-range sensors," said Hendricks. "That do it?"

"If it's doable, it would require a serious software upgrade. Throwing rocks might be better if they choose to dodge aside. If Trem's right, they have manoeuvring thrusters. Just the smallest adjustment, and we're done. I mean, they've sent a very expensive missile to catch an unarmed snail."

Rebekah squeezed the bridge between her eyes, trying to push away the outpour of emotions filling the ship. She felt every nuance of the twins' worry, and it grated on her own.

"The containment unit," said Arin, wheeling about to stare at the black coffin behind ZZ3. "We don't have the wetware, but we do have their real target. Asham."

She'd been waiting for this moment, unsure in her own mind what other options they had. But Arin had explained ZZ3's opinion of what lay in that box, and she had locked that away. Bricked it behind her mounting worries over surviving the next few hours. Was Asham's knowledge – the Scourge and the Butcher – worth their lives? What would the Bustan do with it? Fuck, she didn't even trust what was in there with her own people. The crew of the *Scourge*, and the Skyriders, deserved more than them just giving it up. They had died horrendously at the hands of Asham, and instead of destroying what he created, the Court hid it away.

"No." she said. "It dies with us."

Arin nodded. "Thought you'd say that. But hey, someone had to bring up the coffin in the room."

"I am crew," said ZZ3, and it sidled around, almost, but not quite, part of the circle. "I have two concepts to share."

Arin looked up at the bot with a shake to his head. "Even you ain't fast enough, ZZ3."

Rebekah felt the bot's red eyes on her and nodded her assent. "Go ahead."

"Not me. The probes. Drop them behind on the missiles' approach ..." The voice was flat, but insistent.

Arin filled in the pause, eyes widening. "You mean link them to the debris cannons? It'd give them a fighting chance."

"Not waiting for the sensor return, but acting on a direct trigger burst," said Hendricks, excitement rising in her voice. "It'd take some serious timing. Are these fuckers nuclear?"

Rebekah checked the slate, drawing out the data to project into the hold. "They can take a nuclear warhead. But the corvette will hit its wake, get the full radiation wash. Wouldn't make sense to screw themselves over. And expensive. We're a fly to squash, not a warship."

"This could work," said Arin. "I'll get on the changes. Can I get Heki to help?"

"Both if it helps." Rebekah looked up to ZZ3's pulsing eyes. "You said two concepts."

The pulse stopped, and ZZ3 stilled. "I have the answer to your question, my Captain."

CHAPTER 35

"I'm getting bored, Captain Khan," said Ormsk. "I want *my* wetware. You haven't taken the hint about how much I want it. Perhaps ..."

Rebekah cracked a thumb, and side-eyed Heki who was pointedly staring at her console exactly like Savvo would whenever he knew there was a storm coming. She'd checked on him on the way past, unable to keep away. She needed to keep them all alive so they could get drunk together again. Well, all but two of them. No, three, if ZZ3 was truly crew.

"We don't have it, Lieutenant."

"You taunted me on a lie? Come, come, Khan. Surely not?"

She considered selling out the shuttle, and Scarva, the whole lot. But would Ormsk believe her story? Or even consider tackling Scarva and his Senti ship. No one truly knew their capabilities. The *Unpronounceable* could likely jump away. And besides, she had a strong sense this bastard would just blow them up and then go look.

Heki looked her way, eyes slightly downcast, a catch in her breath. Rebekah muted the comms.

"What?"

"The missile is accelerating, closing in." The fear rolling over from the twin battered at her mind. There was no way Rebekah would be able to focus if Heki couldn't keep herself under control. This wasn't the time for sensitivities.

"I can't save us if you can't keep yourself together." She winced, self-loathing joining the throng battering at her earworm. "Please, Heki."

The girl looked at her, wide-eyed, a tremor in her cheek as a tear rolled down. "I'll be back," she said, unclipping, moving almost at a run in her magboots as she headed out the cockpit.

Rebekah swore, then unmuted the comms. "I take it you've upped the ante."

"You could say that. Last chance. My beautiful missile versus your stubbornness. I do hope you make the right choice." Ormsk's self-satisfied tone grated, but she couldn't let herself react. "Five minutes. Slow your engines, transfer me the cargo. And you can go on your merry mercenary way."

Heki dropped back into her co-pilot seat. Tentacles rippled at the back of her neck. Her cheeks were flushed, but her face wore that determined teenager look. The one Rebekah used to use whenever her Pa mentioned her choice of clothes, friends, or the gods forbid, grades. The cockpit was calm, no emotional earthquakes, and in the middle of trying to save their lives, the reason why slotted home.

Perfect time for a symbiote revelation.

"Nothing to stop you from blowing us out of the black afterwards," she said to Ormsk.

"True. But that's a risk you'll have to take. The more you ... how would a roughneck term it ... piss me off, the less likely I am to be forgiving. Five minutes to live, while I accelerate that missile and we both lose." The comms went dead.

She glanced at Heki, but ignored the symbiote. "Okay?"

"Yes," she said, the monotone back with words spoken through tight lips.

It would have to do.

"Tremil, you ready?" she said. "I think everything is about to happen real fast. I will need you to work with Arin as you have the data and the links."

"Speeding up," said Heki. "Missile strike in four minutes and thirty seconds."

"Yes, Captain. I'm ready, but its Dricks on the probe drop. Arin is busy." Tremil stated.

"Busy? Arin, come back. Speak to me."

"Busy, Cap. Plan B. Do your thing."

"Fuck," she said. "*Arin.*"

"No time. Trem and Dricks are on it. Be ready to hit hard burn." His comms cut out, and she slammed a fist onto the console, making Heki jump and the symbiote's colours ripple.

"Four minutes," said Heki.

"First probe away," said Trem. "Tracking."

The comms crackled, and hissed. "How are we doing, Captain? Not the least bit tempted to sort this little problem out face-to-face? Oh look. Three minutes and forty seconds. Tell you what, let's add a little more juice."

"Accelerating," said Heki. "Three minutes."

"Fuck!" shouted Rebekah. She had no control. None.

"Second probe released," said Tremil, her voice flat. "PDCs firing."

She gripped the sides of the console monitor, willing the data feed to pronounce a hit. Anything. In her mind, she could feel the rattle of the guns, the power of the slugs as they spun through space. Only space was big, and the missile small and fast. They were screwed, and she sat there impotent, heart aching.

"Second probe contact. Continuous fire engaged," said Tremil.

The feed showed no explosions, no in-space spark of light to announce their safety. Everything had escalated so fast. Lieutenant Ormsk had them dancing on a string, or was it a hangman's rope?

"I calculate I have one minute before I can no longer disengage the missile, shame," said Ormsk. "Fifty seconds, forty ..."

"Multiple hits," announced Trem.

"The missile is using thrusters to dodge the main slug pattern," added Heki. "One minute fifteen until ship contact."

"Goodbye Captain. A sad story comes to an end."

"Probes away," said Tremil. "Proximity countdown. Five, four ..."

"What?" she said. "What's happening?"

Rebekah swiped her screen, pulling up a visual of the rear of the ship. Multiple probes scattered from the ejection system, trailing behind.

"Plan B. Hit hard burn!" bellowed Arin.

Rebekah engaged, the ship's engines ramming up high, thrusting the ship into hard and vicious acceleration.

"Two," continued Tremil, her voice strained. "One, proximity contact."

Space, for the briefest of moments, was no longer black. Instead, it lit with yellows and hues of orange as multiple probes exploded at once, forging a cloud of shrapnel, battering at the faint sliver of metal speeding their way.

Rebekah's heart thundered in her chest. Rapid acceleration rattled her ship, pressed its captain into her chair, while she watched her crew's future unfold on the monitor.

And a second flare lit space.

"Yeehaw!" shouted Arin. "Whap! Got the bastard!"

"How?"

"Cut the burn," Arin said, wheezing.

Rebekah's fingers reached out and disengaged the acceleration, letting the strained breath trapped in her lungs escape. "Arin? What the hell happened?"

"I strapped ZZ3's engine disengagement explosives to the last of the probes. Worth a shot according to Trem. Just call me 'our glorious saviour' from now on and I'll be satisfied with that."

"So tell me, our glorious saviour, can you do that again?" Rebekah pressed a hand to her chest, one part of her revelling in the strain of her lungs as it meant she, and her crew, were still alive.

"Shit out of probes," he said. "At least you can call me hero for the next few minutes."

Ormsk cut through on the Bustan frequency. "Can you hear me clapping? No? That was a very expensive missile you made me waste. Hang on a minute, training a new bridge crew. Yes, Ensign, I said shoot the bitch down with the PDCs on my command. Where was I? Oh yes. I want my *fucking* cargo. You have thirty seconds to comply."

Heki yipped. A flinch and cry laced with fear, hands white as they gripped her chair. Rebekah reached out and squeezed the girl's arm. That they lived was down to Arin and Trem's flash of ingenuity. But life was full of shit luck. The PDCs would rip through them.

"ZZ3, you're up."

"Yes, Captain."

Rebekah ground her teeth, a dual crack of her knuckles followed, then she activated her comms. "Okay Ormsk. You win. I am dropping the cargo in five …"

"Dropping? Wait …"

"Three, two …" She eyed the cargo hold doors on her internal feed, the Almaarian Navy stamped box Davina had added to their manifest only a few months back, locked in the jaws of the cargo loader. It no longer contained the armoured spacesuits Duboit had obtained. Instead, a warbot balled as tight as it could, sat inside, promising a last hope on a whim and a prayer. Images of the searing plasma torch mere centimetres from her visor flashed into her head. The breathing, the malevolence. ZZ3's expressionless face lit by the glee of its dreadful eyes.

Good luck. Be crew.

"One. Cargo away. Hope you have a fucking big net, Ormsk. Khan out."

"PDC cannon fire engaged. Coned around the cargo box," Heki stated.

She eyed Heki, and shook her head. They were going to suffer. "Belt up, batten down. Hard burn in three, two, one. Mark." Engaging additional power, and ramming on the manoeuvring thrusters, she started to steer the ship and its crew through another hell. Taking the *Solar Flame* née *Sunstar* on as rapid a curve as she dared away from Ormsk's trajectory. He had a choice: follow and miss the offered cargo, or chase them down.

"Now who's raising the ante, fucker?"

Target sensory sweep detected. Passive sensors active.

Estimated outside temperature remains, as our glorious leader puts it, cold. Space cold. Death's touch. Bloody freezing.

I'm rambling.

What is this? Am I remembering fear?

Is this what being crew means? To fear for yourself, as well as others?

Is that right, Asham? Did you know fear?

'Of virtual prison, yes. Of being locked away, my brilliance sealed from the world.'

ZZ3 experienced that fear, and considered whether the main part of Asham that remained in the containment unit would be experiencing it right now. A virtual cell, with no contact with the outside. Alone. What would a brain patterned mind be thinking? He had taken the prison brought by the Skyriders, and extended its touch and influence across his hollow asteroid. Forging himself into what was not an AI, but a virtual Asham. His mind spread across the mainframe and the containment unit, his limbs the bots, and fingers those of his personal guard he had operated upon. Sealed their fate with bastardised wetware. And ZZ3 was to be his legs. Armoured, powerful. A reflection of how he saw himself.

Temperature adjusting. 90% likelihood I am entering a ship's hold.

The storage box came to a sudden halt. ZZ3's head section jarred, quivering slightly as the only part of the warbot not pressed in against the box sides. Its motion sensors began to recalibrate, and the warbot could feel the box shudder and then move rigidly in a straight line.

Clamped. But how? By the lid? The sides? 100% certainty we are aboard the Bustan Corvette registered 23/CV/BSN.

More data required.

ZZ3 pressed one limb against the box, haptic and other sensors feeding its electronic brain, running through the computations while Asham moaned and groaned impotently about being on a Bustan ship.

Pacified hate. Such a strange thing. You hate the Bustan, but are incapable of taking action. It was they that wanted you in a virtual prison, and here you are, inside a virtual prison on a Bustan Navy ship. Does your lexicon include irony?

Temperature changes noted. Assuming hold is being pressurised for human access.

Waiting protocol engaged.

Pacified warbot protocols remain pacified. Attack and destroy negated.

We are crew.

Self-devised protocol activated.

Waiting…

A second sensor sweep washed over the box. The first had been out in the black, the corvette checking what might be inside. Their first concern would be for a bomb of some form. Their next whether the cargo contained inert equipment as expected. ZZ3 had reduced all activity down to a single shielded processing unit.

The lid disengaged.

And ZZ3 no longer waited.

I am crew.

The warbot exploded from the box, limbs grasping the lid from the jaws of the cargo loader. Sensory information filled its fully activated mind. Three Bustan Navy crew stood around, a variety of tools in their hands, while a fourth held a weapon that twitched its way.

ZZ3 lifted the lid, guiding it into the path of the streaming bullets. The metal dented, the pattern analysis sweeping through the warbot, and it threw the lid towards the Bustan Marine. It crashed into his chest. The Marine had been over-cautious in their magboot setting of choice, as the snap of his shins echoed through the hold.

Overzealous.

'Checking lexicon now. Image sent.'

Yuk. Asham. You have issues.

'Had. Pacified, remember. Our glorious leader has altered my algorithm.'

ZZ3 thrashed a limb out, knocking the crew members aside. The adjusted strength, direction and speed applied maintaining their life signs while removing their threat level.

Two lower limbs pulled the bot from the storage box, and sensors swept the hold, identifying the camera systems. The warbot grabbed the screaming Marines' discarded weapon and destroyed every camera in the immediate vicinity, and ran for the airlock doors. Thankfully, the hold had been pressurised, so crashing through wasn't an issue. It rammed into the outer door, the metal bending and snapping back. ZZ3 took hold, ripping the remains of the door from its runners to use as a battering ram against the inner airlock.

A faint memory slipped from its system, of a time when it would have targeted the enemy, flesh or machine, with impunity. What would it have to do to save the crew? Kill again?

Maybe.

The airlock door curved under his assault, and a final punch with a servo-powered limb sent it flying inwards. The corridor was filled with noise and colour. Red alerts flashed; alarms blared.

'Knock, knock. Killer robot on the loose.'

Suppressing interaction. Shut up.

ZZ3 ran left, its bulk pounding along the metal deck. It ran through the schematic Tremil had found, analysing and recalculating the route based on the alert thundering through the corvette. Bullets slammed into its back plate, pinging away. The question was, would they risk anything heavier? The corvettes were not big ships, and anything with the power to destroy a warbot, may also do the same to its hull. Their best bet was to trap the bot and blow it out an airlock.

Part of ZZ3 was counting on it.

It reached a stairwell, Navy personnel running down the steps, with more pounding from above. These carried weaponry, and ZZ3 ducked beneath those stairs and out of the line of fire. Crashing downwards, the bot analysed the fear present in the atmosphere. Sweat and pheromones associated with terror triggered its own bone-shattering and blood-filled memories.

"Move, Bustan bastards!" ZZ3 bellowed in perfect, monotone Bustan. "I will crush your bones."

Panic spread below, and ZZ3 continued to career downwards, finally forced to clamber sideways along a cramped section. Crew threw themselves aside or heaved others in its way, desperate to escape the whir of his servos and the looming threat. ZZ3 shoved and yanked, driving towards its goal. There would be bruises, broken limbs, blood. The pacified warbot tried desperately not to kill; it would solve nothing.

The target lay at the rear of the corvette, and the warbot left the stairwell. Ahead, a crew member backed into the bulkhead, pulling at the door with eyes locked on the approaching warbot. ZZ3 lumbered on, unable to reach its full speed. If the wheel-lock spun into place, things would get seriously difficult. Another stride, and the door continued to close. ZZ3 lifted a limb, the barrel of its arm gun clicking out from beneath an armoured plate. The bullets clattered against the hull wall, pinging off to slam into the meat and flesh behind the closing bulkhead. Another stride, and another limb wrenched the door wide open, the inner wheel smothered in blood.

ZZ3 strode over the body. A casualty. A life for a life. It stored away the sensory data pouring into its system for later analysis. It needed to understand what it was and how *this* taking of life *felt*.

The corridor beyond the bulkhead had cleared, the crew having scattered behind locked doors. A squad of four Marines faced the warbot, their rifles poised. Two knelt, two stood, all four fired.

ZZ3 grabbed the dead body, the flesh, and hurled it towards the threat. Following in behind, bullets rattling off its armour, the bot crashed into the Marines, scattering them like bowling pins. Choosing to ignore whatever mayhem it left behind, ZZ3 pounded towards the target. The huge door to engineering was closed and the palm-lock glowed red. One of the warbot's metal limbs snaked out and slapped wired pads against the lock screen.

Engaging emergency entry protocol.

As the program worked away in the background, the bot readjusted its limbs, an action its captain found revolting as each limb reversed, bending in the opposite direction as the head spun about. The Marines were broken.

Threat analysis nil.

ZZ3 checked left and right along the corridor, each appearance of Bustan crew met with a volley of its weapon aimed to send them scurrying.

The door beeped, and ZZ3 rapidly readjusted to look ahead again as it slid open. Gunfire battered its armour plate, focused and concentrated on one spot. A tactic used on Bustan 8 that had, on occasion, been very successful. ZZ3 leapt, rolling itself briefly into a massive ball, and smashed into the nearest engineers. They scattered, limbs cracking, screams echoing about the room. ZZ3 ignored the small arms fire, ramming upper limbs into the manoeuvring thruster console. The bot tore wads of electronics free, destroying whatever it could get hold of, before a secondary limb's plate popped open.

"I advise you run," the bot said, again in Bustan, lifting what appeared to be a mining charge for the remaining engineers to see. Another volley of weapons fire hit the bot, scarring the plate at close range. ZZ3 pretended to set the charge, but instead withdrew the smallest of bots – a creeper – once inserted by the *Maverick*'s cam-bot into the *Sunstar*'s navcom and so nearly wiping out the entire crew. Using the frequency Tremil provided, ZZ3 activated the tiny bot and placed it inside the main engine's controls.

"This will go kablooie in five…" The pounding of magboots caused the bot to check its sensors. The engineers had gone. ZZ3 stopped counting and ensured the creeper acted as expected. Once satisfied it was off seeking the targeted section of the engine controls, the bot swivelled towards the door.

And there stood a pair of Marines, a rail gun pinned to the deck.

CHAPTER 36

"Cutting burn," Rebekah said, lips stretched thin, teeth hurting like the rest of her body. "In three, two, one ... Mark."

The acceleration lessened, relief spreading through her body allayed with concern for the unconscious girl and the sickly-looking symbiote. After adjusting their course, she unbuckled and took Heki in her arms. Rebekah disengaged the girl's magboots and carried her along the corridor, heading for the twins' cabin where she expected to find a similar story with Tremil.

"Dricks, Arin, sit rep," she said, the comms set still resting on her head, pressure welts around her ears from the hard acceleration.

"Am I alive? Yes, I am. I'm good, Captain. Dricks is looking a little sickly, but that's because she's old ... Ow."

Rebekah tried to suppress the smile, but it broke out on its own.

Dricks cut in. "I'm as fit and healthy as they come, Captain. But two hard burns in a row without retardant is gonna mess anyone up if we keep repeating it."

"As Arin said, we're alive. Dricks, can you take care of the girls? Heki is out, Trem is," she entered the cabin, "looking rough. I think she may be hurt." Tremil sat strapped into her console chair with her head against the monitor, a swelling rising on her temple.

"On my way. Arin's checking on Savvo. Any news on the Bustans?" asked Dricks.

"They went for the cargo. I'll check as soon as the girls are sorted." She eyed the symbiote, its skin a sickly grey, tentacles unmoving. With a twist of her lips, she set Heki down and took the symbiote in hand, feeling its tentacles latch onto her palm. By the time Dricks arrived, it had begun to feed.

"Don't ask," she said, waving Hendricks' enquiry away. "Let me know how they are."

Rebekah dropped into the cockpit chair. TB mithered before adjusting position and eventually settled on the exposed lower part of her forearm. With a shrug, she checked the ship had altered to the new course, pleased to see the slow curved trajectory was active. They were headed once again for the vicinity of Durnat, just not in Ormsk's path. She considered resetting the transponder to throw the Navy further off their scent, but she needed a plan for Scarva, and the alien only knew the ship as the *Solar Flame*. That was if the bastard had not upped and run.

She ran over Tremil's data on the shuttle, estimating it would arrive an hour before them after their burst of acceleration to avoid the PDC weapons fire. That saved an additional hard burn, which no one needed right now. If the shuttle arrived before they did, she suspected Scarva may cut and run. Unless the mind-sucker had some well-hidden cajónes under those frills, and was greedy enough to see through their contract. If the alien chose to abandon them, the sweetener of their war memories she'd promised for future transport would be lost, and the alien would have a pissed off ship of humans to worry about. She doubted they'd be the first with a grudge, and placing human morals and emotions onto a Senti mind seemed wrong. It would be easier to predict what the fuck was happening to ZZ3.

The scan for the corvette mapped its position relative to theirs. There was no attempt to turn their way, nor was it speeding up. Drifting was the wrong term, the Navy ship still hurtled through space on a heading similar to theirs. The difference being ZZ3. Whatever the warbot achieved on board was a bonus. The Bustan had chosen to retrieve the cargo they'd dropped, and in turn throw enough slugs their way to shred their hull as a reward. Now it appeared locked onto the same flight-path, matching the shuttle's, and taking it towards Scarva. If ZZ3 managed to engage the creeper, they wouldn't be able to decelerate in time.

Now space was big. But they had all been headed for Durnat, and as she projected Ormsk's path, his would bring him closest to the planet, particularly one of the unnamed moons and its additional gravity. That was going to be rough.

"Shame," she said, and clicked over to the internal comms. "Arin, Dricks, I have the start of a plan."

"You do?" replied Arin. "Does it involve big guns? I mean big fucking guns? I've got an urge to purge, so to speak, with a Senti mind-sucker in my sights."

"There is that possibility," she said.

"I'm in. The more dangerous the better." His voice was eager, with a heavy dose of angry undercurrent.

Rebekah's eyes drifted to the cockpit ceiling. He was taking ZZ3's likely demise hard, despite whatever this new version of the warbot was. "Don't you want to hear it first? It includes powered armour and everything."

"It gets better and better."

Rebekah cut out the comms and eyed the symbiote whose tentacles shuffled against her skin. There was a red mark beneath, though she felt no pain, and TB's skin glowed with what she took to be metallic pleasure.

"What are you?" she said. "Friend or foe?" The feeling that swept over her was of calm. Of two precious girls, their dreams muted and content.

"Okay. You get one chance."

The Senti transponder refused to engage, and Rebekah swore. The crux of her Plan A depended on Scarva's greed or curiosity. Would it be tempted to allow them on board? The answer was clearly no. The mind-sucker was taking no chances.

Plan B then.

Arin's favourite.

"Scarva, you fuckwit, why are you not engaging. We have a contract." She focused on her tone, trying not to give anything away as she ran her suit checks, the HUD firing up to run through safety protocols.

The comms kicked in, the familiar Senti standard voice filling the frequency. "Sorry, there is no one here of that name. Please leave a message and we will get back to you in a millennium or two."

"Scarva, you have five minutes before I open up my PDCs. Understand, you mind-sucking alien piece of shit?" Her suit visor hit green, and Rebekah engaged the in-built weaponry, running down the ammo. Arin, as usual, had prepped it well.

"No way. You may have some juicy memories inside that bone cauldron you call a head, but you also have a high degree of human recklessness and stupidity."

She had to admit Scarva, if it was Scarva as they all sounded the same over comms, had a point. But she was shit out of patience. The carbine clicked onto her back, locked and loaded.

"We need out," she said, and nodded to Hendricks as the engineer slid into the pilot's chair. "We got the Bustan Navy on our arse. And we have a contract." Rebekah clomped along the corridor and engaged her helmet before entering through the hold airlock. Arin awaited her, two jetpacks set up ready. The containment unit sat in the centre of the hold; one corner scorched where the plasma torch had proved fruitless in its attempts to cut through. Assuming the Senti ship was constructed of the same metal as the shuttle, and therefore the Butcher's coffin, it had forced a rethink.

"Contract negated due to the aforementioned Bustan Navy in relation to your recklessness and stupidity. Scarva out."

"You scumbag!" She shouted and checked her counter. "Four minutes and thirty seconds you shit, before I pepper your hull with metal confetti."

She checked her HUD, Arin's feed sitting in the top right of her visor, top left filled by the *Sunstar*'s view of the *Unpronounceable*.

"Ready, Dricks. A token blast towards the comms arrays, then follow the pre-programmed path, understand? Don't deviate. Too much risk with the shuttle and the Navy incoming. We fuck up, head back to Benetai. Heki will get you there."

"You don't have to do this," replied Hendricks. "We could cut and run."

Rebekah thought of Hanna, the sobs, of the thousands on board fearing for their lives as the alarms rung, or later when the Bustan Navy had opened its missile ports. The dead Baja faction, heads twisted, vertebrae snapped. Savvo. Then Ormsk.

"Honour and duty," she said. "No one ..."

"Breaks a Breaker," they both replied.

She engaged the jetpack, rising from the deck, Arin ahead and leading. He had by far the greater experience, and as they entered the black, she knew it was the right choice. The sheer beauty of the void took her breath again, drawing her eyes as it always did. How Hendricks hated it so much, she wasn't sure. Similar, perhaps, to the vertigo many suffered up a mountain, while others hopped like sure-footed goats from precipice to precipice.

In the lee of the *Sunstar*, they dropped gently, matching arcs, and waited. The starboard debris cannons opened up, the Senti ship an easy target but in her heart of hearts she doubted they would even graze the plate. However, that comms array was a tempting target. They dropped away as the slugs flew, using gas jets rather than thrusters to propel them towards the ship. A second burst of PDC fire rose a spark or two, and an antenna bent and warped, but refused to break. Arin clamped to the outer hull of the *Unpronounceable*, and added a mag-hook, tethering to it. Rebekah followed suit, and they began a very gentle walk towards the central, rotating portion of the ship. No ships were currently berthed. Arin waited at its edge, facing in towards where the nose clamp would engage with any docking ship.

"In you go," she said. Arin didn't hesitate, timing his movements as the central portion spun, the groove of their target berth appearing from beneath the ship's outer hull. It was huge, big enough to swallow a ship twice the *Sunstar*'s size. Large enough, in fact, to carry the corvette steaming their way. He jetted in, aiming for the floor, that would be the ceiling for a docked ship. He'd made it by the time the next docking berth swept into view, and Rebekah waited for it to return.

Thanks to Senti efficiency, she noted the markings of each berth as they rotated by. Having checked the ship's recording, they knew where the shuttle had docked previously, guessing that it would likely end up in the same place. If not, they'd find a way in through an airlock. Reckless and stupid? Scarva had missed stubborn as hell from the list.

Arin came into view, and she activated the pack, flying down to meet him. He engaged a tether, and they locked both jetpacks to the berth walls. Arin unwrapped his prize possession, the EM tarp he'd printed. It was unlikely the shuttle would be scanning the bay as they came into dock – the whole system was automated through transponders – but he'd insisted.

They hunkered down beneath it, boots maglocked to the bay as the gentle rotational force tried to throw them off, and waited. A check of her feed confirmed the *Sunstar* had begun to move away.

"Last time I did this," said Arin. "I was sat in a hole with Savvo and ZZ3 after it saved our lives. Funny how things come full circle."

Rebekah knew where he was leading, and couldn't blame him despite the weight lifted by the warbot's absence. "ZZ3 wanted to go," was all she managed to say.

"Brought a picnic?"

She slapped his arm, unable choke off back a laugh.

CHAPTER 37

With the shuttle flipped, the main engine cut off as the transponders navigated the small shuttle into the V-shaped bay. Rebekah checked over the rad levels and its strange lack of heat on her HUD. The suit remained in the green, but gave a warning about the rise in radiation while the vibration of the docking clamps' engagement vibrated through her boots.

She risked a glance, saving the dual drones should things go shit-face down when they attacked. The transport had come to a rest, gases being expelled port and starboard, lights flickering along the shuttle's hull before dulling out. The nose was scorched as if it had seen too many re-entries, but apart from that it presented as a typical shuttle. One built from Senti metal, or had, perhaps, an inner skin of the material to deaden all radiation emissions. How it activated and deactivated piqued her curiosity but not as much as who was inside, and what their plans were for the wetware.

Arin wrapped and stowed their cover, and they approached the extending airlock tunnel. They had no idea what it would be made of, trusting their hand cutters would see their way in. By the time it engaged, they were four strides away, and it was clear someone was clambering through, their shoulders scraping against the grey material. A second form emerged, this one without the shoulders, but the unmistakable spread of wide tentacles.

Pshwa.

Anger coursed, but she had to control it. They needed to take out the shuttle first in hope the wetware remained on board, and to remove any threat from the rear. Breakers to the end.

The movements stopped, and she assumed the airlock had cycled through.

"Now," she said, and fired up the hand torch, Arin following suit. They slashed at the material, and it parted, the edges melting like metal, yet the material did not catch fire. Two slashes and they were in, with the shuttle airlock still cycling and the outer hatch slowly closing. Arin threw himself at the door, ramming his hand cutter into the gap, and pressed down. Mist briefly coalesced, flooding the remains of the tunnel just as it had at the Butcher's lab when they exposed it to space. He sliced through the lock.

Rebekah stowed her cutter and yanked out the dual-sided mining clamps they used to wedge open automining ship doors when things had gone to hell. She cranked the complaining hatch open, wide enough for Arin to enter. He discarded the damaged cutter, clamping it against the internal wall. Carbine in hand, he entered the airlock.

With a wedged outer door, alarms were blaring inside. Arin withdrew two handmade charges and was about to place them against the inner airlock when Rebekah gestured for him to wait.

"Give it a second," she added, and removed the clamps. The hull door slid shut, only partially locking after Arin's attack. The airlock alarms quelled, and the system swiftly cycled through. The two ex-Marines were inside, carbines up, synced and ready. It had been quick, but whoever remained on board would know there was an issue. What happened next depended on how they would react. The answer came quickly, bullets raking down the corridor and along Arin's shin plate. He pulled back, Rebekah checking his suit's integrity as she bypassed him.

A junction. The left turn taking them towards the cockpit, the right to the hold. A check showed the shots had come from the hold, and she withdrew a ration pack from her hip pocket. With a heave, she threw it but didn't follow, shoving the carbine around instead. The sight gave her a full view of what they faced. A head popped out, brown-haired, mid-thirties, male and in a flight suit. The rifle in his hand old but well kept. Human. Almaarian. Bullets shredded the ration pack, but she had what she wanted.

"Lay down your weapon. We are well-armed and in space-rated armour. One crack in that airlock, and you're sucking vacuum." The speaker projected the voice, and she signalled Arin back to the airlock.

"Huh," came the reply. "You're gonna kill me anyhoose. May as well go with a gun in my hand."

She didn't have the time to mess about, needing to know whether any message had been passed to those inside if she could. The speed of their assault was key. Rebekah dropped to her haunches, and assuming the man hadn't moved, eased the muzzle around the corner. She swept a hail of bullets across the deck. Pain echoed back, and she stepped out, still low, carbine ready and finger poised on the trigger. The man was down on all fours, both legs bleeding profusely, his weapon still in hand as he stared at her. She fired again, smashing the rifle out of his grip, and probably hitting a finger or two as he squealed again. The look in his eye hinted at another weapon, another attempt to survive. Rebekah stomped down the concourse to slam her boot onto his hand, then lowered herself down, muzzle pressed against his head.

"I don't want to kill you. But I will." And she stared at his forearm. Acid rose at the base of her throat. "What unit?" she said, eyes on the tattoo staring back at her. She pressed the gun in tighter. "What fucking Marine unit?" she asked again.

"I'm dying 'ere," he replied, pulling back his sleeve further as Rebekah removed her boot. "7th and High."

She gawped. Memories flooding back of a time that felt an age away. Before the twins broke the Breakers and forged a family. "Segfi's love-in troops. What the hell are you doing on a Senti ship? More to the point, working with fucking Scarva and Pshwa."

The man's eyes fluttered, and he began to sink, arms folding beneath him. Rebekah swore, placing her carbine on the deck but out of his reach. She drew out a stim gun and unceremoniously slammed it into his neck.

Sorry. I need answers.

"Sit rep. Are we clear, Arin?" Her voice urgent, demanding the facts.

"Can't see no one but we left a hole in their tunnel. Got to be some comeback from that. What's pertaining back there?"

"I have an ex-Marine, 7th and High, dying on me right now before I got answers."

"Wha—"

She cut him off, the ex-Marine's eyes fluttering. Things were coming back to her, and they smelt like trouble. The type where you checked your boot to see what you had stepped in.

"Hey." She tapped his cheek, restraining herself despite the urgency. "Listen up, Marine. State your unit."

"7th and High, Captain, sir."

"Under whose command?"

"Captain Brint. Assigned to—"

"Pilot-sergeant Rubel Carmen," she finished, the image of the man at the forefront of her mind. "I heard you were dead, Marine."

A glance, recognition in his eyes, and he fainted.

Now what?

"Fuuuucckkkk." She battered the deck, furious at herself and the forced delay. No one left behind. She ripped open two medpads, slapping them onto the splintered shin and ankle. They sealed, the blood flow easing, and after shoving his feet up against the nearest seat, Rebekah gathered her carbine.

It was no longer simple.

Rubel Carmen, fuck.

Arin waited, clamped to the hull next to the *Unpronounceable*'s airlock, with Rebekah hidden behind the flapping tunnel. She kept her camera fixed on the entrance, the Senti encounter suit on the other side currently cycling through while holding repair boxes in two tentacles, and a roll of the grey material in another.

Lights flashed above the airlock.

It cycled open.

"Now," she ordered, and Arin sliced open the encounter suit with the remaining hand cutter. Morally, she felt like shit. But these Senti were working for Scarva, Pshwa, or both. Senti who had screwed them over, then cut and run, leaving the Benetai station to its fate. Not only that, she had no clue about how to disable or to knock out a Senti, and she wasn't willing to risk anyone else after Savvo's near miss. The alternative would have been to blow the airlock and then how many would have died?

Arin kicked the encounter suit away, the alien's tentacle flailing at the slash, desperate to try and stop the precious gas from gushing out. She couldn't watch, turning away as Arin entered the airlock and restarted the sequence.

"Me too," he said, staring at the panel. "We're constantly second guessing what the hell's going on. And now we're a bot down, Savvo in medbay and we're killing Senti. What's so damn important about this wetware?"

Rebekah eyed him, her suit's visor displaying his face. No smile sat there, only a determined but angry sliver. Nostrils flaring.

"Let's find out," she said as the door cycled, and they emerged into the dank corridor they had used the last time they had been on the ship.

Seawater and cabbages if I remember right. Except that time, I had no armour to shield me, Scarva.

The corridor maintained the hull's curve, and under half standard grav, they moved quickly. It was as empty as before. The odd square doors with their hemispheric lintels still sealed shut. She had no mind to investigate further, instead focusing on the information her HUD fed her about the corridor.

"Oh hell," she said. "Stop. Arin, on cover."

"Copy that, Captain. You okay?"

"Wishing I had Savvo with us." She began to flick through her menu, seeking the correct subsection, and annoyed she was struggling with the navy suit's systems. "Arin. Swap over. Do a frequency sweep for—"

"Segfi's squads. Brilliant. On it."

She dropped down low, easing her eyes along the curved route, trying to recall where they had walked with Yat. Was that the alien they'd just killed? She shook away that thought and walked herself through the route to Scarva's lab. An idea came to mind, a devious backup plan to threaten what the Senti mind-fucker valued most: memories.

"It's as weak as a newborn kitten," came back Arin. "But I have three signals. Sending."

Rebekah checked her HUD. Arin's link implied a direction, but no more. "What range are you thinking?"

"About ten metres to get an exact location. It's this weird-ass metal everywhere, so don't rely on it if we're talking in another room."

"Take point," she said. "I'll keep track. I want to make sure we have a bead on Scarva's lab before we go all in."

Arin swept past, and she let him lead off by a few metres. She monitored their rear, occasionally comparing their direction against what she remembered. The ship felt as eerie as before and devoid of life. Mould flourished everywhere, though less grew as they approached where she thought Scarva's lab lay.

After turning in towards the central hub, Arin signalled a stop. "I'm thinking we're near," he said.

"Two doors down," she replied, eyes running over the sections between each door, and noting the scrape on the architrave she had marked on their first visit.

This is what happens when you don't clean up after yourself.

So far, no alarms had blared, but her HUD was flashing a change. A glance told her the Marines were on the move, and fast. They must have noted the missing Senti or called the shuttle and were responding to the silence. Which way were they heading? Without a map, she was working on a mental picture of the ship. Being a pilot helped, the need for constantly thinking in 3D, four if you included time and velocity judgements.

"Marines are heading for the shuttle. We sweep the lab, then leave Scarva a surprise." Rebekah reached out for the door, repeating the scrapes across it that Yat had made. Two, was it? No, three, and the door swung open. Empty and as filthy as she remembered. Was this how the Senti normally lived? Presenting the shiny version for humanity?

"Take station," she ordered, and entered, heading past the dentist-like chair set up and towards the machinery in the far corner. It presented as a series of dials and knobs, sheathed in the Senti metal that reached up to the convex ceiling. Scarva had brought the symbiote here after draining the last of them, placing the creature inside a panelled opening. On the Senti Orbs, the symbiotes had rested after each mind-suck on a flat panel much like the absorbent decking, beneath which slabs of dull grey metal sat. Not exactly the same as the one they had delivered to Pshwa, but too much of a coincidence for her to dismiss.

With her chip engaged and HUD sensors full on, she began to attune to the machine. Initially, she had come to set Arin's charges, a backup plan to threaten the Senti with should things fall flat. But curiosity was gnawing at her, and when her wetware and HUD agreed, she worked a panel clear hidden beneath a section of dead electronics. A yank at an inert dial and knob combination exposed familiar blocks of metal. Perhaps they were blanks, or contained sucked memories of value to the Senti. Either way, the Senti would be mighty pissed to have them blown up.

"Arin, I need a charge setting," she said, pocketing as many of the metal blocks as she could.

"We introducing the Senti to Wrecking Squad fireworks?" he said, moving back as she took a cover position.

"More like Breaker attitude. You got a range estimate." Rebekah checked on the Marines while she spoke. An educated guess placed them at the airlock. They would be on their way soon enough.

"Range? These are cobbled together printed Arin specials. Range is asking too much. Timer only, no remote detonations. *Those* babies stopped a Bustan missile hurtling towards our sorry-asses. Remember."

"Yes, our glorious saviour."

"Too right. I can give you timing in five-minute intervals, up to an hour. And for that you should also be grateful." The tone was smug, and a glance to her feed showed him focused on setting the charge. She could accept a return to his banter – for now.

"Grateful? It was the twins' idea to request a printer."

"Yeah ... that just sped things up. Let my genius flower."

An alert flagged on her HUD, and Rebekah shifted position, eyeing the corridor back the way they had come. She now had two figures showing, the third remaining at the airlock.

"Forty-five minutes," she said. "And they're on approach. Hope they haven't brought weedkiller."

"Har bloody har. Done." Arin stepped in beside her. "Now what?"

"We hope Carmen has forgiven me."

CHAPTER 38

Hendricks watched the sensory data flow across the screen in multiple windows, while the main visual feed tracked the spaceship hurtling their way. The corvette was sending out all sorts of signals in a fervent cloud of hope. Hope that the gravity of the small moon and the planet it orbited wouldn't cause too much damage, or yank them on an even more dangerous course. Hope that other ships were listening to them and were steering away.

Hope.

It smelt more of desperation, and she couldn't help but chuckle.

"Fucking stick-up your arsehole Bustan got a taste of ZZ3 medicine. You'll never break a Breaker." The navcom confirmed they were clear of any repercussions as long as the corvette didn't deviate too far. She let out a sigh.

"Dricks," came a tight voice along the corridor, and she spun around to find both twins heading her way. They looked rough, but then they all did after multiple hard burns.

"You should be resting," she replied, and pushed herself out of the seat. "Orders."

Both girls gave the briefest of smiles before collecting a flask of water each. That was about all the answer Hendricks was going to get.

"We checked on Savvo. He's still out," said Heki, taking a sip. And then she froze solid, eyes wild.

"What?" Hendricks stared, taken aback. Even for the girls, the behaviour was strange.

The cockpit console blared an alarm.

Heki shook herself and was swiftly by the engineer's side, fingers running over the information the monitor had ringed in red. A glance told her Tremil was running for her cabin.

"Is that ...?" she said, and dragged up dual windows.

"If you mean lifeboat, no. It's a bloody dropship. Two, in fact. How the hell?" Hendricks slapped the back of her neck, eyes distant. The Bustan were insane. "Shit."

"Trem, go back over the sensory data, see what you can find about those ships." Heki tapped at the screen, nibbling at her lip, while waves of her concern washed over Hendricks.

"Heki, one was dropped recently and fired ahead. They're heading straight for us, full burn." Trem's voice cracked, and Hendricks waited expectantly for the crash of fear that never came. Nothing.

"It's a suicide run, a ramming. Heki, rapid burn, now. Tremil, debris cannons up and fire on that dropship. "

She ran, pounding down the corridor, heading for engineering as the *Sunstar* shifted into high burn. The vibrations shaking deck and ship alike, threatening to throw her against the walls. A second engine burst yanked her forwards, and she disengaged the boots, letting the momentum hurtle her past the cabins to crash into the T-junction. Having twisted to let her legs take the impact, she engaged the magboots, knees calling for her immediate execution as they throbbed in anger.

"Stopping PDCs, we'll die in the debris field!" shouted Tremil over comms.

Hendricks hobbled through the door, and righted herself, then attached magboots in front of the manoeuvring thruster console.

"Thrusters, Now!" she shouted down the comms, the rattle of engines drowning her words. She slapped down on the override with her left hand, hitting the boost she'd wired in after the *Maverick*'s boarding. And prayed.

Rebekah aimed and fired, the burst of carbine fire rattling off the curved ceiling above the two approaching humans. In the damp, green-laced corridor, their echoes sounded dull, but the effect remained as she'd planned. They stopped, backing off against the wall. The leader's hand signal was familiar, telling the trailing Marine to move to the far side. The handlebar moustache and tufted beard, however, were not.

"Is that Rubel? He's got ugly," said Arin. "I mean that combo shouts failed space pirate. He just needs a hooped earring."

"Stow it," she ordered, despite agreeing.

"Throw down your weapons." Her speaker thrummed along the corridor. "You are outmatched and outgunned."

Rubel sniggered. She forgot how much that had endeared her to him at first. "You can kiss my ass first."

"I didn't mention the third part, Rubel," she said. With her carbine up high and synced, she stepped out, firing again, this time at the floor. "We're also armoured up."

Rubel flinched, whether it was at the mention of his name, or at the Navy-issue armour, she wasn't sure. He was in an ancient flight suit, exposed and under armed.

"Drop the weapons. Both of you."

A gunshot echoed from behind, one round, and a grunt told her Arin had seen something he didn't like. The second ex-Marine had crumpled to the floor, holding her shoulder as blood spilled to mix amid the deck's rust brown and green.

"Now, Rubel." She stepped towards him, watching his expression crumple. Anger and hope draining. He stood, arms held wide, and threw his old carbine aside.

"Who the hell are you, man? Don't tell me you're that bitch Segfi's dogs. She abandoned us, not the other way around. I ain't no deserter." His lips twisted into a growl under the ugly moustache. That, at least, was familiar.

Rebekah demisted her visor, enjoying the realisation in his eyes.

"Khan? What the hell? They sent you, the asswipe Breakers to come get me? I'm honoured they thought I was that dangerous." The arms dropped, but she jabbed the carbine back at him.

"Keep them up. Arin, patch your bullseye."

"Copy that." Arin edged past, keeping his own visor clear and giving Rubel a grimace on the way past.

"Enterman. You still alive? How the hell? I had you pegged for two months, tops. Don't tell me Dricks is still going?" He again went to lower his arms. Rebekah repeated the hint he shouldn't.

"I know what you're doing. What you always do. Now shut the fuck up a second. Arin?"

"She'll live. Now if Savvo had shot her, who knows. Yeah, Rubel, Savvo lives on, no thanks to your new playmates." He sent Rubel a glare as he stood up, dragging away the injured woman's rifle.

"Bek." There it was, that fucking nickname. She shook her head.

"That was a long time ago."

"Angel," he said, the words slipping from his lips like poison.

Fuck.

"I'm sorry, Rubel. She's dead. I couldn't … I got there too late. And the rest of the Breakers. All gone."

And me in the middle. First, I steal her fucking man, then I dump the bastard when I realise what a shit he really was. What a shit I was.

His eyes dropped to the deck. A genuine emotion, and it hurt.

"How …?" he started, and then the Senti ship rocked, yawing to the side, throwing Rubel to the floor with his lack of magboots. A scraping sound reverberated through the corridor, metal upon metal, and Rebekah could have sworn she heard tearing. Perhaps her speakers playing tricks. It went on for far too long, fraying already ragged nerves.

"Shiiiit," said Arin, eyes cast up as if he could see through the hull. There was no answer there.

Rubel's eyes narrowed as he pressed his hand to his ear where a comms unit sat. "No way," he shouted, glaring at Rebekah. "I don't know what the hell is happening here, Khan. But a Bustan dropship just slammed into us. Scarva's frills are in a twist."

"They're here for you, me, and that wetware Pshwa, and apparently Scarva, stole. Tool the fuck up, Rubel. This ain't about you. It never was."

The grinding sound slowly came to a halt. Clangs ensuing, repeated, thunderous strikes against the *Unpronounceable's* hull.

"Hope you got some spacesuits handy," Arin said.

"They're in the shuttle," replied Rubel. "As is all our kit. Scarva doesn't want human contamination on board this beautiful ship." He pressed a hand to his ear again, eyes distant as someone, Rebekah assumed Scarva, spoke.

"They're trashing the airlock to Bay Four." Rubel looked sickly, colour-draining as he spoke in his comms. "Let them in, Scarva. Close off the bulkheads, but let those Bustan ass-kissers in. They breach this ship, we're all dead, and get in your fucking encounter suit." He stopped talking, looking to Rebekah. "Scarva says they're Marauders, recognises them from some of the Bustan memory slugs. We're fucked."

Rebekah shook her head. "Grown soft in your old age. Show me where they're coming in." She picked up his old carbine, handing it over. "Take point."

"Bloody hilarious," he replied. He took the rifle and headed back down the corridor, muttering.

Rebekah followed, Arin at her rear after propping up the injured ex-Marine. Rubel turned twice, the increase in grav indicating they were heading towards the outer part of the rotating hull. A creeping worry about Hendricks and the girls tried to worm its way in. If they had managed to send one ship, why not two? She wrapped the kernel of dread in memories of the *Maverick*, and the twins' determination to live, tying it up with Hendricks' tenacity. It gave a little hope while hating the separation.

Rubel halted at a curved corner, fist up, signalling wait. A check to her feed showed Arin had seen, though there was no way anyone could have taken their approach as silent and subtle.

"Scarva's crew. Wait here, they'll be jumpy." Rubel straightened and walked out into the corridor.

Rebekah eased her visor around, not risking the weapon's sight and the threat it may imply. Two encounter suits were at the sealed bulkhead door, one of their shoulder tentacles holding what appeared to be a short spear, or club, tipped with a glowing, diamond head, the other a more familiar appearing gun with a Senti-shaped grip.

The bulkhead shook as Rubel approached, and she could have sworn a dent appeared. A second hit to the side shook the door's housing. The silence that ensued was more ominous than the attacks, and Rubel was already backing off, barking orders at the Senti to do the same. They had just begun to respond when a dull thump shook the door a third time.

Rebekah's HUD blared and flagged a rapid heat increase around the door's edge.

"They're cutting through. Move Rubel!" she shouted, but too late. Another dull thump, and the door began to topple, her suit flashing up multiple traces of chem charge particulates amid the smoke filling the corridor. Her visor compensated as the bulkhead crashed to the deck. In normal grav, the encounter suit beneath would have popped like a shaken bottle, firing Senti everywhere. Instead, it happened as the huge Space Marine boot crashed down onto the metal door. The encounter suit gave all at once, brown liquid and half a Senti gushed out, a squeal emanating amid the horror. The other Senti drove on, ramming its spear into the knee joint. The diamond tip flashed, and the knee jerked, while the Senti pointed and fired its gun. Nothing appeared to emit from the barrel, but the Space Marine staggered briefly back, before swiping out with a huge armoured hand to slap the Senti against the outer hull. A snap, and the encounter suit began to collapse, but the Marauder hadn't finished, its second fist swinging around to crash into the Senti's helmet. Brown liquid spurted briefly from the cracks, the Senti's head splattered blue and green against the mouldy metal behind.

"No, no," said Rubel, backing away.

"Rubel, run!" shouted Rebekah.

He glanced her way, and his face changed. Fleeting memories of their good times together washed painfully away by the reason she left him in the middle of the night. Trust. She always felt there would be another to turn his head. After all, she had so easily enticed him away from Angel.

"They're there," he shouted, throwing away his carbine along with his honour. He pointed straight at Rebekah. "They have what you want. The wetware. Khan has it."

Rebekah lifted her rifle, aiming straight for the weasel's head when the Marauder stepped into view, their helmet clear. Inside, a female head lolled, dead eyed, the neck broken with blood leaking from ears and nose.

Oh fuck.

"Your assistance is duly noted," came the robotic voice in perfect Almaarian. An armoured fist shattered Rubel's sternum, caved in his ribs. Blood splattered the Marauder's arm, and Rubel's already dead body hit the far wall.

"Target acquired." And the Marauder turned her way.

"Run!" she ordered.

CHAPTER 39

Hendricks coughed, moaned, then bumped gently against something hard. Her eyes fluttered, brain daring the red lights flashing within engineering. A second try saw them fully open, and nausea hit. She knew she was going to be sick, a truly unpleasant experience in a contained room with zero grav. Too late, she threw up. Throat raw, Hendricks disengaged her magboots, stepping away from what she had released, then blinked, and rubbed her eyes to reveal the source of the flashing lights. The thruster console blared accusingly back at her, silent alarms declaring the damage her boost had done.

"Quit your complaining. I'm alive."

I'm alive. But ...

Wondering how long she'd been out, she reached for her slate clamped to the wall. A swift diagnostic told her the ship's engines hated her guts, but were still working. The manoeuvring thrusters had moved from hate to seeking vengeance, but at a pinch, gentle adjustments were possible. The hull, however, was showing signs of distress. The boost had shifted parts of the metal skeleton the plates were welded to. It would hold for now, but anything sudden could see severe issues with hull integrity in far too many places.

"But I'm alive. And if I live ..."

A brief look in on Savvo informed her he had suffered far less than her, the medbot injecting a retardant the moment Heki's hard burn had kicked in. Further along the ship, she knocked and entered the girls' cabin, finding Tremil groggy but waking up, strapped to her chair. TB, however, was on the bed, tentacles curled in on itself – skin grey and dry. She feared the worst and made to approach when Tremil's cry cut her short. And she blacked out again as pure anguish raked through her soul.

"Dricks." Water splashed onto her forehead, aided by a gentle hand that repeated the gesture against her cheeks. Throbbing music played in her ears. "Dricks, wake up."

Her eyes fluttered open, greeted by Tremil's concerned gaze. She reached up and gently touched the girl's face. She didn't flinch, a wet hand wrapping about hers in response.

"You with us?" she said.

Dricks nodded, not trusting herself to speak, and realised she was strapped down as she tried to rise. A glance around showed she was in medbay, flashes of the last time she'd been in there causing ghost twinges in her back and hip. Unbuckling, she twisted about, magboots connecting to the deck and carefully removed the headphones.

"TB's not dead," blurted Tremil, a tear rolling from her eye. "He's ... he's cocooned."

Hendricks replaced the headphones, just in case, and squeezed Tremil's hand again. "Heki?"

"She's okay. We both are."

"You did good belaying the cannons," Hendricks said, and stood, ignoring the memory of pain. Another dropped in its place. "The dropship? Where is it?"

"Out into the black, still on a high burn rate."

"And the other? Tremil, the other dropship," Hendricks said, a sudden urgency to her voice.

"They were on a rapid slowdown … It was released sometime before the ship that came for us. They were within human survivable parameters. But not by much," replied Tremil.

"Shit. Has to be Marauders." Hendricks rubbed at the sweat beading on her forehead. "Have we heard anything from Scarva's ship?"

"No. It's been eleven minutes since we avoided the collision. But Heki has something to show you." Tremil produced her slate. "Hek, you have the feed? The one for Dricks."

"Sending," she said, and space appeared. The black. Empty except for the streak heading towards them and slightly off to one side. "That's the first dropship release. See how it drops low, and engages reverse thrust immediately. On a slow down trajectory."

"You told me, Trem."

"Watch." She swiped ahead, and the corvette streaked by. Again, she swiped, revealing the second dropship as it slowed towards Scarva's ship. The screen suddenly filled with their attacker blazing towards them, and the feed shook. Tremil paused the image and slid it back a little before zooming in. "There."

"What the hell?" said Hendricks, focusing in again. "Is that?"

"ZZ3? Yes."

"How is that possible?" asked Hendricks.

Heki spoke over comms. "ZZ3 must have clamped to the dropship – and we're guessing here – then been shaken free towards the end. The corvette's speed and locked flight-path brought it towards us, so I think it was logical for ZZ3 to hitch a ride. With all that additional computation speed we added, maybe it worked out what to do."

"Or is turning too bloody human and took a risk a bot normally wouldn't. Hoped we'd be here. Shit. Is it broadcasting?"

"Not on ZZ3's normal frequency," said Heki.

Tremil blinked, eyeing the screen and the shuttle rotating about Scarva's ship. "Try the probe frequency."

"Aha," replied Heki. "Patching through."

Hendricks shook her head as the monotone voice echoed over comms.

"I am crew."

"Staggered retreat," she ordered, the suit's servos powering her along the corridor. Arin slid to a halt, turning about and firing. Carbine slugs flew by Rebekah, striking something behind that shook the deck each time a boot landed. She ran on past, counting to ten, and repeated Arin's manoeuvre.

As she dropped, she engaged the secondary trigger and accessed her wetware. "Grenade. Run fucking faster."

She fired, the explosive round spiralling through the air to crash into the Marauder's suit. Except the Space Marine was dead. They weren't facing a human, but an Artificial Intelligence tuned for battle, with no living meat inside to worry about anymore.

The grenade struck above the hip, a few centimetres off her targeted area. The explosion vibrated through the plate, and the left half of the Marauder appeared to flail back. But the powered suit compensated, its servos forcing the hip and leg to reattach to the deck and carry on its momentum.

Like a pissed off armoured tank on legs.

Arin ran by, and she got to her feet, bullets raking along her calf plate and up onto the corridor wall.

Where from?

Arin was ahead, kneeling at a junction, sighting. "Grenade," he shouted. "Down."

Despite her best efforts, she must have been in the way, and threw herself to the deck. A brief self-congratulation leaked into her mind as she ducked under the grenade, hands and shoulders hitting the floor as she rolled, thanking Duboit for her suit. Servos strained as she regained her feet and sprinted past Arin.

"Grenade," he repeated, and she swore. Glancing to her feed, he had delayed, thinking he had time for a second strike. He hadn't, and in his feed the combination of Marauder and explosion sent him flying backwards.

"You stupid f—," Rebekah shouted, and slammed into a doorway, bringing herself to an instant stop. Turning, ignoring the pain, she pressed down on the trigger, spraying the Space Marine as it staggered from Arin's grenade. It toppled to its knees as Arin struck the corridor wall, twisting away to crash into the other side before he landed on the deck.

"Grenade!" she bellowed, striding forwards and releasing the explosive. Ignoring its impact, she grabbed Arin's carbine while dropping her own and felt for the second trigger. "Grenade," she repeated, and as the Marauder rose, with chest plate cracked, one arm loose by its side, the explosive struck dead centre. The huge suit flew backwards. Whatever meat it still contained, splashed against the walls as it hit the deck.

"Fucking *AI*," she growled. "Deleted." Ordering her visor to run an analysis of the Marauder, Rebekah reloaded the grenade launcher. She ignored the groan over comms. A good sign, but Arin had put them at risk. An inconclusive response from the HUD didn't help.

"Fuck me." She turned side on, reaching for Arin while watching the heap of metal they'd created. Arin's vitals were in the green. His suit, not so much. One breach sealed, but his chest plating had received its own funeral. Scorched shards lay on the deck as he rolled over onto his back.

"Ouch," he said, half-a-wince accompanied by a grin. "That didn't go so well."

"You think?"

Angry red alarms flashed in her HUD, and Rebekah spun, raising her carbine and firing into the pile of metal. Sparks flew, pattering against the corridor walls, but the HUD continued to pulse. A second Marauder appeared further back, the inside of its visor blood red, a long, thick-barrelled rifle in its hand. A ship-killer. A rail gun designed to drill through the hull at close quarters. She shuddered at what it would do to her suit.

"Oh," was all she managed, and the weapon turned her way.

Arin fired, holding Rebekah's carbine up from the deck, bullets spraying across the Marauder's visor. A human would have flinched, turned away as fear-induced adrenaline forced them to act. At that moment, she realised Arin didn't know, and she had failed to inform him. Funny what comes to you as death stares back at you with no face.

The Marauder's gauntlet twitched, the finger curling about the trigger, and it pulled. She watched it all in slow motion, her chip elevating her senses, urging her to respond.

She hit the deck, a heavy whack into her knees forcing her down, helmet clattering against the metal as it blared its distress. Blood poured over her visor, viscous and red, and her mic picked up a human sigh. No time, she rolled away, trying to work out why there was no pain, why she wasn't dead. She nudged into Arin, the ex-Marine up on his feet and pouring the remainder of his clip into the mountain of metal turning his way. A strange noise echoed in her comms, a glance at her HUD declaring danger to her suit – ion-radiation forming a cone by her side, washing over the Marauder.

So much input. But she had been a Breaker. Cut through the noise. Act.

She fired. The grenade slammed into the Marauder, and it staggered back. Joint motors twitched, and its visor flashed, highlighting a foul and bloody internal coating. The explosion roared through the corridor, and Rebekah grabbed Arin's arm.

"Back, get the fuck back and cover my retreat," she ordered. Arin turned about, running down the corridor. A glance to her side revealed a Senti, the strange gun in its hand and a hole through its encounter suit she could have put her fist through. It stood, tentacle on trigger, continuing to fire when a second round burst through its visor and struck between the soulless eyes. Rebekah looked away, leaping the bloody body on the floor. Her saviour, and she didn't even know her name. The ex-Marine who had accompanied Rubel.

Someone who retained their honour.

And she ran, pounding for the far side of the corridor, adrenaline coursing through her.

"Khan," sounded in her comms. The voice Senti. "Khan, your ship sent a message."

Relief amid the storm, and she crashed against the wall as Arin shouted grenade again. The explosion threw her forwards, a ship-killer round sailing overhead, cutting through the corridor walls like a knife through butter.

"Busy," she said. "Get on with it."

The message dropped in her visor, and as she swung around to fire, the words seared into her head.

"What do you mean, ZZ3 approaching?"

Metal hit metal, a screech that scraped along Rebekah's spine and on into her brain. The Marauder hit the corridor wall, bouncing back, multiple limbs wrapped about its upper body. ZZ3's red eyes peered over the Space Marine's shoulder, and a flare of plasma ignited behind the warbot's head. The Marauder slammed a powered elbow into ZZ3's face, shattering an eye unit, leaving a dent. A second elbow crashed into the bot, and its limbs seemed to hesitate, half-releasing the AI controlled Marauder.

Arin was up and firing, short bursts focused on the shoulder joints. Round after round pummelled the suit, shattering plates. A third elbow smashed into ZZ3, and it reeled back, limbs releasing as the plasma torch twitched behind.

Rebekah shoved Arin aside, grabbing the Senti's weapon splattered with blue-green goo, and wrapped her hand about the strange handle. She leapt, twisting in the air, and depressed the button on its top. Nothing happened, no warmth, no stutter or release of a round. Instead, her visor screamed at her, highlighting the cone of ionised radiation she poured into the Marauder's legs, causing it to stagger. Hoping she had missed ZZ3, she hit the deck, looking up just as the plasma torch emerged from the Space Marine's chest plate, slashing upwards. The sizzle of the already dead Marine filled the air as the helmet split apart to reveal the warbot's eyes gleaming behind.

"I am crew," stated ZZ3.

"Yes, you fucking are," replied Rebekah.

CHAPTER 40

Scarva hovered above its four tentacles, little to show on the alien's face other than the usual Senti blank expression. Rebekah wondered what it was thinking. Perhaps calculating just how much her memories of the Marauder battle were worth? What would the Senti addicts pay to have the deaths of three of their own wired straight into their brain? Perhaps double when layered with human emotions as they fought two AI controlled Space Marines and a ship-killer weapon.

The traitorous shit is probably working out if it could buy a new ship after hoovering my brain.

"You brought them here," the alien said.

"No, Scarva. You did. I can show you whatever feeds you want. In the end, they were after the wetware. The knowledge of which you stole from our memories and sold to Pshwa. Or, more likely, commissioned the dream-pedalling bastard to acquire the wetware for you both. Neck deep, if Senti's have necks, in your own shit," Rebekah said, her eyes solely for the mind-sucker.

"Caught red tentacled," added Arin, his carbine never leaving Pshwa who hovered in the corner of the lab. "So to speak."

"It won't take them long to make their repairs, and then they're going to come looking for you." Rebekah pointed at the alien, scowling for effect.

Scarva off-gassed. "No, you. They think you have ..."

Rebekah wagged her finger, the beginnings of a smile creeping across her face. She had no idea if the Senti scumbag knew that particular piece of human body language, but the alien shut up fast.

"My crew have spliced all the lovely evidence of your behaviour together, parcelled it up in a neat data packet, and have their finger hovering over the send button as we speak." She paused, letting the smile creep further across her face. "They of course may view it with a little disbelief. But with your rep, only a little."

"Khan you can't ..." began the Senti, until she raised her finger again.

"Can, and have. You have a ship in one piece due to me and my crew. You lost some brave Senti on the way. I don't want to besmirch their sacrifice or ..." she turned to face Segfi's ex-Marine. Bruised and bloodied from the battle inside the shuttle, he sat in the corner with shins wrapped in medpads.

"Annit," the ex-Marine replied. "Her name was Annit." There were tears in his eyes, and not from the pain.

"Annit. I want the wetware, and I want the 7th and High's memory slugs. You have ... thirty seconds to comply, or Arin shoots Pshwa. Sixty, and I space you."

The Senti's chin tentacle lashed at the deck, Rebekah surprised but not taking the display as a direct threat. Something about it appeared false and overblown. But then, she knew little about how the Senti showed anger. They revelled in human emotion fed directly into their brains, and Scarva's greed parasited off those addicted to it. But the Senti remained truly alien in mind and body, and familiarity with Scarva did not mean she could read him any better.

"And then I drop you off in the Almaarian system. And may I never see your fleshy face again," said the Senti. Rebekah took that as a request.

"Nearly. One more thing." She watched as the tentacle lashed again, a weird wet sound emanating from the triangular mouth.

"Ask."

"I want to know why the wetware is so special that Pshwa and the Bustans are willing to murder everyone in their path for it. Why the hell all this madness over chips?" She stepped closer, knowing she was in range of Scarva's tentacles, but exerting her power. Trying to dominate the alien into answering.

"From the Senti perspective that is easily answered, but harder to explain. I want them because you were sent to find them."

Rebekah glanced over to the injured ex-Marine, Michaels, and then to Arin. "Take them both out of here," she said.

"Secrets, huh?" Michaels said. "Mine are in this fucker's memory slugs. Remember that." He allowed Arin to help him up, and they hobbled through to the outer corridor, Rebekah hanging back, her carbine on Pshwa until she knew Arin was ready.

She shut the door, and the Senti dragged itself across the deck to tap at the strange machine with the knobs and dials. Arin had already removed the charges, though he'd made no promises to the alien that there weren't more. A drawer popped open, and Scarva withdrew a wrapped set of wetware baring a label. As it tore the bag open, she caught sight of the consignment number and the *Scourge*'s ship code.

The Senti's tentacles manipulated the wetware and eventually placed the set on the machine.

"It is adapted Senti tech." Scarva seemed deflated, and off-gassed extensively as it worked. "This part has been added."

"And?"

"If you want me to fully check it over, I will need trust."

She made to speak, and then sensed a shift between them, its frills puffing up as the Senti spoke again.

"I know you were sent by a man called Duboit. But from your surface memory, you regard that as a front for one of the Emperor's Enforcers. I do not want to anger such an agent any more than I already have. It was opportunistic, now it is not. A sellable asset, no more, no less. Of value, because it is wanted." The Senti off-gassed, disturbing Rebekah's thoughts. "If *I* had the wetware, your Duboit would pay me for it. Or someone else, more. Now I am in deeper than I want to be."

Opportunistic? Like with Carmen. A way to twist something to your advantage. But Pshwa's violence, and the giving up of its addict's den, smelt worse than Scarva's off-gas. It stank of something they both wanted keeping hidden.

"Bullshit," she replied. "Pshwa murdered an entire gang to retrieve it."

The Senti didn't react. "If you want to know what the adaptation is, then you understand we both hold something over each other." The Senti's eyes glistened, a sign, she thought, of a keen interest. Whether that was greed was another matter. But she needed to understand why Erikson had sent them, what the hell all this had been for.

She nodded. "And I want what's on the 7th and Highs' memory slugs."

"That I cannot do. I sold them on after wiping one specific portion ..."

She was convinced he was lying now. But there was only so far she could push, the need to ensure they could all get home at the back of her mind.

"Give me something, Scarva. My crew member's finger is likely getting twitchy by now."

"I do not wish to clash with your Enforcers, any more than I wish to clash with Countess Segfi." She flinched, and the Senti's eyes glistened a little more. "So let me go as far as saying I wiped something the Countess would not want sharing with others when Carmen begged me for passage. I sold the rest. I say no more."

"Begged? He deserted?" Her mind cast back to what he'd said when he'd not known who she was. It fitted.

"Begged. I needed the memories to sell on. The official Orbs were monopolising the war market, leaving me bereft of source memories. Whatever he'd seen, scared the human soul from him and his squad. Even I didn't look."

"On Bustan 8?" she asked, needing to know despite Scarva having already revealed more than he agreed to. "The rumour was you left Carmen and his squad to die. I heard the comms recording."

The Senti chin tentacle quivered. "If it rebuilds a little trust, so be it. No, we faked that to hide them from your Warmonger. I collected his dropship from near Trazor. No more talking. Shall I proceed?"

Shocked, she nodded.

Trazor, the Almaarian gas giant and its multiple moons. Barren. But not apparently empty.

Rebekah eyed the stim gun, thoughts of Rubel on her mind. He had turned on her, on them, attempting to save his own skin in return for selling his honour. What had Scarva said? Whatever they saw on Trazor had scared him down to his human soul. An interesting phrase. Rubel had always been an enigma, but honourable to his squad. Earned a good rep despite being part of Segfi's favourites, and that bad boy persona had endeared him to whoever took his fancy. She had fooled herself into thinking that she had lured him away from Angel. But in truth, he'd let it happen. Encouraged it. But *that* Rubel had deserved a slap, not a shattered rib cage. What lay on Trazor must have turned him somehow.

She injected the stim and rolled her shoulders. "Whatever. Done is done."

"Captain," said Tremil over comms. "Are you ready to send the message now? You asked me to remind you. I've forwarded the encryption key already."

"Thanks, Trem," she said, and selected her frequency. "This is Captain Rebekah Khan. Hannos, we have recovered our cargo and pissed off Lieutenant Ormsk. I doubt the Bustans will be returning to Benetai, but be warned if they do. No need to thank us for the risk we took to save your people, I think we brought that down upon you. However, a small favour would be greatly appreciated. There was once a girl called Hanna, and she deserves to be remembered. Rather than flowers, I bequeath you Pshwa's dream den to sell on, that particular Senti won't be returning. Some petty revenge in her name would help my peace of mind, too. Besides, Tensei will no doubt sell you out first chance he gets. Khan out." She left it at that. Benetai was Hannos' to govern, and she could only nudge.

She pocketed the near empty stim gun. No one but the girls were sleeping through the entry to Senti void-space, warnings or not. Scarva was as likely to commit murder, on the evidence of Pshwa's behaviour, and steal back the wetware, as the alien was to take them to their destination. A risk, but they'd taken a few lately.

"Arin, you're on first watch. Dricks, the second. Eight hours each, in rotation. Anyone of you misses an alarm, you'll have me and my new toy to answer to."

"Aye, El Capitaine. Shouldn't you lock the ship-killer away somewhere safe? Those girls are always sticking their noses where they don't belong." Arin added an air of distaste to his voice.

"Hey, no fair," replied Heki and Tremil together.

"Oh yeah? I go off hunting Bustan Marauder bots, and come back to find someone stole my last Danish. Life on the line, and that's the thanks I get."

There was a cough, and a pause, before Hendricks came on comms. "That was me."

"Bloody traitor!" cried Arin. "I thought Scarva was the lowest of the low, but you could teach that mind-sucker a lesson or two about betrayal."

Rebekah shook her head, clicking off the comms and headed for the cargo hold. Taking a long breath, she entered, and found herself by the box of wetware. She drummed her hand on top, feeling ZZ3's regard despite the inert eyes – minus one, of course.

"Go on," she said. "Say it."

The warbot shuffled, moving to look her way. "What do you wish me to say?"

"What you know, or the Butcher knows, about the wetware." She placed her back against the box, hands on the lid edge, eyeing the bot. "Help me understand."

"Only part of Asham's memories are retained in my system. The rest resides in *that*." ZZ3 gestured towards the containment unit. Asham's coffin.

"It has to be the same wetware Asham used on his guards. Is that information inside you?"

The warbot's eyes pulsed, settling into a pattern. "Somewhat. Perhaps if you explain what Scarva told you, I can piece the gaps together."

Rebekah licked her lips and eased back a little against the metal lid. "Scarva said there was a stored set of memories, and they had the taint of being copied multiple times. That the chip was not designed to record, but transmit. Rough, compared to true Senti tech, but functional."

"That ... helps." The bot paused, eyes swirling in a muted pattern.

Rebekah waited, impatient, but they had time.

"My data bank would suggest Asham had operated on his personal guards to improve their wetware. That, I believe, is an Asham subjective response. By 'improve', he means 'replace'."

"You mean, the memories are more like commands or orders. Why, when you have experienced soldiers already?" A bad taste appeared in her mouth, a disgust. Intrusive thoughts that made her shudder. "Do you think ... the wetware was meant for the hybrids? To make instant soldiers out of them?"

"A super soldier? Asham labels such a thing a folly. Whether that means he tried and it was a failure, is another matter. The image I see is more of a ... factory." The voice was flat, but Rebekah sensed the bot's dislike for whatever it was experiencing. "I will think on this some more."

Rebekah pushed herself up from the box. "You do that, crew."

"I am crew ..." replied the bot, shuffling back into its previous position. "Captain. The coding on the original storage box. Did you run a manifest check on it?"

She stopped, turning back. "No, why would we? It's from the *Scourge* ... Oh shit. You mean the destination coding. Are you going to save me some time, ZZ3? Where was it originally going?"

"The *Segfi*, of course. The Warmonger's flagship."

Heki held Tremil in a tight embrace, tears streaming down her cheeks, eyes wide as the void filled her mind. Empty, black. Dread rippled through her, merging with Tremil's, to forge them as one, holding out together against the sheer nothingness that threatened her sanity.

A tentacle landed upon her thigh, gentle, pulling itself along as more joined in. The touch was loving, caring, but tiny. A mere flutter compared to TB's usual caress, not enough to eat away at the fear hardening her heart and mind.

Void-space.

Well named.

And her thoughts expanded, searing out into the cold, streaking into the space between the stars. Tremil's touch upon her neck retained her focus, an anchor in the merciless black, and they entwined their consciousness as the emptiness threatened to overwhelm them both.

And the nothingness became something, a barrier, a wavering fold of space. Stars pricked the blanket of black, and Heki braced herself as she crashed headfirst into the wall, only to emerge whole upon the other side.

In the distance, the Almaarian sun shone bright.

Her sister's mind leaked into hers, memories unbidden riding the void, merging – and Heki's eyes opened wide. Sat upon her sister's shoulder was TB. No, a much smaller symbiote. Metallic colours fluttering in perpetual motion, tentacles meshed with a carbon-copy on her own arm.

A twin.

"What?" she said, but there was no answer forthcoming. She had just emerged from void-space, leapt from one place to another in the arms of those she loved. Tremil looked as stunned as her.

Star travellers, riders of the void.

And they had witnessed it all. Experienced how the Senti bent space, and in effect, time.

Wide-eyed, they sat up on the cabin bed, unable to articulate their shared experience.

The *Sunstar*'s comms clicked, a familiar voice echoing through the ship. "Well, that was a yawn-fest," said Arin. "Void-space, the most boring forty-eight hours of my life. Anyone for breakfast? Got a Danish-sized hole to fill."

EPILOGUE

Erikson's slate pinged, flagging up the recording he'd been desperately waiting for. He ignored it for the moment and finished reading Davina's confirmation of M4's docking schedule and the subsequent cargo manifest. With some relief, the handover of the stolen wetware the Breakers had recovered was complete. His Enforcer handler had acknowledged receipt, so its care was no longer his responsibility. And of course, Khan's information about where the wetware had originally been heading was an unwelcome addition to his growing sense of unease. Countess Segfi.

For later.

He swiped over to the flagged message and pulled up the new camera feed – recorded aboard the *Maverick* – trying to understand what the shadow across the asteroid field might be.

"Oh," he said when he finally worked it out.

He gulped the water at his side. A small, uncharacteristic shake to his hand causing the liquid to spill onto his desk amid the secure SCIF he prayed kept prying eyes from witnessing what displayed on his screen.

At first the shadow, blocking out the vestiges of the Almaarian sun's light. And then, as the camera panned, a giant comms spike pierced the void just as the huge bow of a battleship appeared. Its solidity against the backdrop of the sun held Erikson in awe, before the reality of it struck home.

A death knell sounded amid the silence of the black.

A warning, soon followed by the shimmer of Point Defence Cannons that tore into the salvager's hull. The briefest of fireballs filled the camera, a vestige of oxygen within the tin can having released as the rounds pierced the smaller ship's engines. That, at least, provided a little hope. Evidence of his involvement partially reduced by the deaths of the lowlifes inside, but he had already viewed the relayed footage of the salvagers' penetration of the *Scourge*. The markings had been removed, but the correlation with his stored image left no doubt as to whose ship lay derelict on the asteroid.

A conspiracy uncovered.

The house lights dropped, instantly ending as if snuffed out by the hands of the gods. The shake that had invaded his hand rumbled through his body, and he let out a long, resigned sigh.

And his world collapsed.

The End of Butcher's Folly, Book 2 of The Wrecking Squad series. Watch out for Book 3, Warmonger's Wrath.

The Wrecking Squad Series

Thank you for choosing to spend your precious time reading Butcher's Folly. It's an honour as an indie author to have written stories readers such as yourself have taken the time to read.

This series has been taking up my headspace for some time. I knew I had a great set of characters to work with and a story premise that had weight. The trick is to marry the two while keeping the flow. To achieve that, the world must feel 'lived in' and by people who feel real. That means imperfect, as we all are, yet striving to do their best. I hope I achieved that, and you want to keep on reading about the events they get embroiled in. Next up is Warmonger's Wrath, which will bring this section of the series, Part One if you will, to a conclusion while setting up the next three books. Yes, these characters are too good to let go yet.

Reviews and ratings are the lifeblood of any author, and vital to indie writers in particular. They help new readers make up their minds when searching for new authors and books. Ratings are your chance to bring a little starlight and attention to my scifi books that are a somewhat different from the norm.

If you enjoyed my novel, please consider leaving a star rating on Amazon and/or Goodreads.

And if you wish to know more about the members of the Wrecking Squad, their origin story is absolutely FREE. Just flick to the end of this book to find out how you can download Redemption Tour - A Wrecking Squad Story.

ABOUT THE AUTHOR

Nick Snape has been steeped in Science Fiction and Fantasy since his friends first dragged him from his schoolwork and stuck a book under his nose. Lost to the world of imagination, he became a teacher by accident, though he thoroughly enjoyed developing the joy of reading and writing in his pupils. Having retired after thirty years, he thought it was high time to practise what he preached.

Nick's books feature everything from all out, heart-pounding, fast-paced action to thoughtful, character driven twists on the fantasy and sci-fi genres. Genetics to Artificial Intelligence, Artifice Dragons to Soul-Eating enemies, nothing is off the menu.

BOOKS BY NICK SNAPE

The Wrecking Squad

Warmonger's Wrath (Book 3)

When the Warmonger steals something precious, how far will The Wrecking Squad go to get them back?

Like hounds on an Enforcer's leash, Rebekah and the crew of the *Sunstar* are bullied into a punishing schedule. Returning from an intense, sickening mission, they are immediately sent out to infiltrate the secret bases of Court nobles hiding their intent as they play at war with real troops and weapons. But the Warmonger is stirring, Countess Segfi flexing her muscles as the truth about the *Scourge*'s secrets are exposed. The ex-Breakers have something she wants, and she'll stop at nothing to retrieve it. With Rebekah and The Wrecking Squad caught up in deadly Court politics, the Countess takes a step too far, and the dogs of war slip their leash. You may shatter a Breaker's heart, but they sure as hell won't stand around and let you do it twice.

Weapons of Choice Series

*'A truly epic saga of riveting sci-fi thrill*ers...'

It started with a failed military training exercise and an alien incursion, desperate and on the hunt. But survival was just the beginning...

After encountering a buried spaceship and its rogue AI on Earth, Finn, Zuri, and Corporal Smith (deceased) take refuge on an alien home world where they unravel the truth about the forced colonisation of Earth-like planets. With the ship's AI providing advanced nano-weaponry and evolving alien battle tech, Finn and Delta blaze a trail through the galaxy seeking a way home, walking a fine line between vengeance and redemption in this thought-provoking action sci-fi series.

Over 20,000 books read in this 'superb scifi series'

Hostile Contact

Return Protocol

Zuri's War

Finn's War

Alien Rebirth

Invasive Species

Legion Earth

Nemesis Earth

Weapons of Choice Box Set Bks 1-8

The Scorching Standalone Series

The World in My Hands

"A deeply nuanced sci-fi standalone with slow-burn suspense, a diverse and unorthodox cast of characters and a spaceship straight out of your worst nightmares"

The world is heading towards global collapse as the Scorching takes full effect. Salvation vessels orbit the Earth, waiting to transport the chosen few away from danger and to start again; ten plantships grown by an alien species for the wealthiest and most powerful, or those lucky enough to be selected by lottery. Yet not all is well on board. Dark secrets lurk in the corridors and depths of their respective ships, dragging Jenna and Seth into a world of malice and violence they thought they had left far behind.

Just Press Play

"Staggeringly original and timely release from a masterful voice in modern sci-fi."

On a devastated Earth, the Drathken arrive with the promise of healing the planet. When anti-alien terrorists threaten the accord, Cop and Vlogger Josh Nkosi, and his MARC unit, chase terrorists into the Burnout Zone only to come face to face with humanity's stark future when the hunt takes a devastating twist. As a conspiracy emerges, Nkosi is forced on a dark path of discovery.

Warriors of Spirit and Bone

A Dragon of the Veil

"An INCREDIBLE start to anew, dark epic fantasy series."

In a realm no longer devoid of magic, the fate of a people rests with Laoch and Sura, and the Gods' weapons they bear – a thousand years of faith and lies reconciled in a single moment of hope and redemption. With whispers of an ancient evil's return, they are left reeling by their enemy's power, one even the Gods' weapons fear. For cast in iron and spiritfire - here be dragons.

A City of Ashes

"A work of coal-dark fantasy that is continually surprising, provocative, and compulsively entertaining."

With the Veil Dragon, Nathair, seemingly under the Spirit Captain's control, Laoch pushes away the grief of his first encounter with the metal beast and hunts for a weapon his new and distrusted ally insists they can use against the coming Constructor invasion. For an Emperor consumed by revenge has a new artifice, one that hungers to enslave.

A Queen in Blood

" A dark ambience largely unmatched by anything else I've read."

As the invasion of Brandshold begins, the realm is haunted by the Infected – devastated and spirit-poisoned townsfolk who hunger for flesh and souls to salve their pain. When the city of Jense falls to a wave of bloody teeth and foul claws, the Constructor's Emperor strikes, shattering city walls with his artifice dragon, and the dreaded *Kraken* soulship. For a queen bathed in the blood of her own people, hope lies in the alchemy of the meisters, a traitorous mechanical dragon, and loyal but broken soldiers.

ACKNOWLEDGEMENTS

As with all authors, this book would never have existed without the dedicated friends and family who were there by my side throughout the entire process. The least I can do is give them a mention for their patience with my obsession! My Beta readers, supporters and fiercest critics have been Pak, Paul Derwent, Martin Lejeune, Bryan Chaffin and TK Toppin. Amazing friends who have put that aside to make sure whatever I put out there was something they wanted to read

Julie, my wife, needs a special mention. Over the past few years she has kept me going, being there at every step through the dark and joyful times. I can't believe how lucky I am.

Finally, the New Year and Pub Night Crews. Wouldn't be here without you.

Thank you all.

WRECKING SQUAD FREE NOVELLA

My new series, The Wrecking Squad, involves a squad of ex-Marines on the run. Their origin story is available in a FREE novella, Redemption Tour, which you can download by subscribing to my newsletter. Yes, absolutely free alongside another book detailed below. Subscribing will also provide further information about this series, and my plans for more exciting science fiction and fantasy novels in the future.

The Lost Squad - A Weapons of Choice Novel

The Stratan Marines who we first meet within Hostile Contact have a surprise in store. A second squad followed them to Earth, those who appear later in the series in Book 7, Legion Earth. The Lost Squad, a FREE full-length novel, details their arrival soon after Yasuko's ship left the Solar System in Hostile Contact. The novel charts the alien Marines' action-packed experiences as countries and mercenaries vie for their technology and knowledge. They are a superb bunch of characters and were a real joy to write.

If you wish to learn more about their history on Earth, and I suggest you do as it's an excellent novel, then please subscribe to my newsletter and receive your FREE novel via the link below:

www.nicksnape.com/subscribe